Fantasy M[illegible] the Classroom

Essays on Teaching with Film, Television, Literature, Graphic Novels, and Video Games

Edited by Emily Dial-Driver, Sally Emmons and Jim Ford

McFarland & Company, Inc., Publishers
Jefferson, North Carolina, and London

Also of Interest

The Truth of Buffy*: Essays on Fiction Illuminating Reality* edited by Emily Dial-Driver, Sally Emmons-Featherston, Jim Ford and Carolyn Anne Taylor (McFarland, 2008)

Library of Congress Online Catalog Data

Fantasy media in the classroom : essays on teaching with film, television, literature, graphic novels, and video games / edited by Emily Dial-Driver, Sally Emmons and Jim Ford.
p. cm.
Includes bibliographical references and index.

ISBN 978-0-7864-5921-6
softcover : acid free paper ♾

1. Popular culture — Study and teaching (Secondary) — United States. 2. Mass media — Study and teaching (Secondary) — United States. 3. Fantasy fiction, American — Study and teaching. 4. Motion pictures in education — United States. 5. Television in education — United States. 6. Fantasy films. 7. Fantasy in mass media. I. Dial-Driver, Emily. II. Emmons, Sally. III. Ford, Jim, 1972– IV. Title.

2012002167

British Library cataloguing data are available

Front cover: *The Dark Knight* (2008) Poster Art (Photofest)

Manufactured in the United States of America

McFarland & Company, Inc., Publishers
Box 611, Jefferson, North Carolina 28640
www.mcfarlandpub.com

Table of Contents

III. New Directions: The Joys of Fantasy Classes

Preface

EMILY DIAL-DRIVER

It's been a "long strange trip," or so Robert Hunter would characterize it. Or, as John Lennon (among others) would say, "Life is what happens to you while you're making other plans."

Certainly many challenging and often interesting detours occurred on the trip to the completion of this volume. We had complications of all kinds: personal problems, technical problems, weather problems. (We didn't have robot invasion or zombie attack, though, so we were actually fortunate.)[1]

As we worked around and through those complications, some of what we thought we were going to do became "other." We added, subtracted, multiplied, and divided. In the process, we discovered that we were not just writing about how to use fantasy and pop culture in the classroom. We were writing about how to teach "big" concepts, such as analysis, interpretation, criticism and critical thinking, and to discuss "big" issues, such as cultural similarities and differences, human relationships, social mores, cultural conventions and moral issues. We were writing about how to encourage students to think about the "other." Krista Tippett on the radio show *Being* says that it is "when we are able to see the other, to see the welfare of the other as somehow linked to our own, that we are able to rise to these moral ideals" (qtd. in Thompson 4).

Much of fantasy literature and film and pop culture literature and film is about "the other" and how we are both "the other" and not "the other." We found we were trying to discover how to transmit an understanding of this conundrum — an understanding so vital to the development of an educated human. We kept discovering new and vital uses for "the fantastic." Jimi Hendrix said, "You have to use fantasy to show different sides to reality. That's how it can bend" (qtd. in Shapiro 457). And, it is through the venues of fantasy and pop culture that we, as teachers, aspire to illuminate reality.

The character Dirk Gently in Douglas Adams's *The Long Dark Tea-Time of the Soul* says, "My methods of navigation have their advantages. I may not have gone where I intended to go, but I think I have ended up where I needed to be" (106).

On our trip, we've had strangeness, we've had life, and yet we think we've ended up where we needed to be. We hope you think so too.

Notes

1. One thing was not a complication. On our trip we've had some invaluable help, from Meggie Espey, Kelsey McBride, Larelie Leuellen, Brooke Martin, Julia Dial Sheppard, Valorie Vernon, Rebekah Warren, Jeana Lee Driver Starbuck, and Todd Starbuck. (You have our grateful thanks for all your hard work.)

Works Cited

Adams, Douglas. *The Long Dark Tea-Time of the Soul.* New York: Simon & Schuster, 1988. Print.

Hunter, Robert. "Truckin'." *What a Long Strange Trip It's Been: The Best of the Grateful Dead.* Perf. Grateful Dead. Rec. 1977. Warner, 1990. CD.

Lennon, John. "Beautiful Boy (Darling Boy)." *The Very Best of John Lennon.* Rec. 1980. Capitol, 1998. CD.

Shapiro, Harry, and Caesar Glebbeek. *Jimi Hendrix: Electric Gypsy.* New York: St. Martin's, 1995. Print.

Thompson, Ann. "From the Executive Director." *Oklahoma Humanities,* Winter 2011: Print.

Introduction

Jim Ford

Fantasy can make you a better teacher. This is a study of various works of fantasy, and how best to use those works in the classroom. It combines close analyses of several popular television programs, films, and graphic novels with practical applications for the classroom. The focus throughout is on specific ways in which fantasy works can enhance teaching and learning. We want to show not only *why* teachers should consider using outstanding works of fantasy and science fiction, but especially *how* to use such works — the pedagogy of pop culture.

One of the more common misconceptions is that professors who use popular culture in the classroom have abandoned the classics. The image of the lunatic professor who spends all his time teaching trash instead of Shakespeare looms large and is a common bogeyman for critics of higher education. Nothing could be further from the truth, at least for the contributors to this volume. We teach in a variety of contexts, classrooms, and disciplines — from high school to college, from freshman composition to senior seminars, from English language and literature to computer science, philosophy, and politics. As is clear from the essays that follow, most (if not all) of us remain dedicated to the classics. The goal is not to replace an established curriculum, but to continue expanding and enriching the curriculum through the judicious inclusion of fantasy materials.

Similarly, we reject the idea that everything is equally worthy of study. Just because something is popular does not mean it is good. There is good and bad in pop culture, and, while it is true that anything can be a useful object of study in the right situation, not everything should be. The emphasis here is on the finest works of fantasy and pop culture, ones that have been proven in the classroom. Some works recur frequently in the chapters that follow, films like *The Matrix* and *The Dark Knight*, television shows like *Buffy the Vampire Slayer*, and graphic novels like *Watchmen* and *Blankets*. Even the fourteen contributors to this volume would disagree about the relative merits of some of the works discussed, such as *Avatar* or *Twilight*. What we share is the belief that such works are valuable tools for the classroom. *Fantasy Media in the Classroom* describes many of these tools, and how best to implement them through specific topics, works, and assignments.

Everyone has favorites, and so the choice of which pop culture works to teach will of course be to a fair extent idiosyncratic. As for the category of "fantasy," we construe it as broadly as possible. In some sense, anything that has even a hint of the fantastic is a work of fantasy. While magic, mystery, and the supernatural are often present, they are not required. Several of the essays touch on the difficulties presented by a narrow conception of fantasy, and some will offer their own definitions. In general, though, our category is not exclusive, and the lines between fantasy, science fiction, and the rest of popular culture are blurry at best. Many of these works are nontraditional in genre, vision, or execution; some are all three. The important thing is not categorizing these works, but utilizing them for educational purposes.

The book is divided into three sections, based on the type of class and the way in which fantasy material is incorporated. The first section, "Seeing the Classics in a New Light: Using Fantasy as a Lens in Traditional Classes," focuses on the ways in which fantasy material can enhance student learning about traditional texts, themes, and topics. What is important is seeing those classic texts in a new light. In these three chapters the fantasy materials build on the same materials professors commonly use, from *Hamlet* in an English literature course to presidential speeches in an introductory government class. The second section deals with similar classes, but treats the fantasy materials as important in their own right (not just for understanding the existing material). "Integrating New Works: Using Fantasy to Enrich Traditional Classes" contains seven essays which highlight the value of studying works of fantasy, from the use of science fiction films like *Inception* for introducing philosophy to the videogame *World of Warcraft* in a computers and culture course. The third section, "New Directions: The Joys of Fantasy Classes," extends the use of fantasy materials past the traditional curriculum. These five essays discuss new possibilities for courses, focusing entirely on works of fantasy. Of course, several of the essays bridge these topics, and the sections have a fair amount of overlap in subject and scope. All fifteen essays emphasize the practical issues in teaching through fantasy: the strengths of particular works, the advantages of specific assignments, and the challenges of integrating pop culture.

The first essay is by Jesse Stallings, a high school English teacher. Despite the fact that it is easier to assign traditional works, for which there are voluminous study materials, teaching aids, and ready-made assignments, he explains why he uses a variety of fantasy and pop culture works. In "Pop

Pedagogy," Stallings argues that such works are ideal for showing students how the skills practiced in English class apply to life outside the classroom. His essay sets the stage for everything that follows. Even though he uses contemporary works like Scott McCloud's *Understanding Comics* and Craig Thompson's *Good-bye, Chunky Rice* to elucidate traditional concepts in literature, both are also studied for their own sake, and Stallings implicitly makes the case for their own literary merit.

The second essay, "Added Interest, Added Value," continues this dual emphasis. In it Laura Gray discusses the ways in which non-canonical works can be applied to established literary classics. By watching the film *Pleasantville* after reading *Fahrenheit 451*, or considering the fantastic elements in Ursula Le Guin after seeing similar tendencies in Poe and Faulkner, recent works serve to extend and illuminate literary themes of more classic texts. Gray reviews the application of this technique in both freshman composition and senior literature courses. In both cases, she demonstrates how canonical works are the basis for a wide variety of contemporary works — and vice versa. Students in her classes read the classic texts, but their experience is enhanced by the careful addition of pop culture.

The final essay in the first section, "Bruce, Bill, and Barack," is a direct application of fantasy to political science. Comparing the words and images of *The Dark Knight* with those of Bill Clinton and Barack Obama, Carolyn Anne Taylor demonstrates how a close reading of a particular scene can shed new light on political speeches and campaign advertisements. Taylor's essay is a great example of how even the occasional addition of popular culture can enhance a traditional course (in this case, Introduction to Government).

The second section opens with "Flights of Fantasy," Jim Ford's discussion of some thirty science-fiction and fantasy films perfect for humanities courses in general, and Introduction to Philosophy in particular. Here the emphasis is not just on the ways in which fantasy materials can help students understand the classics, but also on the new venues fantasy provides for the traditional classroom. This essay describes how to create a film experience for students, ways to integrate science fiction films in any introductory philosophy class, and the merits of those thirty sci-fi classics. Contemporary films like *Eternal Sunshine of the Spotless Mind* and *Inception* supplement rather than replace traditional readings from the great philosophers.

The second essay in this section, "Fusion Curriculum," continues this blend of traditional and contemporary. In it Emily Dial-Driver uses her honors seminar on the "Dark Side of the Mind" as a model for how to fuse canonical and fantasy works. Combining *Dr. Horrible's Sing-Along Blog* with Kafka and the BBC's *Jekyll* with the original enables an interdisciplinary examination of this theme. While this particular class is an unusual one, in that it has a special set of students and no pre-determined discipline or content, the principle of fusion is valid in a variety of courses and contexts. By blending these two types of work the smart teacher engages her students on a deeper level, and elevates the learning experience.

The third essay in this section is from our second editor, Sally Emmons. "We're Not in Kansas Anymore" reviews three different classes, each of which involves a distinct approach to pop culture. Emmons explains the benefits of using pop culture to expand the study of Native American literature, as a supplement to a largely traditional composition course, and as the subject of another course entirely focused on fantasy. In each case, she provides detailed teaching tips, from discussion questions and writing prompts to student comments and homework. She also relates how students were able to learn from, build on, and ultimately critique Todorov's conception of fantasy in the course dedicated to that theme. Emmons's essay demonstrates the various ways in which one professor can adapt pop culture to distinct situations, contextualizing fantasy as appropriate. Even the most faithful aficionado will tailor her use of pop culture to her students' capabilities, interests, and needs. In all three classes fantasy serves as a "gateway" to a deeper understanding of classic texts and problems.

The fourth essay in this section also features a composition course, this time one that uses post-apocalyptic literature to deepen students' critical thinking and to translate that into clear writing. Mary M. Mackie's "Critical Thinking and Post-Apocalyptic Literature" establishes the rationale for such a course, and includes close analysis of a number of excellent texts, including Kazuo Ishiguro's *Never Let Me Go*, P.D. James' *The Children of Men*, and Cormac McCarthy's *The Road.* Mackie argues that dystopian and post-apocalyptic texts are perfect for helping composition students ask themselves "What if?" Her essay includes a number of specific techniques and assignments as well as final exam questions.

The next essay is the first of two team efforts. "Corruptible Power," by Frances E. Morris and Emily Dial-Driver, recounts Morris's move from traditionalist to fantasy enthusiast. Including *The Daily Show* in her classroom helped her students recognize the nature of satire, enabling them to appreciate Jonathan Swift more easily and deeply than they ever had before. Dial-Driver is no traditionalist (as should be obvious by now), but she does love the classics as well as pop culture. This essay describes the magic of both, from *Frankenstein* to SpongeBob (seriously). These two English teachers explore great literature, classic and contemporary, and supply a number of great ideas for classroom texts, films, and television shows.

The next essay in this section, "Breaching Barriers Between Work and Play," highlights a number of unconventional approaches. Shaka McGlotten uses the phenomenally popular video game *World of Warcraft* as a central learning activity. Doing so encourages students to transgress boundaries "between work and play," to see learning as participatory in the highest sense. In some ways the course itself, Computers and Culture, violates the boundary between traditional and fantasy class, and McGlotten's assignments challenge a litany of preconceptions about education. In doing so, it is a worthy bridge between the second and third sections.

The final essay in this section, "Fantasy Classics: Hobbits and Harry in Interdisciplinary Courses," also bridges these two sections. In it Jim Ford shows how the classic works of J.R.R. Tolkien and J.K. Rowling can enhance traditional courses as well as provide new opportunities for fantasy classes. Because of their wide appeal, their readability, and the scope of their worlds, Tolkien's *Hobbit* and *Lord of the Rings* and Rowling's *Harry Potter* series are ideal for the interdisciplinary classroom. Whether used in conjunction with more traditional classroom materials or as the focus of a fantasy course, these stories are easy to integrate into a variety of courses.

The third section suggests the possibilities of new fantasy classes, beginning with J. Renee Cox's "Hansel, Gretel, and Coraline." Based on her work with a Fairy Tale in Literature and Film class, it begins with Tolkien's essay "On Fairy-Stories." Cox makes several intriguing connections between "Hansel and Gretel" and *Coraline*, revealing a number of key lessons for instructors along the way.

The next three essays all involve the work of Joss Whedon in some fashion. *Buffy* is a favorite work for several contributors, having been the subject of our previous book. In her essay "The Fantastic Classroom: Teaching *Buffy the Vampire Slayer*," Emily Dial-Driver describes a course devoted to *Buffy*, and the long list of discussion themes possible in a Buffy class. As she explains, traditional literary principles and techniques are easy to apply to a television show with as rich and full a history as *Buffy* (particularly if the entire series is available on DVD). A number of other series could serve the same purpose, using Dial-Driver's *Buffy* class as a model.

The third essay of the section, "Buffy Versus Bella: Teaching about Place and Gender," shows how two similar works can be combined to enhance student learning. Written by Jacqueline Bach, Jessica Broussard and Melanie K. Hundley, it provides a host of specific assignments and approaches for using *Buffy* and *Twilight* as classroom texts. The authors also provide a list of other strong young adult works that feature vampires, as well as close readings of particular episodes, themes, and issues. In doing so they show how these contemporary series serve as the basis for a fundamental questioning of place and gender.

The fourth essay in this section, "Brave New Classroom: Using Science Fiction to Teach Political Theory," returns to the political science classroom to show how science fiction can be used to teach political theory. Kenneth S. Hicks briefly reviews developments in the teaching of political theory before analyzing John Scalzi's futuristic novels and Joss Whedon's *Firefly* series and

Serenity movie as resources for teaching. Such works, Hicks argues, remind political scientists of the power of narrative, and can restore imagination to political science.

The final essay is by Emily Dial-Driver, and it suggests a number of new approaches to the fantasy classroom. "Incarnations of Immortal Creations" tracks a number of reimagings and retellings of classic stories like *The Wizard of Oz* and *Alice in Wonderland.* Either one could be the focus of its own new fantasy course, or a more general course could track the incarnations of several such stories. In either case these contemporary retellings enable students to understand timeless tales in new ways.

All in all, these fifteen essays provide a wealth of ideas, techniques, and assignments. The goal is to inspire teachers of all kinds to consider new ways to include pop culture in the classroom. Fantasy books, films, graphic novels, and television shows can dramatically enhance any classroom experience, providing new materials to engage students' interest, improve their critical thinking skills, and deepen their appreciation for great literature in all its many forms. We hope that the ideas, assignments, and works discussed in these pages will engender your own creative teaching with fantasy.

I. Seeing the Classics in a New Light: Using Fantasy as a Lens in Traditional Classes

Pop Pedagogy

JESSE STALLINGS

The dirty little secret of the high school English classroom is that the classics can be much easier to teach than contemporary works. The path of explication is well worn, teachers have likely taken classes covering the works, and materials to "enliven" a unit are always close at hand. A quick Internet search for *Lord of the Flies* contains enough analyses, classroom presentations, video interpretations, games, worksheets, handouts, PowerPoint slides, articles, and student essays to keep a teacher's weeknights free throughout the unit.[1] But a liberal use of ready-made units can have unintended consequences: give students enough photocopied handouts and textbook readings and they begin to question the teacher's enthusiasm and the material's relevance.

In no other vocation as important as teaching can a professional fall into the rut of copying the same material from a binder for decades, pages accumulating Xerox detritus as the years go by. In addition to making the teacher seem at best lazy (at worst disinterested), the frequent use of worn-out materials sends signals to students that the answers have already been found — that they have little to offer in the way of new interpretation. This leaves them looking for "the answers" in study guides and essays from last year's students rather than applying the skills and knowledge they acquire in the classroom.

Granted, the reasoning for the use of these materials is understandable — they save time, they have been proven effective, they are pre-aligned to state guidelines, and they may contain genuinely good ideas. But how far do they take the students? The difficulty lies in the fact that out of any number of students a teacher comes into contact with, only a small number will view the subject with the reverence and fervor of an educator. This excitement is vital and certainly can be contagious — a teacher at my school graduates year after year of seniors in love with *David Copperfield*— but can also blind us to the reality that the majority of our students will not continue to consume[2] *anything* after graduation at the critical level we model in the classroom.[3]

This inevitably leads to discussions amongst teachers that include statements like "If they never pick up a book after graduating, at least they will have read____." This is terrifying to me for a number of reasons (making the teacher the arbiter of "good fiction" being the least), but primarily: if our students don't consume another work,[4] regardless of difficulty, *and analyze it using the skills we've presented*, we have failed as English teachers.[5] The source of this potential failure, I believe, branches from an overemphasis on *content* (which makes sense, as the stories are what got us here in the first place) and a relegation of the *skills* (induction, analysis, discussion, communication) to quizzes and vocabulary sheets, rushed essays, or rote regurgitation of the teacher's ideas about a book.

If the students do not see the utility of an essay, its purpose, then it stands to reason that they would cling to What They Know, i.e., the teacher's insights, study guides, etc., rather than their innate (if incomplete or misguided) understanding of the work and communication. It is true that step one in the process of educating a high school student is basic literacy, but the second must be thoughtful consumption and communication.

Would it not be more fruitful to promote an environment that engages the students for the same reason we were drawn to literary analysis and communication? How much richer would our students' lives be if, from the moment they were introduced to literary analysis, they were shown how to apply these skills to the world around them? And, with guidance, to the works *they* deem valuable? There is no need in that case for a *Jeopardy*-like game over the main characters. And by the same token, this environment would encourage students to make analytical connections between the works consumed in class and those they consume in their free time—bridging the gap between schoolwork and "the real world." This would result in assignments more inherently relevant to the students and a set of skills and analytical tools that are *immediately useful*— not something they'll "need to know later." Without this sense of immediate application, of usefulness in life, there is no motivation or pathos for students to engage or learn.[6] Finally, wouldn't it be great if we could watch movies or television or go to concerts without the guilt of "putting off" work for the classroom?[7]

The goal of using contemporary works alongside the classics is not to make the English classroom seem "cool," but to show the students how the skills we practice can and should be applied to their lives outside of the classroom. By introducing these skills through diverse media, we can help the students maintain and expand a repository of useful skills applicable to *all* forms of communication and consumption, not exclusively literature and peer-reviewed analyses and criticism.

"Why are we here?"

For some students, the analysis of literary works carries the tinge of useless (or fruitless) work, possibly due to repeated frustrations caused by unclear expectations and poor reinforcement. These are the students who claim they are "not good at English"—a disconcerting statement tantamount to claiming "I don't communicate very well"—but what they really mean is that they don't understand the object of an English class.

Other students have managed to do well in English courses simply because they have learned to "play the game"—rely on synopses, act excited, turn papers in on time, and tell the teacher what they think he or she wants to hear.[8] These are the students who leave the skills practiced in the classroom at the door on the way out—they don't make an anti-hero connection between Gatsby and *Iron Man,*[9] they don't consider the lyrics of the songs they enjoy, instead relying (as they do in the classroom) on their friends' opinions or thoughts they've picked up in the comments under YouTube videos. It simply doesn't occur to them that the skills we present are applicable outside of classroom explication exercises. These students will likely have the "Freshman wakeup call" in college, but how much further would they be if they had been practicing these analytical skills throughout the years leading up to university? More important, what if our assessments precluded this type of cut-and-paste "writing"?[10]

In a world where the student-to-teacher ratio is 1:1, we could conceivably teach to the individual student's interests, motivations, and aspirations; the student with an affinity for the likes of Pynchon, the Decemberists, and Chris Ware could willingly learn and implement the language of literary analysis just as productively as a student of Austen, Proust, and Eliot because he or she would have an application for these skills in his or her life and would experience the teacher's modeling of these skills *on works the student interacts with daily.*

It is this last group that I want to expand in my classroom—students who are engaged in *Pride and Prejudice* for the sake of enjoyment—because that is the only position in which true learning, not rote memorization and regurgitation, occurs. These fantastic English students develop a love of the classics, they seek out complex works on their own time and engage with them at a deep level, but the individual (student or adult) is rare who never consumes popular media, be it television, blockbusters, comics, or popular music.

My solution is simple: Do not ignore popular works in favor of saving time in the classroom. Do not ignore popular works, regardless of medium, simply because they are popular or because they have no *established* literary merit. Challenge your students (and yourself) to establish that merit.[11] Embrace and integrate popular works because they can enrich and enliven the English classroom, can solidify the connection between the literary analyses and devices and the "real world" in the students' minds, and can lead to a lifelong analysis of culture (high and low) by our students.

Empower the students to apply the skills you present and practice in your classroom to works they consume regularly. Once they have a working knowledge of these skills and the confidence to discuss a work, once they trust you as an educator, *then* plop *The Scarlet Letter* in front of them.

One Solution

I begin with the five-paragraph essay. The students have plenty of examples of this method: webs and bubble maps and such. The goal of these formulae is, of course, to assist the beginning writer with the proper structure and flow of an essay, with the thesis statement somewhere prominent and body paragraphs following (or radiating from) it. But, I ask my students, why five paragraphs? Why is it so important that they have a central point with supporting points and elaborations below? The more cynical argue that it is easy for a teacher to grade: the teacher just counts the paragraphs and reads the thesis.[12] My explanation is that this pattern is repeated throughout nearly every learning experience they are likely to come across, from newspaper articles to textbooks, concept albums and novels, episodes of *House* and *South Park*, jazz improvisation, sonatas, the President's address to the nation, textbooks, and every course they will ever take, each an iteration of the Comp. I mantra: "Tell them what you are going to tell them, tell them, then tell them what you told them."[13]

I explain the pattern through the lens of the basic story arc, drawing a bell curve on the board and asking for labels ("exposition, climax, denouement"[14]). Then, taking my cue from Joseph Campbell, I place the basic hero's journey (departure, initiation, return) below, aligning "departure" with "exposition," etc. Below this, I place the basic format of jazz improvisation (head, improvisation, return).[15] By this time, it is clear to most of the students where I'm going with this. They fill out the final sequence: "introduction, body, conclusion." We spend some time coming up with examples of stories, albums, television episodes, and video games that follow this sequence. Then I pose my questions for them, making it clear that while I have some ideas, I don't know the answer, if there is one[16]: What does it mean? Why does this pattern appear in nearly every form of communication? Even better, for perspective: What things do not seem to fit into this pattern?

Our discussion usually makes its way to the nature of communication and learning, and the grin of realization slowly spreads throughout the classroom: it's about the opposing skills of teaching and learning, communication and consumption. Tell them what you're going to tell them (and its mirror: What do you know? What do you not?), tell them (read, consume, watch, research, listen, discuss, rinse, repeat), tell them what you just told them (reflect, apply, return). The hero's journey, the essay, the graphic novel, the improvisation, the television program, the concept album, the video game has its organizational basis in the audience's movement from ignorance and status quo through a series of explanations, examples, and elaborations to insight, understanding, and reflection. After the viewing, listening, heroics, or reading, both the characters and the consumer are no longer the same—they hold a new insight into the world around them, or themselves (Campbell's "boon"). Now all they need are the tools to communicate—the power to tell others, to spread the word, to bridge the gap between the ideas consumed and the wider world (becoming the "Master of Both Worlds").

This is hugely empowering for the students. The goal of this presentation is to unload the negative associations they hold by giving them a realistic, workable answer to the question of why we do this—the opposite of "because that's how it is done" or "because you'll need to know this later."[17] They realize that their essays should be not only a record of their transformation after reading a work, but a transformative experience for their readers as well—and they get to write the journey.

Journals

Journaling is not a new or innovative requirement of students, but it is the cornerstone of all my classes. In asking my students to record a statement about a work, I am essentially asking them What They Know: what stood out to them, what caught their attention. I prefer phrasing it this way[18] for several reasons: first, they own their answer—as a question of opinion, there is no right or wrong answer, and they aren't spending time and cognitive energy trying to imagine the answer they think I'm looking for. Second, and possibly the most important, intrigue[19] is vital to learning *anything*—if they aren't interested, the process is dead at the gate. "What caught your attention?", however, is fertile ground for other questions: "Why?" (which would spawn a personal essay), "Is it part of a larger pattern within the work, or is it an outlier?" (a literary analysis), "Why was it put like that?" (an analysis of cultural context), or my personal favorite: "Where have you seen this before?" (a thematic exploration). Finally, it is a question that will grow with them as they get better at consuming, discussing, and discovering thematic connections and patterns. Students outgrow the five paragraph essay formula almost as soon as it is introduced, but this question and the investigation that follows is vital to all learning: discovering what we know and don't, seeking answers, checking them, reflecting, applying.

It is clear that even at the high school level some students have not completely grasped the fact that every element of a novel is there because the author chose it. I was surprised to note that most of my students took everything in a novel (or movie, song, television show, graphic work) at face value, never considering *why* a particular event took place, why a character acted the way he or she did, or why an author describes a particular moment in such detail.[20] This line of thinking pops up in their writing as well, but the step from book report to literary analysis is merely changing their driving question from "What happened?" to "Why did it happen and what does it mean?"

I eventually adopted the trite mantra of "*Everything* in a fictional story is made up" or, in my nonfiction courses, "*Everything* is there for a reason." This is a classic eye-roll moment for many of my students[21] until we begin questioning the author's motivations: What does it mean that José Arcadio's blood finds Úrsula? Why is Piggy the one who is picked on? Why does Hamlet love Ophelia? Why is Chunky a turtle? *How to Read Literature Like a Professor* is a great resource for these discussions,[22] as the author clearly explains possible meanings behind symbols and choices an author makes, from why a character gets sick to why the weather tends to change.

I turn to Scott McCloud's *Making Comics* when driving home the statement that "everything in a fictional story is made up," primarily because the focus of the first section, "Writing with Pictures," provides a straightforward explanation of the choices an author makes in creating his or her story. Early on, McCloud narrates and illustrates a short story, then proceeds to remove or insert elements that alter the tone and plot (13). The visual representations help a number of the students better understand the purpose with which elements of a story are put together, while the new question "What if this were like *this*, or removed completely?" is added to their tools of analysis.

The journals the students are required to keep move their positions and purposes from passive audience members/consumers to active members of a conversation, and their thinking from fiction as atomic to *fiction as a construct to be taken apart*. Not only does this habit of recording their interaction leave them practicing their analytical skills and active interaction with a text, but it makes discussion more productive: "If you make a statement, back it up." "I need page numbers." This is frustrating initially, but the propensity of teenagers to make unfounded arguments can leave a discussion listing. Direct evidence anchors it, and disallowing un-cited comments gives them practical motivation to keep detailed journals. These journals document varying degrees of detail and insight, certainly, but they know, if they want to discuss,[23] they had better have their journals out.

In going through this process, students aren't intending to make a list of important quotations and their own ideas (even though that is the result)—

they are simply interacting with the text. Like good scientists, they keep track of their insights, deviations, and support. In addition to the "interesting" question, I ask them to record connections — to patterns within the text, to other works, to their lives, to things they are learning in other classes. The discussion of these interesting things, connections, and questions make up 85 percent or so of class time. We discuss, we plot, we illustrate, we connect, we investigate, we go on tangents, we often lose the original question in favor of a better one. The best part occurs after we have finished discussing the first novel of the course and half of the class has a spiral filled with information about the themes, motifs, symbols, strange occurrences, puzzling scenes, and connections to the wider world — their personal study guide. (By the second work, the other half of the class is on board.)

Writing an essay from this material becomes an exploration of What They Know from the quotations and insights in their journals, an organization of this into What They Will Tell becomes Telling in their essays, and often continues with a final oral presentation of What They Told. The recursion of these skills (induction, discovering relevant support, pattern recognition, close reading) breaks the linear progression of the writing process, one that creates writer's block and leaves students staring at the computer playing with fonts because they've finished the previous step in the formula and the next is the only option.[24]

The greatest thing about journals is that they can be an extremely valuable pre-writing step for *any* kind of creation. In my mythology class, the students read and journal Ovid's *Metamorphoses* and Campbell's *Hero with a Thousand Faces*, making connections, finding allusions, and discovering retellings. These retellings often come in the form of television programs, popular novels, graphic novels, and songs. By posing the over-arching question "What caught your attention?" rather than "What figurative devices do you notice?" the analytical process is (again) founded upon their own interests rather than the teacher's.

Towards the end of the semester last year, when I asked them to create an interpretation of a few myths, they already had a wealth of What They Know in their journals — not only the annotations of the stories themselves, but connections to a collection of diverse works. They then distilled the stories into their basic structures[25] and retold them in whatever medium they felt most appropriate. One student created epic movie posters advertising the summer blockbusters *Midas* and *Medusa*, another created a series of limericks from the distillation, while many created short graphic novels based on the stories, placing them in a modern setting or endowing them with even more outlandish endings.[26]

These distillations and applications give them practice in breaking down a work (regardless of medium) into its constituent parts, finding the basic plot, message, or moral of any work, then building it back up (or distorting it) through a series of associations — essentially a reconstruction in the vein of *Into the Woods* or *Shrek*. This strengthens their ability to discover the essential themes and motifs of a work in any medium, as they have witnessed (and taken part in) the application of these themes to diverse types of literature, be it written, drawn, or sung.[27]

"So how does this work in my classroom?"

Just one more iteration. The students come to class brimming with pop culture references (whole conversations are carried out via movie quotations — just listen to the conversations at lunch). If they are able to memorize entire conversations from movies, entire albums of song lyrics, trace the relationships of characters in their favorite television show, and argue the strengths and weaknesses of contestants on the latest reality TV show, why would we not harness these abilities (and works) for our purposes in the classroom? Begin with What They Know, show them how they can apply the skills we want them to master, use those skills to discover other works, *ad infinitum*. In this way the students need not fall back on what the teacher wants to hear, *because* the students likely feel more informed about the works they consume daily than the teacher.

A clear example of this is in my AP English Language and Composition class. For better or worse, students come to me with little to no experience analyzing arguments. But, They Know how to argue, or at least think they do. That is enough. We begin the course with the arguments they come into contact with daily: commercials.

I pull a few from the previous Super Bowl for the class to watch. After doing so, I ask, "What caught your attention?" and all have an opinion.[28] They understand credibility, they understand emotional and logical appeals — they just don't have words for them. That's where I, the older and more experienced member of this rhetorical expedition, act as a guide — clarifying discussion, questioning those a bit too sure of themselves, and translating their insights into the jargon of rhetorical discourse.

Once they are using "ethos," "pathos," and "logos" correctly and without being prompted, we move on, analyzing arguments from their favorite blogs and magazines. In this way we Jacob's-ladder through the skills and content: we begin with content they have an emotional attachment to (What They Know), discuss and introduce skills (analysis of emotional, logical, and credible appeals), then use these analytical skills to expand their circle of experience. By using works they are truly engaged in to introduce tools that deepen their understanding of these works, we have established a platform from which to move to other, less inherently engaging works.

The rub is that as we move forward in the process, away from works and media they are comfortable with, they are left with only the skills to lean on — the skills are What They Know.

Fractals and the Scientific Method

One of the repercussions of the five paragraph essay is that it leaves the students with no concept of the size of an idea — not every insight deserves 1.5 pages of explanation, while others are much too large for this format. Too many times I have looked over a draft by a student struggling to find evidence for a point, only to find him or her attempting to write many pages over an idea that, as proposed, warrants only a few paragraphs.[29] By way of explanation I usually ask the students for a statement from their journal ("What do you know?"), then walk them through the process of molding it into a longer explanation.

Take Craig Thompson's *Good-bye, Chunky Rice* as an example. It is the story of a turtle named Chunky Rice who leaves his home (and the mouse he loves) to find his place in the world. A student might make mention of the story two sisters tell Chunky: "In Beulahlah, when someone feels regret, ... they'll etch their name in a turtle shell and let it drift away in the Beulahlah river" (56). This is shocking to Chunky, being a turtle and all.

The students have a starting point of interest, but not much to say about it. So, we dig deeper. ("Read, rinse, repeat.") I ask them what the story is about, where this seemingly offhand anecdote fits. If they struggle, I ask them to break down the anecdote (back to "What do you know?"—regret, shell, name, river) and search associations with the larger story ("Read"). They might come up with a connection to the regret Chunky feels about leaving his home; the fact that he is traveling away from home on a boat; or perhaps focus on the "shell" word, noting that it implies "emptiness," but is also Chunky's "home" on his back.

In walking them through this recursive sequence (Check what you know, read, check ... a hint of the scientific method here?), I emphasize that we are exploring the text, looking to learn what we can, while keeping an eye on our goal: an explication of the anecdote. I reiterate that we are taking a through-the-looking-glass approach to the essay form. The essay is an explanation, something others explore, while at this point the students are exploring a work in order to explain it to others.

The second year I presented this, a number of students mentioned the fractals they had been discussing in their previous class — which blew *my* mind, and changed the way I presented these concepts.[30] As they take the empty shell floating down the river and find connections to other empty containers in the novel (an empty shell found on the beach; an empty box left on the pier, the protagonist's possessions removed; an empty box used as a hiding place for a lonely child), we continue to expand "what we know," returning to the work for more support, revising, repeating ... essentially discovering the iterations of a central value (we call these "themes" or "motifs" in literature and music; in jazz they are called "standards"; in fairy tales, "morals"; in an essay, the "thesis")—the motif that an empty container in this novel possibly represents the protagonist's sense of displacement and desire for fulfillment. In this sense, the work becomes a set of overlapping fractals,[31] each theme iterated throughout the work.

Once they have a theme or motif, I take up the iteration, placing it in context of larger works: one theme of displacement makes a solid essay, an explication of that theme within several works (*The Arrival* by Shaun Tan, *Asterios Polyp* by David Mazzucchelli) makes for a great research paper, an explication of the larger pattern of discomfort in isolation exemplified by themes (within a family, *Fun Home* by Alison Bechdel and *Hamlet*; amongst superheroes, *Watchmen* by Alan Moore and *The Dark Knight Returns* by Frank Miller; in confronting a father, *Jimmy Corrigan* by Chris Ware [and *Hamlet*]; in self-discovery, *Ghost World* by Daniel Clowes [... and *Hamlet*]; in sexuality, *Black Hole* by Charles Burns) would compose a chapter, an exploration of several themes in many graphic novels would compose a book, and several books about graphic novels united by an exploration of the medium would make a course.

Outlining

While this sounds good when the entire class is consuming a work, the real test is when an individual student sits down to apply it to a work he or she has consumed and an essay the student plans to write. Enter: The Outline. Getting their idea on paper in the form of an outline and watching it grow makes the abstract tangible. In the lead up to their writing, I draw a brain and a book on the board with a sheet of paper in the middle. The goal, I tell them, is to pull equally from their thoughts, opinions, connections, and insights (brain) and from the text itself (book) in the form of paraphrase and quotation in the composition of their essays. Too much brain and there is no proof—they could be making it up,[32] too much book and they are writing a middle school "report" or synopsis.

A student most often begins with a statement that is either paraphrase ("Chunky left his home") or opinion ("Chunky is a fool"). With a little cajoling, we come up with a statement that contains a bit of the work and a bit of the student's idea,[33] which he or she types with a first-level outline designation ("I"). I model the outline as a conversation—ask them to pretend they have just finished consuming this work with a friend, and the friend makes the statement the student has just written down. I then ask how he or she would respond.[34] If the statement is self-explanatory or especially small, eliciting a "yep," we move the statement to the right, placing larger points above it. If it begs explanation, we move downward, branching out, noting the question, finding answers which become subheadings that may elicit further questions. In this way, the creation of an outline becomes an organic process — a conversation, an improvisation.

By creating the outline in this manner the students do not become "stuck" as they would when attempting to begin with a fully-formed thesis statement,[35] and through discussions of their statements with peers in the classroom, the students gain experience in anticipating the amount of elaboration necessary to make a point — a valuable step in understanding the "size" of an idea, reinforcing the point that the essay is an explanation, a bridge between the experienced student and his or her audience.

Giving students a sense of scale, both of their ideas and the place of essays in the grand scheme of communication; giving them the tools to create their own study guides; and giving them the opportunity and tools to break out of the system that has left them with no other option than to "cheat," plagiarize, or turn in material they don't believe in — these are the seeds of life-long learning, of creating a curriculum that is relevant to the students not because it is "hip," or solely because it integrates the things they consume in their daily lives, but because the things we regularly consume are the only things *anyone* writes about, regardless of experience or purpose.

Notes

1. And that last bit doesn't hurt the students' free time, either.
2. I use this verb in place of "read," "watch," listen," etc.
3. Check the adult bestseller lists or the massive collections of poorly written trade paperbacks at a local used book store.
4. I can take at least one cue from the deconstructionists: "Everything is text." We are teaching critical analysis and inductive thinking as well as reading comprehension and literary movements.
5. Imagine a math teacher thinking, "If they never use fractions again, at least they have seen them in my class."
6. Outside of grades and fear of punishment, neither of which promote the internal motivation requisite for continued learning after these pressures are removed.
7. In this, the introduction of popular culture works both ways: students see the analytical tools of the English classroom used on their own lives and interests, and (this is the biggest payoff for our sanity) the teacher's extracurricular activities become fodder for the classroom.
8. I tell my students that this is quite a valuable skill but isn't necessarily one they should be practicing in the classroom. The source of this phenomenon is likely teachers who make clear what they want to hear from students.
9. Or even *Iron Man 2* (2010) and *Sherlock Holmes* (2009), which, beyond the fact that Downey, Jr. starred in both, ought to stir an inkling of connection or familiarity.
10. Even more important, how much *more interesting* would their writing be if they weren't

regurgitating the bullet points presented in class or in a study guide? No teacher, regardless of goals of consistency or *leveled* assessment, wants to read the same essay 40 times.

11. Or refute it.

12. To a point, this is true, and valuable when introducing students to an argument's format. I rail against the formula in class simply because high school students tend to respond to a tearing-down of old forms.

13. This isn't revolutionary, but the goal is to clear the "classroom only" associations in favor of a wider, seemingly relevant, context.

14. Then asking a student to double-check my spelling of "denouement."

15. Huge thanks to Eric Doss for pointing this one out.

16. This kind of question is vital to all we do in the classroom. Rather than making me the Holder of the Answer Key, doling out the Answers when I deem them worthy, I become a more experienced researcher working alongside and giving advice when necessary. This is an exciting way to do things, as it requires me to be as engaged as they are in finding a solution, and I do not have the comfort of a clear vision of where the discussion will go. (But, of course, I do have a clear understanding of the skills that we'll need to master to get there.)

17. The most obtuse explanation ever provided by anyone who has met a high schooler. There are plenty of meanings behind it: "I don't know," "the school board tells me you need to know this," "it is on the state test." All of which boil down to: "I haven't taken the time to research why it is done this way." For all the raging against the bureaucracy and state tests, wouldn't it be easier to tell our students that the comma goes inside the end quotation marks because the tiny bit of lead would too often fall off the printer's block? It may be stupid that it is still done that way in the U.S., but at least there is a reason. Any other response is at best ignorant, at worst dismissive.

18. Rather than "What is important?"

19. Or the establishment of pathos, for my AP Language students.

20. The infamous "turtle chapter" of *The Grapes of Wrath* comes to mind.

21. "You mean fiction isn't real?!"

22. And one most high school students should read.

23. They do want to talk—we are keeping it interesting, right?

24. And of course, this is a microcosm of the essay itself, tucked neatly into the wider frame of consuming the works, which in turn (if I've done my job) fits within the broadest context of the classroom.

25. Pyramus and Thisbe: couple separated, try to come together in secret, then die by dramatic irony; the stories of Phaethon and Icarus: teen ignores father's advice, dies.

26. Many, many contained a "character turning into a tree/bird/river/stone" non-sequitur at some point.

27. One of the best works to come out of this assignment was a song described by the student this way: "The genre was Industrial, and the myth was Narcissus and Echo. I used the title 'Liquid Beast' to represent both the body of water Narcissus stared at and died from, and Echo herself." The song was haunting and repetitive, featuring leitmotifs for both characters, which echoed and reflected until diverging and fading toward the end. How cool is that?!

28. To reiterate: This is a self-leveling question. Students come to a class with varying skill levels, so their insights are going to reflect this. The key is to not only take every statement seriously (especially the flippant ones; the best reaction to sarcasm or irony is a deadpan, literal reaction) but continue the conversation and tie it to the skills when appropriate.

29. Or the converse: a student taking on the definition of "good science fiction." My goal then was to help the student pare it down to, say, patterns within a single author's work. Still a large undertaking, but it was an independent study.

30. We're all learning here, yes?

31. We can only take this self-similarity and iterative loop metaphor so far, of course, but it stands as a great example of the possibilities of interdisciplinary connections.

32. I emphasize the wider audience here: "Of course *I* trust you, but what about the readers who don't know what fine upstanding citizens you are?"

33. Part of this statement is often a placeholder, as in our statement that "The anecdote in

Goodbye, Chunky Rice is relevant." Here, we aren't sure why it is relevant, but posit that it is. Getting the complete statement (part from the work: "anecdote"; idea: "is relevant") on paper is the important step, after which we can dig into why it is relevant.

34. This is especially fruitful when the entire class participates, providing a wide variety of responses and answers. At this point many students have difficulty in putting themselves in the shoes of their audience. An actual discussion helps this.

35. Which is impossible for many reasons — the writing of an essay should be an exploration and a learning process. Presenting the thesis (I use "hypothesis" for their initial thesis statements) as immutable from the start engenders frustration and a tendency to ignore counter-evidence.

Works Cited

Bechdel, Alison. *Fun Home: A Family Tragicomic.* New York: Houghton Mifflin, 2007. Print.
Burns, Charles. *Black Hole.* New York: Pantheon, 2005. Print.
Campbell, Joseph. *The Hero with a Thousand Faces.* Novato, CA: New World Library, 2008. Print.
Clowes, Daniel. *Ghost World.* Seattle: Fantagraphic Books, 1998. Print.
Into the Woods. Dir. James Lapine. Perf. Bernadette Peters, Chip Zien, Joanna Gleason, Tom Aldredge. Image, 1997. DVD.
Iron Man. Dir. Jon Favreau. Perf. Robert Downey, Jr., Terrence Howard, Jeff Bridges, Gwyneth Paltrow. Paramount, 2008. DVD.
Iron Man 2. Dir. Jon Favreau. Perf. Robert Downey, Jr., Don Cheadle, Scarlett Johansson, Gwyneth Paltrow. Paramount, 2010. DVD.
Mazzucchelli, David. *Asterios Polyp.* New York: Pantheon, 2009. Print.
McCloud, Scott. *Making Comics.* New York: Harper, 2006.
Miller, Frank, with Janson Klaus. *Batman: The Dark Knight Returns.* New York: DC Comics, 2002. Print.
Moore, Alan, with Gibbons Dave. *Watchmen.* New York: DC Comics, 1987. Print.
Ovid. *Metamorphoses.* New York: Viking, 2002. Print.
Shakespeare, William. *Hamlet.* New York: Folger, 1992. Print.
Sherlock Holmes. Dir. Guy Ritchie. Perf. Robert Downey, Jr., Jude Law, Rachel McAdams, Mark Strong. Warner, 2009. DVD.
Shrek. Dir. Andrew Adamson and Vicky Jenson. Perf. Mike Myers, Eddie Murphy, Cameron Diaz, John Lithgow. DreamWorks, 2001. DVD.
Tan, Shaun. *The Arrival.* New York: Arthur A. Lavine Books, 2006. Print.
Thompson, Craig. *Good-Bye, Chunky Rice.* Marietta, GA: Top Shelf, 2003. Print.
Ware, Chris. *Jimmy Corrigan: The Smartest Kid on Earth.* New York City: Pantheon, 2000. Print.

Added Interest, Added Value

LAURA GRAY

For many college students, the language, ideas, and burdensome length of traditional texts are so off-putting that they fail to read more than the first lines or pages. When students lack the attention span, critical thinking skills, and motivation necessary to read an entire novel or play, how can they learn to grasp the deeper significance and meanings of these texts? While there are no quick-fix answers to this literacy gap, traditional texts still have value for our contemporary society and should be taught to our students. Not as summaries on a *Wikipedia* page, but as entire works. Good fantasy literature and film, when incorporated appropriately into more traditional course content, can help bridge some of the intellectual and cultural disconnect that impairs many of our students. Whether used to instruct underclassmen in the basics of literary and philosophical inquiry or with more advanced students to further these ideas, fantasy offers a unique lens of understanding for contemporary students. This chapter provides scenarios in which fantasy materials are used in the traditional classroom.

I regularly incorporate fantasy and pop culture literature and film into courses in English and the humanities. In a junior humanities course on autobiography, for instance, the graphic novel *Blankets* and the film *Persepolis* (from the same-named graphic novel) are used as alternative memoirs. These works culminate a semester of traditional autobiographies, like Zora Neal Hurston's *Dust Tracks on the Road,* in which questions of moral choice and personal meaning are explored. *Stranger Than Fiction* is a delightful movie used in an introductory literature course for its discussions of comedy and tragedy, after we have read several classic, literary examples of both. To further illuminate the ways in which fantasy works within the traditional classroom, two courses are discussed in more depth in this chapter.

In a first year composition course, the film *Pleasantville* is used in conjunction with Bradbury's *Fahrenheit 451.* This juxtaposition helps illuminate the problem of happiness Bradbury's novel examines. The danger of self-imposed ignorance for the sake of happiness is particularly powerful for inexperienced readers because the tone of these two works is quite different. This film also demonstrates narrative technique and metaphor in ways more easily accessible to the novice student.

In a senior literature course, fantasy is employed to further traditional literary explorations of humanity, isolation, myth, and justice. The works of Euripides, Sophocles, and Shakespeare provide a foundation of literary exploration in the first half of the semester. Poe, García Márquez, and Le Guin follow as traditional literary forms that incorporate fantastic elements. Students finally tie this semester-long exploration to contemporary films with fantastic elements (such as *Pan's Labyrinth* or works of Tim Burton).

These classes build a foundation upon established literary works first, and then incorporate non-canonical fantasy material to extend and exemplify traditional literary themes, motifs, and explorations. With these examples, it should be clear that fantasy literature and film can easily be used within almost any class in ways that engage students and further their learning experiences, while maintaining a focus on established and traditional course content.

The First Year Composition Course

What should be the role of first year composition? Discussion and modeling of five-paragraph essay? The thesis statement? A laundry list of writing modes? Grammar? While these elements may be part and parcel of the course, the crucial tasks should center on modeling critical thinking and reading, and engaging students in activities and practices that help them translate these skills into effective writing. Who cares if a student can write a model essay that says nothing and means nothing? In my university, first year composition is taught as an expository writing course that utilizes a variety of short reading assignments as fodder for critical thinking and writing. *Fahrenheit 451* is the only long work required in this course. As with most general education courses in an open-enrollment university, many students enter this class with little experience in critical thinking, academic writing, or analytical reading. I use *Fahrenheit 451* as a gateway to the types of discussions in which students will be expected to engage during their college tenure. The futuristic, dystopian society of this novel provides an engaging read for most first year students. Initial discussions focus on the accuracy of Bradbury's predictions, what students think about the society he describes, character exploration, and the like. When asked to explain thematic issues of the novel, however, students most often reduce the text to "that book about book burning." My goal, then, is to model, through a variety of activities, the multifaceted questions and critiques of the novel. Here is a typical first activity:

For each of the three parts of the novel, answer the following:

1. What is the main idea of the part? Articulate this idea in one or two well-developed sentences.
2. What are the *three most important* issues or episodes within each part? Justify your choices. Use one significant passage to highlight each example. Quote the passage and include page numbers. Try to find passages from the course of the part (beginning, middle, end), rather than choosing three examples existing close together.
3. How do the significant ideas of each part work together to lead to the main ideas presented in the novel?

As basic as this assignment is, even my brighter, better-read students struggle with this type of detailed, close reading in the beginning. It is much more fun (and much easier) to gloss the major plot lines of the novel than to dig into the text. If possible, I have students work on this activity within class, often within groups, so that they are not able to run to *SparkNotes* or *Wikipedia* for answers. Importantly, we dedicate class time to discussion and reading of the text, thus modeling the way this should all work. I move from rudimentary assignments like that above to more complex ones like the following:

The Books of *Fahrenheit 451*

> Within the novel *Fahrenheit 451,* many books/texts are referenced and/or discussed. Go back to the novel, select three such texts and find out more about them. Choose these texts from the course of the novel, that is, try to find examples from the beginning, middle, and end of the novel, not just examples that are close together. Once you have educated yourself on the content of these texts, consider why Bradbury has included them in the novel. What is important about these particular texts in the history of knowledge and understanding? Why would they be considered dangerous to the community of *Fahrenheit*?

For this assignment, I allow students to use any legitimate sources they can find. I do not expect that they will read Plato's *Republic* or all of *Hamlet.* I still want them to begin to *want* to read these works, however, or at least recognize their value. This particular assignment is very eye-opening for most students. It is their first exposure to the so-called Great Books. Having such a discussion come from an appealing novel like *Fahrenheit* engages the students in ways that simply assigning *Republic* or *Hamlet* would never do for this population. It is within this context that I discuss the value of the works themselves, not simply the ideas within the works. Bradbury's society had distilled the plot of *Hamlet* to one page, much like our *Wikipedia* entries. While I am not naive enough to believe that my students will avoid shortcuts like this forevermore, I do feel it a worthy discussion to have. A central argument of Bradbury's book is that a society, in the name of happiness, has found a way to take all meaning from themselves, thus leaving them miserable.

It is usually at this point in our work with Bradbury's novel that I show the film *Pleasantville*. Written and directed by Gary Ross, *Pleasantville* features high school-aged twins Bud (Tobey Maguire) and Jennifer (Reese Witherspoon), who are transported to a fictitious 1950s sitcom *Pleasantville* (much like *Leave It to Beaver* or *Father Knows Best*). Ross uses stunning visuals to evolve this black-and-white world to one of vibrant Technicolor, as the twins and the citizens of Pleasantville awaken to knowledge, thanks in part to art and literature. At first Bud loves living in a world free from problems or even discomfort. But as we follow the twins through their journey of self-discovery, we, too, learn that happiness without freedom or knowledge is not worth having.

This film lends itself to a variety of explorations that work extremely well with underclassmen. While we discuss the film as a piece in and of itself, the main purpose for introducing it within the context of the *Fahrenheit* discussion is to illuminate common themes between these very different works. These pieces work extremely well when used in conjunction for both works rely on elements of the fantastic to examine and comment on society — one a dystopian future, the other an idealized past. Both works also make clear that ignorance is self-selected in the name of happiness, which is a poor, and indeed dangerous, choice for society to make. I also use the film to introduce literary elements of narration and metaphor because the visuals of the movie make these concepts extremely clear. We then consider how these elements work within our novel, thus applying something more easily accessible to them (film) to something that may seem less clear (literature).

As I did with *Fahrenheit*, I have students explore some of the references made in the movie. I have to help a bit more with this — telling them what some of the paintings are, who is playing in the soundtrack at pivotal scenes, and what the trial scene is modeled upon. When we are finished with our discussions of these two works, it should be very clear that both rely on intertextual reference to deepen their meanings, thus reinforcing the importance of communal knowledge which figures so heavily into Bradbury.

One scene from the movie is especially useful for close examination, and serves as an example for the types of discussions and assignments I use for this film. This scene takes place in the soda shop, where the students have gathered to ask Bud questions. Two jazz classics, The Dave Brubeck Quartet's "Take Five" and Miles Davis's "Kind of Blue," provide the background music for this scene. "Take Five" is playing as Bud enters the soda shop. The young people of Pleasantville (some in black and white and some in color) begin asking questions about the world that may exist outside of their knowledge. They are amazed as Bud explains that there are worlds outside of Pleasantville and that there are places where the "roads keep going." "Kind of Blue" begins to play as the conversation shifts to books. In this film, all the books in the library contain blank pages. As the students' awakening and curiosity increase, they ask Jennifer questions about the content of these books. Jennifer, the twin who has cared little about her education, tells them what she remembers of *Huckleberry Finn*, and, as she narrates the story, the pages fill in. The young people look to Bud to fill in the remainder of the novel. The visuals in this scene are engaging; we watch the pages fill in as Bud narrates the tale. As he tells the story of Huck and Jim, he explains that "in trying to get free, they realized they were free already." The scene pans out of the soda shop, as another student is eagerly asking Bud to tell him what happens in *The Catcher in the Rye*, and transitions to the public library, where students, many now in full Technicolor, are lined up waiting to enter.

This scene (as does the entire movie) juxtaposes black and white with color to show the citizens of Pleasantville's awakening knowledge. After looking closely at this scene, I have my own students think about the music and books that are highlighted. Most do not recognize the music and know little to nothing about the musicians or the history and importance of jazz. I use this opportunity to explore jazz with them, and its history as an anti-establishment art form. Because the racism of 1950s America is an important underlying theme of this film, I take this opportunity to discuss this within the context of the music. I also have students explore the two novels from the scene, much in the way I had them explore the texts alluded to in *Fahrenheit*. We discuss the reasons why *Huckleberry Finn* and *The Catcher in the Rye* have been on banned book lists and what their literary significance is. While some students may be familiar with these works, most are not. This is yet another opportunity to broaden their literary knowledge. All of these activities lead to important questions that I want the students to explore in various writing activities. What is the role of happiness in society? What is the danger of self-imposed ignorance for the sake of happiness? Why is it important to be keepers of the knowledge and preservers of our culturally significant texts?

Both of these works, *Fahrenheit 451* and *Pleasantville*, are engaging examples of fantasy and pop culture. Students can especially relate to a movie that centers on two teenagers seeking their own path to happiness. Both works illuminate the dangers of censorship, but I think they do something more valuable for contemporary students. They show that great works of art, literature, and music add to our sense of communal values, and personal meaning, and happiness.

The Senior Literature Course

Fantasy is employed differently in a senior-level English course, Literary Traditions, from in the first year writing course. In this course I encourage students to take ever-increasing ownership for finding and making meaning of the texts explored in the class, and fantasy is one tool used toward this goal. The course literature is considered chronologically, thus emphasizing a progression of thought and meanings, while exposing the ways that the great works of literature build upon the questions and ideas of earlier literature and philosophy. Though we look at each literary piece individually, we connect ideas and themes across the works, seeing how the texts ask important questions in various ways. We also tease out recurring motifs and themes across the various selections. Importantly, I do not structure the readings and discussions *because* of these motifs, but rather allow these ideas to emerge organically from the works.

In the first half of the semester, we focus our study on very traditional, canonical works, beginning with the Golden Age of Greek Drama with studies of Euripides and Sophocles. These works serve to ground our studies as I provide clear and structured readings and explorations for these early pieces. In this, I establish the types of close and critical readings and explorations that will be expected throughout the course. From the Greeks, we move to Shakespeare, studying first a tragedy, such as *Hamlet* or *Macbeth*, and then moving to a problem play or comedy like *All's Well That Ends Well* or *Much Ado About Nothing*. We explore traditional ideas of tragedy and comedy, but also discuss the ways in which these categories are played with and defied. I usually include a film of a Shakespearean drama, asking students to discuss the modern applications and appeals to contemporary audiences.

All of these discussions are aimed at pushing students into critical thinking and discussions that underpin our modern use of literary motifs, themes, and works. As in the first year writing class, film is a medium with which students feel more comfortable, and we consistently explore questions aimed at exposing the importance of classical literature as a living, breathing medium that remains relevant to contemporary audiences. It is upon this foundation that we move through the rest of the semester.

Studies of Edgar Allan Poe, which come around midterm, serve as a gateway to the discussions and ideas that I wish to build upon for the remainder of the term. It is here that ideas about the fantastic and fanciful begin. Poe's work is familiar to most students, who study him in high school. For many, Poe is a favorite writer, and I purposefully choose tales and poems that I think will be familiar so that students feel comfortable in taking increasing leadership in the class. It is here that students begin to really shine, confident as they connect Poe to our earlier discussions, but also move forward into ideas and motifs that will be particularly salient for contemporary readers and writers. Here is a typical assignment used to engage the students in class discussion:

The Works of Edgar Allan Poe

Your group is responsible for teaching (leading the discussion) the EAP short story "—." Using *good literary practices*, prepare to lead this discussion by addressing:

- Significant characters
- Important literary techniques
- Language
- Central idea/purpose/effect
- The way this particular story/tale compares to Poe's other works

You may also use any of the scholarly materials within the text (see for instance, the Introduction to "Tales") that are appropriate for helping us better understand this tale.

Such an activity calls on students to apply the skills gained throughout the course in ways that put them in charge of the discussion. Once each story has been discussed individually, I ask the students to draw connections across the works and to discuss Poe within the broader context of the course. In Poe, we acknowledge a thoroughly unique writer who foreshadows contemporary literature while maintaining a timeless quality. Through this, we establish the fantastic as an effective appeal to readers' fears of death, dying, and isolation. Such ideas, we learn, are perpetual states for the modern human.

In our study of modernism, we include William Faulkner. Faulkner is as unpopular with my students as Poe is popular. Most often I teach *The Sound and the Fury*. With few exceptions, my students hate this work. They struggle with the narrative technique and the story itself. Often students challenge my choice to include this work. Up until this selection, most students thoroughly enjoy the reading selections and class discussions. In some ways, they feel betrayed by what they see as a curve ball in our happy semester. I think such challenges are positive and I encourage them, much to their surprise. It shows, I believe, a growing sense of student empowerment and ownership in the course. However, while I empathize with their experiences with the novel, I carefully show them why I think they are wrong, and that difficult and even flawed texts often have important ideas to contribute. This, too, is part of the tradition of literature.

I choose Faulkner not to frustrate my students but because I think his work is a great example of modern literature and because he leads nicely to our discussions of Gabriel García Márquez, who claims William Faulkner as his "master" in his Nobel Prize speech. Faulkner also works well as an example of the ways in which 20th century writers played with narrative structures and language. Some semesters I include the film *Memento* as an example of unique narrative styles. Other semesters, we explore *film noir* and Faulkner's importance to the sub-genre. Regardless of the specific approach, at this point, I want students to see how writers of literature and film build upon and play with tradition, moving in interesting and new directions. We walk this balancing act for the rest of the term as we discover that tradition is important, but innovation is also crucial.

It is within this context that we close out our semester with Ursula K. Le Guin's *The Left Hand of Darkness*. This is the only assigned text of the semester that fits clearly within the genre of fantasy. A typical first assignment begins with me asking students, often within groups, to discern the important philosophical questions of the novel. Then, after brief discussions of specific ideas or motifs, I have each group select one idea or question for further exploration, finding passages from the novel to support their discussions and conclusions. They are then charged again with teaching the class about their particular idea, with specific, textual examples. Students can see that earlier writers like Poe, García Márquez, and Hurston incorporate fantastic elements within their narratives, but Le Guin's use of the genre of fantasy/science fiction allows her to ask age-old questions in new and profound ways. This novel, we conclude, asks complex questions about humanity and explores the themes of isolation, myth, loneliness, gender, justice, and happiness. All of these ideas are examined in the other works of the semester, and I ask students to connect this work to the discussions we have had throughout the term, drawing conclusions and synthesis. While a number of other, more traditional, books could serve the same purpose, I find that fantasy (in this case, science fiction) uniquely engages the students and allows them to see traditional literary ideas as important within contemporary stories.

Many students, though certainly not all, are steeped in science fiction and fantasy literature. They enthusiastically embrace the conversation in which they are often experts because of their familiarity with *Lord of the Rings*, or *Star Wars*, or even *Harry Potter*. For many, these works (whether in the written or film versions) were their first literary loves, and they see them as the stories of their own generation. Relinquishing the discussions for *The Left Hand of Darkness* and the synthesis of the semester to the class is a bit of a risk. If the semester has been successful, however, it is particularly rewarding to sit back and watch the students take ownership of the material and their learning experiences. Typically, the final project of the semester is an analysis of a film, selected by each student, that uses fantasy to explore contemporary themes. Students are called on to draw comparisons and synthesis of ideas, motifs, and themes across literary periods and genres, while recognizing the significance of these traditions to contemporary audiences, and also appreciating the artistry of a contemporary generation. Thus, students are empowered to take an active role in creating meaningful learning experiences.

The activities outlined in this chapter offer but a few suggestions for the incorporation of fantasy literature and film into courses that otherwise focus on traditional, canonical selections. Such additions enhance student learning at any level of the undergraduate experience by showing that great classic works of art, be they literary or visual, provide the fodder for the contemporary ideas so appreciated by modern students. In this way, they engage and educate students on their way to full cultural literacy.

Works Cited

Bradbury, Ray. *Fahrenheit 451.* New York: Ballantine, 1953. Print.

Faulkner, William. *The Sound and the Fury.* 1929. New York: Vintage International, 1984. Print.

Garcia Marquez, Gabriel. "Nobel Lecture." 8 Dec. 1982. Trans. *Nobelprize.org: The Official Web Site of the Nobel Prize.* From "Nobel Lectures: Garcia Marquez." *Literature 1981–1990.* Ed. Sture Allén. Singapore: World Scientific, 1993. Web. 20 Aug. 2010.

Le Guin, Ursula K. *The Left Hand of Darkness.* New York: Ace Books, 1969. Print.

Memento. Dir. Christopher Nolan. 2000. Lions Gate, 2011. DVD.

Persepolis. Dir. Marjane Satrapy and Vincent Paronnaud. 2007. Sony Pictures Classics, 2008. DVD.

Pleasantville. Dir. Gary Ross. 1998. New Line Home Video, 2004. DVD.

Stranger Than Fiction. Dir. Marc Forster. 2006. Sony Pictures, 2007. DVD.

Thompson, Craig. *Blankets.* Marietta, GA: Top Shelf, 2003. Print.

Bruce, Bill, and Barack

CAROLYN ANNE TAYLOR

"I stand upon my desk to remind myself that we must constantly look at things in a different way."—John Keating in *Dead Poets Society*

Politics has historically revolved around concepts, such as identity, emotion, power and community, the same ideas which are the centerpiece of much of fantasy. The use of fantasy in a traditional political science classroom may seem baffling or bewildering or even shocking. It might seem strange or weird. It also causes excitement. It creates emotions of admiration and awe. It connects with imagination. It "shows" and "makes visible" (Panshin 3).

While mainstream political science has typically viewed popular culture as unworthy of serious investigation, this essay will explore the way that science fiction movies can be used as powerful tools for teaching college students about contemporary politics. Analyzing scenes from *The Dark Knight* can be used to uncover the role emotion plays in our decision making and in political life.

Words, images, sounds, music, backdrop, and tone of voice are often significant predictors of political success. The same can be said of the workings of imaginative worlds: format is often as important as content. Dr. Elizabeth Ossoff, a psychology professor at Saint Anselm College who specializes in voting behavior, says voters start from an emotional perspective and then get more rational (qtd. in Keck). To illustrate, what explains Barack Obama's meteoric rise from obscure state senator to presidential aspirant? Obama was successful in framing the 2008 election as a choice between hope and fear. The message was something like "Support Barack Obama because he makes you feel hopeful" or "Support John McCain because he makes you feel safe."

These appeals tap into the same emotional root: escape fear, believe in a brighter tomorrow, and desire the recovery of the American Dream.

Just as the voters in 2008 had to reflect on safety and hope, *The Dark Knight* invites reflection upon the cost of survival and the limits of goodness in a world of corrupted institutions in which, nonetheless, we have no alternative but to preserve and uphold those same institutions (Beattie). This then is the dilemma of our postmodern condition. But we also know that neither anarchy nor revolution can deliver the society we long for; we must work through individual acts of resistance and courage, hoping and believing in the continued promise of the American Dream, the capability it affords, and the protection it promises in order to achieve the kind of society we desire. These same messages and emotions are what Harvey Dent stands for as the crusading district attorney in *Batman* and what Bill Clinton successfully tapped into in the "Hope" ad used in his first presidential campaign.

Emotions, for Aristotle, have an ambiguous, but essential function in human political action and decision-making. Even though Aristotle argues that human beings are rational animals, he does not conclude that political excellence necessitates a suppression of human emotion. In fact, rather than understanding emotions as dichotomous with reason, Aristotle argues ethical action requires that reason and emotion function as partners or in symphony. This is not to suggest that emotions are universally positive for political life. "The emotions," Aristotle states, "are things through which, being turned around, people change in their judgments and with which pain and pleasure come, for example anger, pity, fear, and other such things and their opposites" (26). An additional complexity in Aristotle's understanding of emotions is that, even within a particular political and physical environment, human emotions are not static or uniform. Instead emotions fluctuate with complex interaction of variables, including not only particular individual characteristics, but also the general influence of age and gender (26).

Even Alexander Hamilton, one of our founding fathers, recognized the potential power of political emotion, but he focused on emotion's negative force. "Take mankind in general, they are vicious. What are they governed by, their passions," he wrote in 1787. Likewise, James Madison observed in *The Federalist Papers #51* that "if angels were to govern men, neither external nor internal controls of government would be necessary..." (322).

Images have become increasingly important in eliciting emotion, including political emotion. Even the cinema has become, or maybe always has been, a potent form of political communication. Nonetheless, the idea of using popular art in the form of films to explain/understand and teach politics is still at the margins of pedagogy. One of the first scholars to note the possibilities of film in the teaching of political science was John D. Millett just after the Second World War. But even at this nascent stage of research on the issue,

Millett realized that "there is little advantage in employing a film simply to photograph a classroom lecture" (520). Clearly, even then, there was much more to it than just letting the images do the teaching. And, today, it's not enough to put in a DVD or play a YouTube clip to fill some of the time of the lesson. There must be a rationale for using material, visual or otherwise, in a classroom curriculum.

Movies can be used as a teaching tool in many ways. One approach uses film to portray historical events or, for more recent happenings, to show them occurring. Another approach would be to utilize film to show debates on specific issues or to let portions of programs become the debate. Also, movies can be used as cultural narratives to explain and criticize theories. Some of the benefits of using movies include the fact that students are used to and are generally good at dealing with visual material, and it would make sense to utilize the skills that they already have to help them in other areas with which they may be less familiar.

Most films, fictional or factual, touch people emotionally as they reflect cultural values and historical meanings. Films also engage emotions. Engaging student emotions contributes to the learning process. In addition, using movies can actively contribute to reducing hierarchies in the class and encouraging discussion. It can be difficult in a political science classroom to elicit comments from students who may fear their own political naiveté. By no means am I claiming that movies should replace the reading of primary literature and academic articles and books, but a combination of showing films to reflect the current curriculum, linked with the assigned appropriate reading for each session, can provide a fruitful alternative to a traditional lesson.

Showing a movie in class provides a common reference point to which all participants can refer in order to make their arguments, points and views clear for the other members of the class. It can provide the "hook" with which to open a class discussion. At the same time, films can make challenging abstract concepts, ideas, and theories more concrete. They dramatize an event or idea by bringing a human face to even the seemingly more mundane issues in politics. A scene from a movie, properly selected, can help students "step into the shoes" of a character acting in that scene; more importantly students are led to empathize, to consider the scope of options the characters may have available to them, and to reflect on the choices as well as on the normative implications at stake in complex circumstances. They might also learn that political reality, like drama, is essentially constructed.

This kind of dramatic visual confrontation with political subjects and with sometimes violent issues and theories dealing with topics of war and peace inevitably creates a certain level of emotional engagement among students. These emotions evoke enthusiasm, encourage class participation, and, without a doubt, have the potential to provide the means for animated class debates and discussions. As students are familiar with films and are used to talking openly about them, movies can also work as a "leveling device" between the teacher and the students since students often take on roles of expertise when they find commonalities between the film under discussion and others with which they are familiar.

The positive effect of familiarity with movies is further underlined by the use of science fiction movies or fantasy films as metaphors for political events, issues, or theories. In contrast to clearly political films in relation to which students may be more reserved about their comments, students seem to be more comfortable in participating in a discussion and hypothesizing about the meaning of a metaphorical movie as there seems to be no right or wrong interpretation in the fictional and often fantastic universe of the setting.

Films portray a certain interpretation of how the world works. One of the main strengths of such an approach is that students are compelled to apply the theories they have considered in text and lecture to a much less self-evident object of study. Theories are scientific constructs, and as such they can be much better understood and their explanatory strengths and weaknesses can be much better uncovered if they are applied to a world which is as obviously artificially constructed as the theory itself, such as the world we encounter in a movie or a video game. Sometimes by shifting the center of attention away from the "usual suspects" to an unfamiliar setting (a fictional world), students are encouraged to critically evaluate some basic ontological and epistemological assumptions, and may gain a much better appreciation of closely-held (and otherwise unexamined) assumptions and theories. I have found this directs students away from stereotypes, labels, and personalities such as liberal/conservative, Obama/McCain, etc. That can lead to a deeper understanding of and more critical thinking about the theories' or subjects' potentials and limits. A good starting point is to identify in advance the respective theory's main assumptions in order to help students focus on the selected scenes which display the diverse bits and pieces of the theoretical approach.

For example, students may consider how Gotham in *The Dark Knight* is the postmodern state and further consider how we are the equivalent postmodern citizens: "The choices we face are not those which are arranged around good and evil, right and wrong. They are the dilemmas we face when our own survival is a gamble which pits us against shadowy and unpredictable enemies who infiltrate and infect all our social and political institutions with fear and mistrust" (Beattie).

According to Beattie, "*The Dark Knight* ventures into this haunted space of political and psychological terror. It taps the world of nightmares in which there is no happy ending and no resolution, just a question posed to each of us: how far am I willing to go in order to feel safe, to belong, to survive?"

This is an important question: "It is a question for our bright and hopeful president, Barack Obama. What price is he willing to pay to become part of the system? And what price might he have to pay to resist its corruption?" (Beattie). Students may well want to enter this kind of discussion when what is under consideration has fewer "real" or "immediate" stakes.

The character of Bruce Wayne in *The Dark Knight* understands the visceral side of politics, and successful politicians like Bill Clinton similarly exhibit an intuitive grasp of the non-rational nature of politics. The importance of emotional themes in politics can be illustrated by comparing scenes from *The Dark Knight* and a campaign advertisement from Bill Clinton's 1992 presidential campaign.

To set the stage, I begin by discussing the notion that politics is pervasive in reality as well as in fantasy and that importance can be placed on associations, in other words, on thoughts, feelings, images and ideas that have become connected. I then give them four examples:

- "I was born in a little place called Hope, Arkansas." (The first line in a political ad, "Journey," used by Bill Clinton)
- "I still believe in a place called Hope." (Closing line in Bill Clinton's acceptance speech, "Bill," at the nominating convention in 1992)
- "I believe in Harvey Dent." Bruce Wayne's speech at a fundraiser for Harvey Dent in *The Dark Knight*.
- HOPE poster — Obama 2008 campaign poster image

Next, I show my class a scene from *The Dark Knight*. Natasha is Bruce Wayne's (Batman) dinner date, Harvey Dent is the local District Attorney for Gotham City, and Rachel is Harvey Dent's dinner date and a good friend of Bruce Wayne. The setting is a very fancy restaurant owned by Bruce Wayne. Bruce and Natasha run into Harvey and Rachel and they end up dining together. As they finish up dinner, Natasha asks why anyone would want to raise children in Gotham City, a place that idolizes a masked vigilante. She explains that Gotham needs heroes like Dent, elected officials, ordinary men standing up for what's right, not someone who thinks he's above the law (e.g., Bruce Wayne's alter ego, Batman). Bruce Wayne agrees and questions who gave Batman his power. Harvey Dent asserts that the citizens of Gotham did, when they stood by and let scum take control of their city. Dent explains that, when their enemies were at the gate, the Romans would suspend democracy and appoint one man to protect the city. It was considered public service. He wonders, however, if Batman's looking for someone to take up his mantle, maybe even Harvey Dent himself. At this point, Bruce Wayne is so impressed he offers to throw the district attorney a fundraiser. Bruce makes the point that one fundraiser with his pals, and Dent will never need another cent.

The next scene I show is at the fundraiser in Bruce Wayne's penthouse in which Wayne endorses Harvey Dent's reelection bid. Wayne begins by using humor to win over the crowd, comprised of wealthy citizens who are being asked to write big checks. He says,

> Where's Rachel? Rachel Dawes — my oldest friend. When she told me she was dating Harvey Dent, I had one thing to say, the guy from those god-awful campaign commercials? "I Believe in Harvey Dent." Nice slogan, Harvey, it certainly caught Rachel's attention. But then I started paying attention to Harvey and all he's been doing as our new D.A., and you know what? I believe in Harvey Dent. On his watch, Gotham can feel a little safer, a little more optimistic, so get out your checkbooks and let's make sure that he stays right where all of Gotham wants. [Wayne toasts.] To the face of Gotham's bright future — Harvey Dent.

I have the students identify and discuss the political issues/images/emotions, etc., in these scenes, including the "hope" Bruce Wayne has for Harvey Dent and why Wayne is both interested in and impressed by this new DA. The students then work in groups to design a conference brochure titled "The Politics of Batman." They come up with possible conference session topics, such as "Is Batman a Criminal or Public Servant?" "Where Does Batman's Power End?" "How Does Money Dictate Power in Government?" "Who Is the Joker in Gotham and in Today's Society?" "What Type of Government Does Batman Represent?" "How Do People's Fears about Batman Represent People's Fears about Giving One Person Too Much Power?" These "session topics" then become the themes for my lectures and discussions the rest of the semester. I tell the students, "You designed the semester, not me." This serves to connect them to the material and they feel invested in the subject.

These topics represent an intellectual and emotional investment in the course material, which leads to better learning outcomes. In a similar vein, Drew Westin in *The Political Brain* writes about how voters' political choices are shaped by their emotions. According to a review by Rutherford in *Public Affairs*, Westin's central point is that successful political campaigns "compete in the marketplace of emotions and not primarily in the marketplace of ideas" (87). We, professors, students, voters, citizens, need to pay close attention to the positive and negative images and emotions that become associated with candidates in the minds of voters, whether or not they/we are aware of them. In other words, successful political campaigning — and decision making — is about being attuned to what is being felt, but remains unspoken. Successful candidates tell emotionally compelling stories about who they are and what they believe in. They can move people to tears, laughter, anger, compassion. Candidates who present voters with position statements, and laundry lists of facts and figures, trusting voters to weigh up the information and reach a rational decision, sometimes lose. Alongside a main narrative, successful candidates offer a number of key signature issues that illustrate their values and principles.

Westin pays close attention to non-verbal communication and the way images, words, and phrases resonate in the unconscious. The associations that link thoughts, smells, memories, sounds are familiar to the advertising industry, which has been using them for years to manipulate people's emotions. Politics is not a battle for the center ground; it is a battle for people's imaginations. In politics today, candidates and office holders have to tell coherent, emotionally compelling, memorable stories, particularly about who they are and what they stand for (424). Bill Clinton was masterful at telling such stories.

In order to illustrate the effect of the non-verbal image, I show the class one of Bill Clinton's earliest presidential campaign ads, which is widely viewed by campaign scholars as one of the most effective commercials in the history of American politics. The purpose of the ad was to begin creating a set of positive associations to him and to establish a narrative about the Man from Hope — framed, from start to finish, in terms of hope and the American Dream ("Journey").

Westin asserts that "Clinton's ad was deceptively simple, narrated exclusively by the then-young Arkansas governor. In the background was music evocative of small-town America. Along with images and video clips that music underscored the message" (4). Westin says that, in his first sentence, "Clinton vividly conveyed where he was coming from, literally and metaphorically — from a 'place called Hope'" (5). Further, "he was not content to make this statement just with words. The ad conjured for viewers a vivid, multi-sensory network of associations, associations not to the *word* 'hope' but to the *image* of Hope as small town America in an era gone by, captured and illustrated by the sight of the train station and the sound of hope, captured in Clinton's voice" (Westin 5). Clinton told his own life story, but he told it as a parable of what anyone can accomplish if just given the chance ("Journey"). He tied the theme of hope to the well-established theme of the American Dream, presenting himself not as a man of privilege descending to help those less fortunate (Bruce Wayne) but as someone no different from anyone else who grew up on any street, Main Street (Harvey Dent), in any town (Gotham City) — indeed, as someone who had suffered more adversity than most, being born after his own father's death.

The story line of the narrative might be summarized in three simple sentences: "Through hard work, caring, and determination, I know what it's like to live the American dream. In my home state, I've done everything possible to help others realize that dream. And as your president, I'll do everything I can to help people all over this country realize their dreams, just as I've done in Arkansas." In the closing line, he tied these twin themes — hope and the

American dream — together, describing his desire to bring "hope back to the American dream" ("Journey").

Part of the ad focuses on the time when Clinton was a young boy and had the opportunity to meet the President, John F. Kennedy, in 1963 at the Boy's Nation Program. The association to President Kennedy was instrumental to the emotional appeal of the ad. Kennedy is an American icon, whose tenure in the White House is widely remembered as a time in which America's hopes soared along with its space program. Thus, in the ad, the sequence of visual images is important ("Journey").

The sequence begins with Kennedy by himself, looking young, vibrant, serious, and presidential — precisely the features the Clinton campaign wanted to associate with Clinton. Then comes the segment showing a young Bill Clinton shaking hands with Kennedy, dramatically bringing the theme of the American dream to viewers' eyes, the poor boy from Arkansas without a father finding himself in the presence of his hero. At the same time, this sequence creates a sense of something uncanny, of "fate," of the chance meeting of once and future presidents that seemed too prescient not to be preordained (not unlike Harvey Dent and Rachel running into Bruce Wayne and Natasha in the restaurant). Then in the ad comes a still photo of Clinton's and Kennedy's hands tightly clasped, emphasizing the connection between the two men. This image lasts far longer than any other in the ad and gradually expands until the aspect of the two hands pans out into an image of the two recognizable figures ("Journey").

About the purpose of the ad, Westin says,

> Clearly, a central goal of the ad was to establish Clinton as presidential. In a race against an incumbent president, who needed only to stand in front of a podium with the seal of the presidency to appear presidential, the Clinton campaign seized every opportunity to show what Bill Clinton would look like a president, with the image of his raising his right hand to accept the oath of office (as governor of Arkansas), but also visually implying what Clinton would look like in his swearing in ceremony as president, followed by a photo of him working tirelessly at his (gubernatorial) desk, signing bills (itself reminiscent of photos of Kennedy) [7].

This ad, then, projects Clinton as a presidential figure, eliciting confidence in Clinton and causing positive resonance in the viewers' minds.

No one, not Clinton, not Harvey Dent, has won an election solely by harnessing positive emotions. Franklin Roosevelt, John F. Kennedy, Ronald Reagan, Bill Clinton, and Barack Obama, all remarkably inspirational leaders, did not shy away from sharply criticizing their opponents, particularly in the general elections. Successful campaigns are campaigns that both inspire and also raise concerns about the opposition. An election is a choice, not a referendum, and, because positive and negative emotions both drive voting behavior, they must be addressed by the candidates — and by office holders.

Finally, I ask the students to read the words of President Obama's speech to Congress on health care from September 2009. Obama repeatedly ties the themes of hope, a better tomorrow, and reaching the American dream in his push for universal health care. He also evokes the emotion of the Kennedy family.

He begins by reminding Americans that "we did not come here just to clean up crises. We came here to build a future. So tonight, I return to speak to all of you about an issue that is central to that future — and that is the issue of health care." President Obama speaks of a letter he received from the late Senator Ted Kennedy that Kennedy had directed to be delivered upon his death. In the letter Kennedy expresses his confidence that this, 2010, would be the year that health care reform became a reality. He wrote of "that great unfinished business of our society." In his speech, President Obama shared the information that Kennedy reminded him of concerns that were about more than material things and that health care for all was a moral issue and rested upon the fundamental principles of social justice and the character of our country. Obama spoke then of the large heartedness and concern and regard for others that we as Americans share and that, when fortune turns against one of us, others are there to lend a helping hand; he spoke of a belief that, in this country, hard work and responsibility should be rewarded by some measure of security and fair play; and he gave an acknowledgment that sometimes government has to step in to help deliver on that promise. He called on the American public not to fear the future, but to shape it. Once again, he used the powerful emotional ties of hope and the American Dream to rally the public to finally achieve universal health care.

More attention to how emotion circulates in the political world is worthy of exploration. Given the awareness that emotion can sabotage the best laid public policies, an understanding of how emotion circulates and is represented in public discourse is important. Emotion is not simply a negative force in politics, for a spirited protest can garner popular support and push the state to live up to its democratic ideals, such as universal health care for all. And given that action, reflection and desire (emotion) are entwined; it is naïve to assume that emotion can be bridled, bracketed to allow reason to prevail. Strong feelings of injustice and passionate expressions of commitment inspire and sustain protest movements around racism, sexism, imperialism/colonialism, and globalization. Students can see those feelings and protests reflected in most media which they would choose to peruse.

Toward the end of the semester, I ask my students to think about what they "hope" for, what they think the American Dream means, and what role they think government and politics do or should play. I ask them if our heroes can be elected officials like Harvey Dent, the man that Natasha believes Gotham needs and what it will take for that to happen (later the discussion should keep in mind the corruptive powers of money and revenge and the ultimate role that Harvey Dent takes on as "Two Face"). What role does emotion play in our politics now and how might it be used in the future? These topics always lead to energetic and thoughtful discussions.

The next step I would like to take in the classroom is to incorporate gaming in the study of political science. Video games offer another opportunity to bring powerful imagery and fantasy themes into the classroom. For example, according to Lamb, *Food Force* is a free online game from the United Nations World Food Program that sends children ages eight to thirteen on six realistic aid missions. It's already been downloaded more than 2.5 million times and the Woodrow Wilson Center for International Scholars in Washington, D.C., has founded the Serious Games Initiative to explore how key challenges facing governments and nonprofit groups can be addressed using game play. "A lot of people are looking at video games because of their pervasiveness and because of their really unique capabilities for learning," says Suzanne Seggerman, co-founder of Games for Change, a two-year old nonprofit that promotes games with a social conscience (qtd. in Lamb).

According to Steve York, senior producer at York-Zimmerman Inc., a documentary film company in Washington, D.C., game playing is "a totally different style of teaching, it's 'learn by doing'" (qtd. in Lamb). Together with the International Center on Nonviolent Conflict and Breakaway Games Ltd., a video game maker, York's company is producing *A Force More Powerful*, in which players use peaceful means to unseat a dictator in ten fictitious scenarios (Lamb).

Eventually, "serious games will take over the world" of gaming, predicts Jason Della Rocca, executive director of the International Game Developers Association in San Francisco: "'People will use video games for learning so easily and so often that they won't think twice about it,' he says. 'People using video games will no more be labeled "gamers" than people today who listen to music are labeled "listeners,"' he adds" (qtd. in York).

"Games and stories are generative with one leading to the other," said game designer Will Wright, who added that games allow people to build models in a virtual world that also apply to the real world. He adds, "People can learn lessons about the past, present and future in an entertaining way" (qtd. in Gaudiosi).

Online games aren't just for entertainment anymore. *Fantasy Congress* is the brainchild of Andrew Lee, a senior at Claremont McKenna College. He says the game is not unlike other fantasy sport games. It is designed for users to earn points as their team — in this case, four senators and twelve representatives — push legislation toward a successful conclusion. Based on actual legislation making its way through the hallowed halls of Congress, *Fantasy Congress* gives power to the people and allows its users to draft a team of sixteen real-life legislators ranging across the congressional spectrum to earn points as bills move through Congress and to the President's desk. Adding this game to political science curriculum can give students a better picture of how the Congress and at least two branches of the government actually work and work together — or not (Venkataraman).

As Jesse Schell writes in *The Art of Game Design*, the illusion of internal consistency in video games is as important as it is frail. Unlike story-based entertainment, where the story world exists only in the guest's imagination, interactive entertainment creates significant over-lap between perception and imagination, allowing the guest to directly manipulate and change the story world. This is why video games can present events with little inherent interest or poetry, but the action can still be compelling (Bissell 115).

Released in 1985, *Super Mario Bros.* was a game of unprecedented inventiveness. It was among the first video games to suggest that it might contain a world. Anyone who plays modern games such as *Gears of War* does not so much learn the rules as develop a kind of intuition for how the game operates. Often, there is no single way to accomplish a given task; improvisation is rewarded. The popularity of games like *Gears of War* resides in the "feel" of its game mechanics (Bissell 58). The procedures and rules of a game are what are meant, broadly speaking, by the term game mechanics. As the game designer Jesse Schell writes, "If you compare games to more linear entertainment experiences [books, movies, etc.] you will note that while linear experiences involve technology, story, and aesthetics, they do not involve mechanics, for it is mechanics that make a game a game." The importance of game-mechanics feel is something that designer Bleszinski has made his special focus and passion. He wants a game to have an interesting game mechanic, but "I also want it to be a fascinating universe that I want to spend time in, because you're spending often dozens of hours in this universe" (qtd. in Bissell 58).

Games in classes can lead to many kinds of fascinating experiences for student and professor alike. In fact, games have been used in the "real world" to make political changes. According to Jane McGonigal, a game designer, "There are newspapers that have used games to get readers to help analyze government documents. There was a [British] game called 'Investigate your MP's expenses," [sic] where readers were able to uncover so much stuff that people actually resigned from Parliament and new laws were passed as a result of the game" (Bensen 15). Investigating such games, and using them, in the classroom can lead to increased understanding of the government and of the power of the media, including the medium of gaming.

The desire to spend hours in a fascinating universe can become an integral part of the learning experience and can be utilized by the canny political science pedagogue to enhance and reinforce those principles important to the political process. Students, citizens need to know how and why their government works; they need to be aware of political action and climate. Any tool—film or game—that catches their attention and imagination can be a valuable tool indeed.

Emotion is becoming part of game mechanics and the "worlds" within gaming are increasingly political in nature. Political fiction and fantasy are still relatively alien in the political classroom, and this is to its own detriment. To what extent can the study of politics through literature, film, games, and popular culture serve to engage and educate students as well as citizens who are "turned off" politics by political junkies and politicians? There is no question: a great deal.

Works Cited

Aristotle. *The Art of Rhetoric*. Cambridge: Harvard University Press, 1926. Print.

Beattie, Tina. "The Dark (K)night of a Postmodern World." *Open Democracy*. 21 Aug. 2008. Web. 28 Sept. 2009.

Bensen, Amanda. "Interview: Jane McGonigal." *Smithsonian* Feb. 2010: 15. Print.

Bissell, Tom. *Extra Lives: Why Video Games Matters*. New York: Pantheon, 2010. Print.

Clinton, Bill. "Bill Clinton: I Still Believe in a Place Called Hope [Acceptance Speech]." 16 July 1992. *Democratic Underground.com*. 2001–2004. Web. 16 Sept. 2010.

_____. "Journey (Clinton [Campaign Ad], 1992)." *The Living Room Candidate: Presidential Campaign Commercials 1952–2008*. 2010. Web. 8 Sept. 2010.

The Dark Knight. 2008. Warner, 2008. DVD.

Dead Poets Society. 1989. Walt Disney, 1998. DVD.

Gaudiosi, John. "'The Sims' Creator Eyes the World beyond Games." *Reuters*. 6 Aug. 2009. Web. 16 Sept. 2009.

Hamilton, Alexander. "Article 1, Section 6, Clause 2: Document 1: Records of the Federal Convention [Minutes]." 22 June 1987. *The Founders' Constitution*. Max Farrand, ed. *The Records of the Federal Convention of 1787*. Rev. ed. New Haven: Yale University Press, 1937. Chicago: University of Chicago. 2000. Web. 3 Aug. 2008.

Keck, Kristi. "Angry Voters Could Affect Both Parties." *CNN*. 25 Jan. 2010. Web. 26 Jan. 2010.

Lamb, Gregory M. "Video Games to Teach Peacekeeping?" *Civil, Well-Reasoned Discourse: Rantburg*. 22 Dec. 2005. Web. 16 Sept. 2009.

Madison, James. "*The Federalist Papers #51: Madison.*" *The Federalist Papers: Hamilton, Madison, Jay*. New York: Mentor, New American Library, 1961. Print.

Millet, John D. "The Use of Visual Aids in Political Science Teaching." *American Political Science Review* 41 (1947): 517–27. Print.

Obama, Barack. "Hope Poster." *Amazon*. 2008. Web. 17 Sept. 2010.

_____. "Remarks by the President to a Joint Session of Congress on Health Care." Office of the Press Secretary. *The White House*. 9 Sept. 2009. Web. 23 Sept. 2009.

Panshin, Alexei, and Cory Panshin. *The World Beyond the Hill: Science Fiction and the Quest for Transcendence*. Los Angeles: Jeremy P. Tarcher, 1989. Print.

Rutherford, Jonathan. "Review—The Political Brain: The Role of Emotion in Deciding the Fate of the Nation." *Public Affairs* 2007: 87–90. Print.

Venkataraman, Nitya. "Video Games, Internet Sites Going Political: Playing Politics with Fantasy Congress to Virtual Campaigns." *ABC News*. 14 Oct. 2006. Web. 11 Sept. 2009.

Westin, Drew. *The Political Brain: The Role of Emotion in Deciding the Fate of the Nation*. New York: Public Affairs, 2007. Print.

II. Integrating New Works: Using Fantasy to Enrich Traditional Classes

Flights of Fantasy

JIM FORD

> "The mind is a strange and wonderful thing. I'm not sure it'll ever be able to figure itself out. Everything else, maybe — from the atom to the universe — everything except itself." — Dr. Dan Kauffman, *Invasion of the Body Snatchers*

The use of fantasy films in introductory philosophy courses is not novel; from textbooks that teach philosophy through film to theoretical accounts of film as a novel way of thinking, the academic literature on the relationship between film and philosophy has exploded in the past few decades.[1] Fantasy films are particularly apt tools for teaching philosophical ideas. A good fantasy film creates its own world, with an internal logic and consistency that make that world especially useful for comparison with the world outside the film (also known, occasionally disparagingly and skeptically, as "the real world"). Including such films in a traditional philosophy course can seem daunting, however, particularly for inexperienced faculty. What is the best way to take advantage of fantasy films while providing a strong philosophical foundation for undergraduate students? There are numerous ways to integrate fantasy films in the introductory philosophy course, and I will highlight several of them here. After that I will focus on roughly thirty fantasy films that have proven successful in humanities, philosophy, and religious studies classrooms, from classic candidates like *2001* and *The Matrix* to more recent films like *Eternal Sunshine of the Spotless Mind*, *Pan's Labyrinth*, and *Inception*. These films can illuminate traditional philosophical topics, even as they remain valuable for study on their own terms. The first step, though, is teaching students how to watch and think about film.

The Film Experience, Part One: The Setting

"These aren't the droids you're looking for."—Obi-Wan Kenobi, *Star Wars*

It has become a cliché that students today are awash in visual images. Despite the time spent consuming television, movies, the internet in general, and YouTube in particular, student focus is usually partial and often limited. Teaching students how to watch a film is a crucial task. Even the most obvious rules—no cell phones, no text messaging, no sleeping, no chatting—have to be emphasized to most college freshmen. I find that it is important to model as well as explicitly describe the sort of response a good audience should have. I may have seen a particular movie many times, but I still need to show the students that this film is important by focusing my full attention. It is tempting sometimes to attend to other matters (the old complaint about the teacher who just plugs in a video so she can catch up on grading), but if I want students to treat the movie as important academic work, then I have to do so too.

All of this is part of teaching students that sustained, critical engagement is necessary in order to experience a film in an academic context. Great films often require repeated viewings, something that can be demonstrated by close analysis of particular scenes in a film that the class has just watched. Despite the time it takes, having an entire class watch a film together can be a powerful experience, one that presents many opportunities for learning. But the professor has to get them all to sit relatively still and pay attention first.

I have found that the best way to show a film in class is to provide a very brief introduction first. This is not the occasion to demonstrate one's vast knowledge on the topic, or to critique the movie at length. Lengthy lectures dampen the students' interest (which is bad), but they also tell the students what to think (which is worse). I try to give students the bare minimum of background information—what do students absolutely need to know to make sense of the movie they are about to watch? Sometimes I do try to suggest questions for the students to consider while watching, or to highlight key themes or scenes, but more often than not students report that this distracts them from the film, and makes it more difficult for them to enjoy the film. Since part of why I use movies is to help students appreciate and understand great films, the last thing I want to do is take the joy out of it. While a minute or two of set-up can be helpful—when the movie was made, what sort of movie it is, basically the kind of information a good trailer might provide—anything more than that should be saved for after the movie.

Of course, a lot depends on the setting and timing of the class. Having a screen sufficient for every student to see well and sound quality that draws the audience in is important. If the regular classroom is not conducive to the film experience, moving to an auditorium or designated viewing space is worth the trouble (and it emphasizes for the students the importance of that day's work). It's easiest to utilize films in a once-a-week, 150 minute class format. A brief introduction by the professor, 100–120 minutes for the film, a five-minute break, followed by twenty-five to forty minutes discussion, is ideal. Such a format is unusual for introductory classes (except for cinema), but for the professor who is planning to emphasize films throughout the course it can be worth the trouble to schedule that way. Much more common is the twice weekly course, in which the professor can introduce the movie and show at least the first hour of the film. In such cases it is crucial to find a good stopping point, one that does minimal damage to the flow and action of the film. That leaves another thirty to fifty minutes for the second meeting of the week, as well as sufficient time for discussion at the end. Make sure that the discussion is a priority, and use the full class-time even if discussion is lagging (or nonexistent). Students learn quickly whether they are expected to contribute, or whether a brief awkward silence can lead to early release. Utilizing films in an online or virtual course is more difficult than it seems. It is easy to assign students films to watch on their own, but ensuring that they do so, and then generating a meaningful discussion afterwards, can be a real challenge. But then that is true of most online assignments and activities.

The Film Experience, Part Two: The Advantages of Popular Films

> "I always thought the joy of reading a book is not knowing what happens next."—Leonard Shelby, *Memento*

One of the advantages of using popular films is that students have often seen the movies before. How many students have seen a particular movie varies tremendously from campus to campus, and even from classroom to classroom. I find in most classes that even the most popular movies, whether good or bad (from *Avatar* to *Transformers 2*), have only been seen by a minority of students. There are usually four or five students who have not seen even the best-known science-fiction and fantasy films like *Star Wars* and *The Lord of the Rings*. This is less an issue of genre (that students do not like sci-fi, for example) than it is the diversity of popular culture, and of the lack of shared experiences. That is partly why using film in class can be so helpful, because it provides students (and the professor) a common language, a shared set of examples and topics to draw on throughout the semester. Using popular films makes it more likely that at least some of the students are familiar with the work in question. This enables the teacher to build on what students already know, to use familiar material to sharpen their critical thinking skills. Every time I teach Plato's *Republic* in class, several students immediately respond to the Ring of Gyges by calling it "The One Ring." That moment of recognition draws them into the text, and helps them make sense of the dialogue much more quickly than they otherwise might. While it is not necessary to watch any of the *Rings* movies to understand the *Republic*, it can make it easier.

The best fantasy and science-fiction films create rich, immersive environments. They have their own logic and laws, and the contrast with the "real world" facilitates critical thinking about both worlds. Just as Socrates proposes images to help his listeners understand the just city in the *Republic*, so too a well-chosen film provides an image to teach students about particular philosophical topics. Both "The Allegory of the Cave" and Descartes's evil demon argument become more vivid through a collective watching of *The Matrix*, particularly if students are allowed to make these connections for themselves.

Popular movies are also useful as a break in an introductory philosophy class. I like to have periods of difficult, intense reading interspersed with the shared film experience. Philosophical texts are challenging, but I do not believe that students can learn philosophy without reading some of the classic primary texts. Enjoying several weeks of close reading and discussion, followed by a film (and discussion), helps maintain student interest and gives them a manageable workload. While this is less a problem in other introductory courses (basic humanities courses, for instance), a film still adds variety to the usual class discussion. Since students in non-philosophy courses may have even less exposure to philosophical ideas, using films as teaching tools in those classes is even more beneficial.

Film the Introduction to Philosophy Class

> Joel: Is there any risk of brain damage?
>
> Howard: Well, technically speaking, the operation is brain damage, but it's on a par with a night of heavy drinking. Nothing you'll miss.—*Eternal Sunshine of the Spotless Mind*

There are many ways to approach the traditional introductory philosophy course, but they can be grouped into several basic types. Many professors prefer a **topical** course, often one in which major branches of philosophy are each introduced (usually several of the following: metaphysics, ethics, logic, aesthetics, epistemology, political philosophy, philosophy of religion, though this is not an exhaustive list). I usually organize Introduction to Philosophy **historically**, as an introduction to some of the most important philosophers. Here the emphasis is on primary texts, and on the questions that were foremost for those philosophers in their particular context. The **combination** of the two approaches also works well, in which major areas (of interest today) are approached through key historical contributions. Films can be integrated into any of these kinds of courses.

Showing a film at the conclusion of each branch works well for the topical course. The idea is to give students an opportunity to use what they have learned to analyze the film. The professor guides the students through the texts, and then allows them to process the film for themselves (in discussion, in writing, or both). Another approach is to show a film first, at the beginning of each section of the course, in order to introduce key ideas and themes through the film. This gives the class common examples to refer to as they study the particular area. For instance, if the branch in question is ethics, showing *The Dark Knight* after several weeks studying Mill's utilitarianism and Kant's categorical imperative provides students with an opportunity to test those theories against the movie's various ethical dilemmas. Showing the film first (before any training in ethics) gives students several scenarios to discuss as appropriate. Either way can work well, although I prefer showing the film after the heavy philosophical work. It is much the same story for the combination class, in that it is structured by themes or branches of philosophy. The professor just has to choose which film best illustrates (or challenges) the particular theme.

Integrating films into the historical introduction to philosophy can be slightly more complicated, if only because students have a tendency to think about the films simplistically. It is the teacher's responsibility to avoid making the connections too linear (for example, "We are watching this movie because *The Matrix* is like Socrates' cave in Plato's *Republic*"). Such an account limits not only what they learn from the movie, but also their appreciation for a film. Still, I have had success using films as bridges from thinker to thinker, or from age to age. *The Matrix* functions as a bridge from Plato to Descartes (really *The Matrix* functions well at almost any point in the philosophical timeline, but that's because it is a particularly rich film). Either *A Clockwork Orange* or *Eternal Sunshine of the Spotless Mind* works well for the transition from Nietzsche to the twentieth century, in part because of the ways each film calls into question the role of the mind and the will in what it means to be human. *Memento* is a classic for moving from modernism to postmodernism, both because of its narrative structure and the questions it poses about memory and identity.

Assignments vary based on the size and nature of the course, but I have found the film journal to be an excellent exercise for Introduction to Philosophy students. Before we watch our first film, I give the students several possible topics, such as character, conflict, scene, or theme. I usually require the students to choose each topic at least once during the semester, but it is their decision which topic to address with which film. When teaching cinema, I give the students a similar (but much longer) list. For Introduction to Philosophy, these are manageable tasks. Students choose a particular character, a conflict, a crucial scene, or a recurring theme to analyze more closely in their journals. Near the end of the semester it is good to have the students write a longer essay, using their journal entries as raw material, or to use their journals for reference during an essay exam. The goal here is to encourage the students to think critically about different aspects of a film in relation to their philosophical studies. Sometimes that can be a direct comparison of a philosophical text to part of a movie, but more often it is how both works relate to a common theme or issue. Of course, the journal only works if students are watching several films during the semester (usually at least four). If time is limited (as it usually is), watching one film a month is sufficient, particularly if students choose another film to watch on their own time. Otherwise a more traditional academic essay is the best assignment to use.

Mind-Blowing Science-Fiction and Fantasy Films: Something Strange

> "Well, dreams, they feel real when we're in them, right? It's only when we wake up that we realize something was actually strange."—Cobb, *Inception*

The choice of which films to use in class is obviously a personal one. Later listed are nearly thirty of my favorites, films that have been successful with a wide variety of classes and students.[2] These films work particularly well for highlighting problems in consciousness, raising doubts about reality, and opening the doors of perception. I group them into three categories. The first kind of film is set in the real world, but problematizes what is real. Such films usually (but not always) have the fewest trappings of science-fiction. A second kind of film creates its own fantastic world, usually set in some future time or some far-away place. A third sort of film creates its own sharply defined reality, only to blur the lines in the course of the film. Such a film is set in a future fantasy world where reality is not at all clear or coherent. All of these movies provide a sharp contrast to daily life and enable the class to discuss a number of interesting questions about the mind, the world, and what it means to live in it.

The first group includes a wide variety of films, many of which are not usually classified as science-fiction or fantasy films. These films work with a variety of audiences, in part because they are not completely alien. Some feature technologies that are currently impossible, such as selective memory erasing (*Eternal Sunshine of the Spotless Mind*) or dream sharing and manipulation (*Inception*).[3] These films are particularly beneficial for discussions of memory and mind, as well as love. Others show characters divided against themselves, in ways that raise doubts about perception and reality even when the divisions are ultimately resolved or explained. In *Fight Club* reality slowly crumbles as the narrator (Edward Norton) finds himself increasingly marginalized by Tyler Durden (Brad Pitt); the film is immensely popular, violent, and disturbing. It is an excellent choice for late in a semester or with a more mature class. *Shutter Island* is a similar choice, in which federal marshal Teddy Daniels (Leonardo DiCaprio) investigates a disappearance at a hospital for the criminally insane and is confronted with questions about his own sanity. The main character in *Memento*, Leonard Shelby (Guy Pearce), is unable to make new memories and spends the film searching for his wife's killer. Scenes appear in reverse chronological order, requiring the audience to piece the narrative together for themselves. *Jacob's Ladder* is the story of a man (Tim Robbins) confronted by a series of horrible visions and flashbacks. While these are not strictly fantasy movies, they stretch reality in similar ways.

This first group also includes some more traditional science fiction and fantasy films, from *Invasion of the Body Snatchers* to *Pan's Labyrinth*. The former is of course one of the classic tales of alien invasions. I prefer the 1956 version; even though students often grumble about black and white films, *Invasion* is a clear example of a film so good that students soon forget their doubts. *Pan's Labyrinth* is an intriguing choice, both for its compelling visuals and for its lack of rational explanations. The movie faithfully depicts two worlds, the brutal reality of post-civil war Spain and a mysterious fantasy world of magical creatures. Students will argue (at length) about how these two worlds relate and what the ultimate meaning of the film might be, arguments that are philosophically rewarding. The film is in Spanish with English subtitles; while students may at first be resistant to a subtitled film, most are quickly engaged by *Pan's Labyrinth*. Another film about mortality and perception is *The Sixth Sense*. Of course, it is the story of Cole (Haley Joel Osment), a young boy who can see and interact with dead people. As ubiquitous as it was a decade ago, I find that many students today have never seen the film.[4]

Future Fantasy Worlds: "A Splinter in Your Mind"

> "You've felt it your entire life, that there's something wrong with the world. You don't know what it is, but it's there, like a splinter in your mind, driving you mad."—Morpheus, *The Matrix*

The second group of films feature fully developed fantasy worlds, usually set in the future or in some far-away place. These are the films that most students think of when they hear "sci-fi." Some, like *The Matrix*, have become classics for academics; others, like *Wall-E*, are more rarely used in class.

Presumably anyone reading these words knows *The Matrix*, where the world humans experience is a virtual reality program, created by machines to control those humans. It is a visually stunning film, and one that remains a sound choice for any introductory philosophy class. *Wall-E* is the animated tale (by Pixar) of a trash-collecting robot on an earth abandoned by human beings. The recent blockbuster *Avatar* is another film in this group. Despite some weak dialogue (among other problems), it is another film that many students will have seen and be able to relate to classroom issues.[5] In different ways both of these films highlight the danger of abusing the Earth's resources. All three of these films create rich new worlds as foils for our everyday reality.

Some of the best sci-fi films meet this standard. The original Lucas *Star Wars* (*Episode IV: A New Hope*) continues to resonate with students. Both *Alien* and *Aliens* are excellent films for classroom use, in that they raise a variety of ethical questions, as well as challenging our ideas of what it means to be human. *Terminator 2* is one of the best films for highlighting puzzles about time and fate. (*Terminator* is also a great science fiction film, but it tends not to work as well for classes). *Total Recall* is easy to mock — I hesitate to say whether the scene where Quaid (Arnold Schwarzenegger) pulls a tracking device out of his nostril or the shot of the man with the alien prophet growing out of his stomach is more painful — but it also has some philosophical depth, and, like a lot of sci-fi films, works well in conjunction with the original source material (Philip K. Dick's "We Can Remember It For You Wholesale"). The same is true for *A Clockwork Orange*, the novel for which continues the story in fascinating ways. It is a bit graphic for freshman classes, but in general it is an excellent film for philosophy. Its vision of the future is fascinatingly contemporary. *District 9* is a more recent film in which science fiction intrudes on modern society. Aliens and their technology are handled in a realistic (and disturbing) manner, with multinational corporations and ineffective aid agencies struggling to accommodate the newcomers. *V for Vendetta* is the tale of a young woman (Natalie Portman) who must decide whether to help the mysterious V (Hugo Weaving) in his terrorist campaign against a totalitarian Great Britain. Finally, *Dark City* is an excellent film noir in which the future is not at all what it seems.

Future Imperfect: "Lost in Time"

> "All those moments will be lost in time, like tears in rain. Time to die." — Batty, *Blade Runner*

My third group consists of films that create their own new worlds, only to blur the lines of reality in a way that combines the best qualities of the first two groups. A strong case can be made for including both *Dark City* and

Total Recall here, but these films go even further in questioning the very realities that they initially establish. While these films can be more challenging to integrate into a philosophy course, when successful, these present the deepest possibilities. *2001: A Space Odyssey* is the prototype for such films. While HAL and artificial intelligence dominate the film, human evolution and its cosmic progress provide a number of worthwhile philosophical topics. The ending can be puzzling, and *2001* is a movie that challenges students, one that usually works better as a second or third film (rather than early in the semester). *Blade Runner* is another classic with its treatment of human beings and androids in a grim future. Deckard (Harrison Ford) hunts down and terminates escaped androids, but his own humanity is uncertain. The film exists in several versions, each of which has its own advantages and claims to authenticity (I myself think Deckard's narration works well at times, although I know others are dismissive). *Minority Report* is a film that does not always get the credit it deserves. It raises questions about fate and free will as well as any other film. Like *Blade Runner* and *Total Recall*, *Minority Report* is based on the work of Philip K. Dick.[6] Reading the source material in conjunction with the film enriches the classroom for all three works. It is not at all clear whether the ending of *Minority Report* is real, or a dream of Chief Anderton's (Tom Cruise).

Many of Terry Gilliam's films are excellent for classroom use. *Brazil* is set in a contemporary totalitarian bureaucracy, and is full of bizarre visuals and a number of imaginary sequences and fantasies. Not many students have seen *Brazil*. More popular is *12 Monkeys*, Gilliam's vision of the world after an apocalyptic plague. James Cole (Bruce Willis) is sent back in time to discover the cause of the outbreak, but his grip on reality is tenuous at best. The film is a wonderful collage of insanity, memory, and time travel. *The Fisher King* deals with similar themes, as Parry (Robin Williams) is lost in a fantasy world after his wife's murder, and Jack (Jeff Bridges) dedicates himself to helping Parry recover (what Parry believes to be) the Holy Grail. *Time Bandits* is a fascinating film about a young boy who travels through time with a group of thieves. At times it feels like a children's movie, but it deals with some of the most serious themes and has a real edge to it. It works particularly well for humanities classes, in that it moves through a number of cultures and historical settings that students will have studied. *12 Monkeys* is the easiest of these to include in an introductory philosophy class, but all four are worth considering.

All of these films present new opportunities for student learning. They can be easily integrated into any introductory philosophy course, providing a shared set of examples, images, and metaphors for class discussion or student writing. Whether as an occasional break from heavy reading or as a significant emphasis in the course, using science-fiction and fantasy films in the classroom is an excellent way to enhance students' introduction to philosophy.

Notes

1. Two good philosophy and film textbooks are McLaughlin's *An Introduction to Philosophy: In Black, White and Color* and Litch's *Philosophy through Film*. There is also *Philosophy Goes to the Movies* by Christopher Falzon. I prefer using primary texts (or anthologies of primary texts) and doing the film work myself, but these textbooks can make the process easier. The only danger is that students end up reading summaries of films in lieu of watching films, and it is obviously not the same. Several series that deal with popular culture and philosophy are worth mentioning: Open Court's "Popular Culture and Philosophy" is more than fifty volumes as of this writing, and Blackwell's "Philosophy and Pop Culture" is in the mid–twenties. Each volume focuses on particular works, from *The Simpsons* to Metallica to baseball, through a collection of essays by various authors, the quality and usefulness of which vary widely (the essays, not the authors). Finally, for a good one-volume treatment of some of the intersections between science-fiction and philosophy, look at *Science Fiction and Philosophy: From Time Travel to Superintelligence*.

2. I know thirty may seem excessive ... okay, it is excessive. But even with thirty films, this is not a comprehensive list. It leaves off 2007's excellent *Children of Men*, the recent remake of *Solaris*, the mind-bending *Being John Malkovich*, the classic original *The Day the Earth Stood Still*, and a host of other great science fiction and fantasy films. But I had to stop somewhere.

3. *Pleasantville* is another movie that features impossible technology. For more on using *Pleasantville* in class, see Laura Gray's essay.

4. One could also include *The Dark Knight* here. I find it more fruitful for discussions of ethics and law than for debates about truth and reality. For more on the uses of *The Dark Knight*, see Carolyn Anne Taylor's essay.

5. For some examples of student reactions to *Avatar*, see Sally Emmons's essay.

6. *Blade Runner* is based on Dick's *Do Androids Dream of Electric Sheep?*; *Total Recall* is based on Dick's "We Can Remember It for You Wholesale"; *Minority Report* is based on Dick's "The Minority Report."

Works Cited

Alien. Dir. Ridley Scott. Fox, 1979. Film.
Aliens. Dir. James Cameron. Fox, 1986. Film.
Avatar. Dir. James Cameron. Fox, 2009. Film.
Being John Malkovich. 1999. Dir. Spike Jonze. Universal, 2002. Film.
Blade Runner. Dir. Ridley Scott. Warner Bros., 1982. Film.
Brazil. Dir. Terry Gilliam. Universal, 1985. Film.
Burgess, Anthony. *A Clockwork Orange*. Norton Critical Ed. New York: Norton, 2011. Print.
Children of Men. Dir. Alfonso Cuarón. Universal, 2007. Film.
A Clockwork Orange. Dir. Stanley Kubrick. Warner Bros., 1971. Film.
Dark City. Dir. Alex Proyas. New Line, 1998. Film.
The Dark Knight. Dir. Christopher Nolan. Warner Bros., 2008. Film.
The Day the Earth Stood Still. Dir. Robert Wise. 20th Century–Fox, 1951. Film.
Dick, Philip K. *Do Androids Dream of Electric Sheep?* New York: Signet, 1969. Print.
_____. "Minority Report." *The Collected Stories of Philip K. Dick: Minority Report*. New York: Carol, 1991. 71–102. Print.
_____. "We Can Remember It for You Wholesale." *The Collected Stories of Philip K. Dick: Volume 2*. New York: Carol, 1995. 35–52. Print.
District 9. Dir. Neill Blomkamp. Tristar, 2009. Film.
Eternal Sunshine of the Spotless Mind. Dir. Michael Gondry. Universal, 2004. Film.
Falzon, Christopher. *Philosophy Goes to the Movies: An Introduction to Philosophy*. Stamford, CT: Routledge, 2007. Print.
The Fellowship of the Ring. Dir. Peter Jackson. New Line Cinema, 2001. Film.
Fight Club. Dir. David Fincher. Fox, 1999. Film.

The Fisher King. Dir. Terry Gilliam. Tristar, 1991. Film.
Inception. Dir. Christopher Nolan. Warner Bros., 2010. Film.
Invasion of the Body Snatchers. Dir. Don Siegel. Allied Artists, 1956. Film.
Jacob's Ladder. Dir. Adrian Lyne. Carolco, 1990. Film.
Litch, Mary. *Philosophy Through Film*. Stamford, CT: Routledge, 2002. Print.
The Matrix. Dir. Andy Wachowski and Larry Wachowski. Warner Bros., 1999. Film.
Memento. Dir. Christopher Nolan. Newmarket, 2000. Film.
Minority Report. Dir. Steven Spielberg. Twentieth Century–Fox, 2002. Film.
Pan's Labyrinth. Dir. Guillermo del Toro. Warner Bros., 2006. Film.
The Return of the King. Dir. Peter Jackson. New Line Cinema, 2003. Film.
Schneider, Susan, ed. *Science Fiction and Philosophy: From Time Travel to Superintelligence*. Malden, ME: Wiley-Blackwell, 2009. Print.
Shutter Island. Dir. Martin Scorsese. Paramount, 2010. Film.
The Sixth Sense. Dir. M. Night Shyamalan. Hollywood, 1999. Film.
Star Wars. Dir. George Lucas. Lucasfilm, 1977. Film.
Star Wars: Episode V—The Empire Strikes Back. Dir. Irvin Kershner. Lucasfilm, 1980. Film.
Terminator. Dir. James Cameron. Orion, 1984. Film.
Terminator 2. Dir. James Cameron. Carolco, 1991. Film.
Time Bandits. Dir. Terry Gilliam. HandMade Films, 1991. Film.
Total Recall. Dir. Paul Verhoeven. Carolco, 1990. Film.
Twelve Monkeys. Dir. Terry Gilliam. Universal, 1995. Film.
2001: A Space Odyssey. Dir. Stanley Kubrick. MGM, 1968. Film.
The Two Towers. Dir. Peter Jackson. New Line Cinema, 2002. Film.
V for Vendetta. Dir. James McTeigue. Warner Bros., 2006. Film.
Wall-E. Dir. Andrew Stanton. Pixar, 2008. Film.

Fusion Curriculum

EMILY DIAL-DRIVER

Not long ago a group of us walked down a street in Washington, D.C. D.C. is one of those cities in which a resident can live, shop, and dine all within one block. It seems like heaven to those who live where the nearest anything is a car drive away, unless a two-or-more-mile walk in 30 degrees with a wind of 25 miles per hour, carrying a pepperoni and pepper pizza and black coffee, or, in 100 degree weather, carrying a gallon of skimmed milk and a pint of peppermint chocolate chip ice cream, makes for happiness. But in D.C.—and Vancouver and San Francisco and Seattle and New York and not in Claremore, OK, or even Tulsa—I can walk a half block, buy a pashmina, select fresh plums, and hear a sidewalk drummer. That's a kind of fusion.

Fusion means combining. Fusion in nuclear physics means atoms combining with each other (okay, that's a simplistic way to define that), which may absorb or emit power. Fusion in food means taking elements from different cultural cuisines to make a new cuisine, adding power to the cook and interest to the restaurant—if the combination is successful. Recently I've seen Eddie's Chinese Takeout, Three Thai Sushi, Masala Wok, Danny's Sub and Chinese, and Jack's Mainly Chinese Tapas Café; and perhaps there could be Papa Minelli's Indonesian Fry Bread Shop and Hop Sing's Pizza Palace. Some of those combinations are fascinating and tasty; some might be complete failures.

Finding the correct combination of elements, in food, in physics, in chemistry—and in education—is vital to the process which one might want to initiate.

The Class

Teaching a fusion class can mean teaching a class that uses both traditional elements and non-traditional elements. Such a class was the Sophomore

Honors Seminar that I taught. The theme of the class was "the dark side of the mind." I used two works that have been categorized as philosophy, one listed under the classification of either sociology or psychology, and several works of fiction, some of which are fantasy. Those divisions, however, are misleading. The individual works are far more complex than that.

Reading List

The reading list contained Chinua Achebe's *Things Fall Apart;* Albert Camus's *The Stranger*; Hermann Hesse's *Siddhartha*; Franz Kafka's *Metamorphosis, In the Penal Colony, and Other Stories*; Robert Louis Stevenson's *Dr. Jekyll and Mr. Hyde*; H.G. Wells's *The Invisible Man*; Philip Zimbardo's *The Lucifer Effect*; and Victor Frankl's *Man's Search for Meaning*. In addition to the reading, we watched a few videos: the *Jekyll* series from the BBC, "Out of Sight" from the *Buffy* series, and *Dr. Horrible's Sing-Along Blog*, originally made for the Internet. Each of these added to the impact of the class.

Achebe's *Things Fall Apart* is a novel in which "things fall apart" for Okwonko, our hero, who ends up disgraced after his efforts to attain status in his tribe come to naught because of his own inabilities to assess himself and others. (A summary of this work and others follows in an expanded summary section, in case you'd like more detail.) Thus, *Things Fall Apart* is a work of fiction dealing with cultural and religious clashes, as well as with internal, interpersonal, and societal conflicts.

Like *Things Fall Apart*, *The Stranger* is a work of fiction dealing with internal, interpersonal, and societal conflicts. In *The Stranger*, the narrator Mersault accidentally kills a stranger and is sentenced to death. Mersault, with his flat affect, shows little emotion and, in current parlance, is apt to meet all events and choices with the "whatever" response. Mersault can be read as a dysfunctional personality. *The Stranger* has been studied as a literary work, as a work of philosophy, and as a treatise in existentialism (or as an expression of how not being an existentialist — and making choices — can be destructive).

Siddhartha is also a work of philosophy and contains a discussion of religion. The main character, Siddhartha, is on a quest to find "truth." He seeks truth through Buddha and then through the pleasures of the world and finally concludes that enlightenment is a personal journey. In addition to being studied as philosophy, religion, and literature, *Siddhartha* is the tale of a personal journey of fulfillment.

"The Metamorphosis," a short story from Franz Kafka's *Metamorphosis, In the Penal Colony, and Other Stories*, is also philosophical. In "The Metamorphosis," Gregor Samsa wakes up as an insect. He is first cared for and then spurned by the family he has supported. On his death, he is swept onto the dust heap. Biographers, psychologists, philosophers, literary critics, high school students, and the general public have all adopted "The Metamorphosis" as a compelling read.

"In the Penal Colony" follows the same style as "The Metamorphosis" but features a machine that carves a condemned (and they are all condemned) prisoner's sentence into the body. Studied in religion and philosophy courses, "In the Penal Colony" has a chillingly detached tone and carries a widely and wildly interpreted allegory.

The Invisible Man, characterized as literary and allegorical in some circles, features an invisible man who rampages across the countryside because he can do so with impunity. *The Invisible Man* can be studied not only as a literary work but as a science fiction novel, a psychological novel, a sociological novel, and a historical novel as well.

The Invisible Man is paired with a *Buffy* television episode on DVD, "Out of Sight," in which an invisible girl is on a revenge rampage because she can do so with impunity. "Out of Sight" examines the need for recognition we all have and is a partner to *The Invisible Man* in terms of the morality of invisibility. What might we do if we knew we would never be observed? (caught?)

In *Dr. Jekyll and Mr. Hyde* Dr. Jekyll separates the non-humanitarian part of himself into Mr. Hyde. Ultimately, Jekyll cannot control his out-of-control id's actions. *Dr. Jekyll and Mr. Hyde*, a detective novel, a science fiction novel, an allegory or a fable, a representative of the gothic novel, and a "literary" work, is a classic exploration of duplicity and of the conflict between good and evil in humanity.

Dr. Jekyll and Mr. Hyde is paired with BBC's *Jekyll*, which is a retelling of elements of the *Dr. Jekyll* story in modern times with the addition of wives, assistants, conspiracies, and corporations. *Jekyll* purports to be a continuation of the story of *Dr. Jekyll and Mr. Hyde* but is also a reiteration of the novel's interrogation of the duality of humanity and of the question of responsibility.

We view one other video. *Dr. Horrible's Sing-Along Blog* begins as the blog of Dr. Horrible, who aspires to be evil and famous. Often foiled, he succeeds in killing the woman he loves and joining an evil brotherhood. *Dr. Horrible* is another way to look at the duality of people and to question the realms of comedy, tragedy, psychology, sociology, and philosophy.

Two non-fiction works tie the material together. *The Lucifer Effect* looks back at the Stanford Prison Experiment of 1970s fame and its horrifying conclusion that people take on the roles assigned to them. Although Zimbardo's work has not yet led to legal and social understanding of societal and systemic pressure on behavior, it is studied by scores of people in sociology, psychology, and literary classes.

Man's Search for Meaning by Victor Frankl is the basis for Frankl's psychological treatment called "logotherapy" and discusses people's basic motives in life. Frankl concludes that people choose their actions, but that those choices are necessary every time an action is possible. People can be "swine" or "saints," and at any minute that choice must be made again. The further conclusion is that people's lives are a struggle to find meaning in those lives.

Expanded Summaries of Class Selections

Included here are expanded summaries of each of the selections in case you need a reminder of more of what each is about. Of course, you can just skip this section and go right to the section on class design.

Achebe's *Things Fall Apart* is a novel, the story of Okwonko, an Ibo, who determines that he will earn tribal status. He earns status through physical strength and becomes foster father to a prisoner, Ikemefuna, who learns to look on Okwonko as a father. When the Oracle determines Ikemefuna must be killed, Okwonko, who fears showing weakness more than he fears a warning not to participate in the murder because he is "father" to Ikemefuna, kills the boy. Subsequently, Okwonko accidentally kills a member of the tribal group and is banished and must serve out seven years in exile. Returning from exile, he finds white people entrenched and touting a new government type and a new religion. He is outraged and encourages his fellows to destroy the Christian church, an act for which he is taken prisoner and held for ransom. After his release, he espouses rebellion and kills a government messenger. The rebellion miscarries, and the person sent to arrest Okwonko finds Okwonko has hanged himself, in disgrace, in rebellion, in despair.

Camus's *The Stranger* is a novel whose cold, unemotional narrator, Mersault, remembers his mother is dead but cannot apply any significance to the fact. He goes to her funeral but does not seem affected by her death. After returning to his home, he falls in with a young woman (Marie) with whom he spends much time. She asks him to marry her, to which he agrees without any discernible emotion. He has two neighbors, one of whom has a sick dog and the other of whom (Raymond) beats his Arabic girlfriend regularly. Mersault, Raymond, and Marie go to the seaside to visit a friend of Raymond's and see a group of Arabic men who are angry with Raymond's treatment of his girlfriend. Raymond and Mersault fight them and the men flee. Mersault later sees one of the men and, without thought, shoots him once and then shoots him four more times. Mersault is arrested and tried. His only defense is the testimony of his friends who are forced to admit he is unfeeling. Mersault is convicted and sentenced to be executed. His stay in the prison does not change him: he is angry at the minister who encourages him to find God, but he does come to understand that his mother was, at the end of her life, free and both ready to die and eager to live again, all of which he might also be. Still, he hopes all the witnesses to his death meet him with "cries of hate" (Camus 123).

Hermann Hesse's *Siddhartha*, a novel, is the story of Siddhartha, who finds what he knows of Hinduism lacking. With his friend Govinda, Siddhartha goes into the world to discover "truth." After being transported across a river by a ferryman, the two become "Samanas" (ascetics), learning meditation and how to suppress bodily imperatives. After three years, Siddhartha decides he has not found "the way." He and Govinda go to the Buddha. Govinda, finding his "way," becomes a disciple but Siddhartha continues to seek. He feels lust and takes the beautiful courtesan Kamal as a lover but must become rich to satisfy her needs. He also learns to gamble, to drink, and to accept his own greed. After many years, he becomes ashamed of his life and decides to end it. However, looking into a river, he remembers his own innocence and decides to live. He awakes to see Govinda, still a student of Buddha. Govinda leaves; Siddhartha takes up residence with the same ferryman he and Govinda had met much earlier. The ferryman Vasudeva teaches Siddhartha about the peace of the river and the cycle of life. Siddhartha is satisfied, but, when he meets his son, Young Siddhartha, and the boy does not accept Siddhartha's teachings on peace and the cycle and leaves for the world, Siddhartha is distressed until he realizes everyone must learn truth individually. Vasudeva leaves; Siddhartha becomes the ferryman; Govinda returns. Each of the two has reached enlightenment in his own way.

In Kafka's short story "Metamorphosis" Gregor Samsa wakes up one morning to find himself as a giant insect. His main concern is to get to work on time since he is the main support of his family: mother, father, and sister. Gregor cannot manage to get dressed but does manage to open his bedroom door when a clerk from his office comes to chastise him for his lateness. Upon seeing Gregor's condition, Gregor's family is shocked and the clerk runs away. Grete, Gregor's sister, takes on the chore of feeding him and cleaning his room. Because of the lack of income, each member of the family must find a way to earn money. The family is less and less inclined to pay attention to Gregor, who sneaks out to listen to Grete play the violin. At one point, horrified at his presence, Gregor's father throws an apple that lodges in Gregor's back. Gregor becomes ill. The family takes in three demanding boarders and stores extra goods in Gregor's room. The lodgers see Gregor and, inflamed with horror, decide to exit the house. The family determines that the insect is not Gregor and they must cease to think of it as Gregor. Gregor dies and is thrown out by the maid. The family asks the boarders to leave; the family takes a walk in the country and the mother and father decide Grete, young and nubile, needs a husband.

Kafka's "In the Penal Colony" is a short story which features a punishment machine that carves a prisoner's sentence on his skin for hours before the prisoner finally dies. The officer in charge of the machine describes its use to a traveler and tells the traveler that the machine scheduled for dismantling should instead be retained because its use leads a prisoner to a religious epiphany. The old commandant of the colony designed the machine because every accused is found guilty, but the new commandant has decreed the last use to be that day. The officer begs the traveler to defend the machine to the new commandant. When the traveler refuses to cast a vote on the machine in either direction, the condemned man is released, and the officer puts himself into the machine with the machine set to carve "Be just" on him. Unhappily for the officer, the machine malfunctions and immediately kills him, thus depriving him of the epiphany he desires. The traveler visits a tea house where the old commandant is buried under an inscription prophesying his return and the recovery of the colony. The traveler leaves on a boat, pushing a soldier and the condemned man back from boarding.

Wells's *The Invisible Man* is a novel which begins with a bundled-up stranger arriving at an inn. His actions are odd. The innkeepers, anxious over a series of recent burglaries, snoop in the stranger's room, which seems to be empty—but furniture moves and bedclothes rise. Later they confront the stranger who reveals he is invisible by taking off his clothes and escaping the police and the crowd. The stranger recruits a tramp, Marvel, to steal the materials from the his room in the inn, but Marvel goes to the police. The stranger chases and threatens to kill Marvel. In the chase, the stranger is wounded by a passerby. The stranger seeks help from the doctor, Kemp, and reveals himself as a former colleague, Griffin. Griffin, an albino, sought invisibility after he robbed his father. Griffin succeeded with a cat but had to use the procedure on himself when the cat's owner complained about him. Now he plans a Reign of Terror and asks Kemp to help him. Kemp makes the police aware of Griffin's location; Griffin attacks Kemp, who does not die, and Griffin runs from the police. Kemp plans to make himself bait for Griffin's capture but the plan is foiled by Griffin's interception of the note to the police. However, as Griffin attacks Kemp, who runs, Griffin is struck by a member of the pursuing crowd and, despite Kemp's pleas, is killed and becomes visible. Marvel, hoping to profit from them, has Griffin's notes and formulas and spends his spare time trying to make sense of them.

In the television episode from *Buffy the Vampire Slayer* "Out of Sight" our heroine Buffy discovers that the "something" doing damage to teachers and students is a girl out for revenge because she was ignored so often she disappeared. The invisible girl seeks to harm Cordelia, one of the "queens" of the school, and make her face so awful no one can forget it. Foiled by Buffy, the girl is taken from the high school by men in black and enrolled in a special school of invisible teens.

Stevenson's *Dr. Jekyll and Mr. Hyde* is a novel in which Dr. Jekyll's friend Utterson, a lawyer, learns that Mr. Hyde, a mysterious figure, tramples a young girl and then pays off her family. This is Hyde's first appearance to the reader. Utterson tries to find out something about Hyde. He talks to Dr. Lanyon, a former friend of Jekyll's, estranged because of his condemnation of Jekyll's research. Hyde appears and disappears in a house attached to the back of Jekyll's house. Jekyll has arranged to leave all his possessions to Hyde on Jekyll's death. Hyde, witnessed by a servant girl, beats a man to death. Jekyll shows Utterson a note from Hyde apologizing for the trouble he's caused and saying he will leave. However, the handwriting is similar to that of Jekyll. Lanyon dies after receiving information about Jekyll but leaves a letter for Utterson. Primed to suspect foul play by Jekyll's servants who say the voice in the laboratory no longer sounds like Jekyll, Utterson and his butler break into Jekyll's house. They find Hyde, dressed as Jekyll, seemingly dead from suicide, and in the laboratory a letter from Jekyll. Utterson reads Lanyon's letter and finds Lanyon died of shock on seeing Jekyll drink a potion and transform to Hyde. He reads Jekyll's letter and discovers the story of his experiments with potions that separate good from evil. Jekyll's experiments make Hyde free from morals: that initially appeals to Jekyll who transforms himself regularly. Finding that he cannot control the transformations, that Hyde is growing worse, and that the ingredients for the potion to return him to his Jekyll self are no longer available, Jekyll says he will kill himself or become Hyde forever.

Jekyll is a BBC series of six episodes, starring James Nesbitt, Gina Bellman, Denis Lawson, and Michelle Ryan. The tagline reads "Everyone Has a Dark Side." The Jekyll, named Jackman, of this series has left his family because he has learned he has an alter ego (unnamed at the beginning), whom he releases at certain times under the supervision of the psychological nurse Katherine. The alter ego becomes Uncle Billy to Jackman's two children and wife. A detective who has been following Jackman shows him that the novel *Dr. Jekyll and Mr. Hyde* is thinly disguised truth and that Jackman looks exactly like Dr. Jekyll, who died without issue. Jackman, having been reared with the knowledge that his mother deserted him and is dead, meets a woman who purports to be his mother before she vanishes. Jackman's friend and boss Peter is a co-conspirator, with others, including a man named Benjamin, for a giant corporation which desires to harness Hyde's powers and is willing to kidnap Jackman's wife and children to obtain those powers. Jackman transforms into Hyde, who kills Benjamin and a few dozen cohorts to save his family; because of the extensive damage he receives in the rescue and escape, Hyde may have disappeared, leaving Jackman and his family. Jackman finds his mother and discovers she is the descendant of Hyde and can also transform, she into the head of the corporation. Conspiracies. There is no end to them.

Dr. Horrible's Sing-Along Blog was initially produced for Internet distribution but later released on DVD. Created and written by Joss Whedon (et al) and directed by Joss Whedon, *Dr. Horrible* was posted on the Internet as three individual acts of about fourteen minutes each and was nominated for and won several awards. It stars Neil Patrick Harris, Felicia Day, Nathan Fillion, and Simon Helberg. In the video, Dr. Horrible speaks to his audience through a blog, delineating the evil deeds that he will commit. He tells of his love for Penny, the girl from the laundry, his enmity for the "hero" Captain Hammer, and his plans for the future, in which he hopes to become a member of the Evil League of Evil. He is hampered by the fact that the "good guys" watch blogs also, thus allowing Captain Hammer to continually foil Dr. Horrible's schemes. After Hammer foils one scheme, Penny is attracted to him and they become co-do-gooders, distressing Horrible. Horrible decides to freeze and then kill Hammer at a fete in honor of Hammer's work with the homeless. The plan goes awry and, even though Hammer feels pain for the first time, Horrible only succeeds in killing Penny. Horrible does join the League and sings that he "won't feel — a thing."

Zimbardo's *The Lucifer Effect* is a retrospective look at what occurred in the Stanford Prison Experiment and how the experiment and the conclusions derived from that experiment apply to Abu Ghraib and to abusers and "heroes" of today. Zimbardo first discusses situational behavior and then spends eight chapters expanding on his published article "The Stanford Prison Experiment" and telling, from decades of reflection, his place in the six-day experiment and his view on the events. In two final chapters on the experiment, he muses on the conclusions one might draw from the prisoner/guard/prison society experiment. He then further discusses, in three chapters, social dynamics and how behavior changes in situation. He concentrates in the next two chapters on Abu Ghraib and the systems that allow such events to occur. His final chapter is a hopeful look at how people can resist situational behavior.

Frankl was imprisoned in two Nazi concentration camps. Part One of *Man's Search for Meaning* analyzes his experiences in those camps. He says the camps lead first to shock, then to apathy, then to negative feelings. However, meaning for each person still exists. His core assertion is that meaning does not rest in the situation but in individual reaction to the situation. Suffering still allows choice. One chooses, and must continually choose, to be either part of the "race" of the decent persons or the "race" of the indecent persons. Sometimes a guard in a camp would be a decent person; sometimes a prisoner would be an indecent one. It is a choice. Part Two introduces Frankl's psychotherapeutic theory of logotherapy. Freud believed the desire for pleasure was the motivating factor for people; Adler believed the desire for power was the motivating factor for people. Frankl believed a desire for meaning was the motivating factor for people. Since life is meaningful — always, he says, we need to seek that meaning; we have the choice and the freedom to do so. *Man's Search for Meaning* is, after 60 years, still selling well. Not only is logotherapy still a factor in psychology and psychiatry, the book is studied as a philosophical text, as a literary work, and as a sociological text. In fact, the Library of Congress, with the Book-of-the-Month Club, did a survey, reported in the *New York Times* in 1991, and found that Frankl's book is one of the "ten most influential books" in the United States (Fein).

Class Design

So what's the point? The point is that each of these works illustrates the class theme: the dark side of the mind. Students had several assignments, to all of which Bloom's taxonomy applied: knowledge, comprehension, application, analysis, synthesis, and evaluation.

For example, they had two essay tests, a mid-term and a final. Neither of the tests required regurgitation of data. Each test required synthesis, reflection, analysis, evaluation, and application.

Class members were required to submit two papers. One paper was a research essay that required personal analysis, synthesis, and evaluation. One paper was reflective in nature: the student had to assess how the work chosen had personally affected that student and to connect that work to other works in the class and other works with which the student was familiar. Each of those papers was presented to the class. The presentation included any visuals the student thought would help elucidate and illuminate the material to the class and had to include the process the student used — with false starts, dead ends, and results, as well as the sources which the student used, what the student learned in terms of material and process, what further research the student or others need to do on the topic, and any other material the student thought would be valuable to the class. Each presentation was followed by questions from the class.

Students also kept a reading journal, with entries for each of the works. Each entry necessitated four sections: a bibliographic data entry, a summary, a personal response, and an analytic paragraph, addressing either a literary or film term with interpretation or evaluation.

Each student produced and presented a visual, tactile, imagistic creative project which illuminated the work for other class members and about which each student had to answer questions on the significance of the individual elements of the project, why he/she chose to do the project about the particular work, and how he/she thought the project effectively interrogated the work.

Finally (finally!) each student functioned as a member of a group and presented two works to the class, one prior to and one subsequent to mid-semester. Group work requires collaboration, cooperation, and discovery. Each student evaluated each member of the group and him/herself. In addition, each student evaluated every member of the class and his/her participation. This required not only a point list for elements of participation but also a narrative on aspects of that participation, which was most helpful.

During their leadership experience, each group gave information to the class and elicited class discussion. Between information presented and discussion, the group had to cover 1) an introduction to the material covered in the studied text, 2) the relationship of the studied text to other works in the text's field(s), 3) the relationship of the studied text to other texts studied during the semester, 4) the value of the studied text, 5) an analysis of the work, including literary elements; and 6) the relation of the work to the theme of the class, "the dark side of the mind." One requirement was to reveal the ability to analyze, synthesize, criticize, synergize, and evaluate. Critical and creative thinking were required. Students were asked not to do a biography of the author unless completely relevant and absolutely necessary to the subject matter and theme.

The Results and Literary Findings

So what did those works and activities illustrate? We're dealing with the dark side of the mind as a theme for the class. As examples of that theme, the works seem self-evident. However, the point is that we can use either "traditional," literary works as illustrations or "non-traditional," pop culture or fantasy works as representative of the theme. So the class has a sampling of both. Traditional works include *Things Fall Apart; The Stranger*; *Siddhartha*; *Metamorphosis, In the Penal Colony, and Other Stories*; *Dr. Jekyll and Mr. Hyde*; *The Invisible Man*; *The Lucifer Effect*; and *Man's Search for Meaning*, except that Kafka's, Wells's, and Stevenson's works can also be seen as relatively non-traditional in that they have been, and sometimes still are, considered genre works, i.e., fantasy or science fiction. *Jekyll*, "Out of Sight," and *Dr. Horrible's Sing-Along Blog* are definitely non-traditional and, generally, students were not familiar with them.

Using a combination of types of works helps students learn to synergize and synthesize, to look for commonalities in works that, on the surface, might not seem to "go together." In fact, there's increasing scientific evidence that using material students are more familiar with can help them deal with material that they might find foreign. According to Greene, in an article in *Scientific American Mind*, pedagogy has progressed from rote recitation, which can be helpful in learning facts, "but the message of modern memory research is that the brain is wired to recognize and organize coherent connections, not arbitrary ones. By tying new learning to existing associations — by engaging in contextual learning — we greatly improve results" (28). He maintains that, if students can make connections between what they are familiar with and what they learn, they will develop an "intricate web of associations that will let them weave the lessons of the book into their own thinking" (Greene 29).

So those works in the class which do not seem to "go together," because some are "popular" (or pop culture), some are fantasy, and some are classic, do "go together." Because students are familiar with film, because students watch and enjoy film and TV voluntarily, we can encourage them to study these more easily than we can "harder" works that they have learned to dread, like they dread Shakespeare and Dickens. Because students are generally more willing to deal with genre material, because it sounds and feels more accessible to them, that material can become a gateway to material that might seem more difficult. So mixing the various valuable forms of narrative culture can bring a classroom to life.

Connections

Students begin to see connections and to make assessments of all the works required, looking for elements of "the dark side of the mind" in each. For example, they assess Achebe's novel and find that *Things Fall Apart* deals with the collapse of Okwonko through his desire not to seem weak under any circumstances. This leads him to murder, but it's not just murder that becomes Okwonko's problem. He is unable to have a fulfilling relationship with his family because he is afraid those "soft" emotions, those actions that reveal caring or love, will lead him to lose the respect of others, in essence — to become the man he despised, his father. His clownish, irresponsible, impecunious, but loved by many (even if not by Okwonko), father never received status in the Ibo tribe. His father never seemed to need that validation. However, Okwonko translates his father's disinterest in the trappings of status into an unforgiveable weakness and vows never to be weak himself. This leads him slowly into personal darkness, from never showing his affection for his family and never admitting to being wrong, into the actual murder of his foster son. From there, he goes into exile but learns little about himself or his relationship to power, pride, and rigidity. His return to his village is disastrous for him — and for the village, leading to more murder, increased disintegration of the original culture, and Okwonko's suicide — a disgrace for his family and, for him, the ultimate loss of status.

Students see in *The Stranger* not someone who wants status or even connection. Mersault is so disconnected that he says the equivalent of "Whatever" to Marie when she asks if he wants to be married. He feels nothing for his mother's death. He fails to see the harm in his neighbor beating his girlfriend. He gets overheated, with the sun in his eyes, and shoots (once and then four more times) and kills a person who might mean him no harm. His darkness seems self-inflicted, a result of a personality defect of some kind. In fact, he does not regret the murder, but he hopes the onlookers at his execution hate and despise him, for those would be emotions with which he might be able to empathize — not that he's shown much of those emotions either.

Okwonko and Mersault both commit murders; both have personality "flaws" that lead to their actions. Okwonko is ambitious; Mersault is not. Both are flaws.

In addition to illustrating personal, human flaws, Kafka masters the dark side of bureaucracy. He specializes in the "little man" caught in the web of the faceless and in the uncaring, random events of the universe. In "Metamorphosis," we see obsessions: Gregor is initially obsessed with going to work, despite the fact he has suddenly, inexplicably, turned into some kind of bug. He never questions why this has happened to him, just as he never questions his father's failure and his family's subsequent reliance on him as their only support. His family never questions anything either. Only his sister has the sympathy that allows her to try to care for her brother, but that sympathy soon wanes. His family turns from him and it turns out they really don't need his support at all. In fact, without it, they send the stopgap boarders, horrified and horrible people, away and leave the womb of their apartment, reenter society, and begin to have ambitions for themselves. Which of these characters has a dark side? It turns out that each does, even the poor victim Gregor, who, though "working his fingers to the bone" for his family, has been proud to be their support and has not encouraged their growth since they relied on him for everything. This is not the picture of a person who wants fully-realized people around him. Nor do Okwonko or Mersault, who are not any more aware of the lacks in their relationships than is Gregor.

Kafka's "In the Penal Colony" has darkness all around. The original commandant, like those who conceive of any torture, was inventive in his depersonalization of the prisoners, creating a machine that tortured before killing, a "cruel and unusual punishment," to be sure. The people who administer the machine, as those in *The Lucifer Effect* and *Man's Search for Meaning*, follow the orders of the hierarchy and carry out the torture. One guard is so fascinated with the process and believes so strongly in the "religious experience" the machine affords that he commits himself to the machine, only to be robbed of whatever experience might have existed by being killed by the machine immediately. He does not benefit from his experience, just as no one has benefited from the machine. Only the explorer, who does not choose to defend — or deprecate — the use of the machine, comes away from the incident without being too smeared with guilt. (He, however, seems very close to the "whatever" philosophy of Mersault.)

Dr. Jekyll and Mr. Hyde is the quintessential exploration of the dark side of humanity, carried out in Dr. Jekyll's experiment of splitting his dark side into human form. Trying to make himself more pure and to give his repressed side some license, Dr. Jekyll only succeeds in letting loose the worst part of the human psyche in the person of Mr. Hyde, who, without the constraints of Jekyll's conscience, guilt, and consciousness of consequence, is free to pillage others for what he desires. Hyde carries the darkness in Okwonko and Mersault to the extreme.

To the dual nature of humanity, *Jekyll* adds the layer of the unlawful corporation and the willingness of individuals to buy into the goals of the corporate "being." Here we see the individual acting in the interests of the corporation and in him/herself because the individual has tied morality and ambition to the aims of the corporation. Since what the corporation wants is what the individual strives for, then individual morality is cast aside, as the order-takers cast aside their individual scruples in the face of the orders of their superiors. Here we also have a Jekyll who is invested in not having Hyde in contact with Jekyll's family. Surprisingly, it is Jekyll/Hyde's family that is redemptive in nature, leading Hyde to sacrifice himself to save Jekyll's family from the corporation. This is a more nuanced work than one in which the dark side is separate and "unclaimed." Hyde, the newborne, is selfish and without constraint. However, he learns and grows. Jekyll is the scientist, but he is willing to unleash the "bad" but powerful Hyde to save his family. In *Jekyll* are themes, sometimes gray, of redemption, sacrifice, identity, responsibility, love — and others.

In *The Invisible Man* we see more of what might occur if action had no consequence. Of course, the "hero" of the story is not exactly a sterling character from the beginning, not being connected to society and feeling shunned because of his difference (his albinism). He reveals a certain lack of conscience when he steals money from his father, money that does not actually belong to his father, an action that drives his father, unable to repay the funds, to suicide. He never expresses remorse for his action. He makes himself invisible and, because he can, takes advantage of his condition to prey on society. He takes what he wants and, being unseen, does not have to deal with the effects of his crimes until he is turned on by the crowd and killed, making him visible in his death. He is easily seen when he is dead. The Invisible Man, just as those who follow the orders of others, does not expect a day of reckoning to arrive. It does.

That day of reckoning also arrives in "Out of Sight" when the invisible girl is arrested (captured? detained?) by the men in black. However, they have ulterior motives in that they intend to use her and others to carry out nefarious, government-sponsored actions. The invisible girl is more sympathetic than the Invisible Man, who steals from his father before he makes himself invisible. The girl is "forced" into invisibility by others who refuse to "see" her and acknowledge her existence. Her "curse" does not come at her behest. She is first a victim before she becomes the culprit.

While *Dr. Horrible's Sing-Along Blog* is generally amusing, it is also sad. Dr. Horrible begins with the ambition of Okwonko, to become "someone." However, Dr. Horrible seems on the road to redemption, based on his love and desire for the girl he meets in the Laundromat. Events conspire to prevent him from realizing the fruits of his relationship and even to prevent him from admitting to the girl, Penny, that he wants a relationship. He succeeds in fulfilling one ambition — to hurt Captain Hammer, his nemesis. In that act he also succeeds in accidentally killing Penny — and his softer side. He becomes a noted villain and enters the Evil League of Evil, but is not self-fulfilled. He loses that possibility by his own actions.

Actions do not always lead to negative endings. *Siddhartha,* a positive note in the midst of depressing material, according to one student, shows the overcoming of the dark side. Siddhartha experiences all the worldly evils. He gambles, has sexual relations with a courtesan, is greedy, leaves a son behind — in short, is a typical, not-very-good person; but he is able to achieve enlightenment. This overcoming of humanities' propensity for self-damage is where both the non-fiction books fit.

For some reason, non-fiction is almost always considered "traditional." Frankl's 1946 work and Zimbardo's 2008 book, based on current and 1971 actions, both address the duality of human nature, albeit from different stances.

Zimbardo's *The Lucifer Effect,* based in psychology and sociology, while much of it is depressing, shows the reader that people will do things they would not consider themselves capable of when they are placed in situations that ask of them certain responses. Zimbardo asserts that people will adapt to circumstances and become the kind of people they would have sworn they were not. However, *The Lucifer Effect* goes farther than the locked-into-role-expectations "box" one might assume it predicts. Zimbardo addresses the people who act as anomalies, people who do not respond completely to the expectations, the "heroes," as he characterizes them. He writes of those who exposed the abuses at Abu Ghraib, of those who worked against the socially-separate and socially-accepted apartheid of South Africa, of the Mother Teresa's in the world who do not do what society expects but go beyond the roles imposed on them. He tells of how one can overcome the pressures of situational behavior by realizing that the pressure exists and by making conscious and conscientious efforts to resist the appeal of such behavior.

Frankl's *Man's Search for Meaning* also addresses situational behavior and the exceptions to that behavior. However, Frankl, while, like Zimbardo, basing his work on actual events, takes a philosophical stance, maintaining that it is a person's internal decision-making process that rules action. Both *Man's Search for Meaning* and *The Lucifer Effect* works come to substantially the same conclusions. Guards can act like guards or can be compassionate. Prisoners can act like prisoners or can be compassionate. In other words, people can be caught by situational behavior or can act as responsible individuals, but there are costs and consequences to each.

The class then can discuss what those costs and consequences are to individuals and to groups. And, in response to each of the fiction works, they discuss how each of the characters acted and could have acted differently. If the character had acted differently, what might have been the outcome? What does this mean in terms of each student's own life and responsibilities to self and to others? How is each character both similar to and different from each other character? What characteristics do they all have in common? What characteristics differ?

Conclusions

Each class differs; each class draws its own conclusions on literary works and/or self in relation to human action but generally reaches the same one that Frankl did: we can act as swine or as saints but we have to decide — and it can be a hard decision with painful result, but it is ultimately a decision — and we should recognize it as one.

In addition to interrogating personal reaction and choice, each class studies the works as works. Each text is analyzed and studied for its affective, aesthetic, mimetic impact as well as its originality and integrity and its significance to the fields of literature and culture. Thus, in addition to using the pop culture/fantasy work as "an illuminative tool" (Durand 4) that functions largely in "shedding light on some topic or theoretical framework in a wholly separate setting" (Durand 3–4), we can ask "what intrinsic value may be found" (Durand 5) in each text, traditional and otherwise. Dealing with texts as literary works is the aim of English classes immemorial.

A Sophomore Honors Seminar is not a "regular" class; it's not composition or literature or psychology. However, it is a synthesis class and has elements of all other kinds of classes. It too is a fusion of sorts. It's interdisciplinary in that the students have selected various majors. It's interdisciplinary in that it contains material from pop and "high" culture, from sociology, psychology, film, television, and literature. However, these materials are also the purview of the "regular" literature classes at all levels, which could also deal with the same material in much the same way, but perhaps with increased emphasis on literary analysis and criticism.

No matter what kind of class, upper or lower division, traditional or non-traditional, "regular" or seminar, discipline specific or interdisciplinary, students can benefit from the critical thinking skills demanded of a class composed of different kinds of works.

Thus, Sophomore Honors Seminar can serve as an example of how fusion of elements can lift a class to heights of discussion and can illuminate principles, problems, theories, and possibilities for students at all levels.

Works Cited

Abrams, M.H., with Geoffrey Galt Harpham. *A Glossary of Literary Terms.* 8th ed. Boston: Thomson, 2005. Print.

Achebe, Chinua. *Things Fall Apart.* 1959. New York: Anchor, 1994. Print.

Camus, Albert. *The Stranger.* Trans. Matthew Ward. New York: Vintage, 1989. Print.

Dr. Horrible's Sing-Along Blog. 2007. Internet Distribution. DVD. Mutant Enemy, 2008.

Durand, Kevin. "Introduction." Buffy *Meets the Academy: Essays on the Episodes and Scripts as Texts.* Ed. Kevin K. Durand. Jefferson, NC: McFarland, 2009. 1–5. Print.

Fein, Esther B. "Book Notes." *New York Times* 20 Nov. 1991. Web. 2 June 2010.

Frankl, Victor. *Man's Search for Meaning.* 1946. Trans. Ilse Lasch. "Preface, 1992." "Postscript 1984: The Case for a Tragic Optimism." Boston: Beacon, 2006. Print.

Greene, Anthony J. "Making Connections: The Essence of Memory Is Linking One Thought to Another." *Scientific American Mind* July/Aug. 2010: 22–29. Print.

Hesse, Hermann. *Siddhartha.* 1922. Trans. Gunther Olesch, Anke Dreher, Amy Coulter, Stefan Langer, and Semyon Chaichenets. Winnetka, CA: Norilana, 2007. Print.

Jekyll. 2007. DVD. BBC Warner, 2007.

Kafka, Franz. *Metamorphosis, In the Penal Colony, and Other Stories.* Trans. Joachim Neugrochel. New York: Scribner, 2000. Print.

"Out of Mind, Out of Sight." *Buffy the Vampire Slayer.* Seasons 1–7. 1997–2003. DVD. 20th Century–Fox, 2006.

Stevenson, Robert Louis. *Dr. Jekyll and Mr. Hyde.* 1886. New York: Signet, 2003. Print.

Wells, H.G. *The Invisible Man.* 1897. New York: Dover, 1992. Print.

Zimbardo, Philip. *The Lucifer Effect.* New York: Random, 2008. Print.

"We're Not in Kansas Anymore"

Sally Emmons

"All the works of man have their origin in creative fantasy. What right have we then to depreciate imagination?"—Carl Jung

Like Neo with the Matrix, today's university students are zealously plugged in, but rather than being "jacked" into an elaborate computer program, these students are plugged into the contemporary world. They check each other's Facebook walls several times a day to see what their friends are doing, Skype, blog, search wikis, watch the latest episodes of their favorite TV show on Hulu.com, download and listen to music on their iPods, text on their iPhones, hold *Halo* parties with other gamers, and know exactly what is happening in popular culture the minute—no, second—it is announced.

How is the university world to compete with so many distractions? How is a university English teacher (me) to ask such technologically minded students to deconstruct literary texts in a traditional college class AND expect them to enjoy and learn from the experience as my own college professors did when I was an undergraduate student? The answer is actually quite simple, though it took me a while to warm to the idea: give the students texts of their generation alongside classic texts, and *voila*! their interest is not only piqued but their excitement level goes up too.

In many of my classes, I deliberately choose to include contemporary texts that have a fantasy component to them alongside traditional texts. Why? Because college students are familiar with fantasy in a way that they are not with the works of traditional writers like Ernest Hemingway and Alice Walker. In fact, those works may seem foreign or hard to read to them. Fantasy can be, and often is, the catalyst that inspires these young academics to see the intellectual and aesthetic value of classic elements of inquiry.

Thus, in my upper-division Native American Literature course I ask my students to watch *Avatar* as they are reading James Welch's novel *Fool's Crow* and Sherman Alexie's *Flight*. *Avatar* brings to life the dangers of romanticizing a culture in a way that a lecture usually doesn't. More importantly, it raises ethical concerns about how one society can justify exterminating another society just because it is different and has something valuable that the first wants. Before long, my students leap from talking about the fictional world of the Na'Vi to how the American government betrayed, abused, and virtually annihilated Native Americans, all because their cultures were different and because they "possessed" valuable land (more on this at the end of this chapter). One of my favorite quotes about fantasy is by Terry Pratchett: "Fantasy is an exercise bicycle for the mind. It might not take you anywhere, but it tones up the muscles that can." *Avatar* does that for my students, most of whom have little to no native ancestry and who know very little about the historical atrocities that occurred in America. Moreover, fantasy texts almost always facilitate my students' journeys into self-discovery and questioning. Perhaps writer Peter Shaffer says it better when he states, "I think one of the best guides to telling you who you are ... is fantasy."

This semester I am teaching an Honors Composition I course around which fantasy intrinsically revolves. In this course, fantasy is very loosely defined as anything that contains futuristic or otherworldly elements. We talk about subjects routine in any first-year writing course: what is expected of them in a college essay, how to conduct and identify credible research, how to document sources using MLA format, how to write an annotated bibliography. But, in addition to all of these expected topics, we also have a challenging reading list which marries classic literary texts with the contemporary: George Orwell's *1984* and Ray Bradbury's *Fahrenheit 451* are side-by-side with Alan Moore's *The Watchmen*, Victor Gischler's *Go-Go-Girls of the Apocalypse*, William Gibson's *Neuromancer*, John Wyndham's *The Chrysalids*, and Margaret Atwood's *Oryx and Crake*. The texts share one common thread (besides their fantasy component, that is): their presentation of dystopic societies in which characters are controlled through fear, propaganda, media, commercialism, religion, science, and government. What leads to the dystopia is different in each society, and this is where our in-class discussions begin. My methodology in designing our class discussions revolves around classic forms of artistic, historic, literary, and philosophic inquiry. My goal is to challenge students to examine human experience by looking at the human condition through literature and to recognize that our past is not understood in isolation, but in the context of broader trends and developments.

We begin with *Fahrenheit 451*. The diction is accessible and the action sequences are exciting. Students immediately are drawn to the young character of Clarisse McClellan, wishing in part that, if they lived in a society like

Clarisse's, where free-thinking and individuality are condemned, they too would still choose to be individuals and go against the status quo. However, they hesitantly and guiltily voice their fear that in actuality they are more like Mildred, a character who has completely succumbed to the media propaganda bombarding her daily, for whom originality, creativity, and critical thinking (hallmarks of a liberal arts education) are foreign concepts. They are shocked that a society like the one in *Fahrenheit 451* could exist but are then even more shocked as they deconstruct how insidiously and easily this society emerged and at how similar contemporary Western society (in particular, American society) actually is to Bradbury's society.

When asked to list examples of how our society resembles Bradbury's infamous anti-intellectual community, they cite some of the expected examples: that most people in American society are wholly dependent upon media and would find it difficult to go through just one 24-hour period without a computer, a cell phone, a television, and/or an iPod (they confess that this would be difficult for them to do too); that there have been instances of mass book burnings in world history, making it plausible that censorship on a large scale could occur if the circumstances are right; that the youth of today want to fit in and look like everybody else their age rather than being unique. But they cite more unexpected examples, too: that, when America was terrorized on its home shores in 2001, Americans were quick to allow the government to enact the Patriot Act out of fear; that there are so many aliterate readers in America today who can read but choose not to because they see no intrinsic value in reading; that illiteracy is shockingly high in what is one of the most influential countries in the world; that an anti-intellectual sentiment is frighteningly on the rise as the dumbing down of everything seems to be the new norm; that American voters either forgo their democratic right and duty to vote for elected officials, or vote without being fully informed about an issue or candidate.

During the course of our discussions, I schedule an out-of-class viewing of the contemporary science-fiction film *Equilibrium* in which a futuristic society has been virtually destroyed due to nuclear war, and a totalitarian regime emerges which requires the populace to take a drug known as *Prozium* to stifle their ability to feel hate, anger, love, happiness, joy, sadness — what makes them human. The students immediately see the similarities between the society in the film to Bradbury's society and cringe when they watch the Mona Lisa destroyed (in a scene hauntingly reminiscent of the opening scene of *Fahrenheit 451*, when Montag glories in wielding his flame-thrower to burn books) because it promotes beauty and feeling in a society in which all aesthetics are outlawed. We discuss the film as a cinematic text, analyzing how the theme is developed through characterization, flashback, plot, character epiphanies, and conflict, and compare this to Bradbury's novel. We then analyze basic cinematic techniques that heighten the effects of the movie: visual symbolism, color usage, and music and discuss how the film borrows from the look and feel of other contemporary films, most notably *The Matrix*. Students enjoy the film because it brings something like Ray Bradbury's world to life for them visually. Moreover, both the novel and the film have slightly ambiguous endings (the novel more so than the film) that allow the students to believe that the totalitarian regimes have been overthrown and that a new (and better) society will emerge.

We then begin *1984*, a much less palatable read than Bradbury. Students again see echoes of today's society in the text, especially in its presentation of Newspeak which they liken to today's lack of interest in reading or writing of anything of substance in favor of tweeting, texting (with its abbreviations and deliberate misspellings) and students' readings of condensed versions of texts rather than the real documents. They compare Oceania's rewriting of historical documents to maintain government control to current news events. We analyze passages that develop Orwell's themes of nationalism, sexual repression, and censorship and discuss how different the tone of this novel is from *Fahrenheit 451*. Students read supplemental articles about power and authority, including articles about Stanley Milgram's controversial shock experiment and the Stanford Prison experiment, and we discuss the weaknesses of human nature when faced with the desire to obey. Outside of class students keep a daily creative journal in which they pretend they are citizens in Oceania being watched by Big Brother just as Winston Smith is watched in *1984*. Their entries become progressively more paranoid, fearful, and intense. Surprisingly, the students more often than not depict themselves as being caught by the Party in the last entry or committing suicide rather than of destroying the society or escaping from it.

During one class we watch an episode from Season 5 of *The Twilight Zone* called "Looks Just like You." The opening narration of the episode states,

> Given the chance, what young girl wouldn't happily exchange a plain face for a lovely one? What girl could refuse the opportunity to be beautiful? For want of a better estimate, let's call it the year 2000. At any rate, imagine a time in the future when science has developed a means of giving everyone the face and body he dreams of. It may not happen tomorrow—but it happens now....

In this episode a young woman reaches nineteen years old, the age at which she must undergo her "Transformation." Everyone in this society must look and act alike so when reaching the age of transformation each selects a model from a mandated list and is surgically altered to look like the model. Marilyn, our young protagonist, rebels against this dictum, wanting to remain as she is, but she is condemned for being radical in her thinking and is locked up for treatment. Ultimately, she is forced to transform against her wishes. The episode resonates with Orwell's themes of conformity and punishment. When Marilyn rebels against the status quo, she is institutionalized and treated by Dr. Sig, a psychiatrist who has transformed into the same model that Marilyn's father and uncle both chose (interestingly, Marilyn's father committed suicide after his forced Transformation). Dr. Sig reasons that Marilyn must transform in order to fit in, saying,

> Many years before, wiser men than I decided to try to eliminate the reasons for inequality and injustice in the world. They saw that physical unattractiveness was one of the factors that made men hate, so they charged the finest scientific minds with the task of eliminating ugliness in mankind. As they learned to reshape the features and remold the body, they also learned to eliminate most of the causes of illness, and thus to prolong life... ["Looks Just Like You"].

Marilyn is not tortured and brainwashed as Winston Smith is, but the end result is the same — complete dedication to the society's status quo. After her Transformation, Marilyn looks at her best friend Val and happily gushes, "And the nicest part of all, Val, I look just like you!" Along with a physical transformation is a mental transformation: gone is the rebellious Marilyn who once proclaimed the attraction of being unique.

We proceed through the remaining texts in much the same way. We analyze each text in detail, concentrating on the message, the techniques that the author employs to impart the message, and how the author uses fantasy elements to advance the message and/or plot. As such, we engage in classic elements of literary inquiry. Two discussion leaders are assigned to each text. Prior to our first class discussion together, the discussion leaders prepare and pass out a list of critical questions about the book that they would like for us to use as a catalyst to jumpstart our first discussion session. The students are amazingly successful in writing probing, thoughtful questions that delve far beneath surface elements of the text and which frequently bridge the new text to previous texts that have already been considered in the class. While I act as an overall guide in these discussions, the students are tremendously successful in "owning" and advancing the discussions. I have used the same technique in non-honors-based courses but with less success. For instance, here is a set of discussion questions that one set of discussion leaders (Katie Gray and Kimberly Qualls) organized for *The Chrysalids*:

1. What was the reasoning behind keeping the depicted society "pure"?
2. How does the society define purity? How does this definition diverge from majority opinions today?
3. What major historical events in which "different" people were persecuted can be compared to the events that take place in the novel?

4. In what ways is the society in *The Chrysalids* like the dystopic societies presented in the other novels we have read? How is it different?
5. What are some examples of the symbolism and theme used in the novel? How is the theme of purity ironic?
6. How would the novel be different if written from the father's point of view? Or from Uncle Axel's point of view?
7. Can some of the factors of the fictional society be seen in today's society, perhaps on an international scale?
8. What would you have done in Aunt Harriet's position, being the parent of a "mutant" child?
9. Discuss the faulty reasoning behind persecuting the telepathic characters, relying on the major theme of "made in God's image."
10. What do you think will happen to both societies, both the Old and New People?

In addition to the formal research-based papers that are expected in first-year composition courses, the students in this class also write short, critical responses to each of the texts. These are reflective, personal responses that encourage the students to discuss not only their personal engagement with the text under consideration, but to also comment upon the connections that they see between the texts in the class and on the text's relationships to us today. Some of the questions that I ask the students to consider follow:

1. What do you think are the benefits you've received from reading this literature?
2. What have you found particularly evocative (exciting, interesting) in this literature?
3. How does this literature speak to you in personal ways?
4. What connections are you making to real life and today's society as a result of reading this literature?
5. Does this literature remind you of any classic literature that you've read? Which ones? How?
6. How does the Stanley Milgram experiment (and the other articles about obedience and authority) influence your understanding of this literature?
7. How do the fantasy elements of the text impact the narrative arc? Would the text be as successful without the fantasy components?

In addition, students are required to complete two creative projects during the course of the semester. One of the creative projects asks students to redesign the book jacket of a text of their choice from the class list and to then formally present their new layout/design to us. Students have a great time pushing their creative impulses with this assignment and have created some truly remarkable work as a result. The second creative project asks students to creatively engage with one of the books in a more organic way. The assignment parameters are straightforward:

> The creative project is your opportunity to respond creatively to one of the texts we are discussing this semester. Your creative project may take any form—*the point is to be creative.* Think about what really interested/perplexed/caused you to think in one of the novels—was it a specific character? A scene? A message? A theme? An issue? Use this as a starting-off place for your creative project. After you finish your creative project, write a two page analysis of it. This paper will include: 1) an explanation of why you selected the work you did; 2) how you think your project illuminates/explicates the work you selected; 3) the significance of your project. You will present the project to the class, at which time you will be asked to answer each of the above questions. You must present the project to receive credit. Be creative. Take chances. Enjoy this assignment [Emmons Syllabus].

The resulting projects were surprising in their myriad approaches—I had students compose and perform original songs in class that reflected the psyche of a character in a book; I had students write poems, create elaborate dioramas, paint drawings, and enact scenes from a text; I even had a student choreograph and perform an original dance representing one character's epiphany in a novel! All of the book jackets and creative projects provide moments for further class discussion and instruction, yet also allow the students to stretch their thinking in more creative venues. Moreover, they gave the students permission to use fantasy elements in a creative way as they actively engaged with the themes in the texts.

Using fantasy in this class has been even more successful than I imagined it would be. The students pushed themselves to think about the relationship of these texts to humanity today and it scared them. "Reading this fantasy literature opens my eyes to the imperfections of the society around me," states Jessica Neeley. "[Prior] to reading these texts," she further writes, "I blindly looked over things that are quite possibly detrimental to our society. These novels ... inspire people to change things that don't seem right in society." Kimberly Qualls echoed the same sentiment, writing, "... they are a sort of prediction that speaks personally to me." Byron Schroeder claims, "This literature has provided me with a new and interesting perspective on life. Because of [it] I have started to question society more. I now see the importance of being involved in voting and other government activities.... I also understand the true value of literature ... this literature really makes me cherish all the freedoms I possess." "These novels are wake up calls," warns Katie Gray. Caleb Demarais echoes the same sentiment, "These books have opened my eyes to how imperfect and dystopic our society is. Because of these books, I notice the degeneration of humanity and society more. These books help me to realize what our culture could become if we continue to walk down the steep slope of restricted freedoms and blind obedience." And Brandi Green states, "These novels have instilled a sense of urgency and fear [in me]. They have allowed me to see the things in our society that I never saw simply because I didn't want to."

Moreover, the students pointed out the connections they see between the texts and humanity. Austin Kreps says, "[These books] show the readers the price of indulgence in today's society and help the reader learn how to discover and decide who they are. This is especially true in younger readers who need role models to show them that it is okay to fight for what they believe in, even if it is an unpopular view that goes against an authority figure or society." Wilson Sprinkles chimes in, "[This] gives me a glimpse of what individuals are capable of and sometimes it is not always pretty. I can read this ... literature knowing that not every person is going to have clean hands and that not everything is going to be perfect." According to Chelsea Blackmore, "I have [now] re-examined my current status as a college student as well as my position as a human being. I have become a stronger individual who now takes time to evolve my passions and fight for what I believe is morally right." Imagine how humbled I was when I learned how the blending of classic and fantasy literature in this course altered the mindsets of my students and challenged them to think about their own roles as human beings in today's society. It was not only a proverbial "light bulb" moment for them but an illuminating moment for me as an educator. What began as a pedagogical experiment to see how students would respond to classic literary texts by reading them alongside contemporary fantasy texts has now transformed the way I think about teaching my courses. This course's success has opened my eyes to the possibilities of teaching fantasy in other, more traditional classes.

Prior to this course, I taught a course strictly on fantasy, also a course for honors students. However, our approach in this class was extremely formal. In this course we used Tzvetan Todorov's *The Fantastic: A Structural Approach to a Literary Genre* as a critical grounding and then discussed books as varied as Oscar Wilde's *The Picture of Dorian Gray*, Sherman Alexie's *Flight*, Gregory Maguire's *Wicked,* and the graphic adaption of Franz Kafka's *The Metamorphosis;* films that include *The Matrix*, *Like Water for Chocolate,* and *Pleasantville;* and the television shows *Heroes*, *Lost,* and *Torchwood.* Our focus with all of the "texts" was how the authors and/or film-makers used magical realism to illustrate something broader.

On the first day of this class, after discussing the syllabus and required assignments, I read a children's book, Maurice Sendak's artistic rendering of

Wilhelm Grimm's *Dear Mili*. The short story is a frightening tale of a young girl who goes walking in the woods upon her mother's request so that she will avoid the horrors of war; after much wandering and fright, she is befriended by an elderly man who provides her with food and comfort. During her wandering, references are made to the "guardian angel" who watches over her every move. At the end of the book, the girl is reunited with her mother but something has changed. The narrative states, "The child went to the village but it looked strange and unfamiliar to her. In among the houses she knew, there were others she had never seen before; the trees looked different, and there was no trace of the damage the enemy had done. All was peaceful..." (Grimm). The girl returns to her home, only to discover that her mother is now an old woman and that thirty years have inexplicably passed during the "three days" she spent in the forest. There is no logical explanation for the magical occurrence; readers are simply expected to accept that something supernatural has occurred and that the girl has been spared the time of unrest and "wicked men" that the text alludes to. Shortly thereafter, the mother and daughter die in each other's arms.

Todorov's theory of the fantastic helps to explain the supernatural element. According to Todorov, we (readers) know that we're in the presence of the fantastic when "there occurs an event which cannot be explained by the laws of this same familiar world" (25). "The person who experiences the event must opt for one of two possible solutions," states Todorov. "Either he is the victim of an illusion of the senses, of a product of the imagination ... or else the event has indeed taken place, [and] it is an integral part of reality" (Todorov 25). Todorov concludes by stating that "the fantastic is that hesitation experienced by a person who knows only the laws of nature, confronting an apparently supernatural event" (25).

This is exactly what happens in *Dear Mili*. The opening of the book explains that "the happy life" that Mili and her mother lead is interrupted when "a terrible war overran the whole country" (Grimm). Despairing when "a great cloud of smoke rose up in the distance and a little while later the heavens resounded with cannon fire [and] shouts and tumult rent the air on all sides," Mili's mother sends her into the woods to save her "from the wicked men" and "a fearful storm" (Grimm). After what seems like a great deal of wandering and fright, the young girl is invited into a home: "Good evening, dear child, is it you? I've been expecting you a long time" states an old man whom readers later learn is Saint Joseph (Grimm). After three days, Saint Joseph informs the girl, "Dear child, you must go back to your mother now. Your time here is over" (Grimm) and gives her a rose, saying, "Never fear. When this rose blooms, you will be with me again" (Grimm). Indeed, it is this rose that is in full bloom when the neighbors find the young Mili and her mother dead in each other's arms the day after their reunion.

There is no logical explanation for the occurrence. Either Mili really did stay in the woods for 30 years without aging, or else she is a victim of her own senses and is somehow dreaming. Readers are left to assume the first explanation to be the correct interpretation — we hesitate and then accept the supernatural occurrence. Interestingly, the grimmest of the Grimm fairytales is also one of its most celebrated due to illustrator Maurice Sendak's artistic rendering of the tale which catapulted it to No. 5 on the *New York Times* best-seller list when it was first released in 1988. Sendak modeled Mili after Holocaust survivor Anne Frank, whose home he had visited, and his own Polish family, many of whom died during the Holocaust. Scenes from the children's book evoke imagery from concentration camps, and a general feeling of claustrophobia and fear permeate the drawings from page-to-page. When some complained about the graphic and scary drawings, Sendak replied, "Parents shouldn't assume children are made out of sugar candy and will break and collapse instantly. Kids don't. We do" ("Illustrator" 74).

Todorov develops his theory of the fantastic in more detail, explaining that three conditions must be met in order for the fantastic to exist: (1) readers must accept that characters in a text are "living persons" and must hesitate when these characters experience magical/supernatural events; (2) "this hesitation may be experienced by a character" (Todorov 33); (3) readers must "reject allegorical [and] poetic interpretations" of a text when the supernatural occurs (Todorov 33). It is this final point that my students refuted in the fantasy course. Time and again, they were confronted with characters like Mili who experienced a supernatural occurrence. Why should the metaphoric and figurative quality of that supernatural occurrence be discounted simply because the fantastic is operating, they repeatedly asked?

Case in point: Sherman Alexie's *Flight. Flight* is a powerfully gripping and award-winning novel of a teenager's quest for an identity as he literally "jumps" between the psyches and bodies of different characters as he time travels. During his "flights" he transforms into an Indian tracker in the 19th century, an FBI agent, a mute Native American boy at the battle of Little Big Horn, and even his father, who abandoned him at a young age. The novel is filled with violence and hatred towards native peoples and attempts to understand the complex shared history of America and Native America. Although the novel can be interpreted on a purely fantastic level, to do so undermines its potential for an even greater message. As a group, my fantasy class decided that it was far more interesting and gratifying to imagine that the main character, Zits, actually does time travel and that it is this time traveling that leads him into a greater realization about himself. At the same time, readers are led to a better understanding of human nature, specifically what drives people to kill and what distinguishes those who choose not to kill, hate, or commit immoral acts.

Much of the written work in the course was reflective in nature. Some of the writing prompts that I used included the following.

(1) The fantastic is a form of literature that "bends" natural laws; as such, it is opposite to literary realism. Flannery O'Connor has written, "I am interested in making a good case for distortion because I am coming to believe that it is the only way to make people see." What do you think O'Connor means in this quote? Using one of the texts we have discussed, explore how important elements in it are "distorted" and explain how these distortions actually contribute to the overall effectiveness of the text.
(2) Identify and discuss a formal aspect of one of the texts we have discussed so far that contributes to the "magical" quality of the text. Such a feature could be the author's use of allusions, metaphors, allegories, etc.
(3) Discuss the society that an author presents in one of the texts we have read this semester. Is he/she critical of that society and its standards? If so, what does he/she criticize and how?
(4) Todorov argues that fantastic literature typically (not always) employs three criteria: first, the world in the text is accepted by readers to be "real" and the readers must believe that they see the characters in this world as hesitating when deciding whether an event is supernatural or natural; second, the characters may experience this hesitation too; finally, the reader will reject "allegorical as well as 'poetic' interpretations" of the text (Todorov 33). We have discussed (argued!) over whether these criteria are correct. Formulate your own theory of the fantastic based upon what we have read and discussed so far in the class.
(5) Most of the literature we have read has produced varying levels of confusion in us (in terms of how the fantastic is operating). Discuss how this disquietude is produced in one of these works, and how this confusion actually contributes to the overall meaning of the work as a whole.

Looking back, it is easy for me to see how much of the work in this fantasy class actually shaped my thinking as I developed the honors composition course that I am currently teaching.

I return to *Avatar*. In the online version of my Native American Literature course a year ago I offered an optional assignment, inviting students to watch *Avatar* and comment upon how it might reflect some of the readings we had been discussing in the class. This was prior to my success using fantasy elements in honors courses so I really doubted whether the students would see the connections that I intended. Since I doubted the success of incorporating something popular in what is a very traditional literature course, I made it an optional assignment (in the form of a threaded discussion). The success of this optional assignment has now led me to make the viewing a required part of the course and to think about how a fantasy component can be incorporated into other, less obvious courses. I began the discussion by asking the students what correlations they recognized between what happens in this film and what we've read in this class. Student discussion threads included the following:

> That is so funny that this question be asked.... This was a modern day science fiction "Cowboys and Indians." Right when they showed the Na'vi society and how they lived and their beliefs I knew that they were like Natives.... [Patricia].[1]
>
> The people in Avatar are just fighting a modern day version of Indians vs. Whites again. The Na'Vi ... are being chased out of their own land and for what? A mineral rock that man desires. The Na'Vi people live on the land and treat the land just as the Native Americans did. *Avatar* is just a modern day man vs. Indians story and I think it gives a good depiction of man and how they took from the Indians so many years ago. They were greedy and thought only of themselves and what they needed and not what the Natives themself wanted or had to say. Many lives could have been spared in both cases if they all just talked and didn't take... [Noreen].[2]
>
> I've seen *Avatar* several times and my son loves it. We have discussions regarding the killing that happens in the film, because I want him to understand that killing for stupid reasons ... is unnecessary and a waste of time and life. When the Na'Vi wage war on the Army I thought it was very cool that there were Plains Na'vi, Coastal Na'vi, Forest Na'vi, Horse Na'vi, and Air Na'vi (for a lack of a better word). I could see the different tribes based upon location relating back to the different Native American tribes and their locations... [Crystal Mooney].

The students engaged in the subject quickly. In other required discussions in the class, students frequently waited until the last minute to post a response, but that was not the case with the discussion of *Avatar*. Placing the course material within the framework of popular culture suddenly allowed the students to see connections with the classic texts in the class, with atrocities of American history, and brought to life the injustices that indigenous people face simply because their life ways are different from another segment of the population. *Fool's Crow* and *Flight* (among other texts) suddenly came alive for them in a very real way.

About fantasy, Barbara Grizzuti Harrison, American journalist, essayist and memoirist, stated, "Fantasies are more than substitutes for unpleasant reality; they are also dress rehearsals...." American cartoonist and writer Dr. Seuss has said, "I like nonsense, it wakes up the brain cells. Fantasy is a necessary ingredient in living." By incorporating fantasy elements into some of my classes, I have discovered that the students are invigorated, so much so that it makes me want to explore how to incorporate fantasy into other classes that I teach. Fantasy has proven to be a gateway that allows my students a better understanding of classic literary texts. It has also made my students think seriously about what their roles in today's society must be and reminds them that they must play an active part in being caretakers of individuality, free-thinking, creativity, and philosophic expression, all tenets of a liberal arts education. What more could an educator hope for?

Notes

1. Some students' names have been changed to allow anonymity.
2. Some students' names have been changed to allow anonymity.

Works Cited

Alexie, Sherman. *Flight.* New York: Grove Press, 2007. Print.
Atwood, Margaret. *Oryx and Crake.* New York: Anchor Books, 2003. Print.
Avatar. Dir. James Cameron. Perf. Sam Worthington, Zoe Saldana, Sigourney Weaver. 20th Century–Fox, 2009. DVD.
Blackmore, Chelsea. Interview. 25 Oct. 2010.
Bradbury, Ray. *Fahrenheit 451.* New York: Ballantine, 1953. Print.
Demarais, Caleb. Interview. 25 Oct. 2010.
Dr. Seuss "Fantasy Quotes." Thinkexist.com. Web. 8 Sept. 2010.
Emmons, Sally. Syllabus. Honors Composition I. Fall 2010.
Gibson, William. *Neuromancer.* New York: Ace Books, 1984. Print.
Green, Brandi. Interview. 25 Oct. 2010.
Gray, Katie. Interview. 25, Oct. 2010.
Equilibrium. Dir. Kurt Wimmer. Perf. Christian Bale, Sean Bean, Emily Watson. 2002. Dimension, 2003. DVD.
Gischler, Victor. *Go-Go Girls of the Apocalypse.* New York: Simon & Schuster, 2008. Print.
Grimm, Wilhelm. *Dear Mili.* Trans. Ralph Manheim. Illus. Maurice Sendak. New York: Michael di Capua Books, 1988. Print.
Harrison, Barbara Grizzuti. "Fantasy Quotes." Thinkexist.com. Web. 8 Sept. 2010.
Havens, Catherine. Threaded Discussion Posting. 14 Nov. 2010.
Heroes. Created by Tim Kring. NBC. 2006–2010. Television.
"Illustrator Maurice Sendak Works His Melancholy Magic on a Long-Forgotten Grimm Fairy Tale." *People* 31.23 (5 Dec. 1988): 74. Print.
Jung, Carl. "Fantasy Quotes." *BrainyQuote.* Web. 8 Sept. 2010.
Kafka, Franz. *The Metamorphosis.* Illust. Peter Kuper. New York: Three Rivers Press, 2003. Print
Kreps, Austin. Interview. 25 Oct. 2010.
Like Water for Chocolate. Dir. Alfonso Arau. 1992. Walt Disney, 2000. DVD.
"Looks Just Like You." *The Twilight Zone.* Season 5.1964. Dir. Abner Biberman. Image, 2006. DVD.
Lost. Created by J.J. Abrams. ABC. 2004–2010. Telvision.
Maguire, Gregory. *Wicked: The Life and Times of the Wicked Witch of the West.* New York: Regan Books, 1995. Print.
The Matrix. Dir. Wachowski Brothers (Andy and Larry). Perf. Keanu Reeves, Carrie Ann Moss, and Laurence Fishburne. Warner, 1999. DVD.

Milgram, Stanley. "The Perils of Obedience." *Writing and Reading across the Curriculum.* Ed. Laurence Behrens and Leonard J. Rosen. Boston: Longman, 2011. 692–704. Print.
Mooney, Crystal. Threaded Discussion Posting. 10 Nov. 2010.
Moore, Alan. *Watchmen.* Illust. Dave Gibbons. New York: DC Comics, 2008. Print.
Neeley, Jessica. Interview. 25 Oct. 2010.
Orwell, George. *1984.* New York: Signet, 1950. Print.
Pleasantville. Dir. Gary Ross. Perf. Tobey Maguire, Jeff Daniels and Joan Allen. New Line, 1998. DVD.
Pratchett, Terry. "Fantasy Quotes." Thinkexist.com. Web. 8 Sept. 2010.
Qualls, Kimberly. Interview. 25 Oct. 2010.
Sac, Angela. Threaded Discussion Posting. 14 Nov. 2010.
Schroeder, Byron. Interview. 25 Oct. 2010.
Shaffer, Peter. "Fantasy Quotes." *BrainyQuote.* Web. 8 Sept. 2010.
Sprinkles, Wilson. Interview. 25 Oct. 2010.
Torchwood. Created by Russell T. Davies. BBC. 2006-Present. Television.
Welch, James. *Fool's Crow.* New York: Penguin, 1987. Print.
Wilde, Oscar. *The Picture of Dorian Gray.* 1906. Clayton, DE: Prestwick, 2005. Print.
Wyndham, John. *The Chrysalids.* New York: NYRB, 1955. Print.
Zimbardo, Philip. "The Stanford Prison Experiment." *Writing and Reading across the Curriculum.* Ed. Laurence Behrens and Leonard J. Rosen. Boston: Longman, 2011. 732–43. Print.

Critical Thinking and Post-Apocalyptic Literature

MARY M. MACKIE

When we were young, we played a game we called "What If." We constructed elaborate scenarios based on simply filling in the rest of the blank. "What if we could be cowboys?" or "What if we used the top of the hill for a hospital for the wounded guys from the war?" Those simple questions led to hours of enjoyment as we constructed worlds we knew nothing about, but our imaginations let us take ourselves there anyway.

From those simple questions, our minds created intricately involved storylines. It is most likely, too, from answering an equally simple "what if" question that a scientist or engineer created most of our modern conveniences: the light bulb, telephone, computer. From wondering if we can, indeed, do something, to actually accomplishing that particular quest — it all starts from responding to that one simple question: "What if?"

Too often, however, the child-like curiosity that encourages us to ask that question in the first place gets lost in the shuffle of mundane, day-to-day existence. Exploration of the unknown — of the world around us as well as who we are — takes second (or third) place to one's job, household responsibilities, care-taking, everything that detracts from the discovery of anything else. We too early lose our desire to ask "what if" and as a result stop questioning many aspects of our world and the world around us; it becomes too easy to accept "the way things are."

One of the challenges in composition classrooms today is how to engender critical thinking, but beyond that, how to translate critical thinking into clear, perceptive writing — writing that brings out the discoveries students can make when they are gently directed to critically analyze any sort of writing: essays, stories, novels, poems, academic articles. Perhaps the greatest challenge is stimulating the students, finding writing that they can understand and perhaps relate to, without resorting to turning the classroom into a dog and pony show. While I understand that pedagogically speaking there are places for power-point presentations and showing films, in light of the fact that fewer people read, and fewer students come prepared into college and university with a solid reading background, I prefer to try to get them interested in reading something they can relate to.

Every teacher approaches this problem differently, the problem of engaging one's students in a meaningful way, a way that will ultimately lead to the ability of the student to critically think and then critically analyze any work in question. There may be many answers to the question of the best way to do this. What I want to discuss in the remainder of this essay are some of the ways I have been able to motivate discussion in university composition classes by making the topics and themes relevant to the students and to their lives. This is one of the most important aspects to approaching learning. Having been in their positions and having walked out of many classrooms wondering how anything discussed was actually relevant to the things I was interested in, or the things I wanted and hoped to learn, made me more aware of the needs of my own students. Finding what is relevant to a particular group of students is an on-going challenge; if one looks at the larger world view, this challenge becomes more workable.

Too often, first-year composition students come to the university classroom woefully under-prepared for the rigors of academic writing. But beyond the challenges of making up for whatever skills they may be lacking as first year-university students, comes the understanding that few of these students have been taught either the importance of or the necessity for critical thinking — and thinking for themselves. For one reason or another, they have been told what they should think, from a young age, right up until the time they enter the university classroom. The idea that they can be asked and even answer the question "What do you think" comes as a shock to them.

So facing a roomful of non-critical thinkers who need to become critical thinkers in order for their college years to be fully productive, the question for the instructor is how this is best approached: *How do I teach them how to critically think, to challenge themselves, to ask questions of the material they will be facing throughout their college careers?*

What needs to be done is to engender critical thinking and from there to enable students to translate that into clear, coherent writing. My challenge, as the instructor, is to motivate discussion while making the topics and the themes relevant to these first-year university students. In facing this challenge, one of the most successful iterations of Composition I involved using five different post-apocalyptic, or dystopian, novels. There are a plethora of this type of novel, and the ones I chose reflected the questions I most particularly wanted the students to think, to discuss, and ultimately to write short papers about.

Post-apocalyptic fiction is considered by many to be a sub-genre of science fiction literature. Set somewhere on this planet, post-apocalyptic fiction looks at the world that *might be* after an apocalyptic catastrophe has occurred. This could be a man-made catastrophe (as in Margaret Atwood's *Oryx and Crake* and Cormac McCarthy's *The Road*) or an unknown world-wide phenomenon, as P.D. James explores in *Children of Men*. It could be an incursion into a possible future based on mankind's present trajectory and explorations (both good and bad), as is the case with Ray Bradbury's *Fahrenheit 451* and Kazuo Ishiguro's *Never Let Me Go*. Post-apocalyptic fiction is that which is set after some sort of apocalyptic disaster has occurred. Dystopian literature (and here is where Bradbury's and Ishiguro's novels might more easily be categorized) focuses on civilizations in the future which have, under the guise of being utopias, degenerated into repressed states. Dystopian literature often feels as if it is suggesting to the reader that if society is not careful, this particular state is what it could pass into. Dystopian literature, I feel, is that which asks students to go back to the question of their childhood: "What if?" Because I feel that the line between "pure" post-apocalyptic fiction and dystopian fiction is blurred — because both of these can be seen as cautionary tales — I tend to think of the novels I use to engender the critical thinking and writing my students need to be doing as either-or, or better yet, a combination of both. Argue it how you will, it is not standard fare, and not literature most of my first-year students would have picked up on their own outside of class.

Often, first-year students have not had the opportunity to ask themselves about a number of basic freedoms they have come to enjoy and assume have always been afforded people. At the beginning of the semester, we start by reading *Fahrenheit 451* by Ray Bradbury. While one or two students will admit to a passing knowledge of (or of having already read) the novel, most first-year students have not even heard of it; they will admit to recognizing book titles of novels which have been made into movies, and since the only version of Bradbury's book is a very old (and very bad) adaptation, most students come to *Fahrenheit 451* without any preconceived notions. This is a good thing, because right out of the starting gate, I can shock their sensibilities and get them to start talking and asking questions.

Fahrenheit 451, like most of the other post-apocalyptic/dystopian literature I use in this course, is not set in a specific time. One can conjecture, but it is usually safer to look at this type of literature as "out there" in a time not so very distant from what we can expect to live through in our — and our students' — lifetimes. That is what makes the specter of any post-apocalyptic literature as horrifying as some of it can be — the thought that what is being presented is not just not happening in the present time, but the actions are something that we (or our children) could possibly have to live through. This ultimately takes the students back to their "what if" questions of childhood, and hopefully makes them consider the scenario not as fiction per se, but as something urgent that they need to seriously think critically about.

Fahrenheit 451 asks the students to consider the questions of censorship, free speech, and the evolution of a society that forbids reading. Before we even start discussing the novel and its themes in class, students receive their paper assignments and they know, while reading, some of the things they will need to focus on in order to successfully complete the assignment. Because this is the first paper required of them in a freshman writing course, I make it more about them and their thoughts and their experiences so far — a personal narrative of sorts, but one that is connected to the themes in the novel. They can write about

- their experience with censorship,
- the importance of free speech, or
- what we ultimately get from reading books.

Because students are being asked to talk about themselves, alongside the novel, it frees them, to a certain extent, because talking about themselves is one of the thing they do best. It's what they *know* and what they are comfortable with.

Sometimes, students want to slide in to a compare/contrast type of essay, which involves discussing how the society in Bradbury's novel is similar yet different from our society; and, while that could be used for a future unit in the course (one that deals specifically with a compare and contrast essay), I find that quite a bit of the discussion in the class covers the similarities and differences and a paper at that point would simply be restating what we all have covered in class.

What this particular novel does for students is make them look at themselves and their lives. It makes them realize how dedicated to "the family" they themselves are, as is evidenced by their commentary regarding so much "reality" television that they watch, and how addicting the television really is. It makes them stop and realize how different their lives would be without the freedom to read what they want to (outside of the classroom, of course, they are quick to point that out). But for the most part they are able to also see the problems inherent with that society at their own level. They see what school has become — a place where nothing is learned, where everything is parroted, and where most "teaching" comes in the form of watching movies. Students point this out and that engenders more discussion, again centered around them and around their experiences.

This, ultimately, leads the discussion to censorship and free speech, which the characters in *Fahrenheit 451* have had to live with all of their lives. When

I ask students to talk about their own experiences with censorship and free speech issues, at first they seem to either frown, because they honestly cannot think of any, or they hesitate because they are not sure how much they want to actually share. It has always been interesting to me how, at this point during the first few weeks of the semester, I am able to get them to understand that their free speech will not be hindered in this particular classroom, at least. It's a refreshing experience for them, to understand that being asked "What do you think?" requires of them to decide what they think and share it without fear of recrimination, or laughter, or a bad grade. Students become comfortable discussing all sorts of themes they discover from their reading of Bradbury's novel: censorship, communication problems, lack of respect for life, society's focus on entertainment over human connections, and the importance of reading for knowledge, among others.

By the end of the first unit, by the end of the discussion of *Fahrenheit 451*, most students come out of their shells, feel empowered enough to share their own thoughts, and start to look at their life experiences a little bit differently, all from the discussions about censorship, free speech, and the importance of being able to learn things from books. It's also a freeing experience for them in the sense that they are able to share not only their ideas and experiences out loud during discussion but through the three-to-five page paper they are required to write and share in a small group, a dynamic which allows for more discussion and introspection during the two drafts through to the final product of their paper on *Fahrenheit 451*.[1]

From starting students on the road to some in-depth critical thinking with discussions on the themes in Bradbury's book, the next step takes them into the interesting waters of ethics. English writer Kazuo Ishiguro's novel *Never Let Me Go* is a first person narrative, a story told by a young woman, Kathy, who immediately stirs the interests of the students by using terms unfamiliar to them. They are drawn into Kathy's seemingly-innocuous story of growing up in an exclusive boarding school—called Hailsham in the novel—and they relate to the usual problems children face growing up: teachers, lessons, learning how to interact with the opposite sex, and dealing with children who can be harsh and cruel and judgmental.

When it becomes finally clear that these Hailsham "students" are more than just "special," that they are clones who are being raised in order to donate their internal organs to rich, ill people who need them, the students reading the novel are stunned. They realize—and can verbalize this in discussions—that Ishiguro was quite brilliant in telling the story in first person narration, and doing it in such a way as to draw the reader into personally relating to these characters, bonding with them in a way, so, when the big reveal comes about (which it does from the start in hints the Ishiguro drops through his narrator, Kathy), it opens up the discussion to the ethical question of raising flesh-and-blood people for the purpose only of supplying needed body parts for disease-ridden rich people.

Even though *Fahrenheit 451* ended with a war that obliterated much of the city in which Montag lived and worked, there is a spark of optimism, and the students are quick to point this out. The city may have been destroyed, but the books live on in the memories of the men, the hoboes, who have memorized them. Montag and the men are last seen heading back towards the city, where it could be surmised that they will be able to rebuild society and reintegrate books into lives that had been bereft of them for many generations. The students agree that a "happy ending" is one they tend to look for, above and beyond the thematic (or symbolic) discussions of the works.

After working through *Never Let Me Go* the consensus seems to be unanimously that there is no hope for Kathy and the other children who are raised for their "donations." The discussion rages — angrily at times — because the students do not understand why the Hailsham children, once they learn what they are and what they are expected to do, do not just leave, run away, refuse to "donate." But, ultimately, they work it out, with indirect guidance, and come to understand that the Hailsham children do not have a choice. There is no place for them to go. This is what they have been raised to do, and sadly they continue to fulfill their destinies.

The understanding this raises in my students is how lucky they are to be able to have the freedom of choice, and with that freedom comes the responsibility to make correct ethical choices themselves regarding how they live their lives and how they treat people. They frequently point out that they are not sure how they would have reacted to the clones in Ishiguro's story, or if they would have felt so strongly that what they have to do — to "donate" — is morally wrong, if they had not been brought along to see the clones as people, as young men and women growing up with hopes and dreams much like they themselves are doing. They raise the point that it is imperative in order to fully understand another — another race, culture, sex — that one needs to understand life from that others' points of view. They argue that whoever it is behind the raising of the clones is "playing God," which can never work out well and is a bad ethical (and moral) choice.

Ultimately what my students are charged with writing their second paper over is one of three options, taken from the variety of themes discussed in *Never Let Me Go*. They are given the choice to write over one of the following:

- medical ethics issues,
- the morality of "good" versus "evil," or
- class issues.

When I first raise the issue of class in our discussion, it does not have the same effect as talking about medical ethics or the morals involved in those who are perceived in the novel as "good" versus those who are perceived to be "evil." It takes a closer reading of the novel to get to Ishiguro's point about class. Perhaps that may be because my students are Americans and tend to not see things from a classist point of view the way a British person (which Ishiguro is) might. For the most part, the students at our university tend to be lower middle-class or upper lower-class, so the issue of class differences is a discussion that does not come easily to them. Ishiguro makes it clear, however, that the clones are considered the lowest class of all, to the extent that people avoid them, much like the Untouchables must be avoided — or were avoided — at one point in India. My students come to understand that the other people in Ishiguro's novel must look at the clones that way, they must see them as not-as-good-as-"real"-people, must convince themselves that the clones do not have feelings, that the clones do not have souls. Otherwise, how could they feel comfortable accepting their "donations"?

Using their developing critical thinking skills, at this point, my students are able to make connections between the treatment of the clones in Ishiguro's novel to the treatment of many classes and races of people. The discussion picks up, and they understand how they can develop a thesis and write a paper on the class issues they have read about in this novel. In the Honors Composition I class, where I use these novels for this purpose, often almost half of the class are majoring in some science in order to ultimately pursue a medical degree. The concept that our modern medical science could ultimately evolve to the point where we could actually carry out what Ishiguro writes of in *Never Let Me Go* becomes frighteningly real. The discussion of this novel begins, now, to bring the students back to the "what if" questions of their childhood, and at this point, they start to look at things a little bit differently than they did at the start of the course.

The third novel I assign for this class is an unusual one for British mystery writer P.D. James. In *Children of Men* the apocalypse has not happened yet, or perhaps it has and hit mankind in a way it was unprepared for. The story is situated in the future, not the far-off-distant future, but one near at hand. Basically the "apocalypse" in James's story is that mankind — men, anyway — has suddenly been rendered sterile. No children have been born at the start of the novel for close to twenty years. The "last generation" is referred to as the Omegas, which is the last letter of the Greek alphabet, used to connote the end. With mankind sterile, no one is going to come after the Omegas; they are the end of mankind. As such, they take liberties that man has not taken before; ragged groups of them wander the countryside wreaking havoc, murdering, doing pretty much whatever they want, and the law does nothing to stop them. The ones who inhabit the countryside have become almost like wild men, avoided at all costs. As a result, what is left of British civilization is centered around the larger towns.

As in *V for Vendetta*, this story asks the reader to imagine government gone to the point of dictatorship, under the guise of doing everything for the good of the people. England, as portrayed in *V for Vendetta*, was run by the High Chancellor Sutliff and his range of yes-men deputies. In *Children of Men* there is a similar scenario — although in this one, the small board that runs England can at least be approached by the hero, Theo, who is the unlucky childhood friend and cousin of the ruler of the country, Xan. While Sutliff has his "Fingermen" who are a kind of select group of secret police, who "bag" undesirables and people who would speak out against the High Chancellor, Xan has a more subtle group to keep control of the population. Those found guilty of whatever infraction are simply shipped off to the Isle of Man where they are dumped and left to fend for themselves. Murderers are left there along with people who have committed lesser, non-violent crimes. Out of sight, out of mind.

As the population of England ages, Xan and his board have come to control the end of life in much the same way they have dealt with the problem of crime. The "Quietus" (so named by the few outside of the government who understand what is going on) is government management of the end of life: it is the drowning of the elderly off the shoreline of northern England. Theo and the group of rebels he comes to be with are not convinced that the Quietus is voluntary euthanasia; the rebels — as rebels are wont to do — vehemently oppose Xan's reign and want to see it come to an end. Theo is engaged to help them, somewhat against his will at first. Yet he changes his mind after he himself witnesses a Quietus and sees the elderly wife of a colleague (Theo is a history professor at one of the universities in England) bludgeoned to death because she changes her mind at the last minute about getting into the boat and dying. Ultimately, the reader discovers that one of the rebel band is indeed pregnant — something no one ever thought would happen again. Theo must keep her safe from Xan and the government until after she has had her baby: the rebels know Xan will use this as propaganda and evidence that he needs to remain in power.

Like Bradbury and Ishiguro before her, James is sending a warning of sorts in her novel and the students quickly grasp this. They understand that James is not necessarily saying that this is what will happen: rather this *could* happen in the not-so-distant future. Given the exposure to pesticides, the over-use of antibiotics, the contaminants in our water- and food-supply, it is not that much of a stretch for the students to understand how simply something like world-wide sterilization could occur, although James is clever enough to not explain it; the most brilliant scientists cannot explain it. The world-wide sterilization is one of those instances that pepper post-apocalyptic and dystopian literature for which readers must be able to apply a "willing suspension of disbelief" that Coleridge wrote about in Chapter XXII of *Biographia Literaria* (qtd. in Prasad 211). We may not know exactly how it happened, but we are willing to believe that it could happen — given the circumstances of life as we already know it.

As far as the students are concerned, the biggest outrage perpetrated in the novel is the government-controlled Quietus. They see, quite quickly, that it is nothing more than state-mandated murder of the elderly and infirm, understanding that people are being bribed to bring in their old folk (as a pension is given to the family after each Quietus).

The students also pay close attention to the matter of dumping criminals — no matter what their crime — on the Isle of Man, leaving them to fend for themselves. They grasp that this means the survival of the fittest, with the strongest and most ruthless preying on the weak, stealing what small provisions they come ashore with. It is assumed by the rebel group that anarchy is the law of the land on the Isle of Man. In addition to the outrage of the Quietus, the cruelty of the Isle of Man punishment is what forces the rebel group to want to dispose, somehow, of Xan and his near-fascist rule.

One of the things I have my students pay particular attention to is a discussion that occurs between Julian, the rebel who brought Theo into the group (the woman who is pregnant), and Theo, during a meeting with the rest of the rebels: Miriam, Gascoigne, Luke and Rolf. They are talking about the government sending criminals of all sorts to the Isle of Man. Julian tells Theo, "They shouldn't treat human beings like that. No matter what they've done, what they are, they shouldn't treat people like that. We have to stop it." Theo replies, "Obviously there are social evils, but they are nothing to what is happening in other parts of the world. It's a question of what the country is prepared to tolerate as the price of sound government" (James 64).

We open the discussion to this question: ethically, should we tolerate certain "social evils" as the "price of sound government?" Like *Never Let Me Go*, James's novel asks ethical questions, difficult ones, ones with no easy answers. By discussing these questions in light of the fiction they have been reading, the students are, often without realizing it, stretching their critical thinking skills, opening themselves up to ideas they have not had to face before, and questioning themselves and their own ethics. They look at different social evils that they themselves identify in discussion and try to come to some conclusions as to whether or not they are things they really want to live with as the price of either sound government or their own personal freedoms. It is difficult for some of them. Some have been raised in an environment in which they either do not think of such things, or they are told what to think. They come through censorship and personal freedom issues in *Fahreheit 451*, medical ethics questions and cloning in *Never Let Me Go,* and move through euthanasia, immigration policies, and strict governmental rules that may or may not be morally and ethically sound in *Children of Men*. They are considering questions they never considered before. They are questioning what they are reading, the world around them, and ultimately their own belief systems, and it is a slow, but amazing, process to watch.

One of the last things about the book we discuss is a specific scene in which Theo, who has gone to see Xan at the request of the rebel group, is standing outside after his meeting. It is just he and Xan talking. Xan reminds Theo that they will not be the last two men on earth — Theo at this point is 50, which is considerably older than any of the Omegas — but Xan asks Theo what they should do if they were. Theo suggests they would drink, "salute the darkness and remember the light. Shout out a roll-call of names and then shoot ourselves." Theo adds, "And since we are, after all, English, we could end with Prospero's speech from *The Tempest*" (James 104).

I remind the students that writers — good writers — do not throw just any old reference to any old thing in their writing, so I have them research the speech from *The Tempest*, assuming the reference is to Prospero's "revels" speech:

> Our revels now are ended. These our actors,
> As I foretold you, were all spirits and
> Are melted into air, into thin air:
> And, like the baseless fabric of this vision,
> The cloud-capp'd towers, the gorgeous palaces,
> The solemn temples, the great glove itself,
> Yea, all which it inherit, shall dissolve
> And, like this insubstantial pageant faded,
> Leave not a wrack behind. We are such stuff
> As dreams as made on, and our little life
> Is rounded with a sleep [Shakespeare 4.1.147–58].

They complete a brief assignment in which they write why this particular passage would be important to James's novel, and why Theo — who is trying to save the country — would suggest two Englishmen end the world with this particular speech.

Science may or may not have caused the world-wide sterilization that plagues mankind in *The Children of Men* but, when the students turn to the next novel required in this course, Margaret Atwood's *Oryx and Crake*, it is very quickly clear that science has indeed run amok. Although it may be safe to conclude that it is science (or the government, with science's help) that has caused the problems in James's novel, the students are aware very early on in Atwood's novel that mankind has manipulated scientific advances to cruel and outrageous outcomes. Upper-class scientific people and their families are confined to large, city-like compounds, surrounded by guards, all for the protection of scientific secrets. On the outside are the "Pleeblands" where the lesser society lives, or tries to. This country — never specified, but Atwood subtly suggests it is America — has evolved into a near-wasteland outside of the compounds. The oceans have risen, changing the coastline for hundreds of miles inland, whole states have turned to desert, torrential rains predictably fall each day with tornadoes being a not uncommon occurrence, and people can no longer spend much time in the sun without sunscreen with extremely high SPF. This, Atwood is saying, is what we can come to if we are not careful, if we do not rein in some of our more outrageous thoughts regarding what science can and cannot do, if we give in to the urge to "play God."

Like the people in *Never Let Me Go* who have chosen to play God through the creation of clones for use of their body parts for ailing wealthy people, in Atwood's novel there is a conscious decision by Crake to play God and design his genetically engineered "Children of Crake" to be the ultimate perfect people. These people will not fight amongst themselves, will not fall in love and thus be subjected to heartache, they will not own land or feel the need for any hierarchical body politic to rule over anything. It is through Crake's machinations that the plague which decimates the population of the world is spread through his Blysspluss pills, distributed with the help of Oryx.

The world created by Margaret Atwood is a step beyond the worlds the students have already been reading about earlier in the course — Bradbury's world, and Ishiguro's world, and James's world. But it's the next step in a logical progression, in a sense. As with the other three stories, here is a situation which could, indeed, be realized if the conditions allowed for it. The students are open to such a situation at this point in the semester because of the reading they have already done and the discussions they already had. Their capability for critical thinking has grown as the complications presented by the progression of novels have grown as well. By the time they read Atwood's story, most of them are still hoping for the best, while expecting the worst, and with the world of Crake, Oryx, Jimmy (Snowman), and the Children of Crake, they certainly see mankind at its worst.

Atwood's story, unlike the earlier novels, is not linear. It begins nearly at the end where the reader is presented with Snowman, once known as Jimmy, who seems to be guardian of an odd group of simple minded people who look up to him and who feed him — not as much as he would like, but enough. The story is told from Jimmy's point of view and Atwood weaves back and forth, telling Jimmy's story of growing up in a compound, of what the scientists were creating and splicing together, while at the same time bringing the story closer to a conclusion as Snowman is going on a trek back to a compound to get more food and guns.

Atwood is not saying that science causes all the problems in the world, and the students realize this, after facing a similar discussion with both Ishiguro's and James's works. Rather, they surmise that Atwood tells a cautionary tale and the group usually divides between one side arguing that Crake was just trying to make the world better and the other side insisting that he was a megalomaniac with severe delusions of grandeur who set out to destroy the world and very nearly came close. Both groups of students, if I approached the paper for this novel from an argument-essay point of view, have sufficient evidence throughout the novel to successfully argue their thesis. What they both do agree on is that it is not science *per se* that has caused the problem, but man's misuse of science — man's insistence on taking that one step beyond.

Rhetorically the students started their writing at the beginning of the course with a form of personal narrative; from there they moved to supporting a thesis, and from there to an explication paper. For *Oryx and Crake*, because at this point they have now read four out of the five novels, we move to a compare and contrast essay. As with all the papers the students will have written by the end of the course, for this one, too, they have a choice of topics. Some students are more comfortable with a specific prompt and would prefer to be given just one; they need the structure afforded by such a constricting assignment. Others tend to thrive more on being given a choice, and I am always quick to tell my classes that if they think of something else they would prefer to write about, given the parameters of what we have been discussing in class and the type of essay we are set to write for this particular assignment, they can discuss it with me. I believe, and most of them come to agree with me, students tend to write clearer, more focused, and more interesting papers when the topic is one in which they have the most interest. It comes across in their thesis statements, and in the specific examples they use to back up their theses.

Oryx and Crake lends itself to specific themes, some of which we have already been talking about in our discussions earlier in the course. Class structure is certainly one point that Atwood brings up in the novel; the role of religion is another. Sexuality and sexual mores in Atwood's future world certainly contrast with those which most of my students are comfortable with, and some choose to write about this. Most, however, choose to look at Atwood's novel alongside at least two of the other novels already read. Asked to compare Atwood's overall frightening view of the potential future and with Ishiguro's or Bradbury's or James's (or with two of them), at this point in the semester they are able to formulate a solid thesis and back it up with specific examples from the texts they have chosen to compare.

This is one of my goals and hoped-for outcomes by the end of the semester. By using these particular novels, I have been able to appeal to the students' interests; have enabled them to feel a connection to either the characters, the setting, or the situation; and have gently focused the discussion on the most important themes in the novels, the ones that for the most part ask the students to think through their own morals and ask themselves ethical questions they may not have had to face in the past. Through looking at themselves in light of these questions, they are able to enhance (or start) their critical thinking skills in new ways. They have learned, at this point in the semester, to share their ideas, to think things through, and to back up what points they are trying to make with specific examples, be it from their own lives (which makes the reading and discussion relevant to each of them) or from the text—and at best a combination of both of them. The novels selected are done so to help them to think. They are selected specifically because the scenarios raised in each send the students back to those early "what if" questions that sparked their imaginations as children. All four of these books present that "what if" scenario and ask serious questions, worthy of students' critical analysis.

The fifth and final post-apocalyptic novel I assign for this class is Cormac McCarthy's *The Road*. My students agree that this story is the most bleak of all the possible future scenarios they have been faced with throughout the course. McCarthy's novel is about both a physical and psychological journey undertaken by an unnamed father and his unnamed son. An unspecified catastrophe has decimated the world; the landscape is bleak, gray, overcast, and cold. Daytime is barely distinguishable from night time; there seems to be no color left in the world. While there is a perceived glimmer of hope for mankind in at least three of the four previously read novels, students find it difficult to be optimistic about mankind's future by the end of *The Road*.[2] The horrific things the man and his son see and have to live through on their trek to the sea become more horrifying and dismal as the novel progresses. Yet this novel, more than the others, is the one the students agree touches them the most, although when pressed most of them cannot clearly define why.

The man and his son journey towards hope, towards life, towards something better than how life was where they lived prior to the cataclysmic event that devastated the world. The man progressively grows more ill as they cross the continent towards the sea; the son grows up. Rather than despair, the two give each other courage and hope, even though the man knows he is going to die and wants to provide the best he can for his son before that can happen. The students see this, for the son, as a journey towards manhood and understanding. By the time the father does indeed die, the son is lucky enough to be taken in by another small wandering group of people; the son has to believe that this group are "the good guys" and that he will be able to move on without his father.

This story challenges the students to look at themselves again, just as the other four also made them introspective. The story raises questions not only of "what happened to the world to make it this way" (which they ultimately realize does not matter to the point McCarthy is trying to make) but it encourages the students to put themselves in the situation of surviving whatever holocaust has occurred and to ask the question that the boy frequently asks: Would they be keepers of the fire? (These are the "good guys" as defined by the father and handed down to the son.) Would they be on the side of the cannibals who continue to roam the countryside, terrorizing any survivors they find, in the hopes of sustaining their own lives through the death and consumption of other humans?

The students want to believe that they would stand fast, that they would "keep the fire." They conclude that they are asking to put themselves into an impossible situation, one that they cannot truly grasp because what has happened to the world, what has happened to the humanity of man is something so truly horrible that it is next to impossible to put themselves into that situation and conclude how they would react. Again, moral and ethical questions come into play as the students continue to use their critical thinking skills to argue their positions regarding the themes McCarthy raises in *The Road.* I ask them, in their paper for this novel, to discuss the journeys both main characters take — physical and psychological — and how they grow and change along the way, taking into consideration the different moral and ethical choices they are forced to make on their march to the sea.

By the end of the semester, most students in the course need little prompting to begin critical discussions over themes in the novels. The questions raised, the ideas presented all have touched a nerve, in one way or another, and have helped the students not only to understand themselves better but, through discussion (and a lot of writing prompts), have strengthened their communication skills as well as honed their critical thinking skills. By the time the course concludes, the final exam questions ask them to synthesize everything they have learned and they are able, from thesis through sufficient examples to back up their claims, to clearly organize their thoughts and present them in an organized, logical manner. That they understand themselves better as well as hone their writing and critical analysis skills are the goals upon which the course is based.

The students choose one of three questions on the final exam, each of which allows them to show what they have learned throughout the semester. They are instructed to formulate their own thesis and to use sufficient specific examples from each text to fully support the thesis. I am including the three final exam questions here.

- Many works of literature take the concept of "the journey" and incorporate it one way or another into both theme and plot. A "journey" can be physical as well as metaphorical and/or symbolic. All of the novels we have read this semester use the concept of "the journey" in one way or another. This is the most obvious in McCarthy's novel *The Road.* Using at least three of the novels from this semester (including *The Road*), discuss the correlation between the physical journeys taken by the protagonists and the metaphorical and/or symbolic journeys undertaken in the works. Begin with a clear, well-developed thesis. Using clear, logical progression, back up your thesis with specific references to the three works you have chosen to discuss.

- One theme we did not discuss in depth this semester is one upon which many novels and films are constructed: the concept of good versus evil. There are a number of ways good versus evil can be depicted in literature — sometimes subtly, and other times blatantly obvious. Using at least three of the texts we read this semester (and one of the texts must be *The Road)*, show how the authors have approached this concept, how each incorporates it throughout their work, and what conclusions we can come to about the very nature of "good" versus "evil." Make sure you use specific examples. Clearly explain how each author uses and develops the theme. Do not generalize. Using your critical analysis skills, clearly make your points, following through from your well-developed thesis statement.
- For centuries, writers have been exploring the mysterious and sometimes elusive thing we refer to as "love." Love, as we all know, comes in many definitions and degrees of intensity, from parental love, to familial love, to the love for friends, passionate love, and the love for one's children. The power of love may be one of the strongest powers that we have never been able to contain — elusive and ineffable as it may be. Yet love plays a major role in a number of the works we have read this semester. Using at least three of the texts (again, one of the texts must be *The Road*), formulate a thesis delineating what the writers are saying about the power of/concept of love in each work. How does love manifest itself? How does it free or constrain the characters? What point, ultimately, is the writer trying to make by his/her portrayal of love? Make sure you have a clear thesis statement, a well-developed essay that stays on topic, and sufficient examples to fully support your thesis from each of the texts you have chosen to write about. Do not generalize in your discussion of the texts.

Benjamin, in his essay "The Storyteller," suggests we need distance and we need the story to have an aura of mystery; all of the novels selected for this particular Composition I class certainly deliver that. There is distance and mystery, but threaded through each of the stories is that connecting thread that ties them all together by the end of the semester. That connecting thread is what leads the students back to the "what if" question of childhood: that each plot could actually happen. The possibility is there that our freedoms could be taken away under the guise of protecting our safety; that science will advance to the point that we can create clones for the use of their body parts for the well-being of "real" people in society; that events could occur to render the world sterile; that through our own megalomaniacal drives we ultimately destroy our planet and most humans on it; that we could be reduced to cannibalism after cataclysmic events nearly annihilate the world.

Students read and ultimately ask themselves "what if." By doing so they not only come to a better understanding of themselves and their own morals and ethics, but they are able to put to use those skills learned as they ask those questions in other aspects of their lives and in other courses of study in their time at university. By studying post-apocalyptic/dystopian fiction, students can better situate themselves in the world as we know it now, and become better communicators in the process.

Notes

1. With all of the papers I assign in both Composition I and II, students are required to bring in copies of their drafts to share with a small peer group for review. They read these drafts aloud, and then the group discusses them; they go on to swap these drafts with people outside of their peer groups, and everyone is instructed to write critiques for the two papers prior to the next class. Once students have had both peer group review and critiques, they have at least five opinions and critiques of their papers, which enable them to complete a second draft. With the second draft, the same process is repeated, with the exception of the written critiques. Students form the same peer groups they had with the first draft, which brings continuity, having the same set of eyes see what changes they have made. After the second draft peer group review, students revise their papers for the final time. When papers are due, each student must submit a packet: the final copy, the first draft that they themselves took notes on during peer group review, the two critiques people wrote for them, and the second draft (again, the one with notes from peer review). I take the entire packet into consideration in my rubric for grading, my logic being that it is the entire process that makes for a final paper, not simply the final product. Items missing from the packet negatively impact the students' paper grade.

2. In *Fahrenheit 451*, Montag and the other hoboes choose to return to the city, with the hopes of rebuilding society and bringing back freedom of speech and the return of reading books. In *Oryx and Crake*, Snowman decides to approach the new humans who are met on the beach. Atwood leaves it up to the reader to decide whether or not he will try to kill them or greet them warmly. Students see this ending as optimistic. They want to believe that these people represent the hope of the future and that Snowman will be healed and not die. In *The Children of Men*, Julian has her healthy baby; Theo kills Xan and, by extension, takes down the suffocating government. That the situation on the Isle of Man and the enforced euthanasia of the Quietus will come to an end is assumed as Theo will assume rule in Britain. While reading *Never Let Me Go,* students hold onto hope that life will change for the graduates of Hailsham, as Tommy and Kathy struggle to find Madame and get the answers they seek. After that meeting, the understanding that things are only going to get worse for the clones slowly washes over not only Tommy and Kathy, but the readers as well, and it seems hopeless by the end; no one wants to fight for them anymore, no one wants to prove their worth as real people with souls. They can only continue on as careers and, ultimately, donors.

Works Cited

Atwood, Margaret. *Oryx and Crake*. New York: Anchor Books, 2003. Print.

Benjamin, Walter. "The Storyteller: Reflections on the Works of Nikolai Leskov." *Illuminations: Essays and Reflections*. New York: Schocken Books, 1968. 83–110. Print.

Bradbury, Ray. *Fahrenheit 451.* 50th Anniversary Ed. New York: Del Rey, 2003. Print.
Ishiguro, Kazuo. *Never Let Me Go.* New York: Vintage International, 2005. Print.
James, P.D. *The Children of Men.* New York: Vintage, 1992. Print.
McCarthy, Cormac. *The Road.* New York: Vintage International, 2006. Print.
Prasad, Amar Nath. *Re-Critiquing S.T. Coleridge.* New Dehli: Sarup, 2008. Print.
Shakespeare, William. *The Tempest.* Ed. Gerald Graff and James Phelan. New York: Bedford, 2000. Print.

Corruptible Power

Frances E. Morris and
Emily Dial-Driver

In the spring of 2006, I, Frances, was still a traditionalist. I went to graduate school later in life, and I truly enjoyed studying the required classic texts. I hadn't yet learned the connective power of using strategically-placed pop culture in the classroom. It isn't that I didn't see the quality available in some of popular entertainment, but I felt students were already inundated with what contemporary society had to offer. I wanted them to have a strong theoretical and classical academic foundation to use as a tool to interpret meaningful works.

However, my frustration with teaching the late seventeenth and early eighteenth centuries' pop icon Jonathan Swift found me desperate. For the previous few semesters, I had to actually explain to my students that "A Modest Proposal" was an exquisitely written piece of irony and not a treatise on infant cannibalism. I started with wanting the students to discover the effectiveness of Swift's irony and sarcasm on their own, so I didn't preview the reading; but, after a student cried real tears and after listening to the anger the class voiced over reading about "eating babies," I decided my very literal readers needed background information prior to delving into the piece.

The following semester, before I assigned the reading, I provided a detailed overview of Jonathan Swift's essay, his time in history, and the writing style he used in the piece. Unfortunately, the culminating discussion of "A Modest Proposal" fell flat. Clearly, I had robbed the students. They learned the history behind Swift's writings, and they knew that this essay was considered a classical piece of sarcasm and irony, but they knew this because I had told them, not because they had felt the bite of Swift's sarcasm. I wanted a venue to introduce Swift's essay that would engage them as active thinkers; I wanted to combat complacent learning. I wanted my students to retain a memory of effective political satire. When I think of memory, feeling, and understanding, my mind always turns to Elie Wiesel. I kept turning his words "Think higher, feel deeper" around to say "In order to think higher, feel deeper."

To facilitate the deeper feeling and the higher, less literal thinking that I knew my students were capable of, I stepped out of my traditional comfort zone and turned to a twenty-first century pop icon and political satirist, John Stewart. This was early in 2006, a mid-term election year. There was political unrest in the air, and Stewart's *The Daily Show* with its fake news was very popular. I hoped that my mostly rural Oklahoma students watched or were at least familiar with the show. I decided to show a clip titled "Level of Taint" that first aired January 17, 2006.

The excerpt was a many-layered political satire—*The Daily Show* at its best. The show's Ed Helms reported on the "taint" in Washington, D.C. The fake reporter posted an anatomical looking graphic of the taint in D.C. Helms pointed out that the taint, pictured as light brown shading, spread from the Pentagon, pictured with a hole in the middle resembling an anus, to a very stiff, phallic picture of the Washington Monument, surrounded by the Capitol and the White House balled up at the bottom. Helms was very serious and very literal in his reporting, but his words combined with his body language had layers of meaning. Helms claimed that he had done some "serious poking around" to find the taint because "people in Washington try to hide their taint, but it's there and it's dirty." Near the end of his report the camera focused back on Helms and, in case anyone had missed the message, his hands were positioned in the very juvenile "read between the lines" fashion. My students laughed and appeared to get the irony in the piece. It was time to dismiss class, so I had no time to discuss the clip or to discuss the reading assigned for next time. All I could do was to ask them to think about the clip while reading "A Modest Proposal."

I am no longer a traditionalist first. My students returned to class ready to discuss Swift's essay. The majority had actually read the essay and they understood that it was political satire. They were ready to dissect the piece. We were able to look at how Swift used symbolism and motifs to develop his themes. We even had an in-depth debate on whether Swift's piece is more sympathetic to the English or to the Irish. The students decided he was equally acidic to both. It has been several years and I have taught many classes in the interim, but I remember the energy in that discussion. Oprah would have called this discussion a "teachable moment" or, to be more precise, "teachable moments"; it was by far the most amazing seventy-five minutes I had had as a composition instructor: It certainly beat trying to explain what irony is and spoon feeding why and how Swift uses it. Consequently, I was on a quest to reproduce this engaged-student experience; I rewound and reversed my lesson plans: study popular entertainment pieces first and then introduce the more traditional pieces. I enlisted the assistance of someone I consider to be an educated pop-culture aficionado, someone who I knew was not a traditionalist.

No, I, Emily, am not a traditionalist, never really have been. That's not to say that I'm not excited about teaching the classics. I am. I'm enamored of Jane Austen's works; I think Dostoevsky is a genius. It makes me happy even to think about, much less read and engage with, Spenser and Milton and Shakespeare. I *love* the "classics." However, I also love pop culture. And I remember that, at one time, Dostoevsky and Austen were pop culture. That is, they were authors of their time. They sold novels to the public. And Dickens! Dickens was so popular that, according to *The Victorian Web*, "one out of ten Britons who could read his works, and then read them aloud to many others" (Cody). Dickens was the essence of the Victorian pop culture novelist. For me, that means one shouldn't discount a work simply because lots of people read it, even if those lots of people reading it are reading it today and not in the Victorian era.

And I love the pop culture fantasists. Fantasy is just an extension of fiction, which is "not true" to start with. Michael Chabon is something of an authority on "real" literature and on pop culture, having written both "pop culture/entertainment" and "serious literature": he has won the Pulitzer Prize for *The Amazing Adventures of Kavalier and Clay*; written for the *New Yorker*, DC Comics and films; and written a detective story (*The Final Solution*), a young adult fantasy (*Summerland*), and non-fiction (*Maps and Legends*), among other works ("Michael Chabon"). He should know what he's talking about.

He says, "Literature, like magic, has always been about the handling of secrets, about the pain, the destruction, and the marvelous liberation that can result when they are revealed" (167). He further says that, in the academic mind, and perhaps in the mind of most "educated" people, entertainment/pop culture "means junk, and too much junk is bad for you — bad for your heart, your arteries, your mind, your soul" (13).

Why is pop culture/entertainment so discounted? Chabon asserts, "It's partly the doubtfulness of pleasure that taints the name of entertainment. Pleasure is unreliable and transient. Pleasure is Lucy with the football. Pleasure is easily synthesized, mass-produced, individually wrapped. Its benefits do not endure, and so we come to mistrust them, or our taste for them" (16).

Specifically, he defends science fiction, fantasy, ghost stories, and horror works: "Horror fiction proceeds, generally, by extending metaphors, by figuring human fears of mortality, corruption, and the loss of self" (120). However, he continues, entertainment bridges "the gulf of consciousness that separates each of us from everybody else ... a two-way exchange of attention, experience, and the universal hunger for connection" (17). In fact, he says, "perhaps all short stories can be understood as ghost stories, accounts of visitations and reckonings with the traces of the past. Were there ever characters in fiction more haunted by ghosts than Chekhov's or Joyce's?" (132). Thus, Chabon says, the "tale," the fairy tale, the fable, the fantasy are worth consideration: "The words 'once upon a time' are in part a kind of formula for invoking the ache of this primordial nostalgia. But serious literature, so called, regularly traffics in the same wistful stuff" (68) and "it is from the confrontation with mystery that the truest stories have always drawn their power" (67).

Chabon, in my case, is preaching to that proverbial choir. If the text is "good" ("to be desired or approved of," "having the qualities required for a particular role," "possessing or displaying moral virtue," "giving pleasure; enjoyable or satisfying," and "thorough"), we should consider reading it, enjoying it, using it.

If the work under consideration is "good," that is, if the work with which we want to deal has our approval (and perhaps the approval of critics), has the qualities we need in order for it to function for us in the role in which we envision it, has pleasurable aspects for us and for students, is thorough in that it deals with the themes or elements with which we want to engage, and, finally, displays the moral virtue — has the weight and importance and credibility — that we require of any text used for educational purposes, then it is an appropriate work to use in the classroom.

In the Composition II classes we both teach, we study three real-world classic experiments which deal with obedience to authority. In "The Stanford Prison Experiment" Philip G. Zimbardo discusses his controversial 1971 prison experiment. Just as a reminder, Zimbardo, a psychology professor at Stanford University, designed a mock prison in the basement of Stanford University's psychology building to replicate the psychological effects of prisons on both the prisoners and on the guards. Ten prisoners and eleven guards were chosen; all were young college age males who were tested and "judged to be emotionally stable, physically healthy, mature, law-abiding citizens" (Zimbardo 734). The prisoners were dressed in feminine smocks, were not allowed to wear underwear, were referred to by their numbers and not their names, and were purposely confused as to what time of day it was. In fact all the rules were designed to force the prisoners into a "childlike dependency" on the guards (Zimbardo 735). The guards, too, were made to wear uniforms and instructed to wear sunglasses to obscure their eyes in order to "deindividualize" the guards (Zimbardo 735). The guards received no formal training but "their symbols of power were billy clubs, whistles, handcuffs, and the keys to the cells and the 'main gate'" (Zimbardo 735). The guards were told to "maintain 'law and order'" (Zimbardo 735).

Both prisoners and guards adapted to their roles very quickly: for both groups, the prison became their reality. The prisoners acquiesced to the humiliating and often sadistic demands of the guards, and the guards reported "being delighted in the new-found power and control they exercised" during the experiment. Zimbardo stopped the experiment after only six days: "We were caught up in the passion of the present, the suffering, the need to control people, not variables, the escalation of power, and all the unexpected things that were erupting around and within us" (Zimbardo 742). At the end of the article, Zimbardo draws parallels between his experiment and the roles we willingly accept in our daily lives. He ends by asking if we are choosing "to remain prisoners because being passive and dependent frees us from the need to act and be responsible for our actions?" (743).

In "Opinions and Social Pressure" Solomon E. Asch reports on his early 1950s "vision test." Asch, a social psychologist, details the findings of his 1950s experiments on the influence of peer pressure on the individual. In the study all except one member of the studied group were confederates of the experimenter. The naïve subject in each all-male group was told this was a "psychological experiment in visual judgment" (Asch 726). The stated task of the group was to match the length of a "standard" line on the control card with a test card on which there were three lines of different lengths. The test lines were numbered 1, 2, and 3. The confederates orally reported their choices; the subject was always the last member asked to choose.

The first few tests were conducted without deception. However, the confederates, as instructed by Asch, soon began to unanimously choose an incorrect line. Essentially, the subject was given two choices: The subject could decide to choose the line that was obviously the correct line and disagree with the group, or the subject could deny his own judgment and choose the erroneous group choice. Asch reports that "the minority subjects swung to acceptance of the misleading majority's wrong judgments in 36.8 per cent of the selections" (728). Asch repeated the experiment with differing numbers in the group.

He reports that, when there was only a two person group, the subject trusted his own interpretation and almost always gave the correct answer. However, when the number of confederates was increased to "three the subjects' errors jumped to 31.8 per cent" (Asch 729). Asch also reports that the compliance of the subjects was greatly affected when the unanimity of the confederates was altered. Even the addition of one confederate instructed to give the correct answers resulted in subjects answering "incorrectly only one fourth as often as under pressure of a unanimous majority" (Asch 729).

In "The Perils of Obedience" Stanley Milgram writes about his much maligned 1963 research into what extent people will follow "immoral" orders. As another reminder: Milgram, a Yale University psychologist, set up an experiment to see how ordinary people responded to orders from an authority figure. The experiment consisted of the authority figure, the experimental scientist; an actor playing the part of the learner; and the subject assigned the role of the teacher.

The participants were told the experiment was investigating memory and learning and, in particular, the study was interested in investigating "the effects of punishment on learning" (Milgram 693). The "learner" was strapped in a chair "to prevent excessive movement and an electrode [was] attached to his wrist" (Milgram 603). The subject was instructed to shock the "learner" each time an incorrect answer was given. After each incorrect answer the subject-"teacher" was instructed to increase the voltage. The shock generator consisted of switches ranging from slight shock to severe shock. As the experiment progressed and the voltage was increased, the "learner's" (actor's) behavior went from showing signs of mild discomfort to demanding to be released from the experiment to what "can be described only as an agonized scream" (Milgrim 695). After the scream at 285 volts, the "learner" stopped making any sounds. If the subject showed any desire to stop the experiment, he was prodded by the experimenter to continue: "Continue. Go on, please." ... "The responsibility is mine. Correct. Please go on" (Milgram 698).

In the end, twenty-five of the forty subjects obeyed the orders from the experimenter so that they had administered the maximum 450 volts three times to the errant "learner." Milgram states that "the extreme willingness of adults to go to almost any lengths on the command of an authority constitutes the chief finding of the study...." (693).

Milgram's article emphasizes the pressure of authority; Asch's article emphasizes the pressure of the peer; and Zimbardo's experiment emphasizes the pressure of the role (or social behavior). Zimbardo maintains that, when one cedes authority to the role — of the submissive prisoner or of the sadistic guard — one has the perception of also ceding responsibility, leaving one without the "onus" of choosing action. Thus, each article deals with the problem of power and authority.

Typically, we follow the "Power and Authority" unit with Mary Shelley's *Frankenstein* — not exactly 21st-century pop culture material since Shelley wrote in the 19th century. Most of the time neither of us deliberately relates the issues in *Frankenstein* to the three pieces on power, authority, and responsibility. However, one semester, in order to see if I had actually taught — and the students had learned — the ability to connect themes in dissimilar materials, I, Emily, used *Frankenstein* in a final essay examination, asking the students to write an essay on how the three pieces relate to *Frankenstein*. I thought I was taking a big chance on this assignment. However, I was delighted — and a bit surprised — to discover that the students did an amazing job on this. They connected the themes beautifully, concluding that Frankenstein himself avoids taking responsibility for his creation. In addition, they decided that he gives in to fear of peer pressure and social pressure when he does not defend Justine but allows her to be executed for a murder done by the creature; and he allows his role as a student and a "good family member" to overcome his responsibility as the creator and deserter of the creature. The three non-fiction articles dovetail nicely into the study of the 1818 pop culture phenomenon that became a "classic" piece of literature for the 21st century.

Those same themes can be illustrated by 20th- and 21st-century pop culture pieces. The genesis of this chapter was our quest to find pop-culture venues that would ease our students into an understanding of classic and difficult material. We wanted gateway pieces which would engage the students and in so doing would provide them a lens to self-discovery and ownership of the knowledge presented in both the popular pieces and in the more traditional materials.

One assumption we feel comfortable in making is that our students have spent many hours with pop culture; Malcolm Gladwell in his book *Outliers* claims that success has more to do with time spent engaging in or practicing the desired activity than with having innate talent or a genius IQ. He calls this the "10,000 Hour Rule," which works out to spending ten hours a week for 20 years (or 20 hours a week for 10 years) engaging in a specific activity. It's probably safe to say most of our students have spent at least this much time watching movies and television and reading popular fantasy, often in the form of young-adult novels. To put it in composition terminology, we decided to address our "audience" of successful pop culture connoisseurs.

We can see the problems of responsibility and the acceptance of that responsibility and the subsequent consequence in many venues in pop culture. Fiction is the timeless lie that tells the truth. The lie may be timeless, but perhaps the fiction needs to be timely for students to make the first connection. Thus, having the students watch and discuss the cult classic science fiction movie *The Matrix* before they are introduced to the obedience to authority themes may facilitate a connection to the timeless reality present in the three experiments: in theory individuals may identify with Neo, but, in reality, their choices often mirror the comfort-seeking Cypher's choices!

As you may recall, in the 1999 movie *The Matrix,* the main character Neo is caught in two worlds—one real and one brought to him in "living" color by the "Matrix." The movie depicts a small renegade group of citizens who have discovered the truth behind the "Matrix": The Matrix consists of all-powerful (authority figure) 21st century race of machines creating an illusion for the people of 2199 that they are living "normal" lives in a bright sunny 1999. In reality the machines grow people in fields of pods. These pod people have cabled umbilical cords that transfer heat and electrical power from each human to the Matrix's power grid. Essentially the humans are batteries.

Neo, a mild-mannered computer programmer by day and a wily computer hacker by night (shades of Superman, Batman, et al.), hacks his way to the question of the movie: What is the Matrix? Soon he is contacted by the renegades. He has to choose to return to the dream world and live the role assigned to him (there's that role problem) or to fight the Matrix and live in what Morpheus, leader of the renegades, describes as the "desert of the real" world. Neo chooses to fight and fight and fight. He proves to be "the one" who can fight and beat the Matrix because he sees it as the lines and lines and lines of binary code it actually is.

The film forces the characters to make choices that reflect the themes we see in the three power and control essays. After learning the truth, Neo, the character we all would like to identify with, accepts his role as "the one" to lead the renegades in the battle against the Matrix to enter reality. Cypher, on the other hand, is originally one of the renegade members and is the character we never want to be like.

In fact, even Cypher's name evokes several ideas: a cypher is zero or a nonentity, that is, a person of no value or importance; a cypher is, at the same time, an encoded message or the key to such a message, that is, a Trojan horse, of sorts; in addition, if Cypher's first name is Lou, the name implies Lucifer himself ("Cypher"). ["Oh, the thinks you can think" (Seuss) about that name!]

Cypher tries to sabotage the group so that he can return to the easy "life" in the Matrix. In the end Neo hacks a message to the Matrix. He promises that he will show the pod humans the truth — show them the real world and give them a choice.

In the Zimbardo, Asch, and Milgram real-life experiments, Neo characters who refused the pleasures of the false world were rare and Cypher characters who wanted the taste of steak, however imaginary, abounded, for the subjects all too often chose to be blindly obedient to authority. *The Matrix* ends with a question: Will the pod people choose to live a real life that will be a very meager existence, literally under a cloud and bereft of sunshine, or will they cede responsibility to the Matrix, as Cypher, the soon-to-be nonentity, does, and "live" a life of no accountability (save powering the Matrix as recyclable batteries), a "pleasant" but not real existence?

A Composition II class discussion of whether the citizens of this fictional society will choose to give the Matrix a system's failure notice or not provides a good segue to the study of Zimbardo, Asch, and Milgrim's real-life experiments. Comparing why the Neo character chooses to claim his "personal power" and to take on the responsibilities and, yes, the risks (with attendant consequences) involved in denying the Matrix control to why the Cypher character chooses to cede his "personal power" back to the Matrix allows students to think about issues without thinking about themselves — a "comfort zone." And that lays the groundwork for moving beyond comfort for students to consider their own responsibilities and actions in the face of authority —

or even perceived authority. Perhaps after attendant discussion, the students will not be so dismissive of the results of the three experiments — the instant Neo "bravado" replaced by the knowledge that inside most of us there lurks a comfort seeking (and subservient) Cypher.

If we want something less weighty, we can turn to something as simple as a cartoon. In the episode "Hall Monitor" from *SpongeBob SquarePants*, Mrs. Puff, the boating school instructor, finally allows SpongeBob to serve as hall monitor, a position he has craved with all his spongy heart. However, his lengthy acceptance speech prevents him from actually functioning in that capacity, and Mrs. Puff, in a moment of weakness and generosity, allows SpongeBob to keep his sash overnight. SpongeBob, inflated with the power of the sash, and with the "help" of Patrick as "deputy," begins to monitor Bikini Bottom inhabitants; it turns into chaos — with traffic problems, "maniac" sightings, and spilled ice cream. SpongeBob is identified as the "maniac" and arrested, but Mrs. Puff defends him, saying, "I'm the one who gave him the uniform in the first place. He's my responsibility." This statement results in her arrest for allowing SpongeBob to cause so much trouble.

Mrs. Puff acts irresponsibly in giving SpongeBob the sash to wear home. SpongeBob and Patrick, in their usual clueless ways, cause the mayhem resulting from SpongeBob's misrepresentation and misuse of power. He is blown with perceived power and *has* to use that power because he has it. However, his power does not actually exist, a hall monitor not really being a position of authority. Even so, the fact that SpongeBob *acts* as if he has power is enough for some people to do as he demands. This is a scary fact, even in areas outside Bikini Bottom. In the above water world, if one speaks in an authoritative voice, some people are likely to respond to that voice as if it were, in fact, authority. When SpongeBob is finally stopped, his misuse of his perceived power should garner him punishment, but Mrs. Puff, realizing the initiating action was hers, defends him and takes responsibility, leading to another consequence: her arrest. The episode ends with Mrs. Puff teaching from her cell and telling SpongeBob that, when she actually returns to the school, they will talk about this — a resulting consequence even for SpongeBob.

This short cartoon can initiate discussion on most of the elements in the three non-fiction pieces. In relation to Asch's and to Milgram's work, we see Bikini Bottom inhabitants, even when there is no real authority invested, responding to the orders of the "hall monitor," because the monitor tells them what to do. They doubt their own validity and accede to his orders. Patrick and especially SpongeBob act as the guards in the Zimbardo experiment, taking on the role of authority that they think they actually have. Thus, one might use this cartoon to initiate discussion of the non-fiction pieces and how the material corresponds not only to the cartoon but to other works of literature, film, or television and to students' life experiences.

The Matrix and *SpongeBob SquarePants* are not the only possible choices. Elements from popular culture abound that allow discussion of the topics of power and authority. For example, one might consider *One Flew Over the Cuckoo's Nest*, Ken Kesey's novel and/or the film; the film *The Shawshank Redemption* and the Stephen King novella "Rita Hayworth and Shawshank Redemption"; *Hudsucker Proxy*, and even *Ikiru* (*To Live*) (an award-winning Japanese film written by Kurosawa and Hashimoto which deals with a man whose knowledge of impending death changes his life and allows him to find meaning in existence). However, it might be more rewarding to use fantasy works to open discussion on the themes.

A recent article in *The New York Times* reported that varying the context of information helps with the retention of new knowledge. The paper cited a study of both college students and adults of retirement age reported in the journal *Psychology and Aging*. The study found that both college students and retirement-age adults who studied a group of artists did better on a test that required them to identify the individual style of the artists than students and retirement-age adults who studied one artist thoroughly and then moved on to study the next artist. According to Nate Komell, psychologist and researcher, "The finding undermines the common assumption that intensive immersion is the best way to really master a particular genre, or type of creative work" (Carey). Kornell goes on to say, "What seems to be happening in this case is that the brain is picking up deeper patterns when seeing assortments of paintings; it's picking up what's similar and what's different about them, often subconsciously" (Carey). Kelly and Johnson agree with the basic premise of the brain locating patterns: "Really, we should think of ideas as *connections*, in our brains.... Ideas aren't self-contained things; they are more like ecologies and networks. They travel in clusters" (122).

Making connections possible, moving students onto unfamiliar, shaky ground by beginning with that with which they are familiar, means using that pop culture with which they have done their "10,000 hours." Adding pop culture varies the cognitive context and helps students pick up on "deeper patterns" and to make "clusters" and "networks" of, and lasting connections to, the information presented in the Zimbardo, Asch, and Milgram essays.

Blade Runner or, alternatively, Philip Dick's *Do Androids Dream of Electric Sheep?* makes perfect sense when talking about power and authority. *Blade Runner*, which is based on Dick's novel, has several entities with power: the company that developed the replicants — androids that are so human-like they are mistaken for humans; Rick Deckard, the bounty hunter who is the main character and who is hunting down the replicants who have escaped from slavery to come to Earth; the replicants with brute force possibilities; the government that dictates the environmental effects in a desolate environment; technology itself. The questions are which entities are the moral ones, which entities have the most power, which ones are at the mercy of others, etc.

If using both *Blade Runner* and *Do Androids Dream of Electric Sheep?* in a class, one might ask the students to consider why the filmmakers emphasize an origami figure which does not appear in the novel, why the Mercer religion of the novel is ignored in the film, and why the environment and extinct animals, which are so much a part of the novel, are simply images in the film. A further discussion might ensue in relation to how power and authority differ in the two works and how the changes in emphasis from novel to film also emphasize the power/authority themes in both works.

District 9 is another film that might be a perfect initiator for discussing the three non-fiction works. In *District 9*, the people of Johannesburg, South Africa, accept what they're told about the aliens stranded on Earth and interned in a camp outside the city. The aliens are denigrated as "prawns," and the population of Earth accepts that they are disgusting creatures unworthy of concern. In fact, the slum in which the aliens are detained is on valuable property, and they are to be removed, more or less illegally, to a less (less?) hospitable location. The "hero," Wikus van de Merwe, is in charge of the move. However, he discovers, to his great surprise, that the aliens are intelligent and even helpful when he falls into alienness himself. He ultimately aids the escape of most of the aliens (it being possible they or their race will return for revenge for their imprisonment). Wikus remains on Earth, still in an alien body: human on the inside, alien on the outside (can we see a metaphor here?). We see in this film the power of the organization, the corporation, and the government, with individuals enthusiastically cooperating in their roles in each of the former until Wikus at least is forced to confront his own complicity and culpability.

Using the film *District 9* as a way to interrogate the issues of power and authority and individual responsibility can be useful to initiate discussion. Discussion could emphasize how Wikus could have avoided complicity at the onset of the situation before further discussion introduces "real life" examples. Using a fictive universe and fictional actions can allow more freedom for discussion, critical thinking, and judgment than immediately approaching what might be sensitive areas before students are comfortable talking about concepts.

Fantasy novels are also valuable ways to approach sensitive topics. "Even" young adult novels can be useful in a college classroom. First of all, young adult novels can have very adult themes. Second, young adult is simply a label. In fact, according to Diane Roback at *Publisher's Weekly*, the Pulitzer prize-winning novel *To Kill a Mockingbird* might have been published with the young adult label if it were published today ("What If" 78). So books published under the young adult label, such as *The Hunger Games* and the *Uglies* series, might be useful for college classes. Film director Gary Ross, speaking of *The Hunger Games*, says the author, Collins, "has created something that's just so unbelievably universal that it doesn't really know an age" (Valby 40). In fact, one advantage of the "young adult" genre would be that the novels are typically quick and engaging reads. This means students are more likely to actually read them, and read them to the end.

The Hunger Games is a series written by Suzanne Collins that includes the subsequent novels *Catching Fire* and *Mockingjay*. In *The Hunger Games* the main character, 17-year-old Katniss, volunteers to take part in the games in place of her younger, frail sister. The Hunger Games are a spectator sport televised for the masses' enjoyment. One male and one female participant from each district are chosen by lot (and must participate) and only one of the 24 will be left standing at the end of the game. It's the rule of the Thunderdome: "two men enter, one man leaves" (*Mad Max*) except that 24 enter and one leaves. At the novel's conclusion, Katniss and the other participant from the district, Peeta, remain: one must die. Katniss cleverly "games" the situation and the two survive, to the chagrin of the game makers and, consequently, the government.

In *Catching Fire*, the two winners take a victory tour and learn that Katniss's action has caused rebellious overtones. Because of the unrest, the next Hunger Games includes 24 winners of the previous games, including Peeta and Katniss. Cooperating with other participants, Katniss destroys the arena but is struck unconscious. She wakes to discover her family safe but her entire district destroyed.

In *Mockingjay*, the darkest of the trilogy, Katniss becomes the "face" of the revolution, sometimes with and sometimes without her cooperation. She must fight the leaders of the rebellion and the game-making government in order to achieve even rueful success.

All three books emphasize authority and power used to bad ends and personal independent action in the face of that power. Part of the independent action Katniss takes is linking herself with others. This is *Survivor*, a media entity with which most students should be eminently familiar, with food—and continued life—as the prize. In the Hunger Games, the penalty is death. However, without the alliances, without the pity Katniss takes on other participants, her struggle would not be as meaningful or as compelling to the viewers of the Game. And it is her struggle, her alliances, her pity, that lead others to rebellion against the ubiquitous power and authority of the government. This exciting and evocative series should connect with students and help them empathize with the characters' actions. In fact this might facilitate the "feel deeper, think higher" metamorphosis we see in Wiesel's words.

Like the Hunger Games, the Uglies is a series of novels: *Uglies*, *Pretties*, *Specials*, and *Extras*. In *Uglies*, we meet Tally, an "ugly," an unmodified teen who aspires to join the "pretties," older teens who have been modified for beauty. She learns that the pretties are "bubbleheads," unable to hold thoughts for very long and most interested in pleasure. She becomes friends with a girl who runs away from the modification to the "outside." Tally must track her down and retrieve her in order to qualify for modification. In the process of her search, Tally meets a true "ugly," an older unmodified teen who lives outside the current society and whose family, although fugitive from the society, works to change it. Even in the face of her new-found knowledge, Tally, through circumstance and guilt, agrees to become "pretty."

In *Pretties*, Tally takes part in all the wild pleasures available but discovers a pill that cures her bubbleheadedness. She escapes the city and reconnects with the unmodified people she met in the previous book but is recaptured and informed she will become a "special," which she does in *Specials*. She is enhanced with special powers, such as strength, and begins to serve the government. The Specials grab control, curing the "bubbleheads" but causing other problems. Tally rebels and becomes a "free" Special.

Tally, heroine of the first three novels, is not the central character in *Extras*: Aya Fuse, a teen who wants to be a famous media journalist, is the protagonist. Aya learns the price of fame and learns how to deal with the real world, meeting Tally along the way.

Of the books in the Uglies series, *Uglies* is a good selection for use in a class as it is the most coherent and thematically sound of the series. Discussions can be based on individuality, free will, appearance (in which case one might involve the topics in *Frankenstein*, of course), role manipulation, environmental issues, power, authority, and responsibility. Another good selection would be *Extras*, which, in addition to the subjects in *Uglies*, could lead to discussion on the effect of various forms of media and their ubiquitous, and informative and perhaps misleading, presence in both the novel and our lives and how they contribute to or stand in opposition to issues of power and authority.

Episodes of pop culture fantasy television series that also might be useful include *Doctor Who*, *Warehouse 13*, *Primeval*, *The Walking Dead*, *The Gates*, *Eureka*, and *Being Human* (the BBC version, NOT the U.S. version), all of which deal with questions of authority and/or use/misuse of power of various kinds in most of the episodes. For example, in the BBC's *Being Human*, Episode 6 from Series 2 fits agreeably into the discussion. In that episode, we see two main characters, Lucy and Mitchell. Lucy, a doctor at the hospital where vampire Mitchell also works, has become Mitchell's lover. Mitchell is trying to live a virtuous, killing-free life.

We discover Lucy to be in league with a revenge-set priest who is determined to wipe the "plague" of vampires from the Earth. Lucy learns from Mitchell that all the vampires of London (who have pledged to follow Mitchell's "no kill" lead because of peer—and power, Mitchell's power—pressure) will gather. She has a decision to make: is she going to give the order to blow up the meeting place or will she accede to her feeling that there is good in some of the despised and desperate beings despite their historic reputation and refuse to kill them? In response to the pressure of authority (on the part of the priest), she overcomes her impulse to refuse and orders the explosion. She makes the choice many would make because she thinks the decision might be right and she knows it is expedient, valuable points of discussion.

The topic of how media reveals power and authority influences on moral choices can be mined in many venues. For instance, according to theologian Stevenson, the series *Buffy the Vampire Slayer* is an "exhortation to make better moral choices" (260), to choose what is right rather than what is expedient. Another series with the same "exhortation" is *Dollhouse*. Also a Joss Whedon creation, *Dollhouse* features an illicit organization that contracts people for five years. Those people leave their "real" lives and are wiped to mindlessness in order to become commodities, products that serve the needs of the corporation's clients.

The main character in *Dollhouse* is Echo. She is a "Doll," mindwiped so she can "become" the role requested by the client and set for her by the organization. (That is, she "echoes" the imprinted personality.) Having agreed to a five-year contract, she can become whatever is necessary to meet the needs of the client. However, she is an anomaly in the Dollhouse, having vestiges of memories and retaining an "echo" of each "person" she becomes. She keeps this "ability" a secret because its revelation would banish her to the Attic, a place for damaged Dolls.

The major characters struggle with issues of morality and expedience. The Dollhouse director and the personality programmer do what they are asked to do, initially without question. Echo's "handler" becomes concerned with how she is being "used" by clients. However, he is, within the arms of the corporation, without power or authority and is, thus, helpless. An outsider, an FBI agent, loses his position because he has revealed the Dollhouse conspiracy and is considered either a lunatic or a foe by various constituencies. He goes inside the Dollhouse to overset it, becoming in some senses co-opted by circumstance. Various situations and complications ensue, ending with the overthrow of the corporation in a world that has been destroyed by the dissemination of the mindwipe technology. Whether this is a satisfactory ending or not is a viewer decision.

One of the central struggles, aside from issues of identity and humanity, is against the amoral power of the corporation and/or the government, staffed with people who fulfill the roles in which they are immersed. We can see the same themes in the Whedon production of *Firefly* and the subsequent film *Serenity*. Both the television series, now on DVD, and the film deal with rebellion against governmental authority and desire to protect the innocent and helpless and to make the most moral of choices in difficult situations. In each of these series we see Zimbardo, Milgram, and Asch again played out in a fantasy setting.

In the past our Composition II students have too quickly dismissed the reality of how seamlessly the subjects in the three studies relinquished their own autonomy. They often think that in Zimbardo's experiment the subjects too quickly played the role assigned — be it aggressor in the guise of a guard or be it victim in the guise of a prisoner. Even though current research shows us that "individuals in groups are more competitive than they are by themselves.... [G]roup members feed off the emotions of other team members, amplifying their drive to win and desire to eliminate rivals" (Anthes 40), students are unlikely to connect information on competition — or even be aware of it — in relation to Zimbardo's groups of guards and prisoners. These groups are rivals; and, as Jabr says, "rivalries not only bias our thought processes but also can corrupt our moral code" (44). In fact, this is true in situations outside experiments: "Because we encounter people we consider rivals quite often — both in and outside of direct competition — rivalries may alter our motivation and moral code on a regular basis, Kilduff [social psychologist] believes" (Jabr 44).

Beyond not understanding how people bend to situational pressure, our students may see, but not necessarily accept, that in Asch's essay subjects who clearly know the right answer bend to peer pressure to give an erroneous solution. They often scoff at Milgram's study in which the subjects willingly surrendered their own judgment to an authority figure and continually administered the shocking punishment.

All three studies took place decades before most of our students were born, so the lessons learned in the studies can seem dated to our twenty-first century students (perhaps as dated as a "Modest Proposal" seemed to the students mentioned earlier before the John Stewart "Taint" episode made the impressive ironic connection).

Understanding human nature — our own and that of others — and recognizing the pitfalls of being a blind follower can be useful to our futures. Understanding that ceding personal power to an authority figure is always a choice, and should be recognized as such, is important. Sometimes it is necessary and right to follow, but it should always be a conscious and purposeful choice. When it is not, it can lead to fanaticism. Anything that helps the students understand that ceding personal power to an authority figure is always a *choice* is useful. Anything that helps students understand that, while it is sometimes necessary to follow, following should always be a *purposeful choice,* is useful. Anything that helps students "remember" the lessons learned from studying the "Power and Control" experiments and connect the knowledge to a *purposeful choice*, is useful. As Wiesel says, "Let us continue to remember. For memory may be our most powerful weapon against fanaticism" (Wiesel 692).

Students — and all of us — have to deal with issues of peer pressure, societal pressure, role expectations, and responsibility in "real life," outside of the realms of film and literature, classic or pop. We all need to be aware of our propensity to allow others to direct our actions. A really bad move on our part can be giving our decision-making to someone else, such as joining the People's Temple Agricultural Project and killing our children and then dying at the direction of Jim Jones in Jonestown, Guyana (Ross).

Delegating decision making can also be positive. When another professor wants to run a class that is taught by the two of us in concert, that's really no problem because I understand his/her credentials and appreciate the purpose of the action. When my sister comes for Christmas to my house where I should be the organizer and orchestrator, she brings her own lists of what to buy and where to go and what to do and when to do it. I don't have a problem with that. I'm perfectly willing to give up my decision making to her. It's very comforting not to have to make a decision.

That's the problem. Comfort is appealing. We all need to know when it's "right" — and smart — to sit back and let someone else direct our lives. Part of that is trust. I trust my colleague(s) and I trust my sister. That trust is based on a long history and a knowledge of motives and abilities. Judgment should be based on experience and on knowledge of human nature — our own nature and that of others, both of which are a matter of experience and education.

Even with the experience and the knowledge, we need critical thinking abilities to assess that experience and knowledge: that means education. Education involves looking at various materials, assessing what the materials say and how they say it and determining how what they say relates to our world and our lives — in the past, right now, and in the future. Investigating, interrogating, considering, assessing, concluding: those are the skills we want our students to learn — and to remember, to reawaken the childhood curiosity that asks the world, "Why? Why? Why?" And they are the skills that we can try to instill using fiction and non-fiction, classics and pop culture, "reality" and fantasy.

Works Cited

Anthes, Emily. "Their Pain, Our Gain." *Scientific American Mind* Nov./Dec. 2010: 39–41. Print.

Asch, Solomon E. "Opinions and Social Pressure." *Writing and Reading across the Curriculum.* 11th ed. Ed. Laurence Behrens and Leonard J. Rosen. Boston: Longman, 2011. 726–30.

Being Human. BBC. BBC America. 2008–11. Television.
Blade Runner: The Final Cut. 1982. DVD. Warner, 2007.
Carey, Benedict. "Forget What You Know about Good Study Habits." *The New York Time* 6 Sept. 2010. Web. 7 Sept. 2010.
Chabon, Michael. *Maps and Legends: Reading and Writing along the Borderlands*. San Francisco: McSweeney's, 2008. Print.
Cody, David. "Dickens's Popularity." *The Victorian Web: Literature, History, and Culture in the Age of Victoria*. 8 June 2007. Web. 15 July 2010.
Collins, Suzanne. *Catching Fire*. New York: Scholastic, 2009. Print.
_____. *Hunger Games*. New York: Scholastic, 2008. Print.
_____. *Mockingjay*. New York: Scholastic, 2010. Print.
"Cypher (*Matrix* Character)—Definition." *WordIQ.com*. Web. 14 Feb. 2011.
Dick, Philip K. *Do Androids Dream of Electric Sheep?* 1968. New York: Del Rey, 1996. Print.
Dr. Seuss *Oh, The Thinks You Can Think!* New York: Random House, 1975. Print.
Doctor Who. BBC. BBC America. Television. 1963–89, 2005–present.
Dollhouse. Season One. DVD. Twentieth Century–Fox. 2009.
Dollhouse. Season Two. DVD. Twentieth Century–Fox. 2010.
Eureka. Syfy. Television. 2006-present.
Firefly. DVD. Twentieth Century–Fox. 2003.
The Gates. ABC. Television. 2010-present.
"Good." *Oxford Dictionaries*. 2010. Web. 12 July 2010.
"Hall Monitor." *Spongebob SquarePants*. Season 1. 28 Aug. 1999. TV. 2010.
Hudsucker Proxy. 1994. DVD. Warner, 1999.
Ikiru. [*To Live*.] 1952. DVD. Criterion. 2004.
Jabr, Ferris. "Meeting Your Match." *Scientific American Mind* Nov./Dec. 2010: 42–45.
Kelly, Kevin, and Steven Johnson. "Where Ideas Come From." *Wired* Oct. 2010: 120–24. Print.
Kesey, Ken. *One Flew Over the Cuckoo's Nest*. 1962. New York: Penguin, 2002. Print.
King, Stephen. "Rita Hayworth and Shawshank Redemption." *Different Seasons*. New York: Viking, 1982. Print.
"Level of Taint." *The Daily Show (with John Stewart)*. Comedy Central. 17 Jan. 2006. *YouTube.com*. Web. 11 Feb. 2006.
Mad Max Beyond Thunderdome. 1985. DVD. Warner, 1997.
"Michael Chabon [Author Biography]. *Book Browse: Your Guide to Exceptional Books*. 16 May 2007. Web. 12 July 2010.
Milgram, Stanley. "The Perils of Obedience." *Writing and Reading Across the Curriculum*, 11th ed. Ed. Laurence Behrens and Leonard J. Rosen. Boston: Longman, 2011. 692–704.
One Flew Over the Cuckoo's Nest. 1975. DVD. Warner, 1997.
Primeval. BBC. BBC America. 2007-present. Television.
Ross, Rick. "The Jonestown Massacre." *Cult Education and Recovery*. Rick A. Ross Institute. 2004. Web. 25 Aug. 2010.
Serenity. DVD. Universal Studios. 2005.
The Shawshank Redemption. 1994. DVD. Castle Rock, 2007.
Shelley, Mary Wollstonecraft. *Frankenstein; or, The Modern Prometheus*. 1818. 2d ed. Ed. Susan J. Wolfson. New York: Longman, 2007. Print.
SpongeBob SquarePants. United Plankton Pictures and Nickelodeon Animation Studios. Nickelodeon. Television. 1999-present.
Stevenson, Gregory. *Televised Morality: The Case of* Buffy the Vampire Slayer. Dallas: Hamilton, 2003. Print.
Swift, Jonathon. "A Modest Proposal." *The Writer's Presence*, 5th ed. Ed. Donald McQuade and Robert Atwan. Boston: Bedford, 2006. 825–32. Print.
Valby, Karen. "Let the *Hunger Games* Begin!" *Entertainment Weekly* 14 Jan. 2011. 38–40. Print.
The Walking Dead. AMC. Television. 2010-present.
Warehouse 13. Syfy. Television. 2009-present.
Westerfeld, Scott. *Extras*. New York: Simon & Schuster, 2007. Print.
_____. *Pretties*. New York: Simon & Schuster, 2005. Print.

_____. *Specials*. New York: Simon & Schuster, 2006. Print.
_____. *Uglies*. New York: Simon & Schuster, 2005. Print.
Wiesel, Elie. *Perspectives on Argument*, 4th ed. Ed. Nancy V. Wood. Upper Saddle River, NJ: Pearson, 2004. 690–92. Print.
"What If the Classic Novel Were Published Today? *Mockingbird* Turns 50." *Entertainment Weekly* 2 July 2010: 78. Print.
Zimbardo, Philip G. "The Stanford Prison Experiment." *Writing and Reading across the Curriculum*, 11th ed. Ed. Laurence Behrens and Leonard J. Rosen. Boston: Longman, 2011. 732–43. Print.

Breaching Barriers Between Work and Play

SHAKA MCGLOTTEN

In fantasist China Miéville's most recent novel, *The City & The City*, Inspector Tyador Borlú investigates a murder committed in either Beszel or Ul Quoma, two cities that occupy the same geography but which are separated by powerful veils of reality and perception. Otherwise set in a world much like our own, the novel imagines these cities as having been more or less inexplicably overlaid on top of one other. That is, while some portions of each city belong wholly to themselves, much of the cities are "cross-hatched," sharing an overlapping spatial and ontological existence, yet separated by custom and belief, as well as by political and metaphysical agreement. Outside of strictly regulated travel between the cities, residents are trained from birth to ignore their intimate neighbors, to "unsee" and "unhear" the lives of people who pass by them on the street or live in a cross-hatched apartment next door. To see or hear one another would be to transgress the uneasy truce that allows the two cities to co-exist; it is to "breach" the social contract.

What does this genre-blending novel have to do with fantasy in the classroom? For me, Miéville's novel instantly conjured experiences working with students in my class, Computers and Culture, a class that blends perspectives from the humanities and social sciences and explores the ubiquity of computers in everyday life. In the course I use the online role-playing game *World of Warcraft* (*WoW*) as a central learning activity. By the third week of the semester students have metamorphosed into orc warriors and undead priests, wielding enchanted swords and dark magic, and battling monsters as they quest their way through an expansive virtual world.

"Cross-hatching" and "breach" perfectly capture the disorientation many students feel as the real world of the classroom and the fantasy world of the game collide, challenging many of their beliefs and assumptions about learning, playing, and working. In this essay, I reflect on the ways *WoW* has usefully breached my students' expectations about participatory learning, cross-hatching their ideas about (academic) work and play. Finally, I also suggest that transgressing the boundaries between work and play is an especially vital pedagogical practice in contemporary "information economies" (like gaming, but also the "infotainment" that characterizes so much media-making and consuming) in which work and play appear to go hand in hand.

Playful Pedagogy

Though it is aimed at the general student body (for most of its history it satisfied a college-specific General Education requirement in race and gender), Computers and Culture is tailored for New Media students who are trained in new media production skills (computer science, web and game design, shooting and editing digital video) and contemporary new media art practices (multimedia art that draws on installation, performance, and conceptual art). It examines the impact of computers on culture and situates their effects on everyday life within larger histories of technological and scientific change. In addition to historical and theoretical work about computers, I also use work by filmmakers and visual artists to explore key aspects of computer-mediated life in our digital age. We tackle a range of topical issues including surveillance, privacy, free software, augmented reality, pornography, new media art practices, and social networking, among others. And throughout the semester we are particularly attuned to the ways gender, race, class, sexuality, and other vectors of difference, shape and are shaped by media, science, and technology. We explore these themes through active engagement, including a Do-It-Yourself (DIY) ethos of peer-learning (students co-facilitate class discussions for more than half the semester) and through solo and collaborative play in the virtual environment of *WoW*.

If this sounds a little boring, or like the jargon professors use to justify their teaching to skeptical administrators, then a more explicit, playful, and honest description is warranted. Among other things, in the class I use high theory to blow their minds, the proliferation of online pornography to challenge their assumptions about the politics of sex, and gaming to seduce them into thinking and working better. We use Deleuze's ideas about the rhizome, an underground, horizontally expanding plant organism, or a way of thinking non-linearly and non-causally, to talk about the cultural and individual transformations shaped by new computing and media technologies like cell phones and Twitter. We talk about and sometimes consume artifacts afforded by Web 2.0, like the collaborative and user-generated content represented by slash fiction or the memes generated on 4chan, a popular image message board.

We debate the controversial case of Justin Berry, a former self-broadcasting underage pornographer turned tech consultant. And we draw on the ideas of open-source guru Richard Stallman to learn about the ways open source software models democratic principles and to question whether downloading torrents of our favorite TV shows meets free and open source muster. Along the way, we manage to talk a little about the history of computing and how computers actually work. We also squeeze in two books: William Gibson's *Neuromancer* and Charles Stross's *Halting State*. Each novel captures the excitement — the risks and pleasures — that come with technological change. The former famously coined the phrase "cyberspace" while the latter convincingly explores an immanent present in which gaming and augmented reality devices have become ubiquitous.

At the outset, the collaborative and DIY nature of much of the learning we engage in presents a challenge to those students who expect me to offer a range of facts for them to memorize and regurgitate through lectures and exams. Moreover, the eclectic course materials likewise challenge their assumptions about what a college course looks and feels like. Yet, more than any other learning activity, the time we spend playing and discussing *World of Warcraft* represents a significant challenge for many students' expectations about education and play.

For readers unfamiliar with *WoW*, it is an enormously popular multiplayer online role-playing game, with more than 11 million subscribers worldwide who regularly pay fees to access this virtual world. Players choose from two factions and ten races and classes to create avatars of themselves that interact in real time not only with the artificial intelligence of the game environment but with up to several thousand other players who are logged onto the same realm or server. As Blizzard, the game development company that owns *WoW*, puts it in their introduction to the game, players "undertak[e] grand quests and heroic exploits in a land of fantastic adventure" ("What Is *WoW*?"). Like the earlier role-playing game *Dungeons and Dragons*, users quest their way through an expansive play landscape, working on their own, or with others in small groups or as members of guilds, the latter of which might have many hundreds of members. While the end game goals are constantly evolving as Blizzard introduces expansion packs to broaden the world's scale and the types of gameplay available (the expansion pack "Cataclysm" which features new playable races and zones to explore, will be available by the time this essay appears), for most users, acquiring sufficient experience with the game, which includes learning to navigate one's avatar and employ one's class specializations (hunters have to fight differently from mages), the professions that enable one's participation in the larger in-game economy (one might become an alchemist or a miner), fighting tactics, and teamplay skills, takes weeks, months, or, for inconstant players like me, years. Unlike traditional media, such as radio, television, or film, the degree of immersion and interactivity of multiplayer online games like *WoW* represent what economist and games studies scholar Edward Castronova calls "practical virtual reality" (4). As a player, you don't just play *WoW,* you inhabit and co-create a world.

I could say that I decided to use *WoW* after careful pedagogical deliberation. In fact, it was an insight as much "doh!" as real inspiration. While I'd come to realize that my students' late, bleary-eyed arrival to class sans homework was not infrequently tied to late nights of gameplay, it had never occurred to me to use a game in a class. When I related what I thought was my quite clever idea to a cohort of Computers and Culture students, some of them groaned. "Not a good idea?" I asked. "No," they exclaimed. "This class was alright, but ... we would have waited another year so that we could have taken *that* class!" These were the gamers who had helped me deepen my own thinking about the importance of gaming generally and the specific social and cultural transformations represented by the online gaming that takes place in such a rich and complex world as *WoW.*

My hunch that playing *WoW,* rather than merely studying the cultural significance of this virtual world or others like it, might enable different and deeper learning has been supported by a growing body of research. James Paul Gee, for example, has written extensively on the ways games underscore widely held misunderstandings about literacy. Gee argues that the expertise minority and poor students demonstrate in their gameplay (whether with Pokémon cards and games or online games like *WoW*) challenge traditionalist approaches to improving literacy that largely focus on phonemic awareness. Children's deep mastery of the complex and technical language of game worlds shows that the cultural learning processes games employ are more effective than the instructed learning approaches many traditionalists advocate. That is, "becoming a member of the games culture" is a more "efficient" way to learn critical thinking, problem-solving, and communication skills (*Situated Language* 12). And game environments are frequently more adept at cultivating a compelling interest to participate (more on which below) than many educational settings.

Compelling Interest

Despite the apparent pedagogical value of using games and gaming pedagogies in the classroom, my students unsurprisingly struggled to appreciate the cultural learning process Gee advocates. They were skeptical about whether becoming a troll mage who shoots firebolts at boars and loots corpses for treasure would help them to understand the cultural relevance of computers. Even for students with a genuine interest in the course materials, playing *WoW* represented a sometimes daunting task. In my first semester using *WoW,* for example, several of the most engaged students in the class reported that they felt alienated by the use of the game. They wanted more history, theory, or policy-oriented work; they felt more comfortable with more traditional academic approaches such as lectures, exams, and papers. One very bright student, Ben, actually withdrew from the course when I offered it in 2008 because it didn't meet his expectations about what constituted appropriate in and out of classroom labor. Graciously responding to my query about whether our use of *WoW* contributed to his decision to withdraw, Ben[1] replied that it had. In particular, he felt a cognitive dissonance about the fact that in an already academically-challenging semester, game-play would be the homework he found most anxiety-provoking. In his own words,

> When I realized that the source of my general stress was a video game, specifically the looming prospect of playing it for hours on end to catch up with the class, something kind of popped and fizzled out inside of me. It seemed crazy. I couldn't reason playing *Warcraft* over, say, getting ahead on reading for another class, so I was perpetually putting it off. The worst part was, even with my general engagement in class discussions and positive feedback on my blogs and presentation, I still felt like a slacker in the context of the class overall. When I did play *WoW*, I couldn't help feeling like I was misusing my time—I felt like a slacker in a different way.

Ben and other high achievers who had mastered academic language and the expectations and norms that accompany cultures of higher ed more broadly, sometimes struggled more than my other, less academically-prepared or motivated students, to link the organizing themes of the course, those related to social identity in particular, to our game play. Other students, especially those who had already been immersed in game culture, were afforded a means by which to apply their existing knowledge in a new context. Thus, gamers and "slackers" were advantaged in ways some experienced learners might not have been.[2] Nonetheless, even students who had actively played *WoW* before necessarily re-oriented their previous experiences, to apply their knowledge of the game world and mechanics to questions of culture and society.

At first, though, I don't make it obvious for anyone. While I give students detailed instructions about getting started, from how much the game costs and where they can buy it, to what faction they should join or server to create their character on, I don't tell them *why* we are playing. I let them flounder. This makes them anxious. Recently, a student in the Fall 2010 cohort, Kevin, got in touch with me: "I would first like to ask exactly what is the overall purpose for playing *World of Warcraft*? I will admit that although I do enjoy the game, I find myself feeling less productive when I play." Although, like most faculty, I regularly make myself available to students to discuss their coursework, in this case I stonewalled Kevin by asking him to think about why *he* thought it might be important. I wanted to create a space in which Kevin and other students could fail to understand our use of *WoW*; this, I hoped, would lead them to ask questions not just about the game or course content but also about learning in general. I wanted to have students begin to play the game not as an instructed process with clear aims but as a way to immerse themselves in a whole cultural milieu. That is, I wanted them to begin to transgress the artificially enforced boundaries between thinking and playing, to *cross-hatch* academic and game culture. Students organically began to draw connections between our readings on virtual and augmented realities, noting the ways playing *WoW* drew them deeply into a world simultaneously tied to and separate from our own.

Several students who struggled with playing the game early during the semester later became some of the most advanced players, leveling as many as several dozen levels ahead of the rest of the course! In fact, one student became so enamoured of the game that she far surpassed me in her knowledge and skills. The following year, she became my teaching assistant, and I relied on her to guide me through changes in the game and brainstorm in-game learning activities. Additionally, students tied their in-game experiences to broader Internet social networks, noting the lively fan cultures of machinima (literally "machine-cinema," the fan-produced video captures of game play) and fan fiction, as well as the ways playing the game effectively and frequently, depended on drawing on unofficial strategy sites and wikis (the collaboratively produced, or "crowd-sourced," hyperlinked webpages of which Wikipedia is the example par excellence). Creating what Ken Bain calls a "natural critical learning environment" thereby enabled students to cross-hatch their understandings of how the game reflected and was part of larger assemblages of technologies, ideologies, and commodities (more on which below).

Again, following James Paul Gee, good video games model good learning. In a brief but informative position paper, Gee outlines sixteen ways games model effective learning. I want to briefly touch on four of these qualities — Identity, Cross-Functional Teams, Performance before Competence, and Agency and then elaborate the relevance of the first in relation to the course's emphasis on gender.

"Identity" refers to the deep investment players make in their avatars, "a commitment of self" that begins when they make choices about what kind of person they want to be in the virtual world (Gee, "Good Video Games" 4). "Cross-Functional Teams" describes the ways players engage with others in ways that draw on their particular areas of expertise but also understand others' specializations well enough to work together toward common goals. In the game this means learning how to play together in "instances" or "dungeons," challenging zones in which it is nearly impossible to play alone. When students attempt them solo, they rarely make their way through the front doors. By the end of the semester, though, a successful in-class dungeon run is accompanied by students' cheerful whoops.

"Performance before Competence" reverses common approaches to learning in most educational environments, emphasizing doing before expertise. While in the past I forced students to read the game manual before playing, I soon adopted the method some parents use to teach their kids to swim; I metaphorically pushed my students into the deep end of the game and shouted encouragingly, "Swim!" Additionally, the game itself is structured in such a way as to provide feedback to new players. By providing tips and carefully scaffolding early game play, it instructs new players in the general aims of the game (kill things and obtain items to advance levels and gain new skills and abilities) as well as the basic mechanics of movement and spellcasting.

Finally, "Agency" indexes the ways that students were able to exercise considerable choice in how they would experience the game world. In creating their characters, they selected the gender, race, and class (though these terms don't mean exactly what they might appear to mean[3]), and, to a limited degree, the appearances, of their avatars. In the game, avatars become extensions of my students' wills as they navigate the virtual world.

Informatively, in spite of the choices available to them, students overwhelmingly selected genders for their game characters that matched their own real world gender presentations. This was a trend I had first noticed several years earlier when I had employed another virtual world, *Second Life* (*SL*), in some of my courses. In *SL* students often created "me-but-better" digital representations of themselves. They spent considerable time and energy ensuring that their online self looked like their offline one. This in spite of the fact that in *SL* one has essentially limitless opportunities for avatar creation — one doesn't need to possess a gender or even be human. Some students, recognizing this freedom, transformed themselves into anime characters, robots, or will-o-the-wisps.[4] In the most recent iterations of the course, I have made students' gender choices a central object of our group inquiry with the intention that students would increasingly come to recognize some of their unquestioned assumptions about gender norms.

The Fall 2009 cohort found it almost impossible to answer the question "Why?" Why did they choose genders for their avatars that, with only one or two exceptions in a class of forty students, matched their own? Their answers ranged from the clueless, "I don't know," to the head-scratching, "It's more realistic," to the comically homophobic, "I don't want other guys flirting with me." After offering a few choice reflections of my own, "'I don't know' begins an inquiry rather than ends it," "What's realistic about playing an undead warrior?" and "So you'd rather look at a guy's ass for hours on end?"[5], we began to interrogate gender identity in earnest.

Drawing on early utopian cyberspace discourse that emphasized the opportunities for the dynamic fluidity of gender in online spaces, as well as key insights from trans/gender studies that emphasizes the constructedness of gender and sexual categories, we questioned why the game designers offered players the choice of only two genders rather than many. In a fantasy world in which users become trolls and elves, shape-shifting druids and shadow priests, why did gender remain obdurately "natural"? We also looked carefully at the ways the avatars conformed to adolescent male fantasies about sexual dimorphism: all the male characters are broad-shouldered, narrow-hipped, and possess enviable muscular definition, while all the female avatars are curvaceous and busty. And we also discussed a controversy about the introduction of a Horde race, the Blood Elves, with the "Burning Crusade" expansion. Earlier designs for the male blood elves were deemed "too-gay" because they didn't evidence the hyper-masculinity of other male characters (Timsy).

We moreover examined the way in-game interactions between players differed. That is, students with female avatars tended to be offered help in the form of tactics and money more often than those with male avatars. Indeed my student Michael created a female avatar rather than learn an income-generating profession because he found that other players would give him more money than he could earn on his own. What did these interactions teach us about the power of gender stereotypes? And how did this behavior transgress gendered norms insofar as gamers assume, and research has shown (for a selective overview, see Ferreday and Lock; for *WoW* specific data, see Yee), that many players (if not my students!) virtually cross-dress, assuming gender identities in-game that differ from their real world ones. While challenging gender stereotypes and examining online interactions proved fruitful, I also wanted students to have the experience for themselves, so I had each student create a new avatar with a gender opposite his/her own.

In this way, I hoped students could use the virtual world to expand their own internal repertoire of simulated experiences, thereby gaining insight into identities different from their own. Although, when given the choice, most students returned to their original avatar, our discussions about gender norms and variation enabled students to recognize the ways our ideas about gaming are mutually shaped by ideas about gender (Williams et al.; Taylor), identify the underlying heteronormative logic to the game, and challenge their own investments in the naturalness of their own gendered identities. More specifically, they learned that women were active participants in gaming cultures, while female bodies were overwhelmingly represented in stereotypical ways. They became more attentive to the exaggerated gender dimorphism, the absence of gay themes to the game's narrative, and the virulent use of epithets like "fag" and "gay" within many of the in-game social forums. And students came to understand something about how gendered presentations in the real world reflect and drive the constructedness of gender in a simulated one.

Taken together, this learning supported the learning objectives of the class, that is, understanding how gender matters in the context of a ubiquitous computer culture, but it did so through an immersive cultural learning process over instructed learning. By *doing* gender, by cultivating an investment in a gendered avatar and experiencing the game world via male and female avatars, they breached their investment in gaming and working as separate worlds and learned to see how their real world gender identities cross-hatched their virtual ones.

Breaching Expectations

In the remainder of the essay, I want to return to the ways gameplay transgresses student expectations about learning, and how this breach relates to the real world of work many of them are already a part of or anxiously anticipating. Of course I don't believe that teaching or learning are only about producing "flexible" laborers for advanced capitalism. It is also about helping students enjoy the pleasure of learning *as* play. However, trends in higher education do force me to think, however reluctantly, "practically" about how my learning outcomes prepare students; and this thinking is likewise informed by the earnestly plaintive queries of my students, "I'm interested in this, but what can I do with this major?"

Again, Ben, whom I quoted above, found playing a game, especially outside of class time, disorienting. Although he appreciated the ways *WoW* could be employed to articulate key class themes, he suggested this might have been as easily achieved by playing a demo during classtime. This would be too superficial an engagement though. Only full immersion would provide a meaningful appreciation for the ways the game illuminated key points about how computers affect and are affected by social life. The fact that this student found playing the game hard work is illustrative and requires elaboration. Clearly willing to work hard in the course (he'd completed nearly all the course requirements by the time he withdrew), for him the problem lay with the *sort* of work demanded of him: "It seemed crazy. I couldn't reason playing *Warcraft* over, say, getting ahead on reading for another class, so I was perpetually putting it off." Reading represented real work, but game play did not; yet, at the same time, the game demanded more work in that it required him to engage in an unfamiliar activity.

Other students shared this feeling that playing was hard work. And I admit that I sometimes felt strange, too, effectively issuing the demand, "YOU MUST PLAY TO SUCCEED IN THIS CLASS." I was also confused and frustrated by their resistance to having fun! Playing *WoW* required students to engage in an unfamiliar mode of learning. Students adept at traditional modes of learning found themselves failing; other students found that reaching certain benchmarks (typically by level or time played) required they put in more time into the "coursework" than they might otherwise.

As education researchers and experienced teachers alike understand, failure is essential to learning. Learning happens at the often-frustrating seam where one's capacity encounters its limits. Typically, however, students are not afforded the opportunity to fail gracefully, that is, without negative feelings like shame or embarrassment. But in play environments, failure is *built into* the acquisition of new skills ("Good Video Games"). In Computers and Culture, the stakes for failing in *WoW* are low; when your avatar in *WoW* dies, you're resurrected, you can resume your play, and you are able to build on your new knowledge. As many progressive educators have come to learn, encouraging students to fail is to facilitate a challenging perspectival shift. On the level of pedagogy, the success and failure of different students was illustrative for me insofar as their experiences helped me to better understand students' beliefs about coursework (variously, that it should encompass reading and writing but not playing, or that it should demand only the barest effort), develop opportunities for productive failure, and frame more meta-level epistemological questions about effort, fun, and instrumentality.

In *Play Between Worlds*, an ethnography of the multiplayer online game *Everquest*, T.L. Taylor writes about an organizing paradox of pleasurable play. Namely, the harder one works at play, or the more instrumental one's game play, the more pleasurable gaming can become. Her focus on "power gamers" emphasizes the ways serious gamers complicate the lines between leisure and work: "The simple idea of 'fun' is turned on its head by examples of engagement that rest on efficiency, (often painful) learning, rote and boring tasks, heavy doses of responsibility, and intensity of focus. Indeed, many power gamers do not use the term 'fun' to describe why they play but instead talk about the more complicated notions of enjoyment and reward" (88). In the context of my course, it was essential that students spend significant time in *WoW*, so that they could experience for themselves the ways their deepening knowledge led to different sorts of experiences, including the feelings of empowerment and achievement as they successfully leveled, the frustration they felt when they encountered problems they had not yet learned to solve, and the excitement that came with the coordinated group play necessary to defeat the high-level bosses in "instances." The more time they spent in *WoW*, the harder they worked, the more fun the game became. (If only the same applied to academic reading and writing!)

Returning to China Miéville's novel, cross-hatching is such a compelling idea because of the ways it foregrounds simultaneity and recognition as transgressions. In the book, two cities occupy the same space and time, yet residents of each city have learned not to see one another, and this unseeing is governed by shared social and legal agreement. Similarly, in students' college lives, learning and play overlap one another, but educators and students themselves fail to see this cross-hatching except in cursory ways. Students are engaged in a good deal of meaningful learning at college, but much of it takes place outside of the classroom when they are engaged in other activities, including, among other things, the forms of play they engage in when "hanging out," an open-ended practice that encompasses a range of activities, from study groups and watching TV to dating and smoking weed. Our ideas about learning are shaped by years of experiences with compulsory schooling and especially the notion that classrooms are spaces for the relaying of facts that students are somehow meant to absorb, often without any context in which to apply those facts. But learning, happily, also takes place outside of the classroom.

By playing the game for the duration of the semester, constructing relatively persistent identities for their avatars, and interacting with one another, my students eventually cross-hatched their understanding of play and work: their gaming came to inform our readings and discussions and vice versa. They learned that virtual worlds are not separated from real ones but rather operate in a world in which gaming and social networking are daily organizing activities, that virtual and real are altogether more situated definitions. They learned that rather than represent an alternate world in which anything goes, online environments continue to be deeply structured by categories of race, gender, and class, as well as other social distinctions. They learned that learning, rather than operating only as a set of official discourses (knowledge) imparted by experts (like professors), is a situated process over which they exercise considerable agency. In *WoW* they shaped their avatars' lives.

And in the classroom they learned that they are responsible for their own learning. One New Media major, Miles, didn't take the course seriously until just past the halfway mark. Then he experienced something like an epiphany. The different elements of the course — our gameplay in *WoW* and the student led co-facilitations — gelled for him; he came to understand learning as a process that depended on his active engagement. In an email, he wrote, "I finally grew up and stopped pretending I wasn't capable of writing papers and properly articulating my thoughts and myself any more because I'm a 'new media major.'"

Finally, students develop skills to breach the veils that separate learning from labor. It is to this last point, the ways playing *WoW* cultivates skills necessary in an era of increasingly "flexible" and "immaterial" labor, that I now turn.

Transformations in global economic structures and flows have been well documented by others (for only two examples, see Harvey; Hardt and Negri). Global capitalism has increasingly penetrated into realms both sovereign and intimate (the language of self-help encourages us to "grow" or "expand," while our emotional and sexual intimacies are "investments"), economic inequalities continue to accelerate, and labor practices are increasingly divided by geographic location as well as by whether they take place in the network or the factory (a "good" job traffics in ideas, others depend on grueling physicality). In the words of my students, "shit is fucked up." Here, my interest in these transformations is practically and pedagogically oriented. While institutions of higher education have increasingly adopted neoliberal philosophies and managerial strategies, I am less certain that what happens in the classroom has effectively responded to corporatization of education or highlighted the many ways it's being actively contested. I have found it essential to persistently ask how the learning my students are engaged in will help them to develop as full people, with a range of intellectual, political, and practical approaches and skills at their disposal, with the capacities to survive, even thrive, in a frighteningly uncertain economic reality.

Given the liberal arts context in which I was educated, am currently embedded in, and remain, despite reservations, politically committed to, this is not so much about identifying specific pre-professional skills but empowering students to develop the critical reasoning and communication abilities that best enable them to engage in the exchange of ideas in a vast array of social circumstances, and to do so in a way that contributes to a common good ("Education in the Liberal Arts"). Computers and Culture is a course through which students encounter a range of materials and learning approaches that, while challenging their expectations, nonetheless aim to help them to think and communicate in increasingly complex ways about technology and culture, race and gender, fun and labor.

Playing *WoW* helps them to hone these abilities. They come to understand how *WoW* is one technologically mediated example among many that models many unspoken capitalist ideologies and practices, namely those related to competition, conquest, and accumulation. That is, they can cross-hatch worlds and breach norms, learning to see and hear anew, seeing, for example, the ways media practices like video games reflect cultural values (like the belief in endless growth) and the way a more reflective awareness of these patterns can help to breach these often unquestioned assumptions. Thus, an organizing meta-level learning objective for Computers and Culture, and the specific employment of *WoW*, centers on the ways gaming represents a challenging, fun, and foundationally *ambivalent* media practice.

In their recent book *Games of Empire*, Nick Dyer-Witheford and Greig de Peuter argue that "*video games are a paradigmatic media of Empire*— planetary, militarized hypercapitalism —*and* of some of the forces presently challenging it" (xv, italics in original). While I have offered a series of examples above about the ways *WoW* is a useful learning activity, stressing for students the relationship between their identities and learning, as well as encouraging them to see notions of play and work differently, Dyer-Witheford and de

Peuter offer another important perspective to understand gaming in more global historical and political economic terms.

As they observe, "a media that once seemed all fun is increasingly revealing itself as a school for labor, an instrument of rulership, and a laboratory for the fantasies of advanced techno-capital" (xix). Many games implicitly and explicitly instruct players in identifying with and glorifying imperial power and authority. And in this view, game play reflects our complicity with and consent to the logic of advanced capitalism. I tend to adopt a more optimistic view toward the use of the game — hoping that it meets students where they are in the wholeness of their selves, and that it can empower them toward more adept modes of reflection and interaction.

I understand, however, that from a more critical point of view, the use of *WoW* can be seen as a direct practical engagement, even if it is a playful one, with the ideologies of "Empire," especially the increasing emphasis, especially in the high technology hubs, the marketing firms, customer support lines, and call centers, of the industrially and economically "developed" and "developing" countries on "immaterial labor." Immaterial labor refers to those modes of creative cooperative work that do not so much lead to the production of value-laden goods as traditionally understood, but rather what sociologist and philosopher Maurizio Lazzarato calls the "the production of worlds," the forms of work (research, communications, strategy, among others) that go into articulating commodities as modes of expression or lifestyles (187). This sort of world-making is powerfully creative and expressive, and it also, in lifestyle branding or the broader promise for "the new," insidiously reaches into the nooks and crannies of ordinary life from birth onward.

Yet, in the course, and resonant with the views of Dyer-Witheford and de Peuter and others (Galloway), the time students spend in *WoW* cannot only be understood as a cynical hands-on training in 21st Century "digital labor and governability" (xix), but as an educative immersion that highlights the many layers of coercion and consent that shape work, pleasure, and political resistance in a globally-networked world. By the end of the semester, I hope that students have obtained new understandings of the relationships between work and play in their learning and that they possess a more sophisticated analysis of their own complicity in global regimes of power without falling victim to political paralysis.

More Than Mere Escape

Most students drop the game around the same time they start selling their textbooks for vacation cash. Some keep playing, though, developing research projects that elaborate their own ideas about the game's relevance. I have continued to work with students whose interest in the game has led them to work on capstone research projects related to the ways global mass media (including gaming) matters, how interpersonal and erotic intimacies emerge in *WoW*, and the convergent relationship between *WoW* and the offline fan cultures that manifest in cosplay (costume play) and conventions. In this way, students continue to breach the lines that divide the overlapping practices of work and play, while expanding their evaluative and social repertoires. For me, their engagements also usefully highlight the importance of fantasy as more than mere escape from and/or into the dark heart of advanced capitalism.

I have found fantasy to be a powerful genre not just for its analogical commentary on contemporary life when, for example, texts grapple with issues of war or politics (as in *The Lord of Rings* books and films or the *Buffy the Vampire Slayer* mediaverse) but learning about cultural values like faith, courage, and loyalty. If this seems unduly optimistic in an era of increasing inequalities, permanent states of political exception, and global terror, then I would suggest we (and by we I mean well-meaning academics and pedagogues), reevaluate our roles as interlocutors enabled to point to the still immanent potentials of modernity as much to its tragic failures and injustices. That is, we are positioned to engage our students (or our colleagues, or anyone else in our respective social milieu, for that matter), in productive fantasies, in, for example, the ways inspiration and enchantment are as much the material of social transformation as set-jawed and steely-eyed political resistance. Put differently, imagination remains as a vital resource for "sussing" out how things might be different and for breaching the perceptual veils that separate worlds of work and play.

Notes

1. All student names have been changed to allow anonymity.
2. This is not to say that many high achieving students didn't also do well in the class; they did. But they had to work harder at "unlearning" more traditional academic methods.
3. In creating one's avatar, one is able to choose whether one is male or female. Race in the game refers to one of the 12 races now available for game play, which includes humans, dwarves, night elves, and orcs among others. Class refers to the type of adventurer a player becomes, such as mage, priest, warrior, hunter, rogue, and so on. One's racial choice also determines the available classes. Blood elves for example can be hunters but not shamans. The racial politics of the game are evident in two other ways. First, players are able to select from a range of hues for some in game races; but these choices don't, for example, enable a player to apply Asian or Black features. Second, and more problematically, several *WoW* races are racialized apriori. Trolls, for example, are a mashup of African diasporic; they speak with Jamaican accents, yet talk about voodoo and practice the Brazilian dance/martial art, *capoeria*. The Tauren, a race of minotaur-like creatures, likewise condense a range of stereotypes about indigenous peoples; they greet others with a solemnly inflected "How," live in longhouses, and articulate a noble, but "primitive," respect for the natural world.
4. The freedoms afforded by *SL* also extend to other aspects of the virtual world, which, unlike *WoW*, is largely created by users. *SL* also offers considerable insight into virtual economies

insofar as much of the user-generated content is for sale and can be easily exchanged into real world dollars. Although I used both *SL* and *WoW* in Computers and Culture, I have switched to the latter largely because *SL* does not offer sufficient structure for my students. Although it frames many compelling questions about identity, virtual worlds, economies, and so on, it is not in fact a game, but a social medium for interaction and creative expression. As a result, it does not have clear aims or effect such a clear sense of accomplishment and empowerment as does *WoW*. *WoW*, by contrast, provides players with regular feedback and rewards them with new skills and areas to explore.

5. In general one views her *WoW* avatar from a slightly elevated third person point of view, from behind.

Works Cited

Castronova, Edward. *Synthetic Worlds: The Business and Culture of Online Games*. Chicago: University of Chicago Press, 2005. Print.

Dyer-Witheford, Nick, and Greg de Peuter. *Games of Empire: Global Capitalism and Video Games*. Minneapolis: University of Minnesota Press, 2009. Print.

"Education in the Liberal Arts." Grinnell College. N.d. Web. 23 Jul. 2010. <http://www.grinnell.edu/academic/catalog/education>.

Ferreday, Debra, and Simon Lock. "Computer Cross-Dressing: Queering the Virtual Subject." *(Queer Online* Ed. Kate O'Riordan and David J. Phillips. New York: Peter Lang, 2007. Print.

Galloway, Alexander. *On Gaming: Essays on Algorithmic Culture*. Minneapolis: University of Minnesota Press, 2006. Print.

Gee, James Paul. "Good Video Games and Good Learning." Academic ADL Co-lab. N.d. Web. 23 Jul. 2010. <http://academiccolab.org/initiatives/papers.html>.

_____. *Situated Language and Learning: A Critique of Traditional Schooling*. NewYork: Routledge, 2004. Print.

Hardt, Michael, and Antonio Negri. *Empire*. Cambridge: Harvard University Press, 2000. Print.

Harvey, David. *Spaces of Hope*. Berkeley: University of California Press, 2000. Print.

Lazzarato, Maurizio. "From Capital-Labor to Capital-Life." *Ephemera: Theory and Politics in Organization* 4.3: 187–208. Web. 23 Jul. 2010.

Miéville, China. *The City & The City*. New York: Del Rey, 2010. Print.

Super Timsy. "*WoW* Overhelmed by Homophobes, Make Blood Elves Less 'Feminine.'" Web. 10 Oct. 2010. <http://gaygamer.net/2006/10/*WoW*_overwhelmed_by_homophobes.html>.

Taylor, T.L. *Play Between Worlds: Exploring Online Game Culture*. Cambridge: MIT Press, 2006.

Williams, Dmitri, Mia Consalvo, Scott Caplan, and Nick Yee. "Looking for Gender: Gender Roles and Behaviors among Online Gamers." *Journal of Communication* 59 (2009): 700–725. Print.

Yee, Nick. "*WoW* Gender Bending." *The Daedalus Project* 7:1 (2009). Web. 7 Oct. 2010. <http://www.nickyee.com/daedalus/archives/001369.php>.

Fantasy Classics: Hobbits and Harry in Interdisciplinary Courses

JIM FORD

"The truth," Dumbledore sighed. "It is a beautiful and terrible thing, and should therefore be treated with great caution."—*Harry Potter and the Sorcerer's Stone* (Rowling 298)[1]

Great fantasy texts work particularly well in interdisciplinary courses. They appeal to a wide variety of audiences, students often have encountered such texts previously, and the texts are more approachable than many other literary mainstays. Even though the works of J.R.R. Tolkien and J.K. Rowling are rewarding literature, they often do not feel like literature to students (largely because they are fantasy works). I have found several successful approaches to using such works, whether as part of a broader selection of "Great Literature," as a focused study of particular literary elements, or as part of a course on the adaptation of literature to film. These works are well-suited to seminars devoted entirely to fantasy classics as well as to broader, more traditional courses. Tolkien's *The Hobbit* and Rowling's early novels like *Sorcerer's Stone* or *Chamber of Secrets* are easy to integrate into a syllabus, while Tolkien's *The Lord of the Rings* trilogy and later Rowling novels like *Order of the Phoenix* and *Half-Blood Prince* require a more sustained commitment. I am more interested in the questions that different texts raise than the conclusions they may offer, and these texts are excellent for raising some of the most fundamental literary questions: Why do we read? What should I read, and what do I want from a book? What makes a book or film great, and what is the relationship between a good novel and a good movie? Traditional humanities topics like identity, love, and friendship naturally emerge from these fantasy texts. Before detailing some of those classroom approaches, I want to take a closer look at why these fantasy classics are so well-suited to interdisciplinary courses and audiences.

Hobbits, Harry Potter, and Interdisciplinary Courses

> "One Ring to rule them all, / One Ring to find them, / One Ring to bring them all and in the Darkness bind them."—*The Lord of the Rings* (Tolkien 272)

I teach a number of courses designed to be interdisciplinary. These are often honors courses, which are targeted at a specific population of bright students from a host of different majors. The works of Tolkien and Rowling are perfect for such courses for several reasons. First, these works appeal to a variety of audiences. They require no special training or experience, and students from all majors can read and enjoy these tales of magic and adventure. Second, many students have prior experience with these works in a non-academic setting. Some have grown up with Harry Potter, and studying their favorite novels in the classroom validates their appreciation. It encourages them to bridge the gap between their private interests and their academic studies. Others have seen the films and are eager to read the books themselves, particularly for the Lord of the Rings series. Even students who have never read one of the books or seen any of the film versions usually have some basic familiarity with the stories and characters. That familiarity helps students move quickly through the texts and overcomes one of the basic problems for introductory courses: getting students to read the material. While a few students may be resistant at first (expect some definite eye-rolling), most students are excited to be reading stories they already appreciate.

A third advantage to these two authors is that they each offer works of varying lengths and difficulties. *The Hobbit* is approximately 250 pages long, and so is easy to include in most semesters even with a great deal of other reading assignments. It is not especially difficult to read; and, while there may be some initial confusion at the subject matter and the various names, most students quickly get into it. It can be covered in as little as one short class period, although a full week is worth the time. *The Lord of the Rings* is significantly longer, with three separate parts (each consisting of two books), a little more than one thousand pages in all. The three separate parts do not work as well individually—it really takes the full trilogy to do the story justice. This makes *The Lord of the Rings* appropriate for more sustained readings. It requires significant class time, usually two weeks at a minimum—six class meetings is ideal, since it enables one class period for each of the six parts. Similarly, the first two Harry Potter novels (*Sorcerer's Stone* and *Chamber of Secrets*) are shorter and easier to read than the others. These are more reflective of the series' beginning as children's literature. A week each works well, but each can be covered in a single class period if necessary. The third novel (*Prisoner of Azkaban*) introduces a slightly darker tone, offers more complex themes, and is slightly more challenging than the first two, although it is still eminently readable. From there the novels are much longer (while *Azkaban* is a little more than 400 pages, *Goblet of Fire,* the fourth novel, is 734, and the last three are all at least 640 pages long). Rowling wrote a total of seven Harry Potter novels, of course; and, while it can be great to read all seven, most classes will focus on a few novels (or one). Most have enough exposition at the beginning to enable readers to make sense of the novel without having read the others, but the last two (*Half-Blood Prince* and *Deathly Hallows*) require some prior knowledge.[2] Otherwise, though, it is easy to integrate any of these works into the average interdisciplinary course.

The fourth advantage to the works of Tolkien and Rowling is that even though these are rewarding works of literature, they often do not feel like literature to students. Partly because they are fantasy works, they seem drastically different from the sort of book one usually reads in a college class. Students learn without being aware of the fact, and what may seem like a break from serious college study is really a tremendous opportunity. Ultimately students realize that a primary purpose of literature is enjoyment. Books are meant to be enjoyed and appreciated, not just studied. The works of Tolkien and Rowling teach students that they can take pleasure in reading works of literature, rather than seeing reading as a chore or something to do because it is "good for you." Of course, some may object that these works are not worthy of study. Even those who may be receptive to works of fantasy and popular culture may dismiss the Harry Potter novels as young adult or children's literature.[3] But these are excellent topics to address in class, and the proof is in the quality of the discussion that these works generate.

Fantasy Novels and the Meaning of Great Literature

> "Even the wise cannot see all ends."—*The Lord of the Rings* (Tolkien 640)

One of my favorite topics for interdisciplinary honors courses (and humanities courses in general) is the nature of great literature, and these works are excellent contributions to that topic. As part of a much larger reading list, one or two books by Tolkien and/or Rowling round out the conversation nicely. I assign these together with classic, canonical texts, anything from *Hamlet* to *Catcher in the Rye*, from Jane Austen to Kate Chopin. Using *The Hobbit* or *Sorcerer's Stone* in conjunction with these more traditional texts highlights questions of the standards and expectations one has (or should have) when reading a work of literature. For teachers who want to add a work of fantasy while maintaining as much as possible from a traditional syllabus, this is the ideal approach.

There are several ways to teach this kind of course. One way is to focus primarily on the more established texts, with one or two works of fantasy added into a much larger mix. This can be done provisionally, with the professor encouraging the students to question what the fantasy texts contribute and how they relate to the more traditional works of literature. In such a course I like to move chronologically, working up to the fantasy works late in the semester. Used this way Tolkien and Rowling do provide a bit of a break after more demanding fare, but still stand as possible great works. Using such works helps students refine their ideas of what constitutes a great work and what the value is in classifying works in various ways. Is it more useful to classify works by genre, as in a great fantasy novel or a great science-fiction movie? Are those genres somehow inferior, as is often assumed to be the case? Raising those kinds of questions helps students reflect on what they are studying and encourages them to appreciate works of literature and art on their own terms. Studying *The Hobbit* or *Chamber of Secrets* in the same class as *The Metamorphosis* enables students to move past judgments based solely on their personal preferences ("this is just what I like") and begin thinking more critically about all sorts of media.

A second way to teach this kind of course is through a balance of traditional literary texts and more contemporary works. With this class I devote the first half to works that an average college-educated person should know, great works of literature from Shakespeare to the early twentieth century. The second half of the course consists of more contemporary works, some that are commonly read in college classrooms and others that are not. One recent course focused on the theme of identity, and included Nick Hornby's *About a Boy*, Jon Krakauer's non-fiction book *Into the Wild*, and Craig Thompson's graphic novel *Blankets,* as well as Rowling's *Deathly Hallows*. In this class the goal is to see how various texts raise similar issues and return to classic themes. Different students gravitate toward different books, but the variety of texts means that almost everyone will have at least one contemporary text to particularly appreciate. The point is not that all of these works are equally valid for raising such questions (obviously *Hamlet* has a richness of language and a depth of thought that many of the others lack), but that even lighter works involve many of the same themes and can enrich the conversation. One way to enhance this discussion is to include Steven Johnson's *Everything Bad Is Good for You*, which argues for the value of popular culture and introduces different ways to evaluate popular works. Doing so gives students some critical tools for weighing the benefits of these various works.

Many teachers resist any talk of a canon or standards of great literature, and it is true that these ideas can lead to frustrating and circular arguments. But discussing with students the how and why of a particular course is a great teaching opportunity. It is a chance for students to become more involved with their education, to reflect on the significance of what they are learning, and to begin the process of becoming life-long learners (a goal of many university mission statements). Even for those few students who do not get interested in books about hobbits and wizards, the issues those books raise about the nature of literature are worthwhile.

Using Fantasy Worlds to Highlight Elements of Literature

> "Of course it is happening inside your head, Harry, but why on earth should that mean that it is not real?"—Dumbledore, *Deathly Hallows* (Rowling 723)

A second approach to using these texts in class is to use the vast worlds that each series of books creates to focus on particular elements of literature. Because the seven Potter novels and the four Rings books (the trilogy plus *The Hobbit*) create their own self-contained worlds, they are conducive to studying individual elements of literature, such as character development or dialogue. This approach is a natural way to organize a seminar devoted entirely to fantasy works. As worthwhile as it is to study such elements in a single book, it can be even more productive to study them across several books by a single author. There are a number of great possibilities for such a class; the most successful one that I have taught is an upper-division seminar called Character in Fantasy Literature, which focuses on the Harry Potter series.

One of Rowling's accomplishments is the creation of memorable and compelling characters. While some readers are focused on the plot of Harry's adventures, I find that many more are attached to particular characters and return to the novels to spend time with their favorite characters. This seminar was a sixteen-week study of major and minor characters in all seven novels. It was a small course, and we devoted roughly two weeks to each of the seven novels. Each week the students presented short papers to begin the class. The assignment was to focus on one major character and one minor character and to analyze that character's development either within the particular novel or across the novels thus far. The line between major and minor characters was deliberately blurry, so students could usually decide for themselves how to classify a particular character.

Characters like Harry, Hermione, and Ron are obviously major characters, but some students resisted their favorite character being called "minor." Several characters who seem minor in one novel take center stage in another;

letting students make the argument for their interpretation is key. One week a student evaluated the growth of Harry Potter in the novel *Order of the Phoenix*, as he increasingly becomes a leader, training the students of Dumbledore's Army to fight the dark arts, and as he struggles to deal with his nascent romantic longings. Another week a student traced the role and confidence of Neville Longbottom, a minor character who is often in the background of the main story, but one whose significance emerges as the series continues. His importance is made much clearer through this comparison of both his demeanor and also his function in the overall plot of all seven novels. That kind of analysis is difficult to do outside the fantasy seminar, simply because other classes will rarely have the time or inclination to read and discuss all seven novels.

This seminar was quite successful, as the students expressed a deeper appreciation for the novels, demonstrated significant progress in their ability to analyze literature, and clearly evidenced tremendous growth as writers. Having a standard writing assignment that they returned to again and again throughout the semester was a real asset pedagogically. They refined their arguments, sharpened their reasoning, and enhanced their diction. The class was great fun as well, both for them as students and for me as their professor. Some students expressed concern early on that studying the books might detract from their enjoyment of them, but this did not occur. It is notable that the students involved had all read the novels previously; and, while most were studying the books for the first time in class, they knew the stories well. This is not a prerequisite for a successful fantasy seminar, but it certainly helps. These students were strongly motivated, and in fact the idea for the course was first suggested by two of those students.[4] A great way to develop this kind of seminar is by teaching one or two fantasy novels in a class, then offer a fantasy seminar on a whole series as a follow-up. The genesis of this particular seminar was actually with students who heard that other classes were studying Harry Potter and did not want to be left out. After the freshmen read one novel (*Deathly Hallows*), the seniors wanted to read them all.

While this seminar focused exclusively on Harry Potter, the world of Tolkien would be excellent for this as well. It is easier to include the *Hobbit* and *Lord of the Rings* in a broader course, if only because the books are more manageable and the reading load is lighter (Tolkien is a slightly more challenging read for most students, but the total number of pages makes the real difference—1300 for the four Ring books versus 4100 for the seven Potter novels). A course that I hope to offer very soon would combine the two, with the first eight weeks devoted to Tolkien and the final eight weeks focused on Rowling. It is always fascinating to study multiple works by a single author, but particularly so when the author is working with the same basic characters and related plots. With Rowling, the same group of friends (Harry, Hermione, and Ron), teachers (Dumbledore, Hagrid, and Snape), and antagonists (Draco Malfoy, Voldemort in one form or another, and Snape again) are present throughout the series, with a few new characters emerging in each subsequent book. With Tolkien, a few characters are present throughout (most notably Gandalf and Gollum), but of course the main character in *The Hobbit* is Bilbo Baggins, who passes the ring on to his young cousin Frodo at the beginning of the *Rings* trilogy. Frodo, his friends (Sam, Pippin, and Merry), and their companions (Aragorn, Gimli, and Legolas) are the major characters in the *Rings* books. With either series, however, there are definite rewards to considering the series as a whole, rather than just studying individual books. A fantasy seminar that practices close reading of both series is a great course for students and faculty alike.

From Book to Film: The Adaptation of Fantasy Classics

> "All that is gold does not glitter, / Not all those who wander are lost...."—*The Lord of the Rings* (Tolkien 186)

My third and final approach to teaching Tolkien and Rowling is to focus on the theme of adaptation. Reading the books in conjunction with viewing the films enables fruitful discussions of a number of important topics and enhances the study of both types of media. Such comparisons introduce the question of quality in both fields. What makes a great novel, and how does that differ from a great movie? What is the relationship between the two, and what are the qualities of a good adaptation? Adaptation can be one theme among many in a course, or it can sustain an entire semester. It works well whether the *Potter* and *Ring* stories are the sole focus (again in a fantasy course), or they are just part of a larger study of the adaptation of great literary works (for which there are many excellent choices).

The two series have had distinct routes to screen. The three films that have been made for the *Rings* trilogy were critically acclaimed as well as commercially successful, with the final film (*Lord of the Rings*: *Return of the King*) winning eleven Oscars in 2004, including Best Picture. All three were directed by Peter Jackson, who is also scheduled to direct two forthcoming films based on *The Hobbit*. The cast and production crew has been basically consistent throughout the trilogy.[5] Despite the number of people involved in each production, the films are clearly Peter Jackson's vision of Tolkien's world. The Potter films are a more complicated and diverse series. One obvious difference is the fact that J.K. Rowling has been alive to oversee production of the films and has been involved in the process. Also important is the fact that a number of different directors have worked on the films, with Christopher Columbus directing the first two, Alfonso Cuarón directing the third (and best) film, and Mike Newell directing the fourth film. David Yates directed the final four movies, including the two based on *Deathly Hallows*, meaning that he has directed half of the eight films. Even as the directors have changed, the same author (Steve Kloves) has written all eight screenplays. Each film has a different tone, a different sensibility, which makes the question of adaptation even more interesting. There is also significant variation in the quality of the Potter films (some are quite good, others are mediocre), whereas the *Rings* films are consistent throughout.

All of which opens up a number of avenues for assignments and discussion. For instance, many of the same elements students analyze in the literary versions can be the basis for intriguing comparisons of book and film. Some characters translate poorly to the screen, while others are more compelling in their film versions. Some scenes are richer in the film versions, while others fall flat. Sometimes the films illustrate gaps or problems in the original text, but more frequently they increase the students' appreciation for the written word. Either way, looking closely at the film and book versions of these two series enhances students' understanding of each media, as well as of the works themselves. It helps students to see the different ways in which character is established on paper and on screen, the importance of theatrical elements like acting, camera angles, lighting, sound, scenery, and special effects, and the results of hundreds of minute changes. Again, while students certainly learn more about the particular works, what they learn about novel and film as mediums is of greater significance.

Conclusion

"I open at the close."—*Deathly Hallows* (Rowling 134)

The possibilities for using popular culture works in general and fantasy works in particular are vast, but the works of Tolkien and Rowling are compelling choices. With the release of the final Harry Potter film, that world is now complete, with seven novels and eight films for academic study. The forthcoming release of two films based on *The Hobbit* (currently scheduled for release in late 2012 and late 2013, respectively) creates additional opportunities for the study of these fantasy classics. It makes this the perfect occasion to devote significant class time (if not a full semester) to these fantasy worlds. The texts are easy to integrate into a variety of interdisciplinary courses. They function well on their own or in conjunction with one or more of the film adaptations. Their mass appeal, the fact that most students are familiar with the stories, and the readability of those texts enhance their classroom potential. These fantasy works are excellent for generating insightful discussions about the nature of great literature or the relationship between novels and their film adaptations. They can be used as contributions to general humanities courses on a number of significant themes, from human nature and identity to love and friendship. Most of all, their use in the classroom teaches students that literature can be enjoyable, fascinating, and rewarding at the same time.

Notes

1. From now on I will refer to Rowling's novels by the second half of their titles, such as *Sorcerer's Stone* or *Chamber of Secrets*, rather than always writing *Harry Potter and the Sorcerer's Stone*. I also use the American editions of the Harry Potter novels. Purists should insert "Harry Potter and the" at every mention of a Rowling title, and transmute *Sorcerer* to *Philosopher* as necessary.

2. I did have a freshman seminar read *Deathly Hallows* on its own, in preparation for the release of the *Deathly Hallows, Part One* film in November 2010. A few students expressed real confusion and had some difficulty making sense of the reading, simply because the seventh book presumes the reader is intimately familiar with Harry, his friends, and the wizarding world. While their fellow students were eager to bring them up-to-date and ultimately all the students appreciated the experience, I would be hesitant in the future to single out the seventh book.

3. The *New York Times* revised its best-seller list in 2000 to prevent Harry Potter's continued domination, creating a separate list of Best-Selling Children's Books just as *Goblet of Fire* was being released.

4. I am indebted to those two students, Valorie Vernon and Rebekah Warren, for many things. I am especially grateful to them for suggesting this class and for their excellent participation throughout that class. I also want to thank Valorie for her capstone project on the adaptation of the Harry Potter novels, which informs several of my suggestions in the next section.

5. Fran Walsh, Philippa Boyens, and Peter Jackson are credited for all three *Rings* screenplays; Stephen Sinclair is also credited on the screenplay for the second film, *The Two Towers*.

Works Cited

The Fellowship of the Ring. Dir. Peter Jackson. New Line Cinema, 2001. Film.

Harry Potter and the Chamber of Secrets. Dir. Chris Columbus. Warner Bros. Pictures, 2002. Film.

Harry Potter and the Deathly Hallows: Part One. Dir. David Yates. Warner Bros. Pictures, 2010. Film.

Harry Potter and the Deathly Hallows: Part Two. Dir. David Yates. Warner Bros. Pictures, 2011. Film.

Harry Potter and the Goblet of Fire. Dir. Mike Newell. Warner Bros. Pictures, 2005. Film.

Harry Potter and the Half-Blood Prince. Dir. David Yates. Warner Bros. Pictures, 2009. Film.

Harry Potter and the Order of the Phoenix. Dir. David Yates. Warner Bros. Pictures, 2007. Film.

Harry Potter and the Prisoner of Azkaban. Dir. Alfonso Cuarón. Warner Bros. Pictures, 2004. Film.

Harry Potter and the Sorcerer's Stone. Dir. Chris Columbus. Warner Bros. Pictures, 2001. Film.

The Hobbit: An Unexpected Journey. Dir. Peter Jackson. In production, scheduled for 2012. Film.

The Hobbit: There and Back Again. Dir. Peter Jackson. In production, scheduled for 2013. Film.

Lord of the Rings: Return of the King. Internet Movie Database. Web. 1 June 2011.

The Return of the King. Dir. Peter Jackson. New Line Cinema, 2003. Film.

Rowling J.K. *Harry Potter and the Chamber of Secrets*. New York: Scholastic, 1999. Print.

_____. *Harry Potter and the Deathly Hallows*. New York: Scholastic, 2007. Print.

_____. *Harry Potter and the Goblet of Fire*. New York: Scholastic, 2000. Print.

_____. *Harry Potter and the Half-Blood Prince*. New York: Scholastic, 2005. Print.

_____. *Harry Potter and the Order of the Phoenix*. New York: Scholastic, 2003. Print.

_____. *Harry Potter and the Prisoner of Azkaban*. New York: Scholastic, 1999. Print.
_____. *Harry Potter and the Sorcerer's Stone*. New York: Scholastic, 1997. Print.
Tolkien, J.R.R. *The Hobbit*. Boston: Houghton Mifflin, 1997. Print.
_____. *The Lord of the Rings*. London: Grafton, 1992. Print.
The Two Towers. Dir. Peter Jackson. New Line Cinema, 2002. Film.

III. New Directions: The Joys of Fantasy Classes

Hansel, Gretel, and Coraline

J. Renee Cox

"Never accept anything from that old woman who lives in the forest."

So responded one of my students when I asked my Fairy Tale in Literature and Film class, on the first day we met, to write a list of the "lessons" they had taken away from the fairy tales that had been read to them as children. I assumed that the student who wrote the clever gem above was referring to the scene in Snow White in which the witch/step-mother-in-disguise offers the apple to Snow White in the dwarves' dwelling in the forest. But when I said, "Oh yes, 'Snow White,'" he looked at me oddly and replied "No, 'Hansel and Gretel.'" We were both right.

I am a big fan of Snow White. The class, however, was keen to discuss Hansel and Gretel. *Really* keen. I had to go with it, but I was a bit resistant. Hansel and Gretel? It's so typical. So *overdone*. Two kids wander into a forest, get into trouble, get out of trouble, go back home. What else is there to say about it? Plenty, as it turns out, if the instructor will close her mouth and let the students run with it.

It was a lesson I learned more than once as I taught that class. Donald Haase addresses this very issue in his essay titled "Yours, Mine or Ours? Perrault, the Brothers Grimm, and the Ownership of Fairy Tales," and we will return to that essay at the end of this chapter. As it was, it was only the first day and we had already stumbled upon a "classic" (read: done-to-death) fairy tale that I had intended to merely gloss over as we pursued more "interesting" and "unusual" fairy tales. The best-laid plans.

For the moment, at least, I tried to steer them away from Hansel and Gretel as they offered some of the other "life lessons" they had absorbed as children being exposed to fairy tales: *True love will always break the witch's spell. Old, ugly hags will do anything to stay young and beautiful. Obey your parents, or something very nasty may happen to you. Step-mothers really hate their step-children. That other place that seems so much better than where you live is actually a trap.* "Like the gingerbread house in 'Hansel and Gretel'!" piped up a girl in the back row.

"All right, then," I thought, "'Hansel and Gretel' it shall be."

They were right, of course. Hansel and Gretel is rich in possibility, not only in terms of the range of possible interpretations and interesting avenues it offers for exploration — even for those students who know the story inside and out — but also in terms of how genuinely frightening the story is. Many of my students named this very attraction on the first day of class, when I asked them why they were so enchanted with Hansel and Gretel. "Because it's so terrifying," they responded. "Really?" I asked, "More terrifying than Bluebeard?" "What's Bluebeard?" they asked. A rarely printed Brothers Grimm fairy tale in which a young woman is given in marriage to a king with a blue beard. She is terribly frightened of him. One day, she disobeys his command not to look into a certain room in the castle. When she looks in the room, she sees the hanged and horribly mutilated bodies of dozens of dead women, pinned to the walls on all four sides of the room and in various states of decomposition — murdered by Bluebeard and kept as trophies. Her punishment is to meet the same fate, which she very nearly does, but her brothers come to her rescue at the very last second.

Blood and guts. Mutilated women. A sociopath's trophy room of corpses. "Nope," the students stood firm, "Still not as scary as 'Hansel and Gretel.'"

They were unanimous in their explanation as to why. Bluebeard is a story about an adult woman pitted against an adult man who is, after all, just a man; Hansel and Gretel is a story about children pitted against a supernatural evil — and, when you're a child, listening to a story about two children who are up against something so hugely frightening it's beyond comprehension, that tends to freak a kid out. I had to grant them the point. They then offered up other reasons why Hansel and Gretel deserves the *scariest fairy tale ever* award:

- ✓ innocence taken advantage of;
- ✓ their own hunger used against them as food becomes the lure to draw them in and trap them;
- ✓ desire for the perfect home life betrayed;
- ✓ the ideal nurturer transforming into a monster;
- ✓ youth being devoured (literally) for the perpetuation of that monster's existence.

I listed the reasons on the board as the students rattled them off. I took a step back, looked at what was written up there, and a light went on: *Coraline.*

It required only a few minor adjustments to work "Hansel and Gretel" and *Coraline* into the beginning-of-semester readings and discussions I had planned. For any instructor planning a unit on fairy tales and fantasy — a unit which may fit into most any kind of class — the same plan may be laid out. Students should devote an evening to studying the Brothers Grimm version of Hansel and Gretel published in 1812. They should also then carefully view — preferably in class, if there is time — the film *Coraline* (theatre release date 2009, directed by Henry Selick). Five points of discussion provide paths of exploration for both of these pieces, with supplemental readings providing a framework for students to try out theories and interpretations of their own.

J.R.R. Tolkien on Fairy-Tales and Fantasy

J.R.R. Tolkien's classic essay "On Fairy-Stories" provides a great foundation for prompting student discussion regarding what fairy stories are, and what they aren't, according to Tolkien. One of the first and most productive conversations that can take place in such a class is an exploration of what a fairy tale *is*. How does one define or recognize a fairy tale? What makes it such? When does a fairy tale cross over into being a fable? A folk tale? How are the fairy tale and fantasy connected? "How is it that so few fairy tales *actually include fairies as characters*?" asked one student, and I thanked him silently for giving me the perfect segue into Tolkien's essay. Tolkien argues that the term "fairy-tale" has been ill-defined and, as a result, "used ... very carelessly" (33). He offers his own ideas about the term:

> fairy-stories are not in normal English usage stories about fairies or elves, but stories about Fairy, that is *Faërie*, the realm or state in which fairies have their being. *Faërie* contains many things besides elves and fays, and besides dwarfs, witches, trolls, giants, or dragons: it holds the seas, the sun, the moon, the sky; and the earth, and all things that are in it: tree and bird, water and stone, wine and bread, and ourselves, mortal men, when we are enchanted [32].

Tolkien goes on to write that "faërie cannot be caught in a net of words; for it is one of its qualities to be indescribable, though not imperceptible" (32). At this point, students may decide that Tolkien's "definition" of the term is not so helpful — that it is dodging the nitty gritty, so to speak. But this very element of wispiness is what Tolkien appreciates, and what students should come to appreciate as well. Tolkien does help us out, though, by continuing into a discussion of what fairy-tales are *not*, and which types of stories do not belong in the category of Faërie, to his mind. "I would ... exclude," he writes," "or rule out of order, any story that uses the machinery of Dream, the dreaming of actual human sleep, to explain the apparent occurrence of its marvels ... since the fairy-story deals with 'marvels,' it cannot tolerate any frame or machinery suggesting that the whole story in which they occur is a figment or illusion" (35). The *Alice in Wonderland* stories crafted by Lewis Carroll, then, do not qualify as fairy-stories for Tolkien, because these stories feature a "dream-frame and dream-transitions" (36). Students should hold this distinction in mind, as it will become important.

Several pages later, Tolkien delves into his thoughts about *fantasy*, and he is careful to object to any negative connotations associated with the terms *fantasy* and *fantastic*:

> The human mind is capable of forming mental images of things not actually present. The faculty of conceiving the images is (or was) naturally called Imagination. But in recent times, in technical not normal language, Imagination has often been held to be something higher than the mere image-making, ascribed to the operations of Fancy (a reduced and depreciatory form of the older word Fantasy) ... I am ... glad of the etymological and semantic connections of *fantasy* with *fantastic*: with images of things that are not only "not actually present," but which are indeed not to be found in our primary world at all, or are generally believed not to be found there. But while admitting that, I do not assent to the depreciative tone. That the images are of things not in the primary world (if that indeed is possible) is a virtue not a vice. Fantasy (in this sense) is, I think, not a lower but a higher form of Art, indeed the most nearly pure form, and so (when achieved) the most potent [59–60].

Students who have read carefully can see then, for Tolkien, there is no concrete dividing line between *fairy-tale* and *fantasy*; they touch each other, they blend in and out of each other, and that is as it should be.[1] These passages from Tolkien become a springboard into posing some questions to students. How closely does Hansel and Gretel fit Tolkien's description of a faërie-story? Tolkien specifies that the world of Faërie is exactly that: an all-encompassing realm in which magical events take place *while we are enchanted*. Are Hansel and Gretel (the children, not the tale) *enchanted*? The villain appears to cast no spell. Indeed, she appears to not even need one — the children go willingly into the house of their own volition. The house itself in which the old woman lives need not be a magical creation — in the 1812 Brothers Grimm version which students are studying, the dwelling is in fact *not* described as a gingerbread house. It is described as "a little house ... built of bread and had a roof made of cake and transparent windows of sugar" (187).

It would require some tricky work, but a house such as this could be created without the assistance of magic or enchantment. What about the villain herself— is she of the Faërie realm, in the category with elves, giants, trolls and dragons? Prompt students to observe the language with which the villain is described — is there anything overtly Faërie about her? Might she simply just be a clever, nasty old hag with serial killer tendencies? The manner in which Hansel and Gretel escape requires and uses no magic — Gretel simply pushes the unsuspecting woman into the oven. There is an odd episode toward the end of the story, when Hansel and Gretel encounter "a large body of water" (189) on their way back home after their dark adventure. It's curious that this body of water, which is so large, did not figure into their journey *away* from home, but figures into their journey back toward it.[2] Still, there is no reason to believe this body of water has appeared via magic. The white duck which obligingly ferries the children, one at a time, over that body of water is not overtly Faërie-like either. It does not speak in a human language (it does not speak at all). And as far as being able to carry the children on its back — well, maybe it's just a really big, talented duck.

All these things taken into consideration, if students edge toward a conclusion that Hansel and Gretel doesn't quite fit into our description of fairy-tale as laid out by Tolkien, and that what at first glance might have been deemed *fantastical* elements may actually have naturalistic explanations, now we're looking at an intriguing possibility. Skip down to the section titled "Terror, Horror and the Uncanny in 'Hansel and Gretel' and *Coraline*" for more on that subject.

Tolkien carefully specifies that stories which work within the frame of a dream-sequence, or even the possibility of a dream-sequence, do not qualify as fairy-tales. I think we can safely assume that he considers any such story outside the realm of true fantasy, as well. This clarification by Tolkien opens up some promising avenues to explore in regards to *Coraline*.[3] Students who've paid attention when viewing *Coraline* will have noticed that Selick and Gaiman have left open a strong possibility that each one of Coraline's "trips" into the Other Apartment is simply a dream. But students who paid *really close* attention to the film will likely argue, successfully, that Selick and Gaiman have left us clues that Coraline's adventures in the Other Apartment did actually take place — and therefore, the story deserves to be classified as a fantasy, by Tolkien's standards. Since *Coraline* can also be interpreted as a modern-day retelling of Hansel and Gretel, perhaps *Coraline* is a fairy tale as well — but only if students have decided that Hansel and Gretel belongs to Tolkien's realm of faërie.

Back to square one then, students might say. Well, maybe. But the journey yielded some great things.

The Power of Food and the Role of Gluttony in Hansel and Gretel and Coraline

A hungry child stumbles upon a wonderful place where food — heavenly, delicious food — is abundant and infinitely available. The nurturer who provides that food is providing a veritable dream come true for the hungry child. Food is the perfect bait. Food lures the unsuspecting child into the perfect trap.

Are we talking about Hansel and Gretel or *Coraline*? Exactly.

In her Norton Critical Edition introduction to Hansel and Gretel, Maria Tatar takes up this very issue of food in fairy tales. "Food — its presence and its absence — shapes the social world of fairy tales in profound ways," she writes, and she points out that

> wish fulfillment in fairy tales often has more to do with the stomach than with the heart ... fairy tales often take us squarely into the household, where everyone seems to be anxious about what's for dinner and about who's for dinner. The peasants of folktales may have to worry about famines, but children in fairy tales live perpetually under the double threat of starvation and cannibalism [179].

As Tatar brings to our attention, Hansel and Gretel is by no means in sparse company as a tale about hunger and the driving need to appease it. She refers readers to several other examples, including the Brothers Grimm story titled "The Children of Famine," in which a desperately hungry mother decides she must eat her own two daughters in order to relieve her misery.[4]

Returning to Hansel and Gretel, Tatar expands on the theme of hunger, food, and the figure which provides it:

> Like many fairy tales, the Grimm's "Hansel and Gretel" is set in a time of famine.... While the stepmother at home was intent on starving the children, providing neither food nor nurturing care, the witch in the forest initially appears to be a splendidly bountiful figure, offering the children a supper of pancakes with sugar, apples, and nuts and putting them in beds so comfortable that they feel as if they are "in heaven." But it quickly becomes clear that the witch is an even more exaggerated form of maternal malice than the stepmother, for she feeds the children only in order to fatten them up for her next meal [180–181].[5]

Hansel and Gretel, students will concede, certainly live under — and directly experience — what Tatar describes as "the twin dreads of starvation and the fear of being devoured" (182).

This is a natural moment to pose the question: to what extent does Coraline live under the same double threat? Is she starving, per se? Well, that depends. She and her parents have just completed a tiring move from Michigan to Oregon, and this in the midst of a looming deadline which both her parents are racing to meet. In the days after their arrival at the 150-year-old house (sectioned off into three separate apartments, collectively known as "The Pink Palace"), Coraline's parents spend all their time furiously typing away on their computers as they each attempt to finish their chapters for a garden catalogue. They have unpacked only the essentials — and even barely that — so viewers get the sense that once the professional movers have driven away, the first and only boxes unpacked were those containing the computers, and all else fell by the wayside.

Coraline's bed is not even properly made up — she has just a blanket and a pillow atop a bare mattress. There is practically no food in the kitchen. Coraline's mother makes several references to food shopping — it needs to be done, but there just hasn't been time. As a result, the first several meals in the new house are rather pathetic (limp pasta and over-boiled vegetables for example), and in each case Coraline turns up her nose at the meager meals and refuses to eat. So, yes, she is starving in a sense when she first makes the trip into the Other Apartment.

Upon completing her first "voyage" through the glowing tunnel/duct which connects her real apartment to the Other Apartment, Coraline stands up and looks at the Blue Boy painting across the room. The Blue Boy is joyfully licking a huge ice cream cone. This same Blue Boy in Coraline's real apartment doesn't appear with this treat. The message is clearly stated via the Other Blue Boy painting: this new, mysterious place will be all about food. Coraline sniffs the air and murmurs, "Mmmm. Something smells good." She immediately finds the Other Mother in the kitchen, cooking a fantastically huge dinner: a massive roast chicken, corn on the cob, gravy, dinner rolls, mashed potatoes, sweet peas; and, when Coraline asks through a stuffed mouth, "Got any gravy?" the Other Mother replies, "Well, here comes the gravy train! Choo, Choo!" as an actual miniature train chugs across the table, train cars full to the brim with gravy. The Other Mother then offers Coraline more of every item on the table, to which Coraline responds, "I'm real thirsty."

"Got any requests?" asks the Other Mother. "Mango milkshake?" says Coraline, and the chandelier lowers itself to Coraline, with each arm of the chandelier offering a different flavored milkshake. Coraline has barely taken a sip when the Other Mother sweeps a large, freshly baked cake with a thick layer of frosting on it in front of Coraline. In an equally direct parallel with Hansel and Gretel, when Coraline indicates that she is sleepy and wants to go to bed, the Other Mother chirps, "Of course. It's all made up." She leads Coraline upstairs to her Other Room, where the bed is perfectly made up, with clean sheets, fluffy pillow, and fluffier comforter. Coraline, like Hansel and Gretel, sinks into a blessed sleep in a bed that feels like it was made in heaven.

This pattern is repeated for the next two visits that Coraline intentionally makes to the Other Apartment. In each instance, she steps out of the tunnel/duct and goes directly to the kitchen, where the Other Mother is either preparing food in abundance or has left food for Coraline in abundance. The theme of hunger and starvation is also emphasized directly in the dialogue: during her first visit to the Other Apartment, when Coraline is sent to fetch her Other Father because dinner is ready, the Other Father responds with "Who's starving? Raise your hand!" When Coraline first bites into the chicken and says, "Mmm, this chicken is good," the Other Mother replies, "Hungry, aren't you?"

Students should pursue these connections about hunger, food and satiation between Hansel and Gretel and *Coraline.* The exploration of food being used as a lure, as a trap set by a sinister "provider" who intends to consume the child naturally follows. When we read Hansel and Gretel and when we watch *Coraline*, it's hard not to notice that the kids in both of these stories are, quite literally, constantly stuffing their faces—or having their faces stuffed—and they do this voluntarily (at first). Some students might call this gluttony, while others might insist that the children do seem to be genuinely in need of food. Encourage students to explore whether or not the children are eating in excess (the typical definition of "gluttony") and whether their all-consuming desire for food signifies some kind of psychological bugaboo. Adolescent children with psychological bugaboos were one of the many specialties of Bruno Bettelheim, and this moment in the discussion is an ideal time to introduce his essay on Hansel and Gretel.

Published originally in 1976 in his collection of essays titled *The Uses of Enchantment,* Bettelheim, a student of Freudian psychoanalysis and a child psychologist, takes up the issue of (you guessed it) oral fixation. No discussion of fairy tales is complete without deciding that someone in the story—maybe even *everyone* in the story!—is struggling with an Oedipal complex. The Freudian approach to fairy tales which shapes Bettelheim's essay may seem quite alien to students, especially if some of them have never encountered Freud. But that initial alienation should fade, especially if the students understand that, while they are free to agree with *everything* Bettelheim writes, they are also free to question the essay, and free to decide that, while it's interesting, they don't have to buy it hook, line and sinker. But they can certainly exercise their intellectual muscles while they listen to the salesman's pitch.[6] Bettelheim begins with setting up the symbolism of the mother in the story:

> The mother represents the source of all food to the children, so it is she who now is experienced as abandoning them, as if in a wilderness. It is the child's anxiety and deep disappointment when Mother is no longer willing to meet all his oral demands which leads him to believe that suddenly Mother has become unloving, selfish, rejecting [159].

Some pages later, he expands on this idea of how the child feels when Mother has suddenly demonstrated such a change; the child is

> devastated by the ambivalent feelings, frustrations, and anxieties of the oedipal stage of development, as well as his previous disappointment and rage at failures on his mother's part to gratify his needs and desires as fully as he expected. Severely upset that Mother no longer serves him unquestioningly but makes demands on him and devotes herself ever more to her own interests—something which the child had not permitted to come to his awareness

> before — he imagines that Mother, as she nursed him and created a world of oral bliss, did so only to fool him.... Thus, the parental home "hard by a great forest" and the fateful house in the depths of the same woods are on an unconscious level but the two aspects of the parental home: the gratifying one and the frustrating one [163].

Students can read this passage and link it directly with *Coraline,* if they were careful to note Coraline's own perception of how her parents (especially her mother) have been treating her since their move to the new house. She tries everything to get their attention, only to fail. They are busy trying to meet their deadlines, and so do not have the option or inclination to devote all their attention to her, and Coraline appears to resent this. She tries her mother first, only to have her mother respond with "Coraline, I don't have time for you right now." She then tries her father; in an effort to get his attention, she swings back and forth on a door which squeaks loudly every time its hinges open. Her father snaps at her, "Just let me work!" A double rejection. Then, that evening, a meager and unappetizing dinner. Coraline's first three experiences in the Other Apartment provide exquisite balm for these wounds. Not only is there abundant food, but there is also a set of parents who devote all their energy and attention to Coraline. She is the very center of their world, every moment. This is evident in the final lines of the "Other Father Song," which her Other Father has composed especially for her and which he sings to her.

Coraline quickly comes to understand that, when she's in the Other Apartment, she will be fed, she will be cared for, she will be fawned over, and she will be listened to. This desire to be listened to comes up repeatedly in the film. In the front yard of her real apartment, Coraline's friend Wybie is absorbed in playing with a banana slug that he's found. Coraline complains, "You are just like them.... My parents. They don't listen to me either." And when the Other Mr. Bobinsky makes a last ditch effort to keep Coraline in the Other Apartment, he taps into her deepest desires when he tells her that if she breaks away from the Other Mother, "You'll just go home and be bored and neglected, same as always. Stay here with us. We will listen to you. And laugh with you. If you stay here, you can have whatever you want, always."[8]

The Other Apartment is a tremendous temptation to Coraline because she knows, when she's there, none of her demands or needs will be denied. Hansel and Gretel make the same assumption about the mysterious house they've stumbled upon. Bettelheim argues that "[t]he house stands for oral greediness and how attractive it is to give in to it" (161) and since

> in dreams as well as in fantasies and the child's imagination, a house, as the place in which we dwell, can symbolize the body, usually the mother's ... the house at which Hansel and Gretel are eating

> away blissfully and without a care stands in the unconscious for the good mother, who offers her body as a source of nourishment. It is the original all-giving mother, whom every child hopes to find again later somewhere out in the world, when his own mother begins to make demands and to impose restrictions [161].

Hansel and Gretel find this longed-for mother-replacement figure, and so does Coraline. But here is where the danger lies for our young protagonists. They are all three deeply immature, deeply self-absorbed, entirely wrapped up in the satiation (gluttony) of their own desires and needs. To continue for much longer in this mentality, Bettelheim argues, will pose a serious threat to their development into healthy individuals, as well as a direct threat to their very lives:

> But as the story tells, such unrestrained giving in to gluttony threatens destruction. Regression to the earliest 'heavenly' state of being—when on the mother's breast one lived symbiotically off her—does away with all individuation and independence. It even endangers one's very existence, as cannibalistic intentions are given body in the figure of the witch [161].

These same cannibalistic intentions are given body in the figure of the Other Mother, whose intent all along has been to draw Coraline in so she may trap and eat her.

Hansel, Gretel, and Coraline now face a critical choice: to remain immature and die, or to mature and live. Bettelheim sees this moment as one of great potential growth:

> The witch's evil designs finally force the children to recognize the dangers of unrestrained oral greed and independence. To survive, they must develop initiative and realize that their only recourse lies in intelligent planning and acting.... Only when the dangers inherent in remaining fixed to primitive orality with its destructive propensities are recognized does the way to a higher stage of development open up [162].

"Hmmmm. All that from a little fairy tale?" the students ask. Welcome to the world of Freudian psychoanalysis. But even the most skeptical of students will likely come to appreciate that while Bettelheim's argument may at first seem pretty bizarre (especially since he is obviously taking this all so very seriously), he is bringing up intriguing, valid possibilities and interpretations that we can apply to Hansel and Gretel, as he did, and that we can now also apply to *Coraline*, with all manner of interesting results.

Terror, Horror and the Uncanny in Hansel and Gretel and Coraline

As long as the class is on the subject of Freudian psychoanalysis, we should see what the man himself might contribute to our discussion of the fairy tale and the film. In particular, Sigmund Freud's 1919 essay titled "Das Unheimliche" (translated and known in English as "The Uncanny") offers an examination of what it is exactly in life and in literature that can — for lack of a better phrase — spook the bejesus out of people. Hansel and Gretel, my students insisted, is the most frightening bedtime story ever penned. *Coraline*, in the opinion of many, is deeply disturbing on more levels than one can really count — so disturbing that many of my students stated that even with its PG rating, they would not consider allowing their children to see it. A perusal of this cornerstone essay by Freud yields much fertile ground for stimulating discussion about these very issues.

Freud writes that "the 'uncanny' ... belongs to the realm of the frightening, of what evokes fear and dread" (123) and that "an uncanny effect often arises when the boundary between fantasy and reality is blurred, when we are faced with the reality of something that we have until now considered imaginary" (150–51). He also states that he agrees with E. Jentsch, who wrote that "one of the surest devices for producing slightly uncanny effects through storytelling is to leave the reader wondering whether a particular figure is a real person or an automaton" (qtd. in Freud 135).

Students will likely see an immediate link between Freud's claim that we become frightened — or at the very least, really uncomfortable — when we can't quite be sure that the line between reality and fantasy hasn't been punctured somehow and the feeling which Hansel and Gretel certainly had when they first perceived the delicious house in front of them. Coraline demonstrates this same hesitation when she first sees the Other Living Room which is so much like hers, and yet so different. Coraline appears to feel real fear a minute later, when the Other Mother turns and looks Coraline fully in the face for the first time. There are large black buttons on the Other Mother's face where her eyes should be. This bothers Coraline, but she quickly recovers (at least outwardly). We, however, do not. Buttons instead of eyes: it is deeply bothersome. It is unnatural. It is familiar and yet not familiar; the buttons and the eyes they hide are known and yet unknown. It is uncanny.

It's an interesting question to pose to students, to ask them to clarify and articulate as best they can exactly *why* the button eyes strike us as so uncanny, so frightening. Do they make the Other Mother appear, as Jentsch describes it, as some kind of automaton? What are the buttons hiding? To what extent do we judge another individual's intentions via what we can see in their eyes, and to what extent have we (and Coraline) been robbed of that perception — even robbed of the ability to sense danger — by the bizarre presence of the black buttons?

Freud also devotes some time in his essay paraphrasing a story written by E.T.A. Hoffman titled "The Sand-Man." For Freud, the fact that the Sand-Man tears out the eyes of children leads to the overwhelming sense of the uncanny in Hoffman's piece, because it directly addresses the fear which many children have (according to Freud) of "being robbed of one's eyes" (138): "Psychoanalytic experience reminds us that some children have a terrible fear of damaging or losing their eyes. Many retain this anxiety into adult life and fear no physical injury so much as one to the eye. And there is a common saying that one will 'guard something like the apple of one's eye'" (140).

Coraline seems to be a case in point for Freud's claim. After one particularly satisfying visit to the Other Apartment, the Other Mother innocently says to Coraline, "You could stay here forever if you want to." "Really?" Coraline asks. "Sure," responds the Other Father "We'll sing and play games, and Mother will cook your favorite meals."

"There's just one tiny thing you have to do," says the Other Mother. "What's that?" asks Coraline. The Other Mother places a box with two black buttons inside it on the table in front of Coraline. It takes a few moments for Coraline to figure out what's going on. As soon as she does, she yells, "No way! I'm not letting you sew buttons into my eyes!" It's a moment of genuine terror, and it's at this point that Coraline is (ironically) suddenly able to see that the Other Mother, and the whole world she's created for Coraline, is not even remotely benign. Coraline soon learns that the Other Mother has in the past successfully seduced three children into allowing her to sew buttons into their eyes — and after doing so, she ate the children up, and callously tossed their souls into a deserted room in the Other Apartment. Coraline understands completely that what is about to ensue is a battle for Coraline's eyes — and for her very soul. Her dream life has abruptly become the stuff of nightmares.

To the subject of dreams and nightmares Freud naturally turns in his essay, as he expands upon the theme of children suffering a deep-seated terror of losing their eyes: "The study of dreams, fantasies and myths has taught us also that anxiety about one's eyes, the fear of going blind, is quite often a substitute for the fear of castration..." (139), and that, for children, a "particularly strong and obscure emotion is aroused by the threat of losing the sexual organ" (140). This is what Freud calls "the infantile castration complex" (140).

At this point, students may laugh out loud — out of nervousness perhaps, or because they might already be aware that Freud rarely wrote anything without managing to claim that a penis is the most precious possession on planet earth, even to infants. It's a bit of a stretch to make Freud's castration complex theory fit *Coraline*; the main challenge being, obviously, that since she doesn't *have* said precious penis, she probably doesn't fear losing it.[9] But remind students that, just because it is a stretch, does not mean it's impossible. That's what interpretation is about. Using an element in interpretation doesn't mean having it perfectly fit every single detail and element of the story to which it's being applied: adjustments are allowed for. If the shoe fits, wear it. If it doesn't fit, cut your toe and your heel off, like Cinderella's stepsisters did, and *make it fit!*

Returning to the problem posed in our earlier discussion of whether or not Hansel and Gretel fits Tolkien's descriptions of what constitutes a fairy-story and what constitutes fantasy: if students seem to be leaning towards a conclusion that Hansel and Gretel is neither, then we are faced — through process of elimination — with an intriguing possibility. Intriguing, as in truly horrifying. The story is real. It's not remotely "outside" the realm of possibility. These events could really happen. Maybe they *did* actually happen — perhaps are happening as we speak. Children are lured into murderer's homes every day all across the world, and how easy it is to offer a child something he delights in — a teddy bear, a video game, an ice cream cone — to get him to come with us. This is why, as my students convinced me, Hansel and Gretel deserves the *scariest fairy tale ever* award: because it isn't a fairy tale. It's the reality we live with, the daily reality of the most horrific betrayal — children whose innocence and trusting nature are used against them for the fulfillment of an adult's atrocious intentions.

It isn't necessary to go into specific examples by name of children who have been lured by adults into traps from which they never escaped. When I asked earlier if the old woman in Hansel and Gretel might simply be a clever, nasty old hag with serial killer tendencies, I was only partially joking. She *is* a serial killer of children. The Brothers Grimm tell us that she lays in wait for children and "she had built the little house of bread just to lure them inside. As soon as a child was in her power, she killed it, cooked it, and ate it" (188). So we don't know how many she's murdered and eaten — but it's definitely more than one.[10] As for the Other Mother, our serial killer of children in *Coraline*, we learn for certain that her current number is three children murdered and eaten — working on the fourth, Coraline — and her bloodthirsty rampage will only end if Coraline manages to defeat her.

When we consider the horrible spectacle of children pitted against sadistic adults, we see that the playing field is so desperately uneven, it sends a shiver down the spine. The situation becomes all the more menacing when other adults, who should be present and offering their help to the child, turn out to be useless — or worse, participating in some way in the attack on that child. Undoubtedly the most chilling moment in the film *Coraline* takes place when the Other Father chases Coraline down in the garden. He is at the helm of a huge, mechanical garden mantis/machine, with razor-blade sharp pinchers and snapping jaws. As the Other Father steers this deadly machine toward Coraline, he whines helplessly, "Sorry. So sorry. Don't wanna hurt ya. Mother making me."

For all the sugared-window fairy tale imagery in Hansel and Gretel and all the brilliance of stop-motion animation in *Coraline*, stripped of these decorations and bows and held up before us in their purest forms, these stories are — to quote one of my students — "damn scary." Your students might agree.

Maternal Poison and the Toxic Female in Need of Regeneration

"All will be well, soon as Mother's refreshed. Her strength is our strength," mumbles the wilting Other Father to Coraline.

At first glance in Hansel and Gretel and in *Coraline*, we appear to be dealing with a simple matter (?) of cannibalism. The villains in these stories trap and eat children. Simple ... maybe. The old woman/witch in Hansel and Gretel eats children — no mistake about that — but she does not subsist on children exclusively. She can live on other things during the weeks in between those lucky days when she can snag a kid (or two). This is evident in the description of the witch's mode of operation: "As soon as a child was in her power, she killed it, cooked it, and ate it" (188). Four weeks go by during which the witch (alliteration!) tries to fatten Hansel up (188). She obviously had to have been eating something else in the meantime in order to stay alive.

Not so the case with the Other Mother. When the Other Father makes the comment to Coraline about Mother needing to be "refreshed," we know for certain now even if we weren't sure before: the Other Mother is one big, creepy parasite and the host of choice to whom she has leeched herself is her "daughter," Coraline.[11] Regeneration is the name of the game here, and Coraline is the key ingredient. The Other Mother is failing in strength as the hours go by — she loses her capability to remain in the shape of Coraline's real mother, and as her physicality changes, she also begins coughing: a sign of degeneration. The other "people" who populate the world created by the Other Mother begin to fade as well, hence the Other Father's statement that "her strength is our strength."

The tables have turned dramatically for Coraline. The all-giving maternal figure has become poisonous, has latched onto her, and now demands Coraline's body and soul in order to sustain her own toxic existence, just as she consumed the bodies and souls of the three ghost children trapped in the mirror-room. Explaining to Coraline how they came to be there, one of the ghost children tells Coraline that the Other Mother "ate up our lives." This is something more than just basic cannibalism. It's at this point that students can start exploring the metaphorical aspects of this relationship between Coraline and the Other Mother.

Coraline doesn't notice it during her first several visits to the Other Apartment, but students might have: that Other Mother is way, way too into this whole Mother/Daughter thing. Coraline is the consummate reason for the Other Mother's existence — she hovers over Coraline, spends all her time and effort cooking for Coraline, making clothes for Coraline, setting up wonderful evenings of entertainment for Coraline, gazing at Coraline with adoration whenever Coraline is near. It's creepy. It's unbalanced. One might be tempted to use the expression that the Other Mother needs to *get a life*— to exist in some way outside of and away from the child. In her struggle to understand the trap that's been orchestrated by the Other Mother, Coraline asks the Cat, "Why does she want *me*?"

The Cat replies, "She wants something to love, I think. Something that *isn't* her. Or maybe she'd just love something to eat." Coraline says, "Eat? That's ridiculous. Mothers don't eat daughters." The Cat replies, "I don't know. How do *you* taste?"

Mothers don't eat daughters, literally. But mothers can certainly consume daughters, figuratively. Children who find themselves under the yoke of over-bearing, over-involved, and desperately needy parents have to find their own way out of that suffocating environment. These children have to navigate all manner of awful guilt, as they try to establish their own identities and lives while being sabotaged by the parent — often the mother — who doesn't want to be left alone. Coraline finds herself in this very position, but she is quick enough to use this twisted situation against the Other Mother. In proposing a deal, by which if Coraline wins a game she will have won her own freedom, she offers to the Other Mother the following: "If I lose, I'll stay here with you forever and let you love me. And I'll let you sew buttons into my eyes." (In other words, I'll never leave you, you'll always have me to fawn over, and I'll let you cripple me for the rest of my life.) "And if you somehow win this game?" asks the Other Mother. "Then you let me go," answers Coraline.

The stakes could hardly be any higher. In order for Coraline to succeed, she must make a complete break away from the Other Mother — not a partial one. She must give up entirely the home that seemed so blessedly perfect. Then, she'll have to demonstrate initiative, resourcefulness, courage, and stamina in order to wage and win the battle for her freedom. It may appear at first as though Coraline fights this battle on her own, but she does not — she seeks out and is gifted with the help of neighbors from her real apartment, as well as the mischievous black cat which can wander back and forth between the two worlds, and the Other Father. Bruno Bettelheim touches upon this subject of combining resources in his essay on "Hansel and Gretel": "These stories direct the child toward transcending his immature dependence on his parents and reaching the next higher stage of development: cherishing also the support of age mates. Cooperating with them in meeting life's tasks will eventually have to replace the child's single-minded reliance on his parents only" (166).

He is referring in this passage to the teamwork demonstrated by Hansel and Gretel as they work for and gain their own freedom from the nurturer-turned-monster in the cottage and as they find their way back home to their real (i.e. non-threatening) family members. He continues, "No more will the children ... seek for the miraculous gingerbread house. But neither will they encounter or fear the witch, since they have proved to themselves that through their combined efforts they can outsmart her and be victorious" (165).

Coraline does eventually outsmart the Other Mother and gain her victory, but not without pain or struggle, and not without guilt. When Coraline shuts the Other Mother up in the Other Apartment and then escapes with the only key, we hear the Other Mother's bloodcurdling screams from behind the door: "Don't leave me! Don't leave me! I'll die without you!"

Denouement and Ownership: Tolkien's Ideal Endings and Claiming Stories for Ourselves

Naturally, the classroom discussion should eventually turn to the endings of these stories. Within that discussion may also appear questions such as: *Are these "happy" endings? Has our time been spent productively, being that we are adults studying children's stories? Have we arrived at the right answers and interpretations?* J.R.R. Tolkien and Donald Haase can assist us in addressing these queries.

Before pursuing the question of whether these stories offer us "happy endings," it is necessary to go backward a bit into Tolkien's essay "On Fairy-stories." He states that fairy tales "offer also, in a peculiar degree or mode, these things: Fantasy, Recovery, Escape, Consolation" (59). Students should already be familiar with his thoughts on Fantasy, since they have discussed it in class. He encapsulates the idea of Recovery when he writes, "Recovery (which includes return and renewal of health) is a re-gaining—regaining of a clear view.... We need, in any case, to clean our windows; so that the things seen clearly may be freed from the drab blur of triteness or familiarity—from possessiveness" (67). Encourage students to discuss what Tolkien means in this description of Recovery: what does he mean, we need "to clean our windows"? Can aspects of our own lives "be freed from the drab blur of triteness or familiarity" through the experience of fairy-stories? On the subject of possession, Tolkien writes that too many elements of our lives "have become like the things which once attracted us by their glitter, or their colour, or their shape, and we laid hands on them, and then locked them in our hoard, acquired them, and acquiring ceased to look at them" (67). Do students agree that experiencing a fairy-tale/fantasy story can bring back a sense of appreciation for what we had locked away and forgotten? Have the stories about Hansel and Gretel and *Coraline* impacted us in this way?

Moving into Tolkien's section on Escape, he specifies that he doesn't approve or agree with "the tone of scorn or pity with which 'Escape' is now so often used" (69). Put simply, he sees nothing shameful in the human desire to escape into fairy-stories and fantasy. Escape has forever been an integral part of fairy-tale and legend, in the view of Tolkien:

> There are other things more grim and terrible to fly from than the noise, stench, ruthlessness, and extravagance of the internal-combustion engine. There are hunger, thirst, poverty, pain, sorrow, injustice, death. And even when men are not facing hard things such as these, there are ancient limitations from which fairy-stories offer a sort of escape, and old ambitions and desires (touching the very roots of fantasy) to which they offer a kind of satisfaction and consolation [73].

Tolkien clarifies that this consolation is not limited to

> the imaginative satisfaction of ancient desires. Far more important is the Consolation of the Happy Ending. Almost I would venture to assert that all complete fairy-stories must have it ... this joy, which is one of the things which fairy-stories can produce extremely well, is not essentially "escapist" nor "fugitive." In its fairy-tale — or otherworld — setting, it is a sudden and miraculous grace: never to be counted on to recur. It does not deny the existence of *dyscatastrophe*, of sorrow and failure: the possibility of these is necessary to the joy of deliverance; it denies (in the face of much evidence, if you will) universal final defeat and in so far is *evangelium*, giving a fleeting glimpse of Joy, Joy beyond the walls of the worlds, poignant as grief [75].

This is quite a tall order for an ending to a fairy-tale or fantasy story. Students may at first struggle to think of example stories whose endings bear out this description of Consolation, but only if they are over-thinking Tolkien's passage. One helpful example that may be offered to students is Tolkien's own *Lord of the Rings* trilogy. The ending of this epic, laid down in the final pages of *The Return of the King,* directly fits his description of the Consolation of the Happy Ending. The extent to which *Hansel and Gretel* and *Coraline* present the Consolation of the Happy Ending is a topic that students should certainly pursue.

In Tolkien's sequences on Escape and Consolation, he seems to be anticipating and answering the question of whether adults have spent their time in a "productive" manner by spending hours in the realm of faërie and fantasy. His reply appears to be an unequivocal "yes." He feels strongly that "Fantasy ... does not seek delusion, nor bewitchment and domination; it seeks shared enrichment, partners in making and delight, not slaves" (64); and, in a comment that might surprise some students, he determines that the Fantasy, Recovery, Escape and Consolation which fairy-stories have to offer are "all things ... which children have, as a rule, *less need than older people* [emphasis added]" (59).

Just as there are "lessons to be learned" from fairy-tales and fantasy stories (maybe), there are lessons to be learned as an instructor leading a class on fairy-tales and fantasy (definitely). It may be tempting to approach the class with an "iron fist" so to speak, especially if we have become too enchanted with the idea of our own expertise and authority. In an effort to keep the class "on track," we might approach the class having already made all the value judgments and decisions regarding which stories will be studied, which elements will be examined, which interpretations will be deemed the most valid, and which conclusions will be arrived at. Hopefully, in such a case, the students will challenge the instructor to reconsider, as my students challenged me. In doing so, the students are demonstrating what Donald Haase refers to as Ownership of Fairy Tales. The passage below is illuminating, with its emphasis on children claiming fairy tales for their own. It becomes more illuminating when we substitute the concept of *children* with *students*:

> The opportunity to reclaim fairy tales is as crucial for children as it is for adults. But the right to ownership of the tales may in some ways be more difficult for children to claim. After all, teachers, librarians, parents, and powers in the culture industry exert a certain control over the popular reception of fairy tales by determining to a great extent not only the nature of the tales that are made accessible to children, but also the context of their reception.... Children's responses are expected to conform to the external authority of the tales they read or hear [362].

Haase proposes a way out of this narrow approach: children, he says, should be granted permission to "reread and reinterpret the tales in new ways. By experiencing a wide variety of tales, they can view the stories of the classical canon in new context. By actively selecting, discussing, enacting, illustrating, adapting, and retelling the tales they experience, both adults and children can assert their own proprietary rights to meaning" (363).

Oh, and don't forget: *Never accept anything from that old woman who lives in the forest.*

Notes

1. Students who were looking for the ultimately authoritative answer which put all prior debate to bed and which stated in no uncertain terms "A fairy tale is *this*" and "Fantasy is *that*" may be disappointed, but they will get over it. This isn't a math class, after all. We aren't after the "right" answer—we're after the exploration of the question and what it can yield. It takes some students time to reconcile with this, obviously, especially if they are new to the humanities.

2. See Bruno Bettelheim's essay titled Hansel and Gretel for his evaluation of this body of water as a symbolic baptism/rite of passage for the children (164).

3. On the sites I've consulted regarding *Coraline,* Neil Gaiman's book (on which the film is based) is described as a fantasy/horror novella and the film is described/categorized as a fantasy children's film.

4. She doesn't eat them, ultimately; they fall into a deep sleep until Judgment Day, and the Brothers Grimm end the tale with "Meanwhile, their mother departed, and nobody knows where she went" (651). She shows up later on as the Other Mother in *Coraline,* obviously.

5. Students at this point will likely point out that, in the 1812 version of Hansel and Gretel they are studying, the children's female parent is not a stepmother, as Tatar refers to her in the

passage above, but their natural mother. Remind students that Tatar addresses this change (made by Wilhelm Grimm) in the preceding paragraphs of her essay. For further reading, students should look to Jack Zipes' essay titled "The Rationalization of Abandonment and Abuse in Fairy Tales: The Case of Hansel and Gretel," within which he provides a detailed account of the history of the Grimm's many versions of "Hansel and Gretel."

6. Remind students of the academic proverb "It is the mark of an educated mind to examine an idea without accepting it."

7. Written and performed by They Might Be Giants. Available on the *Coraline* film soundtrack.

8. Of course we know, at this point, that the Other Bobinsky is simply a puppet creation of the Other Mother, and whatever comes out of his mouth has probably been crafted by her.

9. I do sometimes wonder if Freud ever noticed that *all* children were not males. There had to have been female children in Freud's day — I'm sure they had been invented by then. Why doesn't he acknowledge this? It is a mystery.

10. The 1987 film adaptation directed by Len Talan softens the terror of this question: the old witch has encapsulated the bodies of the past children she's caught inside large, gingerbread-man cookies which line both sides of the yard leading up to her house. There are at least a dozen of them. They are not actually dead, though. As Hansel and Gretel escape her house, they are able to break all those children out of their cookie cages. However, the film still has its seriously frightening moments. In one scene, Gretel wakes up in the middle of the night and spies on the grandmotherly old woman, who begins to sing a menacing song about the joys of killing and eating children. As the witch delivers the final line of the song, she quickly turns and looks Gretel directly in the face. It is extremely scary — especially from the point of view of a child — and Cloris Leachman, who plays the witch, deserves much of the credit for this scene's impact.

11. We soon realize that the word *parasite* as a descriptive is not very far off— since the Other Mother is in fact a huge spider.

Works Cited

Bettelheim, Bruno. "Hansel and Gretel." *The Uses of Enchantment: The Meaning and Importance of Fairy Tales.* New York: Vintage, 1989. 159–66. Print.

Coraline. Dir. Henry Selick. Writ. Henry Selick and Neil Gaiman. Perf. Dakota Fanning and Teri Hatcher. Universal Studios, 2009. DVD.

Freud, Sigmund. "The Uncanny." *The Uncanny.* Trans. David McLintock. New York: Penguin Group, 2003. 123–61. Print.

Grimm, Wilhelm, and Jacob. "Bluebeard." *The Complete Fairy Tales of the Brothers Grimm.* 3d ed. Trans. Jack Zipes. New York: Bantam, 1987. 610–12. Print.

_____. "Children of Famine." *The Complete Fairy Tales of the Brothers Grimm.* 3d ed. Trans. Jack Zipes. New York: Bantam, 1987. 651. Print.

_____. "Cinderella." *The Complete Fairy Tales of the Brothers Grimm.* 3d. ed. Trans. Japes Zipes. New York: Bantam, 1987. 79–84. Print.

_____. "Hansel and Gretel." *The Complete Fairy Tales of the Brothers Grimm.* 3d ed. Trans. Jack Zipes. New York: Bantam, 1987. 53–61. Print.

_____. "Snow White. "*The Complete Fairy Tales of the Brothers Grimm.* 3d ed. Trans. Jack Zipes. New York: Bantam, 1987. 181–88. Print.

Haase, Donald. "Yours, Mine or Ours? Perrault, the Brothers Grimm, and the Ownership of Fairy Tales." *The Classic Fairy Tales.* Ed. Maria Tatar. New York: W.W. Norton, 1999. 353–64. Print.

Hansel and Gretel. Dir. Len Talan. Perf. David Warner and Cloris Leachman. The Cannon Group/MGM Home Entertainment, 1987. DVD.

Tatar, Maria. "Introduction: Hansel and Gretel." *The Classic Fairy Tales.* Ed. Maria Tatar. New York: W.W. Norton, 1999. 179–84. Print.

They Might Be Giants. "Other Father Song." *Coraline* Original Motion Picture Soundtrack. Koch Records, 2009. CD.

Tolkien, J.R.R. "On Fairy-stories." *Tolkien On Fairy-stories*. Ed. Verlyn Flieger and Douglas A. Anderson. London: HarperCollins, 2008. 27–84. Print.

_____. *The Return of the King: Being the Third Part of the Lord of the Rings*. New York: Mariner Books, 2005. Print.

Zipes, Jack. "The Rationalization of Abandonment and Abuse in Fairy Tales: The Case of Hansel and Gretel." *Happily Ever After: Fairy Tales, Children, and the Culture Industry*. New York: Routledge, 1997. 39–60. Print.

The Fantastic Classroom: Teaching *Buffy the Vampire Slayer*

EMILY DIAL-DRIVER

I know way too much about *Buffy the Vampire Slayer*. I don't know as much about the series as those people who are fans of, say, *Star Trek* or *Star Wars* do about "their" series. I don't know how big Buffy's house is or how many demons she's conquered in her career. That's not the kind of thing I know. I do know the themes and symbols for episodes and series; I know character arcs and literary and pop culture allusions. And pertinent quotes from the series come to mind at the most opportune and inopportune moments. So, when students who knew we were working on some academic articles about *Buffy*[1] asked whether I could teach a class on the series, I jumped at the chance.

A class on a pop culture show. Not knowing that there is a whole subset of literary analysis called "Buffy studies," skeptics might argue that studying a pop culture/fantasy television series is not scholarly. In fact there are websites devoted to something like "weird classes that colleges allow unsuspecting students to take and poor put-upon parents to have to pay for — basically a waste of money and intellect."

However, as most "Buffy scholars" know, teaching fantasy doesn't mean abandoning the traditional goals and objectives of teaching English. Students — and scholars — can apply the traditional literary principles that they learn in other classes and recognize that the same principles apply to pop culture works.

The Class

When the university and department agreed to offer the class, many students were intrigued and more than willing to sign up for an English class on a show of which they may or may not have been fans. In fact, most who enrolled were not fans and did not take too much convincing that we were not going to investigate *Buffy* from the perspective of fandom, but from the perspective of the literary analysis and criticism. Since the show had completed its seven-season run, the entire oeuvre was available on DVD. Students were asked to watch all seven seasons and to consider each season equivalent to a novel, with each episode a chapter in the work. In addition, they were required to read several works of *Buffy* criticism, of which there is a plethora.

The major program in our department leads to a bachelor's degree in liberal arts. Classes in this program often require a handbook of literary terms, such as Abrams. Students in the Buffy class also had to obtain the handbook. Using this handbook, literary and film terms and definitions of literary and film criticisms, the students investigated *Buffy*'s visual elements, analyzed the series and separate episodes as literary works, and explored how various literary criticisms applied to the works.

To show their progress and achievement each student, in addition to two essay tests on the material, submitted a research essay, a reflective paper, and a creative project. The research essay — not a research report — has to contain not only research into what scholars and critics had said about *Buffy* but also the student's original thoughts on the topic.

A reflective paper is a paper which requires a student to interrogate personal reactions and relationships to the work and the connections that the student makes between that work and other works of his/her reading and/or viewing experience. This paper requires analysis of the works, the student's personal reactions to the works, and connections to the larger world of literature, film, and pop culture.

A creative project is the "equivalent" of a ten-page paper, meaning that the student should spend "ten pages" worth of thought and work on the project. The project should be visual, tactile, and imagistic and should illuminate, explicate, and illustrate the work for other class members. The project is presented to the class with an explanation of how the project fulfills those requirements. One of the items the student has to address is the significance of each element of the project. When the formal presentation is finished, the project is subject to questions from professor and class members. Although this seems intimidating to most students, because it requires two elements many literature and composition students may avoid: creativity and oral presentation, it is an illuminating project for both students and professor. The project requires the student to interact with the material in substantively different ways from research and literary criticism. It requires deep analysis and questioning of how elements can be linked. The project can reveal a student's profound knowledge of the work that sometimes catches class members and professor by surprise and ends in delight.

The students did remarkably well in the class. One commented that she finally realized why it was necessary to learn all those literary and film terms and types of criticisms, that they were actually useful, and that she was looking forward to taking Shakespeare the next semester and using those same terms and criticisms. From *Buffy* to Shakespeare. I thought that sounded like a pretty successful breakthrough for the traditionalists, as well as the pop culture addicts.

Although we dealt with many, many elements of the series, one of the main emphases was theme. *Buffy* is the story of the "one girl in all the world" who has the strength to fight evil. The opening lines of each episode, are voiced by Giles, her mentor, originally a high school librarian at Sunnydale High School, and are approximately this: "Into every generation, a Slayer is born. One girl in all the world. She alone will have the strength and skill to fight the vampires and demons, to stop the spread of their evil." *Buffy* begins when Buffy enters SHS as a sophomore, after being expelled from a high school in Los Angeles for "burning down the gym" (which just happened to be full of vampires).

Buffy does not want to be the "Chosen One." She rejects her calling at every turn. However, with great power comes great responsibility, as Spider-Man might say. She has the power to fight evil and, as a consequence, feels compelled to do so. Buffy has a fairly potent sense of right and wrong. Evidently her mother, who is a character in the series through five seasons, reared her to know she has to choose to do the correct thing. Buffy wants to be a "normal girl," but, when, in the first episode, she discovers that a student has been killed by a vampire, she feels constrained to investigate and to eliminate the threat to "normal people," who, if they knew they were living on a Hellmouth, would look to her for help — or run screaming to an alternate location.

She is a secret hero, however, and must do her good deeds in the metaphoric dark, a dark which is lightened by the presence in her life of several people who not only know who and what she is but who also feel compelled to do the right thing and to aid her to the best of their abilities. Her "Watcher," Giles, of course, is in her corner — as a non-combatant, as an advisor, as a mentor, as a nag. Some of her fellow students inadvertently discover her secret and become the "Scooby gang": Xander, a not-in-the-in crowd underachiever, and Willow, an achiever and computer whiz/nerd, are the first members. Through the series, they are joined by Cordelia, the popular, snarky cheerleader who can't believe she hangs around with "those people"; Oz, an underachieving, very bright, guitar playing, lover of Willow; Tara, a shy Wiccan, the second lover of Willow; Anya, a former demon cursed to human form and in love with Xander; and Dawn, Buffy's sister, who does not exist until Season Five (yes, really). All of these people are also drawn into the eternal battle.

Each season has a "big bad," a foe that persists through the season, interspersed or in concert with a number of "little bads." Unlike some series, in *Buffy*, as in good novels, the characters grow and change. This change is particularly striking because the characters begin as sophomores in high school and end, in Season Seven, as working members of the community, having weathered the *sturm und drang* of maturation.

One can illustrate any literary or film term by examples from the series, but the most rewarding illustrations include discussions of literary criticism and theme. One can investigate *Buffy* through the lens of feminist criticism, psychological and sociological criticism, gender studies, Jungian and Freudian criticism, religious studies, Marxist criticism, rhetorical criticism, or theoretical or practical criticism, using a formal, expressive, pragmatic, or mimetic emphasis. I could simply list all the formal terms for literary criticism here because one might choose to use any one of the types of criticism through which to view *Buffy*. However, this truncated list should suffice as an example of the wealth of possibilities for perspective.

For example, *Buffy* studies include numerous arguments about whether or not *Buffy* is an example of a feminist series. A short list of those involved in the feminist interrogation include Bodger, Buttsworth, Culp, Daughtey, Greenman, Hollows, Jowett, Stevenson, Vint, Wilcox, Wilcox and Lavery, etc.—and I do mean etc. On one side of the argument are those who maintain that, because Buffy is the antithesis of the helpless blonde victim of the horror film convention, *Buffy* must have a feminist message. On the other side of the argument are those who maintain that the show reinforces the stereotypes of "inity"—masculinity and femininity. One can have a discussion that ranges into detailed examination of each episode in dealing with this interrogation alone.[2]

Thematic Interrogation

The themes, however, are my favorite because discussion of theme can range from detailed analysis of the series itself into the realm of current affairs, sociology, psychology, history, personal reactions and relationships to elements—and the universe.

Among topics for exploration are the following, including questions that will initiate discussion:

Anthropology: What does each episode reveal about humanity? What does each episode reveal about people's relationships to each other and to the society and larger culture? How do the characters behave in line with and in opposition to their culture? What are the characters' cultural motivations for behaving in the way they do?

Community philosophy/group influence: Buffy has a "Scooby Gang." Each member of the Gang functions in a different role. What roles does each member of the Gang fulfill? How does each fulfill the various roles? Does any character break from the role to commit anomalous actions? Are each member's actions the same when a part of the group or do those actions change when he/she is estranged from the group? What is a community philosophy? How does group expectation change the actions of a character? How does disappointing or not fulfilling that expectation change a character?
Culture (including pop culture): What does each episode in *Buffy* reveal about U.S. culture? about southern California culture? about high school culture? How does this revelation correspond to or contradict a familiar culture? What pop culture elements are included in each episode? What elements "date" the episode? What elements are universal?
Ethics and morality: What is right and wrong? In this (choose a situation from any one of the episodes) situation, what is the right thing to do? the expedient thing? Are the two the same? What does it mean to Buffy's development as a person that she has to lie to most of the people in her life? Is lying wrong? What are the results of lying? In a larger sense, what is the morality of the series? of each episode? of each character? Does the morality change situationally? If so, how? If not, why not?
Family and family dynamics: *Buffy* defines family in specific ways. What are the examples of family and family dynamics in each episode? What is a family? How are families formed? What is the function of a family? What is a function of a family in *Buffy*? Must the members of a family be related by blood or law?
Fashion: How is each character revealed through fashion choice? How is change in character revealed through the series by fashion choice? What do the fashions reveal about the larger culture of U.S., California, high school, the turn of the century to the 21st century?
Feminism: Is *Buffy* a feminist series (the eternal conundrum)? How does the episode under discussion illustrate or refute the feminist ideal? What are the stereotypes of masculinity and femininity revealed in the episode/series? What are the contradictions that make the conclusion reached problematic? How has feminism changed? How has feminist rhetoric changed over the last decades, and how is that change revealed in the series?
Film elements: How do the elements of film support the theme of the episode/series? What function do the following have in each episode: camera angle, montage, editing, voice over, *mise-en-scène,* length of shot, length of scene, one- two- or three- shot, pan, framing, etc.? How does lighting function to heighten or decrease emotional reaction in each

scene? How does camera placement function to heighten or decrease emotional reaction in each scene? What effect do the background elements in each shot have? What effect does the setting have? the sound track? the music?

Forgiveness: What characters, major and minor, commit acts for which forgiveness is needed? What then occurs? Why? What is the result of the forgiveness? Is there any act which cannot be forgiven? What examples of forgiveness/lack of forgiveness occur in the episode/series?

Free will and determinism: Buffy is the Chosen One. She did not choose this. In fact, she's usually opposed to anything that means she can't go on a date. And she can't make a plan to shop that's not interrupted by a quest or a mission. She has to lie to most people because her calling is not a public one. How then does free will and determinism play out in the series and in each episode? What free will does Buffy exhibit? Are her actions determined?

Friendship: What does each episode reveal about friendship: its rewards, its dangers, its responsibilities, its difficulties, its benefits, its disadvantages? How do the characters interact with each other? with the larger group?

Genre: To what genre does *Buffy* belong? What, in any episode, corresponds to the genre conventions? How does the episode subvert the genre conventions?

Greek chorus: If the function of a Greek chorus is to comment on the action of the moment and/or the theme of the actions or if the function of the Greek chorus is to comment on the action as the ordinary citizens of the surrounding area would comment, then does the music in each episode function as a Greek chorus? If so (and, yes, it really does), how is each piece of music also commentary? Does the commentary work on aesthetic and thematic levels?

Humor: Are there humorous elements in each episode? What might they be? What is their purpose? their function?

Identity: In the series, how does each character determine his/her identity? What changes in that identity as each character changes through the series? What concrete clues are there to show the identity of each character? If identity is already formed in the minds of others, how does any character change the preconceived identity?

Irony: What are the ironies in the episodes? in the series? What instances of verbal irony appear? What instances of situational irony are evident? What instances of dramatic irony exhibit? What functions do these ironies serve? What is their purpose?

Language: Characters in *Buffy* often use language in innovative and interesting ways. What are examples of the ways in which each character

uses language? What makes each character's speech pattern individual? What examples of unusual word choices are available? What is the function of slang? How does slang function in *Buffy*? What allusions appear in each episode? What is the function of each allusion?
Law: There is natural law and human law. How may we define each? How are the two laws portrayed in *Buffy*? How are they in sync or in contradiction? Which is most important to follow? How is any decision on which is most important reinforced or contradicted by events in the episode/series?
Mythology: What various mythologies are revealed in *Buffy*? How are the elements of that mythology revealed? What differences from the usual mythologies exist in the episode/series? What is the mythology of *Buffy* itself?
Musicology: What is the function of music in *Buffy*? What is the function of music in any medium? Does that function differ in *Buffy*? Why is that so? How does music function in each episode? What is the rationale behind the choice of each musical element?
Narration: Narrative tools include character arcs, plot arcs, points of conflict, foreshadowing, etc. Narration appears in many forms: journal entries, journalism, conversation or dialogue or monologue, interviews, notes, non-chronological or chronological story — which might be biographical, autobiographical, or neither. What form of narration does each episode have? What form of narration does each season have? the series as a whole? What types of narration appear in any one episode or in a segment of an episode?
Opera: If one defines opera as story set to music, with the lyrics moving the plot, then one of the episodes of *Buffy* might be defined as operatic. Is "Once More with Feeling" an opera? What is the function of a musical episode? Why would a director and/or producer want a musical episode in a series such as *Buffy*? Does the episode "work"? Is it effective? Is such an experiment a mistake? Do the lyrics advance the plot sufficiently to please the audience?
Philosophies: Various philosophies are revealed in the episodes. What examples of existentialism are evident? How is nihilism revealed? What other philosophies are exposed? What is the function of each philosophy in the episode/series? What does the philosophy reveal about the events and/or character? How does the episode/event reveal that philosophy?
Redemption: Characters, both minor and major, commit acts for which they require forgiveness, if such is possible. What is forgiveness? What is redemption? What characters need redemption? What characters receive redemption? How is each of those characters redeemed? How do other characters relate to that redemption? Are these events realistic? believable?

Religion: What religious elements exist in each episode in *Buffy*? How is religion portrayed? What function does it serve? How is each character related to the religious element?

Responsibility: What is the responsibility (or responsibilities) of each character? How does each character accept/reject that responsibility? This is also a question with which characters who are not part of the Gang must deal. How do the "minor" characters deal with their responsibility?

Sacrifice: Sacrifice is a theme that runs through the series. Why is this so? What is a sacrifice? How does sacrifice function in the series? Who or what is sacrificed and for what purpose? Does the motive for sacrifice matter? What is the outcome of sacrifice? Does the outcome vary for different characters?

Sexuality: How is sexuality addressed in *Buffy*? What does each episode say about sexuality? What stance might one speculate the series takes on sexuality?

Stereotypes and conventions: What stereotypes does each episode reveal? How does each episode subvert or reinforce those stereotypes? For example, "Pangs" uses some Native American stereotypes and the conventions of the "western" film as an interrogation tool. Many episodes deal with the stereotypes and conventions of high school. Others ask about the efficacy of such conventions and stereotypes. What are the examples of such?

Conclusion

Above is only a short set of examples of the possibilities for discussion in relation to *Buffy*. The possibilities really are endless. People might ask "what intrinsic value may be found" (Durand 5) in *Buffy*. We can find much to value. Studying the series allows us to examine philosophical and literary theories in an atmosphere that may seem less threatening to the student than scrutinizing *The Faerie Queene*. Koontz, in "Heroism on the Hellmouth: Teaching Morality Through *Buffy*," says that "the shared viewing experience [of *Buffy* episodes] removes much of the apprehension students often have toward open discussion of loaded concepts such as morality" (61). Thus, Buffy can serve as a gateway to discussion of important moral and philosophical questions that require the critical thinking and assessment so valued as university, cultural, and personal qualities.

But *Buffy* may also lead to the Queen. Henry Jenkins, in *Convergence Culture: Where Old and New Media Often Collide*, says universities often miss out on the possibilities rife in pop culture, that "more focus is placed on the dangers of manipulation rather than the possibilities of participation, on restricting access — turning off the television, saying no to Nintendo — rather than in expanding skills at deploying media for one's own ends, rewriting the core stories our culture has given us" (259). We can look at Buffy as a quest story, a hero's journey, and go from her journey to the journey of Britomart and Redcrosse in *The Faerie Queene*. Thus, *Buffy* can serve as a gateway to a broader experience in the literary classics.

However, *Buffy* can also serve on its own. Jenkins further asserts that students/viewers should come to think of themselves beyond being simply manipulated by media and think of themselves as "participants and not simply as consumers, critical or otherwise" (259). Studying how to critically weigh the omnipresent material is an important tool to give our students who may be technologically savvy — and in fact blasé — but need help in learning to assess (and not simply "accept") the films, television shows, YouTube videos, and future apps that permeate their lives.

Thus, we can conclude — and I did — that teaching a class about a pop culture element can lead us to the same ends, transmitting analytic and critical abilities to students, as teaching a class with a more traditional curriculum.

Notes

1. See Emily Dial-Driver, Sally Emmons-Featherston, Jim Ford, and Carolyn Anne Taylor, eds., *The Truth of* Buffy: *Essays on Fiction Illuminating Reality*. Jefferson, NC: McFarland, 2008. Print.

2. Others who might be useful in building a class discussion about *Buffy* criticisms, feminist and otherwise, include Alessico, Appelo, Battis, Billson, Black, Dechert, DeKelf-Rittenhouse, Dial-Driver (etc.), Durand, Fowler, Fritts, Green and Yuen, Hornick, Kawal, Korsmeyer, Krzywinska, McDonald, McLaren, Mendelson, Pateman, Pender, Reiss, Resnick, Richardson and Rabb, Saxey, Schudt, Shuttleworth, South, Stokes, Stroud, Sutherland and Swan, Tabron, and West.

Works Cited

Abrams, M.H. *A Glossary of Literary Terms*. With Geoffrey Galt Harpham. 8th ed. Boston: Thomson, 2005. Print.

Alessio, Dominic. "Things Are Different Now? A Postcolonial Analysis of *Buffy the Vampire Slayer.*" *The European Legacy* 6.6 (2001): 731–40. *Academic Search Complete*. EBSCO. Web. 18 June 2007.

Anderson, Wendy. "What Would Buffy Do?" *Christian Century* 17 (May 2003): 43. Print.

Appelo, Tim. "Buffy Slays: Now What?" *Slate* 5 Nov. 2001. Web. 1 Oct. 2007.

Battis, Jes. *Blood Relations: Chosen Families in* Buffy the Vampire Slayer *and* Angel. Jefferson, NC: McFarland, 2005. Print.

Billson, Anne. Buffy the Vampire Slayer*: A Critical Reading of the Series*. London: British Film Institute, 2005.

Black, Robert A. "It's Not Homophobia, but That Doesn't Make It Right." *Dykesvision* 2002. Web. 15 Oct. 2007.

Bodger, Gwyneth. "Buffy the Feminist Slayer? Constructions of Femininity in *Buffy the Vampire Slayer.*" *Refractory: A Journal of Entertainment Media* 2 (2003). Web. 16 Aug. 2007.

Buffy the Vampire Slayer. Seasons 1–7. 1997–2003. DVD. 20th Century–Fox, 2006.

Buttsworth, Sara. "Bite Me: Buffy and the Penetration of the Gendered Warrior-Hero." *Continuum: Journal of Media and Cultural Studies* 16.2 (2002): 185–99. Print.

Culp, Christopher M. "'But ... You're Just a Girl.' The Feminine Mystique of Season Five." *Watcher Junior* 2 (July 2006). Web. 31 Aug. 2007.

Daughtey, Anne Millard. "Just a Girl: Buffy as Icon." *Reading the Slayer: An Unofficial Critical Companion to* Buffy *and* Angel. Ed. Roz Kaveney. New York: Taurus, 2002. 148–65. Print.
Dechert, S. Renee. "'My Boyfriend's in the Band!' Buffy and the Rhetoric of Music." *Fighting the Forces: What's at Stake in* Buffy the Vampire Slayer. Ed. Rhonda V. Wilcox and David Lavery. Lanham, MD: Rowman & Littlefield, 2002. 218–26. Print.
DeKelf-Rittenhouse, Diane. "Sex and the Single Vampire: The Evolution of the Vampire Lothario and Its Representation in *Buffy*." *Fighting the Forces: What's at Stake in* Buffy the Vampire Slayer. Ed. Rhonda V. Wilcox and David Lavery. Lanham, MD: Rowman & Littlefield, 2002. 143–52. Print.
Dial-Driver, Emily, Sally Emmons-Featherston, Jim Ford, and Carolyn Anne Taylor, eds. *The Truth of* Buffy: *Essays on Fiction Illuminating Reality*. Jefferson, NC: McFarland, 2008. Print.
Durand, Kevin. "Introduction." *Buffy Meets the Academy: Essays on the Episodes and Scripts as Texts*. Ed. Kevin K. Durand. Jefferson, NC: McFarland, 2009. 1–5. Print.
Fowler, Heather. "Messages about Sex and Violence in the Buffy/Spike Relationship on *Buffy the Vampire Slayer*." *Associated Content*. 1 June 2006. Web. 8 Sept. 2007.
Fritts, David. "Warrior Heroes: Buffy the Vampire Slayer and Beowulf." *Slayage* 17 5.1 (June 2005). Collins College. Web. 15 April 2006.
Greene, Richard, and Wayne Yuen. "Morality on Television." Buffy the Vampire Slayer *and Philosophy: Fear and Trembling in Sunnydale*." Ed. James B. South. Popular Culture and Philosophy. Series Editor William Irwin. Chicago: Open Court, 2003. 271–81. Print.
Greenman, Jennifer. "Witch Love Spells Death: Was the Killing of Tara on *Buffy the Vampire Slayer* a Bold Plot Move or Just Another Dead Lesbian on TV?" *Sacramento News and Review* 6 June 2002. Web. 16 Sept. 2007.
Hollows, Joanne. *Feminism, Femininity, and Popular Culture*. Manchester: Manchester University Press, 2000. Print.
Hornick, Alysa. *Buffyology: An Academic Buffy Studies and Whedonverse Bibliography*. 2005. Web. 18 Sept. 2007.
Jenkins, Henry. *Convergence Culture: Where Old and New Media Collide*. New York: New York University Press, 2006. Print.
Jowett, L. *Sex and the Slayer: A Gender Studies Primer for the* Buffy *Fan*. Middletown, CT: Wesleyan University Press, 2005. Print.
Kawal, Jason. "Should We Do What Buffy Would Do?" Buffy the Vampire Slayer *and Philosophy: Fear and Trembling in Sunnydale*. Ed. James B. South. Chicago: Open Court, 2003. 149–59. Print.
Koontz, K. Dale. "Heroism on the Hellmouth: Teaching Morality Through *Buffy*." *Buffy in the Classroom: Essays on Teaching with the Vampire Slayer*. Jefferson, NC: McFarland, 2010. 61–72. Print.
Korsmeyer, Carolyn. "Passion and Action: In and Out of Control." Buffy the Vampire Slayer *and Philosophy: Fear and Trembling in Sunnydale*. Ed. James B. South. Popular Culture and Philosophy. Series Editor William Irwin. Chicago: Open Court, 2003. 160–72. Print.
Krzywinska, Tanya. "Hubble-Bubble, Herbs, and Grimoires: Magic, Manichaenism, and Witchcraft in Buffy." *Fighting the Forces: What's at Stake in* Buffy the Vampire Slayer." Ed. Ronda Wilcox and David Lavery. Lanham, MD: Rowman & Littlefield, 2001. 178–94. Print.
McDonald, Paul F. *The Goddess and Her Gift: An Analysis of the Fifth Season of* Buffy the Vampire Slayer. 29 Sept. 2001. Web. 19 Aug. 2007.
McLaren, Scott. "The Evolution of Joss Whedon's Vampire Mythology and the Ontology of the Soul." *Slayage: The Online International Journal of Buffy Studies* 18 5.2 (2005). Web. 8 Sept. 2007.
Mendlesohn, Farah. "Surpassing the Love of Vampires." *Fighting the Forces*. Ed. Rhonda V. Wilcox and David Lavery. Lanham, MD: Rowman & Littlefield, 2002. 45–60. Print.
Pateman, Matthew. *The Aesthetics of Culture in* Buffy the Vampire Slayer. Jefferson, NC: McFarland, 2006. Print.
Pender, Patricia. "'I'm Buffy, and You're ... History': The Postmodern Politics of *Buffy*." *Fighting the Forces: What's at Stake in* Buffy the Vampire Slayer. Ed. Rhonda V. Wilcox and David Lavery. Lanham, MD: Rowman & Littlefield, 2002. 35–44. Print.

Reiss, Jana. *What Would Buffy Do? The Vampire as Spiritual Guide.* San Francisco: Jossey-Bass, 2004. Print.
Resnick, Laura. "The Good, the Bad, and the Ambivalent." *Seven Seasons of* Buffy: *Science Fiction and Fantasy Authors Discuss Their Favorite Television Show.* Ed. Glenn Yeffeth. Dallas: BenBella, 2003. 54–64. Print.
Richardson, J. Michael, and J. Douglas Rabb. *The Existential Joss Whedon: Evil and Human Freedom in* Buffy the Vampire Slayer, Angel, Firefly *and* Serenity. Jefferson, NC: McFarland, 2007. Print.
Saxey, Esther. "Staking a Claim: The Series and Its Slash Fan-Fiction." *Reading the Vampire Slayer: An Unofficial Critical Companion to* Buffy *and* Angel. Ed. Roz Kaveney. New York: Taurus Parke, 2002. 187–210. Print.
Schudt, Karl. "Also Sprach Faith: The Problem of the Happy Rogue Vampire Slayer." Buffy the Vampire Slayer *and Philosophy: Fear and Trembling in Sunnydale.* Ed. James B. South. Popular Culture and Philosophy. Series Editor William Irwin. Chicago: Open Court, 2003. 20–34. Print.
Shuttleworth, Ian. "They Always Mistake Me for the Character I Play! Transformation, Identity, and Role-Playing in the *Buffy*verse (and a Defense of Fine Acting)." *Reading the Vampire Slayer: An Unofficial Critical Companion to* Buffy *and* Angel. Ed. Roz Kaveney. New York: Taurus Parke, 2002. 211–36. Print.
South, James. "On the Philosophical Consistency of Season Seven: or, 'It's Not about Right, Not about Wrong.'" *Slayage* 13–14 4.1–2 (Oct. 2004). Collins College. Web. 3 May 2006.
South, James B., ed. Buffy the Vampire Slayer *and Philosophy: Fear and Trembling in Sunnydale.* Popular Culture and Philosophy. Series Editor William Irwin. Chicago: Open Court, 2003. Print.
Stevenson, Gregory. *Televised Morality: The Case of* Buffy the Vampire Slayer. Dallas: Hamilton, 2003. Print.
Stokes, Mike. "Absolute Power." *Buffy the Vampire Slayer Magazine* 10 (July 2000): 18–19. Print.
Stroud, Scott R. "A Kantian Analysis of Moral Judgment in *Buffy the Vampire Slayer.*" Buffy the Vampire Slayer *and Philosophy: Fear and Trembling in Sunnydale.* Ed. James B. South. Popular Culture and Philosophy. Series Editor William Irwin. Chicago: Open Court, 2003. 185–94. Print.
Sutherland, Sharon, and Sarah Swan. "The Rule of Prophecy: Source of Law in the City of *Angel.*" *Reading* Angel*: The TV Spin-Off with a Soul.* Ed. Stacey Abbott. New York: Taurus, 2005. 133–45. Print.
Tabron, Judith. "Girl on Girl Politics: Willow/Tara and New Approaches to Media Fandom." *Slayage* 13–14 (Oct. 2004). Web. 9 Sept. 2007.
Vint, Sherryl. "'Killing Us Softly': A Feminist Search for the 'Real Buffy.'" *Slayage* 5 (9 December 2002). Web. 8 Aug. 2007.
West, Dave. "Concentrate on the Kicking Moxie: Buffy and East Asian Cinema." *Reading the Vampire Slayer: An Unofficial Critical Companion to* Buffy *and* Angel. Ed. Roz Kaveney. New York: Taurus Parke, 2002. 166–86. Print.
Wilcox, Rhonda. "There Will Never Be a Very Special *Buffy*: Buffy and the Monsters of Life." *Slayage: The Online International Journal of* Buffy *Studies* 5 (May 2002). Web. 27 Aug. 2007.
Wilcox, Rhonda. *Why Buffy Matters: The Art of* Buffy the Vampire Slayer. New York: I.B. Taurus, 2005. Print.
Wilcox, Rhonda, and David Lavery, eds. *Fighting the Forces: What's at Stake in* Buffy the Vampire Slayer. Lanham, MD: Rowman & Littlefield, 2002. Print.

Buffy Versus Bella: Teaching About Place and Gender

JACQUELINE BACH, JESSICA BROUSSARD
AND MELANIE K. HUNDLEY

Since the publication of the Harry Potter and Twilight sagas, fantastical young adult literature continues to dominate bookshelves and, consequently, the way we teach the adolescent literature course at the university level. Works of fantasy, once derided as less powerful or less literary than more traditional fiction forms, are now taught alongside works of realistic fiction, historical nonfiction, and, increasingly, graphic novels. Fantasy literature does not accept the world as it is; rather, it imagines different possibilities for what it means to be a hero, to be a force in the world, to fight for good. Fantasy literature often confronts binary positions and allows characters to be more than they think they can be.

These representations call for a rigorous examination of how we are to treat these texts with our students. We believe recent works, such as *Buffy the Vampire Slayer* and *Twilight* are geared toward a female audience, as opposed to the male-oriented works of the past, changing the way we regard the tradition of the female in this genre. Tamora Pierce, author of a series of fantastical literature set in the world of Tortall, argues that "Fantasy, more than any other genre, is a literature of empowerment.... In fantasy ... however short, fat, unbeautiful, weak, dreamy, or unlearned individuals may be, they find a realm in which these things are negated by strength. The catch — and there's always a catch — is that empowerment brings trials" (51). Fantastical fiction, with its emphasis on characters who are more than they seem at first glance, provides opportunities for challenges to gender roles. Buffy and Bella are two notable protagonists in this field who do not give in to previous representations of women as side-kicks or damsels in distress. According to Kellner, Buffy and Bella provide "a richness of allegorical structure and content in these shows [which] allows the production of meanings and identities beyond more conventional media culture" (56). In particular, given this representation, the focus on gender seems especially important. Because adolescent literature courses often focus on race, class, gender and sexual identity, we find that focusing on the various textual representations of these female protagonists in childhood and adolescent settings, such as school and the prom, helps our students (re)consider the assumptions they and society have about these places.

Buffy and Sunnydale, California; Bella and Forks, Washington

Adolescent media is full of female characters who are closely identified with the places in which they live; these places, in turn, play a large role in defining their characters. Contrary to popular opinion that adolescents must leave their homes in order to find themselves through diverse experiences, these young women show that one can understand oneself by staying put. Buffy and Bella choose to make Sunnydale and Forks their homes after they lose the homes of their childhoods; the move to these new homes signals profound changes in their lives. The characters experience first loves and loss, and discover their own powers, both natural and supernatural, upon encountering the fantastical in each of their communities. Their adventures lie not in the larger, wider world but in the alternative and strange worlds of their homes. The two characters often challenge the gender expectations associated with places like home, school, and work. These representations of gender and place can challenge our students' own assumptions of present and future identity and its relationship with place.

Staying Put: Why Buffy and Bella Don't Leave

In this chapter, we consider approaches to teaching these texts and ask students to consider the rigid associations that often come with gender and place. The fantastical elements in these texts serve to make readers look for the hidden in their own worlds. This chapter examines teaching fantastical texts in which teenage girls negotiate their gender identities in somewhat oppressive small towns; the adolescent literature course with its focus on race, class, gender, and sexual identity provides a place for this to happen.

Feminist geographers, such as McDowell, help question the notion that the home is a haven for women, that the work space perpetuates gender division, and that given a choice, women will choose safety and security over adventure and personal freedom. Their work, when applied to fantastical young adult literature, demonstrates that adolescent males take up a quest which leads them away from home, while adolescent females tend to stay home. Although there are female characters in adolescent literature who participate in quests much like male protagonists (Alanna, Daine, and Keladry in Pierce's Tortall series, for example), their experiences tend to highlight the ways in which they, as females, approach the quest differently than males would, but with equal or sometimes more success. This dichotomy — the feeling that adventure must take place away from home rather than at home — illustrates the ongoing struggles to show strong females in empowered roles. The increasing presence of adventures or growth opportunities for female characters that do not require they follow traditionally-established male patterns demonstrates a growing maturity in the genre. Place and its importance in identity development is being explored in nuanced ways; no longer does a character have to make a break with a home setting in order to be empowered, rather there is opportunity for empowerment within the home setting. Harry Potter and Percy Jackson leave their homes to learn about themselves but Buffy Summers and Bella Swan do not.

One potential reason for this shifting approach to place in fantastical literature is due to the willingness for authors to play with traditional expectations for settings. As Wood points out, it was Anne Rice who was responsible for popularizing the change of setting in vampire novels from a gothic one to less foreboding ones. Rain-drenched Forks is less forbidding than a crumbling castle on a moor and sun-drenched Sunnydale seems an unlikely location for vampires. Bella and Buffy's stories both begin with their moving to new towns; McDowell notes that "studying those in transit ... in the analysis of flux and fluidity, in ways of becoming rather than being a woman, in the making and remaking of identities" (205) that "supports feminist notions that women's identities are unfixed" (205). They move at pivotal times in their development; their previous homes are frequently juxtaposed with their new homes, highlighting the ways in which their identities were fixed in one location but are potentially more fluid in another.

Two Girls in Love with Vampires: Buffy Versus Bella

The movie *Buffy the Vampire Slayer* was written by Joss Whedon and directed by Fran Rubel Kuzui in 1992. In an interview about the genesis of the idea for the leading character, Whedon explained, "The first thing I ever thought of when I thought of *Buffy: The Movie* was the little ... blonde girl who goes into a dark alley and gets killed, in every horror movie. The idea of *Buffy* was to subvert that idea, that image, and create someone who was a hero where she had always been a victim" (Whedon, "Commentary"). Whedon's Buffy is certainly no victim — she slays vampires, eliminates demons, and, in the end, triumphs over even the obstacles in her life. In 1997, the Warner Bros. television channel, the WB, expanded on the film's mythology in the series *Buffy the Vampire Slayer*, which aired in the United States between March of 1997 and May of 2001 (Kellner 60). In 2001 UPN, now the CW (a merged station between WB and UPN), picked up the show for its final two seasons. Like vampires who are written as the ultimate society outcast, Buffy (and Bella) closely identify themselves as outcasts in spite of their attempts to be part of their communities.

Buffy Summers moves to Sunnydale after a disastrous school year in Los Angeles. During this school year, she discovered that she was the Chosen One whose life calling was to slay vampires. While many teens would be thrilled with the onset of superpowers, Buffy just wants to be normal. She was happy with her life as pampered daughter, cheerleader, and social butterfly. Her new role changes all of that. *Buffy*, the television series, is considered by some as a tribute to the outcast teenager. Millman describes the show as "an ode to misfits, a healing vision of the weird, different and marginalized finding their place in the world and ultimately saving it" and Lavery calls it a "surprising series about outsiders who routinely save the world" (Wilcox and Lavery 254). Buffy and her friends, though frequently seen as outsiders and misfits in their school, routinely save the school, their peers, and the world. Bella, like Buffy, is surrounded by friends who do not fit into traditional school or community settings but who, routinely, take on challenges to that community.

Stephenie Meyer's four-part vampire saga, *Twilight*, *Eclipse*, *New Moon* and *Breaking Dawn*, made the *New York Times* Best Seller List for Children's Series Books and incited a large interest in young adult readers looking for more vampire literature. These novels joined a series of notable titles, including L.J. Smith's *The Vampire Diaries* and Melissa De la Cruz's *Blue Bloods*. Meyer's character, 17-year-old Isabella "Bella" Swan, moves to Forks, Washington, to live with her father Charlie after her mom remarries. Her mother's new husband plays minor league baseball and Bella moves so her mother can travel with him. At her new school, Bella becomes interested in a group of outcasts, one of whom is Edward Cullen, a vampire. The story soon involves ancient feuds between vampires and werewolves — and most notably, the love triangle among Bella, Edward, and Jacob Black, a childhood friend turned werewolf. While the action across the four novels takes the characters around the world, most of the story takes place in Forks, Washington. All four books have been made into movies, and *Twilight* has been adapted into a graphic novel.

Buffy Summers is a combination of Barbie-doll beautiful and Xena-warrior-princess strong. She is a petite blonde with fabulous fashion sense who employs her inherent superpowers to save the world. For all of her talents, she seems to feel as though she is incomplete; she wants to be more than the girl who knows her way around a crossbow. Buffy just wants to be a normal teen; she wants to return to what she was in her previous home — a popular, perky cheerleader whose biggest worry centered on what to wear. Buffy's responsibilities as Slayer force her to carry the survival of the world on her shoulders. Though initially resistant to her role as hero, she chooses to accept it. Sunnydale, her home, is both the place she resists and the place she embraces. It's "two hours from Neiman Marcus," complains Buffy in the first episode, "Welcome to the Hellmouth," but she soon defends its schools; teen hangout, The Bronze; and her home from the numerous "big bads" that help her keep her title "Buffy the Vampire Slayer."

Bella Swan, on the other hand, spends most of her time being rescued, even though she "want[s] to be Superman too" (Meyer, *Twilight* 474). She describes herself as not graceful; her clumsiness and frequent falls become something that the people around her comment on frequently. She drives a manual transmission truck and spends a lot of time in the second novel rebuilding and riding a motorbike. Bella was born in Forks, but left it with her mother when her parents divorced. On the first page of *Twilight*, she reveals her feelings about Forks: "It rains on this inconsequential town more than any other place in the United States of America. It was from this town and its gloomy, omnipresent shade that my mother escaped with me when I was only a few months old" (3). Yet, in spite of her seeming distaste of Forks, Bella chooses to live the remainder of her ultimately immortal life in a small cottage in the woods surrounding the town.

In the rest of this chapter, we combine the strategy of comparing print texts with visual ones as a means of discussing the role the locations of our childhood and adolescence play in the formation of our gender identities, community responsibilities, and work and home. Each section begins with a theoretical discussion of place and gender and then moves to a description of a teaching strategy.

Bella Doesn't Do Ballet: Childhood, Nostalgia, and Place

Teachers who encourage the reading of *Twilight* often choose to draw attention to the ways in which Meyer uses language and literary elements, whether it is Bull who focuses on Meyer's use of figurative language or Bruett who focuses on Edward as a Byronic Hero or Robillard who focuses on diction. These teachers examine elements that capture the essence and angst of what it means to be an adolescent. Many consider adolescence to be a time of storm and stress (Hall). Teens do stupid things: they bend or break laws, they date the wrong people, they throw temper tantrums when they do not get their own ways. However, both of the heroines in consideration here are youths by definition of biological age alone. They act as adults. Buffy continually puts herself in danger as only a teen can; however, she does it for the greater good of her community and often the world. Bella acts on a much smaller scale in the initial installment of the Twilight saga. She acts on behalf of her family, both her biological family and her future family of the Cullen clan. According to Valentine, "If we think of childhood not in terms of a biologically defined age group but rather as a performative or processual identity" ("Boundary Crossing" 18), both girls are very adult, even though most of the adults in their worlds do not understand what the girls are doing or why they are doing it.

Unlike Buffy, who has the support of several adults in her life, Bella exists in a more difficult transitional space as she does not have adults there for the bulk of her exploits. Edward, though older than Bella in age, behaves both as an adult and as a teen; he pouts, he tries to get his own way, but he also tries to help Bella think through the consequences of her actions. In addition, he makes choices for what he considers to be Bella's own good. Bella's mother is in Florida for much of the first book/film. Charlie, her father, is often unaware of what Bella is doing. While he attempts to be the father that she needs him to be, and tries to give her boundaries, and introduce her to friends he deems appropriate, like Jacob and the other members of the Native American tribe of the area, she has been previously given too much freedom and generally continues with her planned courses of action. Bella is also not afforded another benefit that Buffy has been given, superpowers. This lack of physical power both acts as the reason why she is in need of constant *supervision* by Edward, and the remainder of the Cullen clan, and why she is able to be Edward's "savior" in a more emotional sense. She is also able to save her parents by protecting them "from information which they may not be able to 'cope' with" (Valentine, *Public Space* 67). The lack of physical power or grace does not stop Bella from attempting to save her loved ones.

In order to protect her mother, Bella rushes to a special place from her childhood at the end of the first book. Alice, one of the Cullen clan, has a vision of the ballet studio where Bella first attempted to learn to dance. The dance studio was significant to Bella and we, as readers, learn about it for the first time then, when Bella traces her fingers over Alice's drawing. Falling into a sort of "reverie" (Meyers 420), Bella describes where all the items in the studio should have been and how they have changed. In the film, Bella recognizes "an archway" which triggers her memory of the dance studio and identifies the Hunter's, James's, location. Philo argues that "certain spaces are likely to be triggers [of reverie] because something about them returns to us the sensations and even contents of these childhood moments" (14). Alice asks Bella if there is a reason to go to the place, if there were some connection to this studio for her: "No," Bella says, "I was a terrible dancer — they always put me in the back for recitals" (Meyer 420). According to Philo, "in any one of us there are different childhood*s*, varying senses of both who we *were* as a child and who we could now have *become* had we been able to pursue different trajectories out of childhood" (14–15). We might speculate on the question: If Bella had been successful as a dancer, would she dress more stereotypically female, be less excited about her truck, or want to go to prom like her both human and vampire female friends?

Pas de Deux: The Metaphor of the Ballet Studio

With our students, we explore how Bella's lack of dance ability and her disassociation with traditional female roles influences her perception of her own femininity, manifesting in her physical clumsiness and lack of grace: "The dancer has been seen as femininity objectified, the embodiment of patriarchal ideology.... The *pas de deux* [a dancers' duet in which the male dancer literally presents the female dancer to the audience], for the ballerina and her lead male partner, embodies the traditional attributes of femininity and masculinity" (Carter 294). In this pose, "she appears to be supported, manipulated, by him; he displays her to the spectator" (Carter 294). In turn, she "conceal[s] her strength, she gives the appearance of fragility and moves with her own kinesphere, the private space around her body" (Carter 294).Then in visual contrast, "he demonstrates his strength and power with soaring virtuosic leaps across the public space of the stage" (Carter 294).

In relation to the topic of dance, Bella, though initially resistant to the idea, agrees to attend prom with Edward. While Edward and Bella are at the prom and he lifts her while dancing, Bella's lack of grace and athletic ability are evident, as is the male dominance. Dance imagery continues in the novel, as, on the way to Phoenix and the dance studio, Bella describes an imagined moment of meeting Edward at the airport. Her description of their meeting sounds much like a dance; she says, "I visualized how I would stand on my toes.... How quickly, how gracefully he would move through the crowds of people separating us. And then I would run to close those last few steps between us ... and I would be in his marble arms" (Meyer 440). Ballet dancers balance on their toes; female dancers run and launch themselves in the air, trusting their male partners to catch them safely in their arms.

Later, the fight scene in the studio between James, Bella, and Edward is a dark and distorted *pas de deux* with the partners constantly changing. It begins with James emotionally positioning Bella on the *stage*—luring her to the studio, then cornering her. In the text, she runs, knowing fully the futility of her attempt to escape. James leaps from a crouched position to stand in front of her, just as the male partners do in ballet; however, his leaps are more than human. Once in front of her he delivers a "crushing blow" (Meyer 449) to Bella's chest, so fast she is not sure if it was his hand or foot; she flies across the room and smashes into a mirror. In a vain attempt to escape, she weakly crawls on her hands and knees. James breaks her leg by stepping on it, leaving her desperate and limp. He then stands over her and nudges her broken leg, letting her scream in agony before raising her hand and biting.

In the film, the scene is visually more intense because the males in the scene continue to show masculine strength and agility by throwing each other through windows and mirrors. After Bella is bitten, the male dominance continues and Bella is left to writhe on the floor both with broken bones and with vampire venom coursing through her veins. As the younger Cullens tear James apart and burn the pieces, Carlisle holds Bella down. Edward comes to the final rescue as he removes the venom from her blood. At the end of this scene, Bella, exhausted from the fight and in pain, is picked up by Edward, "in his arms, cradled against his chest—floating, all the pain gone" (Meyer 457). Her body is controlled by her male lead much like a ballerina's.

With the emphasis on the physicality of the performers, it is easy to forget Bella's strength and her displays of personal power. Yes, Bella is on the floor, weak, fragile, broken, bleeding, and crying out in pain, but all the while she is still doing all that she can to protect her family. She suffers through seemingly intolerable agony so that others will be safe. Her emotional strength is evident in the text but less so in the film version.

Viewing this scene through a feminist lens, we can see both the fulfillment of and challenge to traditional female roles. Bella, though lacking in grace and physical strength, is not necessarily the victim here. She chooses to confront Hunter/James, realizing that she is not as strong as he is. She still has the courage to show up, to go to the ballet studio even though she has not been successful there previously. Bella is not good at being a "girl." The ballet studio is a feminine site for most characters; however, in this novel, it is a space that is dominated by the male characters rather than the female characters. This forces us to rethink notions of feminine spaces by examining Meyer's use of phrases and clauses to recreate, albeit an extremely bloody one, a ballet. Bella, who is not good at fulfilling traditional female stereotypes, makes a stand in this ballet studio, forcing the men to battle in and around traditionally female accessories (mirrors, ballet bars, etc.) in a traditionally female location.

However, even with this identity-altering experience in her history, Bella is still secure in her definition of femininity. Bella is her chosen name. Isabella is what her parents named her but like so many teens, she chooses a name for herself, *Bella*—which means beautiful in Italian. She could have chosen *Isa* which is feminine or she could have gone more with the more androgynous *Izzy*. Isabella (Isabella Duncan) is the name of a famous dancer; in choosing Bella rather than Isabella, she is taking one more step away from the female-as-dancer identity to find a different kind of femininity.

Part of what makes a comparison between a written text and a visual one, like film or graphic novel, so crucial to the development of critical thinking skills is that "there is no such thing as a straightforward 'translation' or adaptation of a text" (Clayton 130). Students must develop strategies to assimilate "re-present[ations of] the text in significant ways, working to produce new meanings which allow for re-interpretation of the source material" (Clayton 130). Naturally, changes are going to be essential when compressing or expanding textual ideas, and it behooves the audience to understand why scenes are written differently, why characters and their relationships morph, and why plot lines may be altered completely. Understanding why these changes are made or what they mean in the context of the format can help audiences recognize how written devices can translate to the screen and change or enhance the original text.

In the Classroom

In this scenario, students would be asked to read both the visual text of the film *Twilight* and the text by Stephenie Meyer. In the dual versions of the scenes, audiences become aware of the different visions of strength, grace, and age and the impact of *not* doing ballet. After watching the scene from the film and reading the scene in the text, the students have seen two very different takes on the same events. Here they should be able not only to see the differences between the events that took place — Bella's experiences in the text versus Edward's in the film — but also what this juxtaposition of scenes means both personally and as a group. We have included a matrix for leading a possible discussion on the two scenes.

Twilight: Interpreting the Fight Scene

Bella's confrontation with the Hunter and her subsequent rescue by Edward are interpreted differently in the *Twilight* novel from the interpretation in the *Twilight* movie. Compare the two scenes and consider which scene shows a more empowered Bella. What is the same about the scenes? What is different?

Twilight Novel: Fight Scene

- How is Bella lured to the location?
- Does the location have special significance to Bella?
- Is the location representative of a traditional gender expectation? If yes, how? Does Bella meet the traditional gender expectation?

Twilight Movie: Fight Scene

- How is Bella lured to the location? Does the location have special significance to Bella?
- Is the location representative of a traditional gender expectation? If yes, how? Does Bella meet the traditional gender expectation?

Twilight Novel: Fight Scene

- Consider the physical positions of the fighters. How does the fight begin? Where is Bella? What happens to her body in the course of the fight? Where is she physically during most of the fight?
- At what point in the fight does Edward enter the fray? What happens to Bella?
- Bella is injured. What happens after this? How does Edward interact with her?
- Based on your reading of the text, what do you think of Bella? Of her rescuer? Of the aftermath? How does the text support your reading of Bella?
- Does the scene fit with the overall interpretation of the character and story by the author? Is the author consistent in her presentation of the characters and the characters' relationships?

Twilight Movie: Fight Scene

- Consider the physical positions of the fighters. How does the fight begin? Where is Bella? What happens to her body in the course of the fight? Where is she physically during most of the fight?
- At what point in the fight does Edward enter the fray? What happens to Bella?
- Bella is injured. What happens after this? How does Edward interact with her?
- Based on your "reading" of the scene, what do you think of Bella? Of her rescuer? Of the aftermath? How do the visual cue and clues (lighting, camera angles, jump cuts, use of color) support your reading/viewing of the scene?
- Does the scene fit with the overall interpretation of the character and story by the director? Is there something missing or added that changes something significant in the characters or the characters' relationships?

Now that you have compared the scenes, consider which of the scenes you think showed Bella as more empowered. Construct an argument, either print or visual, that develops and supports your argument. Use support from both the text and the film.

Mirrors play a role in both the novel and the movie version of the fight scene. In both scenes, Bella sees herself reflected in the glass. In the novel, Bella's body shatters the mirrors. In the movie, she sees Edward as he fights and herself as she is dying. Mirrors are also part of multiple mythologies—including vampire lore. Below is a sample writing prompt for a parallel poem that incorporates the idea of mirroring:

> For the first part of this writing task, you will compose a poem that shows how you think the world sees you or how the world sees Bella. For the second part, you will compose a parallel poem that shows how you see yourself or how Bella sees herself. You will keep the structure and most of the words of the first poem and change

only a few words or lines. [We have included an example of a student piece written in response to this prompt[1]].

We Are Family: Responsibility to One's Community

A character's relationship to his or her community is another topic we discuss in our adolescent literature courses, as young adult authors explore their protagonist's relationship with his or her town or neighborhood. In *Gender, Identity and Place*, McDowell asks if, in this globalized world, people still feel a responsibility to their local areas (3). Local areas, too, are regulated by power relations which determine who can belong, thereby supporting a particular set of beliefs, behaviors, and customs. When gender is seen as binary, places too become gendered: masculine being outside, public, and work; feminine being private, inside, and home. So, what does this mean for Buffy and Bella who feel strong ties to their local communities and ultimately choose to stay (as in Bella's case) forever in these small towns or can only be forced out by their demise (as in Buffy's case). And, how are we to understand their relationship to their schools?

Because school is an integral part of an adolescent's life, it is an integral part of much of fantastical literature. This literature often creates and extends a metaphor for school — school is hell, school is a refuge (Harry Potter), school is a sanctuary (Percy Jackson), school is a musical (*Glee*, *High School Musical*), school is a jail (Hawkins' *Hex Hall*), school is an institution — in all of these metaphorical incarnations, school is a place that shapes part of the character's identity. Literature and pop culture create images of school that reify, romanticize, or contradict how adolescents see school.

School, a significant location in an adolescent's life, is a place of where Buffy and Bella spend a great deal of time. In these places, they meet their friends, develop social connections, and resist the more traditional gendered expectations. They are both part of and outside of the school culture. The metaphor that "high school is hell" is made literal in Buffy's world. When Buffy is kicked out of her L.A. high school, she and her mother move to Sunnydale. Sunnydale High, her new high school, is built over a "hellmouth" and there is daily struggle with demons, both real and imaginary. When Bella sees Forks High School for the first time, she asks, "Where was the feel of the institution? ... Where were the chain-link fences, the metal detectors?" (Meyer, *Twilight* 13). These questions, though whimsical, signal her expectations of school — it is an institution, a place where actions and behaviors are controlled by someone else. For Buffy, high school is hell; for Bella, high school is an institution.

School Is Hell

Sunnydale is the site of both evil and support for Buffy. She finds strength in the support of Willow and Xander, her closest friends, and Giles, her "Watcher" and pseudo-father figure. She is not a strong student, so school is often a site in which she feels inferior. In her previous school, she was a popular cheerleader with an active social life. In Sunnydale, she is an outsider with few close friends. Buffy struggles with her desire to be a normal teen girl in contrast to her role as the Slayer. While other high school girls are looking for something that marks them as extraordinary, Buffy searches for something to make her like everyone else. A conversation from "Homecoming" between Buffy and Cordelia highlights this conflict:

> CORDELIA: I don't even get why you care about Homecoming when you're doing stuff like this.
>
> BUFFY: Because this is all I do. This is what my life is. You couldn't understand. I just thought ... Homecoming Queen. I could pick up a yearbook someday and say, "I was there. I went to high school, I had friends, and, for one moment, I got to live in the world." And there'd be proof, proof that I was chosen for something other than this. Besides, [pumps the rifle] I look cute in a tiara.

Buffy wants the rites of passage that other teens have; she wants school to be something other than hell. School for most adolescents is the place where they spend the majority of their time. It is a central place in Buffy's life; she goes there for eight hours every day, for training and research before and after school hours, and for school events. Many of the epic battles in Buffy's life occur on school grounds. In spite of the way that school is a location of conflict and danger for Buffy, she continues to go, she continues to fight the battles, and she continues to survive. Buffy survives high school and demon attacks much the same way that most high school students do — she shows up, she participates as much as she can, and she has close friends who are there to support her and to make her laugh. There is, of course, an epic battle on graduation day. Oz, a friend of Buffy, tells her, "Take a moment to deal with this. We survived." Buffy replies that it "was a hell of a battle." Oz says, "Not the battle. High school" ("Graduation Day").

Although school is a daily struggle for Buffy, it is also the location of many of her greatest adventures and the site of most of her physical and emotional growth. She does not have to leave Sunnydale to engage in epic battles or to make choices to save the world. School, for Buffy, is a place that demonstrates her own duality; it is the location that shows her as both a typical high school student trying to fit in, to learn, and to make friends and as a warrior fighting to slay demons, to rescue her friends, and to save the world.

School as Institution

Like Buffy, Bella spends a great deal of her time at school. She sees school as an institution in the lives of teens. She doesn't feel as though she fits in and, unlike Buffy, makes no real effort to be a part of the community of Forks High School. She has friends there; but, until her relationship with Edward develops, she doesn't put much effort into any of her relationships. Bella is a better student, academically, than Buffy. While Buffy spends a great deal of time in the library at Sunnydale High School, she only checks out one book (a book of Emily Dickinson's poetry) and she does this to impress a boy. Bella is clearly a reader. She talks about the texts she read in her previous English classes and professes a love for Jane Austen. Much like many girls in high school, she is a quietly successful student and performs the role of "good student" as a way to keep herself invisible. Bella understands the rules and roles of high school and is aware of them, even when she does not meet those expectations. She goes to class and she does her work. She does not, however, actively participate in the other rituals of high school (homecoming, prom, etc.). Although she attends prom, it is not by her choice. She attends in tennis shoes and a borrowed dress.

In the Classroom

School as a place is easy to identify; school as a cultural concept that helps shape our identity is more challenging to identify. In order to help students connect with the ways in which school shapes the identity of characters, it is useful for them to think about and discuss the ways in which school shaped them. Place, though frequently difficult to pinpoint, is important for examining the ways in which it helps shape a character's identity and choices, for what it makes possible in the life of the character, and for what it limits.

Consider using the following observations when thinking about the space/place of school with students:

- Although the physical shapes of schools are different region to region, there are certain commonalities — classrooms, black/white boards, lunchrooms, gyms, libraries, etc. These are distinctive physical features with cultural expectations attached to them. List the physical features of Buffy's and Bella's schools. What do they reveal?
- The people within the physical space of school are divided into groups and subgroups. The groups and subgroups often attach themselves to particular areas — band students frequently hang out near the band rooms, drama students may choose to hang out near the theater. Common locations — cafeterias, libraries — are sites where these groups meet. What groups are visible in these locations in these works? Where do the protagonists fit in?

- School is a place that often has its own language. Groups and subgroups often have slang particular to them. Examine the different types of language used in these works. Perhaps focus on one exchange (for example, between an adult and an adolescent). What do we learn about these characters through their use of language?
- Navigating the multiple locations and groups within a school is often part of a character's challenge. The choice to embrace, challenge, resist, or escape particular elements of school will shape how a character develops. Think about ones that are usually tied to one's gender identity, such as the bathroom/locker room.
- Although Buffy and Bella engage differently with school, it is still a large part of their identities. What are the locations in their respective schools that they share? Which locations are unique to Buffy or Bella?

That Special Night: The Prom

One point of entry into this large subgenre of fantastical young adult fiction is to examine the role transitional places play in the gender identity of its characters. Place, here defined as "made through power relations which construct the rules which define boundaries" (McDowell 4), includes high school proms, which transform ordinary places, like school gymnasiums into other places with their own rules and codes of conduct, especially in its rigid gender roles for males and females (for example, in most "real-life" areas in the current climate couples must be male-female or controversy results). Overstreet argues that teenagers are partly fascinated with these vampire tales and the possibilities of "escape and growth" found in the stories of humans "who associate with these powerful creatures" (13). Paying attention to where those events, which mark milestones in adolescent lives, take place is one way to question stereotypical depictions found in this genre. When students situate novels like *Twilight* (and shows like *Buffy*) within the genres of both young adult literature and vampire tales, those discussions can lead to deeper reflection about significant symbolism and metaphoric meaning—and a good place to start is the high school prom.

In "The Prom," Buffy discovers that someone is planning to set a pack of "hellhounds" on Sunnydale High School's prom. After hearing the Scooby Gang contemplate not attending their prom because they will need to help prevent mayhem, Buffy exclaims, "I'm going to give you all a nice fun normal evening if I have to kill every person on the face of the earth to do it." Although she tells Angel, her vampire quasi-boyfriend, she's attending the prom strictly in "chaperone capacity," Buffy attends the last moments of her prom after disposing of the hellhounds, and she also experiences the perfect prom night she hoped her actions would ensure for the rest of her classmates. They award her the Class Protector Award — the first one ever, and Angel makes an appearance for the quintessential slow dance.

Bella doesn't intend to attend her prom because she is disgusted by what it stands for — the same reasons why Buffy seeks to protect it. Instead, Edward, her vampire boyfriend, insists that she attend. In the film, right before Edward and Bella leave for the prom, Charlie and Edward face each other across the kitchen table. They get up and as they watch Bella descends the stairs, her cast noticeable. Edward says, "I'll take care of her, Chief Swan" to which Bella's father replies, "Uh, huh, I've heard that before." From what Edward will protect Bella is unclear because, after a very civil conversation with Jacob, the rest of the evening is routine-prom: pictures, DJ, slow dancing. Perhaps Edward meant he'd protect Bella from himself as the film closes on the two of them dancing, he having refused making her a vampire. However, the film shows the viewer that trouble is indeed waiting for Bella, as Victoria (whose lover was killed by the Cullen clan) has been watching them in their idyllic scene.

English teacher Candence Robillard was surprised to find that her high school students found nothing questionable about Bella and Edward's relationship. She reflects, "It seemed normal to them that a girl would alter almost every area of her life for a boyfriend" (14). It wasn't until she asked them to think about the traditional narratives found in romance novels and gothic literature that "they began to notice (if not yet to question) the use of such a paradigm in literature intended for young women" (14). Examining Bella and Buffy's experiences with prom illustrates how they "are able to enjoy a type of independence, free of supervision, that they are denied on a day-to-day basis" (Best 118). While prom is a gendered space, it is also a place in which both these characters choose to embrace or resist traditional expectations, another point for class discussion.

In the Classroom

For this activity, students can watch the last half of *Buffy*'s "The Prom," beginning with Scene 9, "Caught in the Act," and the last twenty or so minutes of *Twilight*, starting with Scene 22, "An Important Rite of Passage") and fill in the viewing chart below:

In her book *Prom Night: Youth, Schools, and Popular Culture*, Amy Best observes that proms, like high school graduations are important rites of passage; however, "to what precisely would it be a rite of passage?" (2). On the following chart, note the various representations of each of the proms found in *Buffy the Vampire Slayer* and *Twilight*.

Prom Scene Component	***Buffy the Vampire Slayer***	***Twilight***
Soundtrack (What songs are playing and what might they convey?)		
Setting (Are there themes to the proms?)		
Boundaries/ Rules (Who are the chaperones? What checkpoints are in place?)		
Style of Attire (What are the males and females wearing that stand out? Why?)		
Role of the supernatural (Are the fantastical elements observed by the other students? Is there a risk to them?)		

Discuss the following questions:

1. What do Buffy and Bella's attitudes toward prom reveal about their characters? Do they support, oppose, or complicate stereotypical girls' attitudes toward prom?
2. Now, answer the same question from Angel and Edward's point of view. Think about other proms, including your own (if you attended yours). To what is prom "a rite of passage"?

Best, who conducted research on proms, identifies several characteristics common to most proms and we use her findings to help students unpack the expected gender roles in this formal place and how Bella and Buffy negotiate those expectations.

Conclusion

Whether you choose to design an entire course based on fantastical young adult literature or use fantastic material in just a segment, it is important to consider the ways in which gender roles play out in the fantasy worlds created. Often in these texts, gender roles are flipped, with female characters taking on traditional male roles and expectations (hero on quest), or challenged, with female characters resisting gendered expectations of the hearth-and-home locations. Other materials we haven't discussed here might also prove valuable in discussing gender roles and place, including young adult novels that have female main characters, supernatural elements, and vampires, such as those by such authors as Amelia Atwater, Rachel Caine, P.C. and Kristin Cast, Melissa de la Cruz, Marianne Mancusi, Richelle Mead, Alyson Noel, and Lili St. Crow, among others.[2]

As teachers, we must consider how authors open the expectations tied to place for critique. If the hero-on-a-quest role is usually a male, an author opens up multiple interpretations when she (or he) makes the hero a female. If there is the expectation that females stay home for security reasons, an author opens that up for examination when he (or she) makes home sites dangerous. Both Buffy and Bella face danger in locations that are typically considered safe — school, a dance studio, and prom.

The relationship between gender roles, identity, and place is complicated. Allowing readers of film, television, and text to examine the ways in which these roles are developed, challenged, or reified allows for a more nuanced understanding of the cultural complexity of gender and its ties to place. Familiar locations can be sites of great adventures and expected rites of passage can be fraught with danger. While Buffy and Bella are not the typically questing heroes, they exist in geographical spaces that force them to take on unexpected community responsibilities and roles, to challenge existing gender expectations, and to develop their own definitions of what it means to be female.

Fantastical literature, more than any other literature, offers the opportunity for readers to question and critique current society because it offers a "what if" version of a possible world. This provides both an alternative image of the world and a safe place to examine current expectations. Readers can agree with Buffy that "high school is hell" and kill off metaphorical demons or with Bella that high school is an institution in which they attempt to be invisible without drawing explicit attention to their own feelings. They can question gender roles and expectations without necessarily arguing that traditional gender roles should change. Fantastical literature allows the reader to explore an imagined world and alternative roles.

Notes

1. Below is an example of a response poem written by one of our students:

Reflection
Lindsey Bollinger

In the mirror on the bathroom wall	In the mirror on the bathroom wall
I look for the truth in my reflection	I look for the truth in my reflection
Will I find it there?	Will I find it there?
They tell me I'm	They tell me I'm
smart	stupid
funny	boring
pretty	ugly
but in the mirror I see the truth	but in the mirror I see the truth
my body is bad	my body is good

and that's all that matters
If my clothes are boring enough
no one will look at my body
I will hide the real me
In the mirror on the bathroom wall
our eyes meet
our reflections meld into one
and for a moment I see the real you
and I think you see it too.
There is something of me in you.
I fear the mirror on the wall
for the lie I will see there.
That is not who I am.
But I cannot ignore what I see:
A girl
trying to hide her body
because she is ashamed
I see the truth in the mirror.
I am beautiful.
Inside and out.
No matter what the others say.
I see myself in the mirror
the mirror on the bathroom wall
and the mirror in your eyes

and that's all that matters
If my clothes are flashy enough
everyone will look at my body
I will hide the real me
In the mirror on the bathroom wall
our eyes meet
our reflections meld into one
and for a moment I see the real you
and I fear you see it too.
There is nothing of me in you.
I fear the mirror in your eyes
for the truth I will see there.
That is not who I am.
But I cannot ignore what I see:
A girl
trying to show off her body
because she is ashamed
I see the truth in the mirror.
I am beautiful.
Outside and in.
No matter what the others say.
I see myself in the mirror.
the mirror on the bathroom wall
and the mirror in your eyes

2. Following is a list of additional young adult literature supernatural and vampire novels that have female main characters: Amelia Atwater's *A Demon in My View, In the Forests of the Night, Midnight Predator,* and *Shattered Mirror*; Rachel Caine's *Carpe Corpus, Fade Out, Feast of Fools, Ghost Town, Glass Houses, Kiss of Death, Lord of Misrule, Midnight Alley,* and *The Dead Girl's Dance*; Kate Cary's *Bloodline* and *Reckoning*; P.C. and Kristin Cast's *Awakened, Betrayed, Burned, Chosen, The Fledging Handbook, Hunted, Marked, Tempted,* and *Untamed*; Melissa de la Cruz's *Bloody Valentine, Blue Bloods, Keys to the Repository, Masquerade, Misguided Angels, Revelations,* and *The Van Alen Legacy;* Lucienne Diver's *Vamped* and Re-*Vamped;* Melissa Francis's *Bite Me* and *Love Sucks*; Kailin Gow's *Life's Blood* and *Pulse*; Alyxandra Harvey's *Blood Feud* and *Hearts at Stake*; Rachel Hawkins's *Demonglass* and *Hex Hall*; Carla Jablonski's *Thicker than Water*; Carrie Jones's *Captivate, Entice,* and *Need*; Mercedes Lackey's *Legacies;* Cynthia Leitich-Smith's *Blessed, Eternal,* and *Tantalize*; Marianne Mancusi's *Boys that Bite, Girls That Growl, Night School,* and *Stake That!;* Amanda Marrone's *Uninvited;* Katie Maxwell's *Circus of the Darned* and *Got Fangs?*; Richelle Mead's *Blood Promise, Bloodlines, Frostbite, The Last Sacrifice, Shadow Kiss,* and *Vampire Academy*; Alyson Noel's *Blue Moon, Dark Flame, Evermore, Night Star,* and *Shadowland*; Meredith Ann Pierce's *The Darkangel*; Serena Robar's *Braced 2 Bite, Dating 4 Demons,* and *Fangs 4 Freaks*; Ellen Schrieber's *Coffin Kisses, Love Bites,* and *Vampire Kisses*; and Lili St. Crow's *Betrayal, Defiance, Jealousy,* and *Strange Angels.*

Works Cited

Atwater-Rhodes, Amelia. *A Demon in My View.* New York: Laurel Leaf, 2001. Print.
_____. *In the Forests of the Night.* New York: Laurel Leaf, 1999. Print.
_____. *Midnight Predator.* New York: Laurel Leaf, 2003. Print.
_____. *Shattered Mirror.* New York: Laurel Leaf, 2003. Print.
Best, Amy L. *Prom Night: Youth, Schools, and Popular Culture.* New York: Routledge. 2000. Print.
Bruett, Joyce. "Looking for the Byronic Hero Using Twilight's Edward Cullen." *readwritethink.*

Web. 28 Dec. 2010. < http://www.readwritethink.org/classroom-resources/lesson-plans/looking-byronic-hero-using-1148.html>.

Buffy the Vampire Slayer. 20th Century–Fox, 2001. DVD.

Bull, Kelly Byrne. "Analyzing Style and Intertextuality in Twilight." *English Journal* 98.3 (Jan. 2009): 113–116. Print.

Caine, Rachel. *Carpe Corpus*. New York: Signet, 2009. Print.

_____. *The Dead Girl's Dance*. New York: Signet, 2007. Print.

_____. *Fade Out*. New York: Signet, 2009. Print.

_____. *Feast of Fools*. New York: Signet, 2008. Print.

_____. *Ghost Town*. New York: Signet, 2010. Print.

_____. *Glass Houses*. New York: Signet, 2006. Print.

_____. *Kiss of Death*. New York: Signet, 2010. Print.

_____. *Lord of Misrule*. New York: Signet, 2009. Print.

_____. *Midnight Alley*. New York: Signet, 2007. Print.

Carter, Alexandra. *Routledge International Encyclopedia of Women: Global Women's Issues and Knowledge*, Vol. 1. London: Routledge, 2000. Print.

Cary, Kate. *Bloodline*. New York: Razorbill, 2006. Print.

_____. *Reckoning*. New York: Razorbill, 2007. Print.

Cast, P. C., and Kristin Cast. *Awakened*. New York: St. Martin's Press, 2011. Print.

_____. *Betrayed*. New York: St. Martin's Press, 2007. Print.

_____. *Burned*. New York: St. Martin's Press, 2010. Print.

_____. *Chosen*. New York: St. Martin's Press, 2009. Print.

_____. *The Fledgling Handbook*. New York: St. Martin's Press, 2010. Print.

_____. *Hunted*. New York: St. Martin's Press, 2009. Print.

_____. *Marked*. New York: St. Martin's Press, 2009. Print.

_____. *Tempted*. New York: St. Martin's Press, 2009. Print.

_____. *Untamed*. New York: St. Martin's Press, 2008. Print.

Clayton, Sue. "Visual and Performative Elements in Screen Adaptation: A Film-Maker's Perpective." *Journal of Media Practice* 8.2 (2007): 129–145. Print.

de la Cruz, Melissa. *Bloody Valentine*. New York: Hyperion Books, 2010. Print.

_____. *Blue Bloods*. New York: Hyperion, 2007. Print.

_____. *Keys to the Repository*. New York: Hyperion, 2010. Print.

_____. *Masquerade*. New York: Hyperion, 2008. Print.

_____. *Misguided Angels*. New York: Hyperion, 2010. Print.

_____. *Revelations*. New York: Hyperion, 2009. Print.

_____. *The Van Alen Legacy*. New York: Hyperion Books, 2009. Print.

Diver, Lucienne. Re-*Vamped*. New York: Flux, 2010. Print.

_____. *Vamped*. New York: Flux, 2009. Print.

Francis, Melissa. *Bite Me*. New York: HarperTeen, 2009. Print.

_____. *Love Sucks*. New York: HarperTeen, 2010. Print.

Glee. Writers Ryan Murphy, Brad Falchuk, and Ian Brennan. Fox. 2009–2010.

Gow, Kailin. *Life's Blood*. New York: The EDGE Books, 2010. Print.

_____. *Pulse*. New York: The EDGE Books, 2010. Print.

"Graduation Day." *Buffy The Vampire Slayer*. Season 3. WB, 2003. DVD.

Greenwalt, David, writer and dir. "Homecoming." *Buffy The Vampire Slayer*. Warner Brothers. 3 Nov. 1998. Television.

Hall, Stanley G. *Adolescence: Its Psychology and Its Relations to Physiology, Anthropology, Sociology, Sex, Crime, and Religion*. Vol. 1. 1904. Ithaca, NY: Cornell University Press, 2009. Print.

Harvey, Alyxandra. *Blood Feud*. New York: Walker Books for Young Readers, 2009. Print.

_____. *Hearts at Stake*. New York: Walker Books for Young Readers, 2010. Print.

Hawkins, Rachel. *Demonglass*. New York: Hyperion, 2011. Print.

_____. *Hex Hall*. New York: Hyperion, 2011. Print.

High School Musical. Writer Peter Barsocchini. Dir. Kenny Ortega. Perf. Zac Efron and Vanessa Hudgens. Disney, 2006. Television.

Jablonski, Carla. *Thicker than Water*. New York: Razorbill, 2007. Print.

Jones, Carrie. *Captivate.* New York: Bloomsbury, 2010. Print.
_____. *Entice.* New York: Bloomsbury, 2010. Print.
_____. *Need.* New York: Bloomsbury, 2009. Print.
Kellner, D. "Teens and Vampires: From *Buffy the Vampire Slayer* to *Twilight's* Vampire
Lackey, Mercedes. *Legacies.* New York: Tor Teen, 2010. Print.
Lavery, David. "Afterward." *Fighting the Forces: What's at Stake in* Buffy the Vampire Slater. Ed. Rhonda Wilcox and David Lavery. Lanham, MD: Rowman & Littlefield, 2002. 251–56. Print.
Leitich-Smith, Cynthia. *Blessed.* Somerville, MA: Candlewick, 2011. Print.
_____. *Eternal.* Somerville, MA: Candlewick, 2010. Print.
_____. *Tantalize.* Somerville, MA: Candlewick, 2008. Print.
"Lovers." *Kinderculture: The Corporate Construction of Childhood.* 3d ed. Ed. Shirley Steinberg. Boulder: Westview, 2011. 55–72.
Mancusi, Marianne. *Boys That Bite.* New York: Berkley Trade, 2006. Print.
_____. *Girls That Growl.* New York: Berkley Trade, 2007. Print.
_____. *Night School.* New York: Berkley Trade, 2011. Print.
_____. *Stake That!* New York: Berkley Trade, 2006. Print.
Marrone, Amanda. *Uninvited.* New York: Simon Pulse, 2007. Print.
Maxwell, Katie. *Circus of the Darned.* New York: Smooch, 2006. Print.
_____. *Got Fangs?* New York: Smooch, 2005. Print.
McDowell, Linda. *Gender, Identity, and Place: Understanding Feminist Geographies.* Minneapolis: University of Minnesota Press, 1999. Print.
Mead, Richelle. *Blood Promise.* New York: Razorbill, 2010. Print.
_____. *Bloodlines.* New York: Razorbill, 2011. Print.
_____. *Frostbite.* New York: Razorbill, 2008. Print.
_____. *The Last Sacrifice.* New York: Razorbill, 2010. Print.
_____. *Shadow Kiss.* New York: Razorbill, 2008. Print.
_____. *Vampire Academy.* New York: Razorbill, 2007. Print.
Meyer, Stephanie. *Twilight.* New York: Little, Brown, 2005. Print.
Millman, Joyce. "The Death of Buffy's Mom." 12 March 2001. *Salon.* Web. August 2010.
Noel, Alyson. *Blue Moon.* New York: St. Martin's Griffin, 2009. Print.
_____. *Dark Flame.* New York: St. Martin's Griffin, 2010. Print.
_____. *Evermore.* New York: St. Martin's Griffin, 2009. Print.
_____. *Night Star.* New York: St. Martin's Griffin, 2010. Print.
_____. *Shadowland.* New York: St. Martin's Griffin, 2010. Print.
Noxon, Marti, writer. "The Prom." *Buffy The Vampire Slayer.* Dir. David Solomon. Warner Brothers. 11 May 1999. Television.
Overstreet, Deborah Wilson. *Not Your Mother's Vampire: Vampires in Young Adult Fiction.* Lanham, MD: Scarecrow Press, 2006. Print.
Philo, Chris. "'To Go Back Up the Side Hill': Memories, Imaginations and Reveries of Childhood." *Children's Geographies* 1.1 (2003): 7–23. Print.
Pierce, Meredith Ann. *The Darkangel.* New York: Little, Brown, 1982. Print.
Pierce, Tamora. "Fantasy: Why Kids Read It, Why Kids Need It." *School Library Journal* 39.10 (1993): 50–51. Print.
Robar, Serena. *Braced 2 Bite.* New York: Berkley Trade, 2010. Print.
_____. *Dating 4 Demons.* New York: Berkley Trade, 2010. Print.
_____. *Fangs 4 Freaks.* New York: Berkley Trade, 2010. Print.
Robillard, Candence M. "Hopelessly Devoted: What *Twilight* Reveals about Love and Obsession." *The Alan Review* 37.1 (2009): 12–17. Print.
St. Crow, Lili. *Betrayal.* New York: Razorbill, 2009. Print.
_____. *Defiance.* New York: Razorbill, 2011. Print.
_____. *Jealousy.* New York: Razorbill, 2010. Print.
_____. *Strange Angels.* New York: Razorbill, 2009. Print.
Schrieber, Ellen. *Coffin Kisses.* Katherine Tegen Books, 2005. Print.
_____. *Love Bites.* Katherine Tegen Books, 2010. Print.

_____. *Vampire Kisses.* Katherine Tegen Books, 2003. Print.
Twilight. Dir. Catherine Hartwicke. Perf. Kristen Stewart and Peter Facinelli. 2008. Summit, 2010. DVD.
Valentine, Gill. "Boundary Crossing: Transitions from Childhood to Adulthood." *Children's Geographies* 1.1 (Mar. 2003): 37 — 52. Print.
_____. *Public Spaces and the Culture of Childhood.* Burlington: Ashgate, 2004.
Whedon, Joss. "Commentary: 'Welcome to the Hellmouth.'" *Buffy the Vampire Slayer.* Season One. 20th Century–Fox home Entertainment, 2006. DVD.
Wilcox, Rhonda, and David Lavery, eds. *Fighting the Forces: What's at Stake in* Buffy the Vampire Slayer. Lanham, MD: Rowman and Littlefield, 2002. Print.
Wood, Martin. "New Life for an Old Tradition: Anne Rice and Vampire Literature." *The Blood Is the Life: Vampires in Literature.* Ed. Mary Pharr and Leonard Heldreth. Bowling Green: University of Bowling Green Popular Press, 1999. Print.

Brave New Classroom: Using Science Fiction to Teach Political Theory

KENNETH S. HICKS

Getting students to think imaginatively about politics can be challenging, in part because "developing a theoretical imagination" is rarely listed among the student learning objectives in political science curricula. Introductory courses are taken up with developing students' fact bases. In more advanced courses, the primary concern is to impart the methodological skills and specialized knowledge, with teaching protégés how to become political "scientists." While understandable, this tendency can produce knowledgeable but uninspired students, lacking the practical reasoning skills to be either good social scientists or engaged citizens.

The case for teaching political theory-oriented courses that tap into the canon of utopian literature is well established (Sibley 57–74), and courses focusing on the utopian/dystopian "canon" of Thomas More, Edward Bellamy, Robert Owen, H.G. Wells, Jules Verne, George Orwell, Thomas Huxley, and Evgeny Zamiatin (or Zamyatin) are fairly common in many of the Ivy League schools and the larger state universities. This chapter maintains that political theory in general and the discipline as a whole benefit from the inclusion of courses with names like Science Fiction and Politics or the Politics of the Future. First, such courses afford sustained opportunities to explore in detail the challenges political communities face in educating their citizens; in particular, this essay follows the work of political theorists like the late Isaiah Berlin in arguing for a curriculum that stimulates a sense of political imagination. Second, these kinds of courses can be organized around the transformational potential that technology plays. Science fiction in particular offers numerous opportunities to discuss the dynamic nature of technology (e.g., the Internet, smartphones, iPods, etc.), and think playfully and creatively about the future of technological change. Third, such courses offer opportunities to recognize that technology often creates as many problems as it solves. The myth of the "Modern Prometheus" stands as a uniquely modern myth and can be used to suggest that the facile belief in the inevitable march of progress can have tragic consequences. Planning for such a course, which I intend to teach in the near future, can also add depth to planning for other courses.

Imagination

Political theory has fallen on hard times in recent years. As a sub-field of political science, political theory has endured a nearly half-century slide, largely owing to the behavioral revolution that swept through the social sciences in the 1950s (Easton 36–58). This commitment to behaviorism and to the urge to counting things was not without consequences; while other social sciences like psychology were relentlessly proselytizing the value of quantitative methods for understanding mental processes — the "landscape of the mind," the embrace of quantification among political scientists resulted in increasingly abstract research that did little to help non-political scientists (and others) understand how politics affected their day-to-day lives. In the search to develop a professional culture of objectivity and value-neutrality, the discipline scourged itself of content vital to the development of citizenship and eroded its status as a discipline committed to understanding power and how power can be used responsibly and accountably to help improve humanity's living conditions and life prospects.

Another consequence of the shift to behavioral approaches was a tendency to treat political theory as primarily an exercise in hypothesis-formation. This shift in emphasis elided one of political theory's more important historical tasks: civic education. Within the new paradigm, the liberal/postmodern state — and with it, educators — were duty-bound to profess a neutral indifference to the various contending views of the good life. As a consequence, while virtually every curriculum required college students to take American Federal Government, little to nothing was done up to that point to inculcate a sense of citizenship; routinely, eighteen-year-old students cannot tell the difference between a liberal or a conservative, let alone meaningfully discuss matters related to the perennial issue of politics: justice, equity, and how best to secure a good, meaningful life. As William Galston observed, the "greatest threat to children in modern liberal societies is not that they will believe in something too deeply, but that they will believe in nothing very deeply at all" (Galston 255). People who believe nothing very deeply are often most vulnerable to the siren song of the Father Coughlins and the Glenn Becks of the world.

Political theory provides students with the kind of historical grounding necessary for careful political analysis and the practical imagination necessary to apply historical lessons to the dynamic and fluid present. For theorists like Isaiah Berlin, the rise of Romanticism and the Counter-Enlightenment in the 19th century was an unsurprising — even predictable — reaction to the sweeping transformations of the Enlightenment. Likewise, the two great shaping passions of the 20th century — the faith in technology to solve problems like famine and disease and the fierce, passionate ideological conflicts provoked by the Russian Revolution — were equally informed by the platonic belief that "all genuine questions must have one true answer and one only, all the rest necessarily being errors" (Berlin 5). Against modernity's absolute faith in science or ideology, another set of extremists, value relativists, denied that there was any objective or rational way of adjudicating claims from different moral perspectives. The two extremes appeared to offer irreconcilable choices: politics is either ineluctably about faith or is intractably about subjective conviction, and never the twain shall meet.

Berlin's skepticism regarding absolutes did not inspire him to the despair of relativism. For Berlin, Enlightenment thinkers like Johan Herder and Giambattista Vico had already captured a central insight: while we cannot all agree on how to live our lives, our imaginations provide a powerful link between time, space and culture; we may not understand Pericles's Athens from the perspective of a Greek of the fifth century B.C.E., but some understanding is possible because "what make men human is common to them, and acts as a bridge between them.... We are free to criticize the values of other cultures, to condemn them, but *we cannot pretend not to understand them at all* [author's italics], or to regard them simply as subjective, the products of creatures in different circumstances with different tastes from our own, which do not speak to us at all" (Berlin 9). The capacity for intersubjective understanding suggested a middle path to understanding and explaining human events — which Berlin called pluralism — a belief which fed his conviction that the human urge to certainty is always doomed to fail. Facts may be stubborn things, but beliefs often prove to be even more intractable. Importantly, a central avenue for mutual understanding is storytelling, in particular, using stories to capture essential truths about the human condition.

Imagination is a crucial element to understanding viewpoints from different temporal or cultural perspectives. Berlin suggested that there was a general structure or pattern of existence — a *Wirkungszusammenhang,* requiring a facility for empathy with historical figures when they act; without this facility, the person attempting to construct a narrative of motives is "at best a chronicler or technical specialist; at worst a distorter and writer of inferior fiction" (Berlin 55). Berlin, of course, was primarily writing about historians and political theorists who were intent on characterizing events from the past, but his argument requires recognition that good theorizing, like good history, is not simply a matter of brute description. Moreover, Berlin suggests that there might be more than one way to defy reality: to ignore evidence in the service of a cherished ideology is to indulge in a more damaging kind of fantasizing than the kind of fanaticizing about a more perfect future in which Robert Owen, Edward Bellamy, and H.G. Wells indulged, and which "hard-headed realists" like Karl Marx denounced as "utopian cloud gazing."

Berlin believed that forcing individuals "into the neat uniforms demanded by dogmatically believed-in schemes is almost always the road to inhumanity" (16) and that we have an obligation to think proactively about how to avoid situations in which cruelty is unavoidable. The rationale for speculative political theory is that a course in the politics of the future can provide students with the opportunities to recognize the importance of imagination in conceptualizing future politics. In a similar vein, W. Lance Bennett has noted that, although social scientists all too often relegate the idea of play to the realm of children's activities, the sense of freedom to play with ideas and to "discover the conditions necessary such public celebration of a future political order" is essential to taking a politics of the future seriously (Bennett 356).

Technology's Promise

A course in science fiction and politics can be organized around the political implications of new technological innovations. Is an introduced technology more likely to facilitate or impede democracy? On the one hand, dystopian novels express an overarching pessimism toward technology. Beyond the capacity of cameras and microphones to entrance the masses, the state's burgeoning administrative power is viewed by these thinkers as contributing inexorably to the loss of personal space and individual autonomy. On the other hand, utopian writers tend to express great faith in the emancipatory implications of technology to wipe out disease, eliminate hunger, and effortlessly provide the abundance that would fulfill Marx's dream of a humanity unfettered from want, and free to, as Marx says, "hunt in the morning, fish in the afternoon, rear cattle in the evening, [and] criticize after dinner" (qtd. in Tucker 160).

Of course, technology's record is more Janus-faced. Most technological innovations have been used both to emancipate and oppress. The printing press simultaneously contributed to the spread of literacy and the capacity of individuals for self-governance and self-expression while simultaneously enhancing the capacity of the propagandizing power of the state and facilitating the power of bureaucracy to keep tabs on people. Likewise, the musket ended the monopoly of force enjoyed by the European nobility and also made possible the subjugation of significant portions of the globe at the hands of a new class of gun-bearing Europeans, spreading the gospel of capitalism and the white man's burden.

In his provocative book *The Transparent Society*, David Brin argues that technological innovations are inevitable; the cameras are coming to public squares whether we will it or not. The Pandora's Box of surveillance technology has been opened, and the ability to monitor public spaces will only increase by leaps and bounds in the coming years, with the cameras getting smaller, more mobile, and able to store greater amounts of data. The difference between an open, accountable, and transparent society and a closed, unaccountable and authoritarian society is a simple matter of politics: Who will have access to the cameras, the police, or the people?

For Brin, the key to avoiding technology's centralizing and authoritarian implications is "mutually assured surveillance," in which everyone has the right to shine a light anywhere in the public sphere of choice; this can enforce respect far more so than the other "technology" alternative, which would be for everyone to be armed (Brin 254–55). Crucial to securing mutual accountability is the "rise of an age of amateurs, in which skill and expertise become so widely dispersed that no cabal of professionals can ever become dominant, or indispensable" (Brin 331). At the cost of losing the anonymity of cosmopolitan living, Brin would argue that we gain much greater accountability. Over time, having people know how much you spend on groceries will be "like having people know what color sweater you are wearing" (334). This sort of declaration may offer a useful introductory springboard for how we tend to link our self-conceptions with our beliefs regarding privacy, and how technology can transform how we think about both human nature and privacy.

The Politics of "Old Man's War"

Imagine a possible future in which Earth is a sleepy backwater and, at the age of sixty-five, the citizens of the United States have an opportunity to sign away the balance of their lives after seventy-five by entering into the Colonial Defense Forces to fight humanity's enemies in outer space. The image of Grandma and Grandpa taking up arms and charging an alien position seems ironic; in fact, Earthling recruits have their consciousness transferred into "augmented" human bodies that can be grown in a couple of months. After a few months training, Colonial Defense Forces recruits are thrust into a hostile universe engaged in an anarchic struggle for scarce resources. The recruits' new bodies are robust, green-skinned, powerful, and agile; for ten years, their job is to fight humanity's intergalactic enemies, which turn out to be pretty much whoever the Colonial Defense Forces designates as an enemy.

Intergalactic travel is rendered possible by "Skip Drive." "Conventional" travel between stars is impossible because faster than the speed of light is "just a speedy way to get killed" (Scalzi, *Old Man's War* L3020), as hitting a speck of space matter at greater than the speed of light will blow a hole in any ship traveling faster than the speed of light. Therefore, in order to get from one star system to the next, ships require a device that opens a door in space — which is comprised of multiple universes — to another part of this "multiverse." However, skip drive becomes more unreliable the further the attempted jump, which forces humans and their neighbor races into the same quadrant of space and makes habitable planets exceptionally valuable. Likewise, interstellar communication can only be undertaken using "skip drones," which are essentially skip drives with a data-loaded computer.

Another essential piece of technology in this imagined future is the BrainPal, which are neural implants that enable soldiers to upload and download data to their brains. BrainPal comes with terabytes of already loaded information, ranging from the trivial (cartoons) to the essential (alien language translation programs). To illustrate the importance of BrainPal to a Colonial soldier, rifles are synched to each soldier and cannot be fired by anyone else. The mind-to-implant upload rate facilitates tremendous knowledge acquisition: imagine being able to consume Mary Shelley's *Frankenstein* in eight minutes! Moreover, BrainPal-enhanced soldiers share data through their adaptive interface, allowing Colonial Defense Forces units to form extremely tight, disciplined units.

This is the imagined future of John Scalzi's first novel, *Old Man's War*, and its sequels, *The Ghost Brigades*, *The Last Colony*, and *Zoe's Tale*. Told primarily from the perspective of a seventy-five year old recruit named John Perry, Scalzi portrays an imagined future characterized by soft despotism, in which the state uses the difficulty of interstellar communication to impose a chokehold on the dissemination of information. Colonists themselves are not asked to serve in the Colonial Defense Forces — that was tried and proved to be a disaster: instead the Colonial Defense Forces recruit among the elderly of a marginalized Earth, and predominantly from the United States, whose citizens are otherwise denied access to the stars. The populations of the developing world are shipped out when they rebel or when population density reaches a boiling point.

Over the course of Scalzi's narrative, it becomes clear to the Colonial Defense Forces that the augmented elderly denizens of Earth are not enough to protect humanity's racial security (a significant ratcheting up of the "national security" rationale), and a new technology enables the Colonial Defense Forces to take the DNA of recruits who were recruited and yet died prior to their seventy-fifth birthday and recover portions of their identities. A pastiche of different identities is implanted into even more augmented and BrainPal-enhanced elite troops. These "reconditioned" soldiers are viewed with both awe and suspicion by other Colonial Defense Forces. Given an accelerated "socialization program," these "Ghost Soldiers" have no process of socialization; having never been a child, these Special Forces soldiers are acutely aware that they lack the "humanity" of "real-borns."

These storylines can be used as the basis for class discussions exploring the political implications of the kinds of technology that may or may not be introduced at some point in the future. Is Scalzi's imagined future a kind of utopia, or is the novel primarily dystopian in nature? What is the basis of this future state's power? How does this state maintain control over so vast a territory and so large and heterogeneous a population? How does technology facilitate this control? Is Scalzi's depiction of a single government administering hundreds of billions of people scattered over dozens of planets realistic? Does this society give its citizens the information necessary for them to make informed political decisions? How does technology contribute to the resolution of the governance problems facing this state? What role does technology play in the resolution of the narrative's principal conflict?

Scalzi's texts can also be used to introduce students to issues related to international relations theory. Based on what can be learned from the novel, why is the Colonial Alliance in a state of permanent war with seemingly the rest of non-human civilization? Does Scalzi model intergalactic politics in his universe on the anarchic world of contemporary international relations? How should the aliens in Scalzi's universe be perceived? Certainly, in the early portions of *Old Man's War* the reader is asked to adopt the soldier's perspective; however, as the story unfolds, the reader is cajoled to take on a more nuanced understanding of the different alien species. In particular, the Obin — whom another alien race uplifted to intelligence ... *without providing them with a sense of self*— provide an interesting basis for discussing what it takes in order to be considered a morally autonomous agent. If nothing else, Scalzi's imagined world suggests that human beings will continue to be motivated by the same fundamental issues that require political solutions today; the need for access to land and resources will eternally produce the kinds of conflicts that have justified ethnic cleansing in the recent past.

Scalzi's narrative also provides an excellent basis for discussion of the nature of socialization and the relationship between the state and its citizens. What is the nature of the initial trade-off that the Colonial Defense Forces make to the then-seventy-five-year-old-citizens of the United States? What would you do, near the end of your natural life span, if someone proposed to you that they could transfer your consciousness into the body of a vital, perfectly healthy body; the trade-off is that you must provide ten years of military service, with a guarantee that you would be frequently exposed to combat and instant death? As John Perry, the principal protagonist in *Old Man's War* puts it, by the time he hit the recruitment age of sixty-five, his friends were gone and his wife was dead and the trade-off sounded pretty good:

> Trading that in for a decade of fresh life in a combat zone begins to look like a hell of a bargain. Especially because if you don't, in a decade you'll be eighty-five, and then the only difference between you and a raisin will be that while you're both wrinkled and without a prostate, the raisin never had a prostate to begin with [Scalzi, *Old Man's War* L170].

Other questions relate to the state's right to seize DNA from those recruits who die before their seventy-fifth birthday. If such technology existed, what is the potential for abuse? How "human" are the members of the Ghost Brigades? What rights should "recycled soldiers" have? Does the state's possession of such assets increase the likelihood that the state will resort to force without exploring other options?

In a recent interview, Scalzi conceded, "Every science fiction author is destined to fail on the technology front" (Henrikson). Part of what makes Scalzi's work worth academic treatment is that he takes his science as seriously as the story-telling elements of his fiction. In a similar vein, part of the value of reading older science fiction is to get a sense of what writers of the 1960s and 1970s were actually able to predict, alongside of their glaring omissions of the internet, cell phones, and iPods. Classic science fiction holds its value less because the author gets the science perfectly right — they never do — than because the story being told conveys important insights into perennial questions.

Technology's Peril

Isaiah Berlin commented in his essay "The Pursuit of the Ideal" that "Utopias have their value — nothing so wonderfully expands the imaginative horizons of human potentialities — but as guides to conduct they can prove literally fatal. Heraclitus was right, things cannot stand still" (Berlin 12). Greek mythology is replete with stories of how the search for technology to gain power over nature can have disastrous consequences. For example, the Titan Prometheus stole fire — which could be considered to be humanity's primordial technology — from the Gods and was given the punishment of being chained to a rock and having his liver eaten by an eagle, only to have his liver regenerate at night, to be gnawed at again the following day. In revenge for the theft of fire, Zeus bestowed upon the first woman, Pandora, a box that must not be opened, knowing that human curiosity would eventually cause it to be opened, unleashing all the evils of the world upon humanity. The ancient warning "be careful what you wish for" has always found expression in science fiction.

A course whose topics included this kind of dystopian element could also offer opportunities to explore the Romantic rejection of Enlightenment faith in progress. For example, Mary Shelly's *Frankenstein, or the Modern Prometheus* (1818), one of the earliest examples of science fiction and the progenitor of the dystopian novel, depicts humanity's urge to explore and control nature as bordering on the profane. From the Romantic perspective, the arrogance implicit in the attempt to supplant God could only result in disaster. While myriad books and essays explore dystopian themes and would be appropriate for inclusion in such a course, this section will focus on the world created by Joss Whedon in the brief television series *Firefly* and culminated in the motion picture *Serenity*.

Firefly, Serenity, *and Social Engineering*

The series *Firefly* is premised as a fusion of science fiction and old West frontier narrative. Humanity, having wasted Earth's natural resources, is compelled to seek refuge in space. Using terra-forming, human colonies spring up, some of which become affluent and technologically advanced, while others are poverty-stricken and resource poor. The central planets of the human intergalactic civilization form what is known as the "Alliance," and a resulting civil war between the Alliance and the "Independents" culminates in the Battle of Serenity Valley, in which the Independents suffer a debilitating defeat. The show's main protagonist, Malcolm Reynolds, and another character, Zoe Washbourne, were foot-soldiers in the Independent military. After the war, Reynolds and Washbourne buy a Firefly class spaceship, a transport noted for its durability and versatility, which they name *Serenity*. The principal narrative theme of the show is the crew's attempts to avoid the long arm of the Alliance, moving from job to job in the attempt to make enough money to keep the ship fueled and the more mercenary members of the immediate crew of five paid.

Also on board is a "companion," a trained consort (prostitution is legal in this future) whose presence as the lessee of one of the ship's two shuttles conveys a legitimacy that gives *Serenity* access to space ports where jobs can be had. In addition to a "shepherd," a mysterious religious figure who is taken to traveling, the crew has taken on Simon Tam, a doctor, and (unknowingly at first) his sister, River. Reynolds's determination to avoid a civilization he deems corrupts results in *Serenity*'s precarious course between the edges of civilization and "Reaver territory," with the Reavers described as humans driven mad by the infinite blackness of space, and who periodically subject the border planets to savage raids.

The movie *Serenity* offers several illustrations of how technology can produce horrific consequences. Perhaps the most poignant is River Tam, described by her brother as a prodigy who had been sent to a special school for gifted children; her journey illustrates the impulse to make the best better. The school, however, turns out to be an Alliance-funded program for identifying children with telepathic potential. Simon receives a coded message from his sister telling him that people at the school are hurting the students. Risking a brilliant medical career, Simon breaks River out of the school. In a later episode of *Firefly*, Simon discovers that part of River's brain — the amygdala, the part of the limbic system that controls emotions — had been stripped away and that she had been subject to repeated cranial invasions. The Alliance's experiments left River emotionally damaged, unable to control her thoughts; as a result, she is subject to emotional and increasingly violent outbursts; over the course of the series and movie, River's capacity for effective violence increases exponentially. In the movie, the narrative reveals that the Alliance planned to turn River and other telepaths into military weapons. Why trust a "killing machine"? River's storyline can be used both as a caution against using other human beings as "mere ends" but also can suggest the power of individual conscience and the possibility of redemption and recovery.

The other character who highlights the social engineering impulse is described in the movie *Serenity* as "the Operative," a true believer who dreams of a "world without sin." The Operative is a member of a class of futuristic special agents, a kind of futuristic "black ops" agent. As he describes himself, "I don't exist. The Parliament calls me in ... when they wish they didn't have to." Invariably courteous, the Operative is also completely ruthless and willing to commit any number of atrocities to capture River before she reveals a particularly damaging Alliance secret. After the Operative destroys a village with women and children in it and kills one of Mal's former crew members, Mal and the Operative speak by video. When Mal says, "So me and mine got to lay down and die so you can live in your better world?" the Operative replies, somewhat incredulously, "I'm not going to live there.... How could you think — there's no place for me there, any more than there is for you. I'm a monster. What I do is evil; I have no illusions about it. But it must be done" (Whedon *Serenity* 85).

And when Mal asks him if he even knows why River must die, the Operative states, "It's not my place to ask." The Operative's narrative offers several opportunities to discuss the nature of evil in politics; while the Reavers could stand in as expressions of utter nihilistic savagery, the Operative presents a more banal appearance. As an antagonist that viewers can understand — if not support — the Operative can be used to discuss how most human atrocities begin with political leader's grand but vague promises of a "world without want or sin," but almost always are carried out by functionaries willing to suppress their conscience in the service of some "greater good."

The Reavers, an ill-defined group of savages occupying the fringes of the human-occupied system, could initially be compared to the unrealistic, stereotypical portrayals of Native Americans from movies about the frontier west from the 1940s, 1950s, and 1960s.[1] In the series, Reavers are characterized as madmen who wandered out into space and went insane. For example, when *Serenity* is attempting to bluff its way past a Reaver cruiser during the series pilot episode, and Simon Tam asks Zoe Washbourne what would happen if the Reavers board the ship, because Simon, being from one of the central planets, has only heard of Reavers in "campfire tales," Zoe replies, "If they take the ship, they will rape us to death, eat our flesh, and sew our skins into their clothing, and if we're very lucky, they'll do it in that order" (Whedon).

For much of the remainder of the series, Reavers are a kind of background horror used to signify that "the Black," the series slang for space, is a dangerous place. At no point in either the series or the movie are Reavers depicted as other than homicidal madmen (exclusively men, it appears). Indeed, one could question how such a "society" could form and sustain itself. Warfare is an innately "social" activity: how could maniacs operate spacecraft, navigate from planet to planet, and engage in the myriad cooperative acts necessary to unleash howling savagery on colonial outposts? The reality behind the Reavers, however, is revealed in *Serenity* as the ultimate consequence of social engineering, which is the secret that River Tam learned when top members of the Alliance Parliament visited the laboratory where a behavioral modification specialist was experimenting with River, and showing off his "star pupil." The Alliance, whether attempting to pacify a fractious colony or simply experimenting with planetary population control, introduced a chemical into the atmosphere of a newly terraformed planet named Miranda. Designed to suppress aggression, the chemical worked all too well for most of the population, causing them to just lie down and forget to breathe. However, in about one-tenth of the population, it had the opposite effect, to stimulate aggression "beyond madness." Those first Reavers destroyed the Alliance scientific team sent to investigate what had happened to the planet. The Alliance's ruthless attempts to suppress the truth and the *Serenity*'s crew's attempts to publicize it provide another fruitful avenue for discussing secrecy. When are states allowed to keep secrets: When it threatens the regime? Or when it threatens the state itself?

In any event, the Reavers, far from comprising mere humans-*cum*-savages, are revealed as victims of anonymous, no doubt well-meaning futuristic Dr. Frankensteins.

Conclusion

Cory and Alexei Panshin have argued that science fiction "is a literature of the mythic imagination" (Panshin and Panshin 13). Science fiction and (to a lesser extent) its close relative fantasy, provide important insights into aspects of human behavior that cannot be quantified, but that are essential features of a fully-drawn human landscape. A quote from Ursula K. LeGuin captures the aspirations of this essay:

> I believe that all the best faculties of a mature human being exist in the child, and that if these faculties are encouraged in youth they will act well and wisely in the adult, but if they are repressed and denied in the child they will stunt and cripple the adult personality. And I believe that one of the most deeply human, and humane, of these faculties is the power of imagination: so that it is our pleasant duty, as librarians, or teachers, or parents, or writers, or simply as grownups, to encourage that faculty of imagination in our children, to encourage it to grow freely, to flourish like the great bay tree, by giving it the best, absolutely the best and purest, nourishment it can absorb [LeGuin 38–40].

Science fiction has a past, present and future, and the stories I have chosen are simply two possible worlds that can be used to explore the more subjective aspects of politics; the whole tapestry of science fiction as a genre of literature can be mined for lessons about the malleable nature of the self. LeGuin argues that fantasy is "the natural, the appropriate language for recounting the spiritual journey and the struggle of good and evil in the soul" (LeGuin 64). Political scientists have honed their craft, and burnished their credentials as "very serious thinkers" among the disciplines of the social sciences. The proposition of this chapter is that political scientists need to recall that stories matter and that how the discipline presents itself to other human beings that do not happen to be numerate political scientists is a matter of supreme importance. Central to that endeavor is what can only be viewed as an act of recovery: to recall that dreams matter, and that aspirations are part of the human narrative as much as vote counts and opinion surveys.

Notes

1. Another excellent basis for discussion of the dangers of technology are the Reavers. At first glance, Reavers may appear as the kind of stereotypical Native Americans who attacked white people in western movies like *Stagecoach* (1939). As Whedon notes, "Every story needs a monster. In the stories of the Old West it was the Apaches" (Arroyo). However, Whedon is famous for playing with stereotypes, and his intent is not to pay homage to this kind of racial stereotyping but to subvert the metaphor. Indeed, Whedon attempted to remove any suggestion of racial stereotyping by calling his monsters "Reavers," whose etymology reaches back to 12th century "reivers," who were Scotsmen living along the English-Scottish borders who largely subsisted on "reiving," or crossing the borders to raid and plunder villages (Nebergall).

In the series, Reavers are characterized as madmen who wandered into space and went insane. Except for *Serenity*'s meeting with a Reaver cruiser, for most of the series, Reavers remain a kind of background horror, like the music from *Jaws*. At no point in either the series or the film are Reavers depicted as other than homicidal madmen. Although the Reavers are able to command spaceships and use high-tech weapons, the preference of Reavers is merely to use technology to come to close quarters with their quarry, presumably to eat them and desecrate their flesh while they are still alive. In "Bushwacked," it becomes chillingly clear that part of the Reaver "recruiting strategy" is to leave some captives alive and force them to watch the savage butchery of loved ones and relatives. Mal ruminates that when "a man comes up against that kind of will, the only way to deal with it, I suspect, is to become it."

Whedon's purpose in creating the Reavers is revealed in the movie *Serenity*. The reason River Tam was being hunted so remorselessly is that she came into contact with an Alliance Parliament member while she was a captive, and she telepathically learned a terrible secret about Miranda, a planet on the other side of Reaver territory. Years before, the Alliance introduced a chemical into the atmosphere of Miranda that was designed to suppress aggression. The drug worked all too well for most the population. People forgot to go to work, and eventually simply died. But for about ten percent of population, the drug had the opposite effect, stimulating aggression "beyond madness." These initial ravening hordes (ten percent of thirty million people would comprise close to three million such madmen) destroyed the Alliance scientific team sent to investigate what had happened to the planet. The Alliance then compounded their calamitous mistake by attempting to suppress the truth.

In short, the Reavers offer a number of valuable opportunities for discussing the dangers implicit in social engineering. First, the metaphor of mindless savages offers opportunities for investigating the kinds of stereotypes that are so often present in westerns, action, and military movies. Is such a society of mindless savages sociologically feasible? The show hypothesizes about the psychology of the Reavers, but the sociology is left out. How could such a huge collection of insane individuals form the kinds of social bonds necessary to pilot spaceships and plot raids? Second, Reavers offer an opportunity to explore the power of the state and the need for secrets. What kind of secrets are we comfortable with the state keeping? What kind of secrets must we prevent the state from hording, so that voters will have sufficient information to hold our elected officials accountable? And third, Reavers stand as metaphorical victims of the powerful, paternalistic, and intrusive Dr. Frankensteins implicit in a modern, technologically advanced society, and a warning that humanity's ability to tinker with the laws of nature sometimes outruns our prudential understanding of the powers at our command.

Works Cited

Arroyo, Sam. "Joss Whedon Panel at Wondercon, Comic Book Resources." 20 Feb. 2005. Web. 12 May 2011.

Bennett, W. Lance. "When Politics Becomes Play." *Political Behavior* 1.4 (Winter 1979): 331–59. Print.

Berlin, Isaiah. *The Proper Study of Mankind: An Anthology of Essays*. New York: Giroux, 1998. Print.

Brin, David. *The Transparent Society: Will Technology Force U.S. to Choose between Privacy and Freedom?* Reading, MA: Addison-Wesley, 1998. Print.

"Bushwhacked." *Firefly. Shriftweb*. 27 Sept. 2002. Web. 12 May 2011.

Cobban, Alfred. "The Decline of Political Theory." *Political Science Quarterly* 68 (Sept. 1953): 321–37. Print.

Easton, David. "The Decline of Modern Political Theory." *The Journal of Politics* 13.1 (Feb. 1951): 36–58. Print.

Galston, William. *Liberal Purposes: Goods, Virtues, and Diversity in the Liberal State*. New York: Cambridge, 1992. Print.

Henrikson, Erik. "The *Mercury* Interview: John Scalzi." *The Portland Mercury* 12 May 2011. Web. 15 April 2011.

LeGuin, Ursula K. *Language of the Night*. New York: Harper, 1993. Print.

Nebergall, P.J. "Reiving, Feuding, and Primitive Warfare." Buffalo University. Web. 12 May 2011.

Panshin, Alexei, and Cory. *The World Beyond the Hill: Science Fiction and the Quest for Transcendence*. Rockville, MD: Phoenix, 2010. Print.

Scalzi, John. *The Ghost Brigades*. New York: Tom Doherty, 2006. Print.
_____. *The Last Colony*. New York: Tom Doherty, 2007. Print.
_____. *Old Man's War*. New York: Tom Doherty, 2005. Print.
Sibley, Mulford Q. "Apology for Utopia I." *The Journal of Politics* 2.1 (1940): 57–74. Print.
_____. "Apology for Utopia II." *The Journal of Politics* 2.2 (1940): 165–88. Print.
Tucker, Robert C., ed. *The Marx-Engels Reader*. 2d ed. New York: Norton, 1978. Print.
Whedon, Joss. "*Firefly* Pilot: Serenity, Part 1 and 2." *Whoa: Good Myth*. Shriftweb.org. Web. 1 May 2011.
_____. *Serenity: A Movie Script*. 2004. ScifiScripts: Serenity. Web. 1 May 2011.

Incarnations of Immortal Creations

EMILY DIAL-DRIVER

The return of the soul to earth in another body after the death of the original body is called reincarnation. And, according to reincarnationists, this death/rebirth can happen over and over. Such reincarnation can also occur literarily.

Literary works can be re-embodiments and re-creations. For example, *Beowulf* originated early in English literature and has been retold and adapted many, many times, including the film *The 13th Warrior*, adapted itself from Michael Crichton's book *Eaters of the Dead*; an episode of *Star Trek*; and, according to Sutton, the *Predator* film. The *Predator* film is not as obviously a re-embodiment of *Beowulf* as *The 13th Warrior* but some see them as similar. They are farther apart than Jane Austen's *Pride and Prejudice* is from *Pride and Prejudice and Zombies* by Jane Austen and Seth Grahame-Smith, which is *Pride and Prejudice*, plus added gore.

Other examples abound. *The League of Extraordinary Gentlemen* begins as a comic, becomes a graphic novel, and continues as a film, with the changes in emphasis required by the medium and the craftspeople who deal with the work. Looking at these works — and their transformations — may increase student accessibility and allow students to use literary criticism and other literary analysis tools to analyze and evaluate material.

Dr. Jekyll and Mr. Hyde's transformation to *Mary Reilly* and to the BBC's *Jekyll,* the comic Batman's conversion to the feature film *The Dark Knight,* and the graphic novel *V for Vendetta*'s adaptation to the film of the same name show us how material moves from one medium to another. Studying the movement in narration, theme, character, symbol, image, etc., required by a shift in medium can teach valuable lessons about the demands of the creative medium. *Batman* and *V for Vendetta*, the printed works, carry different impacts and narrative necessities than *The Dark Knight* and *V for Vendetta*, the films.

In addition to the demands of medium conversion, content and context in each of the works can be a useful study. What does *Mary Reilly* say that *Dr. Jekyll and Mr. Hyde* does not? How does each reflect the cultural milieu in which each was created? Which is more effective in what areas? The interrogations of such works can be limitless.

Retelling the story has a long history. Even Shakespeare was in that game. Then there are all those Disney re-embodiments of the fairy tales, with most gore removed. So from the beginnings of literature, there's a long tradition of re-creating the "classic"—or at least the evocative—story.

In addition to the "fairy" tales of Anderson and the Grimm brothers, and the short list of non-"fairy" tales mentioned above, two stories have been told and retold, worked and reworked: *The Wonderful Wizard of Oz* and *Alice in Wonderland*, works that have become iconic in world culture. (And, yes, I can defend that since many U.S. films generally make their way to much of the rest of the world.)

Some, and I do mean only some, of the works that have relied on the original L. Frank Baum's *The Wonderful Wizard of Oz* include musicals, television and film productions, and variations on a theme. Baum's work was published in 1900 and has since become part of an international lexicon of fantasy. Most students assume they are familiar with the work, but what they're usually familiar with is the film made in 1939, starring Judy Garland, Ray Bolger, Bert Lahr, Frank Morgan, Jack Haley, and Margaret Hamilton. The story actually begins with L. Frank Baum's novel for children titled *The Wonderful Wizard of Oz.*

At this point, I should tell you that summaries of works appear at the end of this chapter in a section titled "Summaries." If you're familiar with the work, you certainly don't need a summary and can skip it—unless you're a compulsive note reader like me. If you're not familiar with the work, then you have a quick resource in the summary section. Or, if you're in between, you can refresh your memory of the work in that same note. We begin the summary section with L. Frank Baum's *The Wonderful Wizard of Oz* and summaries follow in the order in which they are dealt with here.

Oz and the Wizard

Baum's story is both more complex and less coherent than the film version. Although Dorothy rides out the tornado in a farmhouse, which lands on and kills the wicked witch, the details differ. Many of the strange creatures of the book are omitted from the film; the silver slippers desired by the Wicked Witch of the West become ruby in the film; the Emerald City is mostly emerald because the inhabitants and visitors wear green-lensed glasses; reality and dream in the film are conflated.

Before the film, there were other recapitulations of the original work. As Gjovaag explains in his website, *The Wonderful Wizard of Oz* was followed by a musical stage play named *The Wizard of Oz* (1902) before the 1939 film of the same name. The first book was also followed by thirteen of Baum's books about Oz and expanded between 1900 and 1963 to a canon of forty books, with authors including Ruth Plumly Thompson, John R. Neill, Jack Snow, Rachel R. Cosgrove, and Eloise Jarvis McGraw and Lauren McGraw Wagner. Copyright on the original work expired in 1956 (Gjovaag), and the world of Oz media expanded.

A 1978 film, made from an earlier Broadway musical, repeats, more or less, the story of Oz. *The Wiz*, starring Diana Ross and Michael Jackson, begins in the Harlem area of New York City and subsequent events and details are updated, flying monkeys becoming motorcycle gangs, the good witch being a numbers runner, the witch's non-motorcycle minions being sweatshop workers. Essentially, however, the themes of the original, the 1939 film, and *The Wiz* remain the same: we already have the things we need to make us complete, home is a good place to be, and a quest can bring realizations, initiations, and benefits.

New versions of the Oz story abound; some are continuing sagas not yet finished at this publication date; others have told their story and ended. Both *The Wizard of Oz* and *The Wiz* are closer to Baum's imagined world than many of the other, later tales of Oz.

For example, Jack Snow, who wrote some of the Oz canon, also wrote a short story called "A Murder in Oz," an event theoretically impossible since nothing dies in Oz. In the short story, Ozma is murdered and the Wizard becomes the detective who seeks the culprit who turns out to be culpable but not guilty.

In *A Barnstormer in Oz,* subtitled *A Rationalization and Extrapolation of the Split-Level Continuum,* a noted science fiction writer, Philip José Farmer, has an airplane pilot come through a rift to land in Oz. Incorporating elements of conspiracy, "science" theory, and "realistic" details, the novel moves closer to science fiction than the fantasy of the other works. This book is no longer being printed—yet, and that's a shame.

In *Dorothy of Oz,* Son Hee-Joon takes the basic concept of Oz and converts it in a Korean manhwa (South Korean comic, print or animated) to a "sideways" story in five volumes, of which four are translated into English. In Volume One, the reader is dropped *in media res* into the adventure. Mara, the main character, is called Dorothy by others even as she insists she is actually Mara. The Tin Woodman is a cyborg. The Cowardly Lion is called Tail and is a chimera (half lion, half human). The Scarecrow is a clone. There are gray areas of motive and action. The story is ongoing so it's not entirely clear what final relationships will occur and what alliances will hold. I can't wait for the next volume.

The Tin Man, a TV production, both continues the story of Oz and transforms it. *The Tin Man*, a 2007 miniseries from director Nick Willing, starring Zooey Deschanel and Neal McDonough, ran six hours on the SyFy channel in 2008. DG (for Dorothy Gale) is the main character, a disaffected teen who falls into the O.Z. (Outer Zone) and discovers companions and truths about her birth, parents, and heritage. Dark and evocative, this retelling functions on several levels: it refers to the original text and to the 1939 film but it also depicts the Tin Woodman as a sheriff (hence, the man with the tin star — the tin man) who has lost his family and thus his heart. Quest for power, justice, revenge, truth, knowledge, redemption — quest is the ultimate aim of the characters. What motivates the characters and what ends they achieve are the central delights of *The Tin Man*.

An odd and fascinating book from John Skipp and Marc Levinthal is titled *The Emerald Burrito of Oz*. The Emerald Burrito is a restaurant in Oz. This book is charming, interesting, and compelling. It includes corporate and government conspiracies, a tin man who is half crazed, people from the "real world" who make their homes in Oz, living computers, good and evil (sometimes hard to decipher), and out-of-the-world entities. It's worth a read — or two!

The *Oz Squad: Volume One* is the first four issues of a continuation of the Oz series in comic book form. Dorothy and her companions, the Scarecrow, the Tin Woodman, and the Cowardly Lion, are members of Gale Force, an organization formed to protect Oz. All the members of the Squad are affected by their sojourn on Earth. Tik-Tok becomes evil. He is the nemesis for the members of Oz Squad who might be conflicted about fighting all out against a denizen of Oz.

In Search of Dorothy/Witch's Revenge/Dorothy and the Wizard's Wish is a series not finished at publication of this volume. The series asks, "What if Oz wasn't a dream?" and, twenty years after Dorothy leaves Oz, we find the Scarecrow, the Lion, and the Woodman traveling in a tornado machine to find Dorothy in the U.S. Meanwhile, the Wicked Witch of the West (who has possessed the body of a U.S. woman) is also on a hunt, again to find those ruby slippers (this series alludes only to the film *The Wizard of Oz*). The first two books end with Scarecrow making a plan to foil the Witch, and that's where we leave Oz until the publication of the third volume. Maybe we want to know the end of the story; maybe not.

Dorothy is a Fumetti comic, that is, a comic made with photographs. Dorothy is a disaffected, disenchanted teen (disaffected teens seem to be in ample supply in these later versions of Oz) in a science-fictionalized retelling of the classic story, with an emphasis on the struggle between good and evil, dark and light. *Dorothy* is chapters one through four of a comic originally published quarterly. Sadly, it remains unfinished.

Although the Dorothy of this photo-comic version is still on a quest to get home, there's more conflict, both external and internal. Does she really want to go home? Is home where her heart's desire resides? I cannot find other issues, but this volume is well worth investigating. With both Dorothy's back story of unhappiness in Kansas and Oz's past told partly through flashback, the graphic novel has a fascinating, evocative, and suspenseful structure.

The series *Lost in Oz (Lost in Oz, Lost in Oz: Rise of the Dark Wizard, Lost in Oz: Temple of the Deadly Desert*—2011 publication anticipated) follows four friends who end up in Oz. Their very presence changes Oz. They meet many of the inhabitants of Oz and travel between the worlds. The first two books of the series leave us with many unanswered questions, not all of which we really care about answering.

Gregory Maguire aided in the resurgence of interest in Oz when he began a series called the Wicked Years, beginning with *Wicked: The Life and Times of the Wicked Witch of the West. Wicked* starts with the birth of Elphaba, who will become the Wicked Witch of the West and tells the story from the point of view of the witch, born green and never really wanting to be evil. It's a dark story (not all green) and contains government policies, politics, conspiracies, decisions, and power struggles, as well as the rebellions and treasons of the anti-government fighters. Elphaba is melted by Dorothy, but the saga doesn't end.

Maguire continues the story with three other novels including *Son of a Witch*, the story of Elphaba's son Liir, and *A Lion Among Men*, the chronicle of the Cowardly Lion.

The initial book of the series, *Wicked: The Life and Times of the Wicked Witch of the West*, became *Wicked*, the musical, which also pays some homage to *The Wizard of Oz* film imagery. The musical begins with a celebration of the witch's demise and the arrival of Glinda in a bubble, reminiscent of the film. Events narrated in detail in the Maguire novel are often only referred to in the musical. Less dark than Maguire's novel and with a happier outcome, *Wicked* is a fascinating retelling.

And this is certainly not the end of the creative uses of Baum's original concept of Oz.

The Wonderland with Alice

Another iconic work appearing in several iterations is *Alice in Wonderland*, which originated in two volumes by Lewis Carroll: *Alice's Adventures in Wonderland* in 1865 and *Alice Through the Looking Glass* in 1871. The original *Alice's*

Adventures in Wonderland begins with Alice on the bank of a river, bored with her book. She follows a watch-carrying, talking white rabbit and falls down a rabbit hole. Among others, she meets the Cheshire Cat, the March Hare, the Dormouse, the Hatter, and the Queen. The whole thing turns out to take place in a dream.

In *Alice Through the Looking Glass [and What Alice Found There]* we find Alice playing with her kittens until she wonders about mirrors and climbs up to fall through the mirror above the fireplace. In *Through the Looking Glass*, she meets Tweedledum and Tweedledee and the Red Queen with whom she runs posthaste over a chessboard. Once again she wakes to find Wonderland a dream and herself perhaps a figment of someone else's dream.

Walt Disney's animated 1951 *Alice in Wonderland* conflates the two books and introduces characters from both: the White Rabbit, Tweedledum and Tweedledee, Queen of Hearts, and Cheshire Cat. Alice's adventures lead her on a quest for home and she finally awakes to reality with new knowledge that fantasy might be too fantastic.

The 1999 Hallmark *Alice in Wonderland* is a departure from both the original and Disney. Alice is a young girl, frightened to sing in front of guests. However, just as most Alices also realize, her trip down the rabbit hole shows her that she has her own strength.

2009's *Alice*, written and directed by Nick Willing (who also directed *Tin Man*), makes Alice grown up and in the throes of romance. Alice goes through the glass to find that Wonderland's calm is a drug supplied by people from our present world who are captured and forced through the glass to slavery in a casino-like factory of emotions. She finds her past, her present, and her future in Wonderland and uses her new-found knowledge to understand what true love really is and who might deserve such a feeling.

Walt Disney's 2010 *Alice in Wonderland* live-action version, starring Mia Wasikowska and Johnny Depp, is again different from other versions, but also features a grown up Alice. Directed by Tim Burton, 2010's *Alice in Wonderland* takes some odd turns. Alice is a runaway from a marriage. In Wonderland, she faces her fears and overcomes the evil queen to restore the order that should reign in such a kingdom. She leaves, promising the Hatter she will return. Having won the fight in Wonderland, she is strong enough to refuse marriage and strike off on her own.

In a departure from the "standard" reworkings of the old story, *Sesame Street* has produced *Abby in Wonderland*. Rhyming to grow bigger and smaller, *Sesame Street*'s fairy-in-training Abby Cadabby is the Alice figure. With Elmo as the Red Rabbit, Abby meets the Counterpillar (who counts) and the Cheshire Cookie Cat (who says "follow the yellow brick road ... oh, that different story"), goes to a "T" party with the Mad Hatter, and plays croquet with His Royal Majesty the Grouch of Hearts.

Non-western countries love Alice too. Japan has several versions of Alice, including the multi-volume mangas *Alice in the Country of Hearts* by Quin-Rose/Soumei Hoshimo and *Alice 19th* by Yu Watase, the graphic novel series *Key Princess Story: Eternal Alice Rondo* by Kaishaku, the television anime *Alice in Wonderland*, and the DVD *Miyuki-Chan in Wonderland*. A new Korean film *Alice* was casting in 2010. Carroll's stories live almost everywhere.

Alice in Wonderland and *The Wonderful Wizard of Oz* are more recent stories than the old "fairy" tales. Yet those old tales still take on new life as they are retold.

Combination Stories

Into the Woods is an amalgamation of fairy tales: Cinderella, Little Red Ridinghood, Jack and the Beanstalk, and Rapunzel, with mentions of Snow White and Briar Rose. The 1980s musical, directed and written (with Stephen Sondheim) by James Lapine, and starring Bernadette Peters, became a DVD in 1997. With a stage narrator, the stories are interwoven. The characters must go into the woods to find their hearts' desires and to save themselves from evils, including giants. The woods are the place where each one comes face to face with his/her own morality and mortality. All the characters (some of whom are dead) return with lessons learned; children listen; children don't listen; actions have meaning and consequence; everyone goes into the woods.

The ten hour mini-series of *The Tenth Kingdom* contains several of the old stand-by stories, woven together, including Snow White, Little Bo Peep, wicked stepmothers, wolves, and trolls. The premise is there are nine kingdoms in faery; the tenth kingdom is the "real world." Mixing the stories together, along with a connecting narrative, gives them renewed life.

Also breathing new life into ancient narratives is Mercedes Lackey, a notable fantasy writer, who has started a new series based on the "classic" fairy tale, updating and sometimes conflating the well-known stories. The Five Hundred Kingdoms series takes place in a logically-illogically constructed universe in which fairy godmothers, evil stepmothers, and handsome princes live — with a twist.

And So?

What can we do with these reincarnations of literary works, these re-embodiments, these re-creations? We can look at changes in narrative, theme, symbol, tone, and audience as different authors of different eras reincarnate old standards. We might start with audience. Each of the works has a specific audience in mind. Assigning one or more works and discussing how the prospective audience affects the content, language, tone, and purpose of the text is interesting. For example, the audience for the original Oz books is small children; the audience for *A Barnstormer in Oz* is adults with some interest in science and science fiction; the audience for *Dorothy in Oz* is early twenty-first century comic book aficionados (at least initially). Asking the questions about how the text changes to reflect the assumptions and conventions of the audience can elicit some remarkable discussions.

Discussing audience leads into the discussion of narrative style and language. The obvious change in language is the use of R-rated words, such as in *The Emerald Burrito of Oz*. But there are other changes as well. Just as *Burrito* does, *A Barnstormer in Oz* uses science and science fiction terms that might not be familiar to a younger audience. Dropping one into the midst of action without an explanation, as occurs in the manhwa *Dorothy in Oz* is not a narrative style typically found in children's stories, which tend to follow simple chronological narratives. We might ask what effect narration sequencing has on the audience and what purpose changing from simple chronology to more complex forms of storytelling fulfills?

Characters also change from one version to another. Why? What is the function of changing characterization? For example, Tik-Tok of the original *Tik-Tok of Oz* book is an inoffensive character with great flaws. He is round and copper and could be useful in many adventures. However, his greatest flaw is having to be wound up to function. He has three separate windings: thought, action, and speech. Each must be wound. The major difficulty in having Tik-Tok as a companion is that his gears often stop working just at the moment he needs to be of aid to his companions.

He appears in other works (*Queen Ann in Oz* by Karyl Carlson and Eric Gjovaag) as the same metallic oddball, but in some, instead of acting as an instrument of good, becomes an immoral monster (*Oz Squad*) or the foil of an immoral element (Grommetik in *Wicked*). Investigating the rationale that drives the change leads to questions: Do our fears of technology drive us to view Tik-Tok as a robot, the metallic unfeeling being that is capable of ignoring humanity and its hard-won morality?

This technophobic reasoning doesn't seem reasonable since we are inundated with technology, immersed in it daily. We are Internet users, on mainframe, laptop, pad, and smart phone, and with texting, e-mail, video, and still pictures on our cell phones. We're never disconnected.

So why is Tik-Tok a creature of fear? Is it because we've seen too many movies with evil robots? Is it because we are familiar with the Terminator films? Is it because technology has progressed to the point that we can see possible negative futures, even if subconsciously, and fear them?

P.W. Singer writes in *Scientific American* about the rise of military robots and the fact that warfare is more and more dependent on robots, which have come to the point that "The human is certainly part of the decision making but ... a decision to override the robot's decision must be made in only half a second, with few willing to challenge what they view as the better judgment of the machine" (63).

Classic science fiction novels and short stories, as well as recent films, have featured robots and androids that act independently and not to the betterment of humanity. "Fondly Fahrenheit," by Alfred Bester, is one of those stories, occasionally reprinted in anthologies. In it an android, his programming affected by temperature, becomes a serial killer, hardly a story that makes for comfortable thought. Then we have many other examples: the 1921 play in which the word robot first appeared, *R.U.R. (Rossum's Universal Robots)*; *I, Robot,* film or Asimov story (in which the evil robot appears in "Little Lost Robot," maybe); the Transformers films, comics, toys, and TV cartoons; *Doctor Who*'s Daleks (which have appeared in more than one medium and whose "Exterminate! Exterminate!" resonates through pop culture); Hal (okay, it's a computer) from *2001: A Space Odyssey,* film and Clarke novel; GLADOS in *Portal*; Data's Evil Twin and the Borg (a combo entity whose saying "Resistance is futile" also resonates) in *Star Trek*; Adam the Frankensteinian cyborg in *Buffy the Vampire Slayer*; Solid State Entity in *Neverness*; replicants from *Blade Runner* and Philip Dick's *Do Androids Dream of Electric Sheep?*; and many, many others.

So manmade technological marvels can be frightening. None of these anxiety-producing elements had yet appeared when Tik-Tok made his first appearance. And the negative imagery of robot/android has become more and more ubiquitous. Perhaps the "old days" allowed a more rosy picture of the rise of technology.

However, in contrast to the worsening image of Tik-Tok, the Tin Man has not made as dramatic a negative transformation. He is not so much feared, appearing in *Tin Man, Oz Squad,* and *Wicked* as a "good guy." He also appears in the *Emerald Burrito of Oz,* in which he is morally gray—having a strange temper and the ability to do great damage in the fight for right. He's "gray" as well in *Dorothy of Oz* (well, he's slightly suspect in this version—and we don't know the final outcome yet). So, he too has been subject to the change in perception of the modern versions. Still, we might ask why he is not as fearsome a figure as Tik-Tok becomes. Is it because he was once fully human? Then perhaps we must ask what being human actually means.

Class speculations could include both metallic characters in their investigations.

Dorothy and Alice also change. Dorothy in the original Oz is a little girl; Dorothy as played by Judy Garland is a teen; Dorothy in the photo *Dorothy* is an older, disgruntled teen. Dorothy in the *Wicked* versions and Dorothy in the original Oz only melt the witch because of an accident. What makes Dorothy generally keep her innocence? What is it about the character that perhaps elicits the authorial perception that she must be kept more likeable and less culpable? D.G. in *Tin Man* and photo Dorothy in *Dorothy*, being the cranky teens that they are, may be less likeable than the original Dorothys of Baum and the 1939 film. However, they still retain the wonder and naiveté, even innocence, and perhaps an absolute belief in goodness, that makes Dorothy a popular and iconic figure.

Alice grows from the little girl in *Alice's Adventures in Wonderland* and *Through the Looking Glass* and Disney's 1951 *Alice in Wonderland* to the grown-up Alice in Disney's 2010 *Alice in Wonderland* and in 2009's miniseries *Alice*. What effect does the age of a character have on the narrative? What effect does it have on the audience? We could investigate motivations for changes in characters in our discussions.

Tone can also change from version to version. *Wicked* is very political, not in the Republican/Democrat/Tea Party/Independent/Libertarian sense, but in the Munchkin/Wizard sense. There are conspiracies within conspiracies. *Alice in Wonderland* (2010) also has conspiracies and alliances on both sides of the rabbit hole. The *Alice* (2009) miniseries is also complex politically, with parties and alliances. What is the tone of each version of the story? How does the author convey the tone? What does the difference in tone mean to the impact of the work?

Symbols may remain the same and they may change. Tik-Tok is a changeable figure that can also function as a symbol. Dorothy and Alice themselves can be symbolic of the initiation quest—and, interestingly, they are girl questers, which is not generally or historically a typical role for that gender. What does that mean in terms of the narrative? What does that say about our culture and the culture of the work?

Themes also morph. From themes suitable to children to adult themes, it is investigation of themes that many of us find most interesting. What are the themes of each work? What themes carry from work to work? How are works tied together by theme? Themes of friendship and betrayal, attainment and failure to attain, and the outcome of various pursuits—successful or not—in terms of personal growth, initiation, courage and cowardice, community, individual choice, and many others are exemplified in the various works. Each of these items can lead to productive discussion.

Why would an author choose to use the mythology of the original book (and perhaps the additions of subsequent mythological rebirths)? One might speculate that using an existent mythology gives a working shorthand to an author. For example, we can see in *The Tenth Kingdom*, as well as in *Into the Woods*, that references to fairy tales function beyond allusions to deepen the impact of the narrative. For example, the princes in *Into the Woods*, even after attaining the women for whom they have striven—Cinderella and Rapunzel—sing about their desire to quest for the woman in the glass casket—

Snow White — and the woman behind the briars — Sleeping Beauty/Briar Rose. The audience recognizes these references and understands not only the allusion but the questing princes as well. It's not attaining the hand of the princess either prince really desires; it's the quest itself. Cinderella refers to the prince she meets at the ball as "charming" but can't seem to find other qualities with which to attribute him, even as the Baker's Wife pushes her for more detail. So the fact that the audience knows "all about" Prince Charming adds humor to this scene. And when Prince Charming himself admits that he's "charming, not sincere," again the audience can appreciate the humor in that utterance beyond a simple allusion.

In *The Tenth Kingdom*, the references to mirrors allude to Sleeping Beauty's stepmother, the evil queen, who, in many versions of the story, asks the mirror who is most beautiful. The *Tenth Kingdom* version of the story, though, gives the queen even more mirror power, the power to communicate and to transport. Magic mirrors are a staple in fairy tales and the mirrors in the Kingdoms are the quintessential mirrors. We also have the Wolf, who is both a bad guy pretending to be a good guy (so that betrayal can ensue), and a bad guy redeemed by love. Then there's the Midas curse suffered by Tony, who, like Midas, thought the curse was not a curse, but a really fine idea. These allusions then add depth to the story by evoking the entire oeuvre of the referenced tale.

Other factors could surface in discussion as each element is debated and each work is examined. So we continue to investigate fantasy works from previous eras, partly because those works can be connected to other works under discussion and used as an "illuminative tool" (Durand 4), "as a way of ... shedding light on some topic or theoretical framework in a wholly separate setting" (Durand 3–4). However, we go beyond simply using the texts as "gateway material" in order to deal with more substantive material; we study those texts in and of themselves. In fact, James Hannaham, novelist and journalist, contends that "Every experimental director goes through an 'Alice in Wonderland' thing" (qtd. in Mead 47). Perhaps this continual reinvention is because, as Brown, who writes about the process and purpose of writing, says, *Alice's Adventures* "can be read as a glorious fantasy, or it can be read as a comment on the powerlessness of a child, of children in society. You don't have to choose — you can read it on many levels...." (Brown 543). In fact, she contends, we study fantasy/pop culture works because "both *The Iliad* and *Alice in Wonderland* ring true. People read them today with as much pleasure as people derived from them when they were first written. A work lives like that if it is morally true" (Brown 543).

We study the original texts and the changes in those texts. The purpose of such study is multi-leveled. We have the "Well, look what Soandso's done with *that* work. Amazing. Isn't that *fun*!" We have, looking only at the new work, the "What does this new creation say?" We have, looking at both old and new works, the "What does this new creation say that the old one did not? What does this new creation mean that the old one did not?" We have the "What is the purpose of re-creating an old work? What are the significances of the changes, additions, and deletions the new author has made?" We have the "Is this new work worth reading and studying? Is it more or less valuable than the old work?" So from amazement to analysis to criticism, looking at old and new, in juxtaposition or alone, discovering new ways of telling old stories, is a valuable exercise for literary students and professors alike.

Changes, even as they make the work perhaps entirely different, illustrate the timeless nature of such creations as those creations are altered and claimed by subsequent generations.

Summaries

I've included the summaries of the major incarnations because even if the devil is not in the details the differences are.

Wizardy Summaries

The original *Wonderful Wizard of Oz* starts with Dorothy, a little girl living in Kansas with her Aunt Em, Uncle Henry, and dog Toto. Dorothy and Toto are caught inside a whirling tornado that carries them, and the farmhouse, to a magical land where the house, settling, lands on the Wicked Witch of the East and kills her. Grateful, the Good Witch of the North gives Dorothy the silver shoes the Wicked Witch of the East was wearing when she died. The Good Witch tells Dorothy that she should go see the Wizard of Oz, residing in the City of Emeralds, and ask him to help her return to Kansas. Dorothy sets out on the road paved with yellow bricks and saves the Scarecrow hanging on a pole, derusts the Tin Woodman, and meets the Cowardly Lion. They all agree to go with her to the Emerald City to get, respectively, a brain, a heart, and courage. Their journey involves many obstacles to overcome, including the bear-tiger Kalidahs and the field of Deadly Poppies, from which they are rescued by field mice.

At the Emerald City, they are asked to don green spectacles, giving the city a green appearance. Individually, the travelers meet the Wizard, who appears in various guises — as a giant head, a woman, a beast, or a ball of fire. The Wizard agrees to help each of them — for the price of their killing the Winkie ruler who happens to be the Wicked Witch of the West. Desperate, the four agree and set out to be beset by wolves, crows, bees, and soldiers. They overcome all but are then captured by the Winged Monkeys, controlled by the Witch through the magical powers of the Golden Cap. The Winged Monkeys disassemble the Scarecrow and Tin Woodman and imprison the

Lion. The Witch tricks Dorothy out of one of her silver shoes. Dorothy throws a bucket of water on the Witch, who melts. The Winkies celebrate their freedom, put the Scarecrow and Woodman back together, and ask the Woodman to become their new ruler. The Tin Woodman says he will return after Dorothy returns to Kansas. Using the Golden Cap, Dorothy commands the Winged Monkeys to take the travelers to the Emerald City. The four travelers, back in the Emerald City, are avoided by the Wizard, whom Toto accidentally reveals as a traveling-show magician who came to Oz from Omaha in a balloon. The Wizard gives the Scarecrow bran, pins, and needles brains (so he will be sharp-witted), the Woodman a silk heart, and the Lion a "courage" potion, each of which satisfies the recipient.

The Wizard agrees to take Dorothy and Toto with him in a balloon, appoints the Scarecrow to rule, and accidentally takes off too soon, leaving Toto and Dorothy behind. The Winged Monkeys cannot cross the desert around Oz and are no help, so the Soldier with the Green Whiskers tells the travelers to appeal to Glinda, the Good Witch of the South. Again, they journey, meeting Fighting Trees, Hammer-Heads, China people, and a giant spider, which the Lion kills, freeing the forest animals from its tyranny. The Lion agrees to return as ruler of the forest when Dorothy has succeeded in making it to Kansas. The travelers finally reach their destination and Glinda tells Dorothy the silver shoes have all along been her ticket to Kansas. Glinda will use the Golden Cap to return Dorothy's friends, who are now rulers of sections of Oz, to their kingdoms and then release the Cap to the King of the Monkeys. Dorothy and Toto return to Kansas, losing the shoes in the magical trip, and rejoin her relieved relatives.

The 1939 film *The Wizard of Oz* (also starring Jack Haley, Billie Burke, Charles Grapewin, and Clara Blandick) differs from the original novel. Dorothy and her aunt and uncle still live on a farm in Kansas, but are joined by three farmhands: Hickory, Hunk, and Zeke. A mean, bicycle-riding townswoman takes Toto away by sheriff's order after she is bitten. Toto escapes and returns to Dorothy, who takes him and runs away, finding an itinerant fortune teller who, checking her possessions, tells her that her aunt is ill with grief. Dorothy, stricken, returns to the farmhouse just in time to be in a tornado and be struck unconscious. She awakes in the house, which is being carried by the tornado: the house drops to the ground and Dorothy opens the door to a Technicolor village of little people, who sing in celebration of the house/Dorothy killing the Wicked Witch of the East. A bubble-riding Glinda, the Good Witch of the North, appears. Her sister, the Wicked Witch of the East, tries to steal the ruby slippers from her dead sister's feet but Glinda magicks them onto Dorothy's feet. The Wicked Witch of the West vows revenge; Glinda tells Dorothy to ask the Wizard of Oz in the Emerald City for aid, and reminds her never to take off the slippers.

Dorothy and Toto start their travels on the Yellow Brick Road, meeting a Scarecrow whom she pulls from a pole, a Tin Man whom she oils, and a Cowardly Lion, who all decide to join her in hopes of receiving their hearts' desires of brains, heart, and courage, respectively, all of which they demonstrate they already possess as they meet obstacles, including a field of sleep poppies, along the Road. In the Emerald City, they meet the Wizard (appearing as a giant head) who agrees to help them if they bring him the Wicked Witch of the West's broomstick, which never leaves her hand. The Witch is aware of their quest and sends the Winged Monkeys to capture Dorothy and Toto. When the Witch threatens to drown Toto unless she receives the ruby slippers, Dorothy tries to remove them to give to her but is unable to do so. The Witch concludes that the slippers must only come off when Dorothy is dead. The three companions arrive at the Witch's castle, overpower some guards, and dress as those guards to free Dorothy. As they all try to escape, they are cornered and the Witch sets fire to the Scarecrow. Horrified, Dorothy throws water on him, also wetting the Witch, who melts. The guards and soldiers rejoice in their freedom and surrender the broomstick,

The travelers return to the Emerald City and Toto inadvertently exposes the Wizard as a fraud. However, the fast-talking Wizard convinces them they had their desired qualities all along and only need the paperwork, which he grants them, to prove it. The Wizard offers to take Dorothy to Kansas the same way he arrived, by balloon, and leave the three companions in charge of his kingdom. Toto, chasing a cat, makes Dorothy miss the balloon. Saddened, she supposes she will stay in Oz, but Glinda appears and explains the ruby slippers have always had the power to return her to Kansas but that Dorothy needed to learn that running away doesn't lead to heart's desire. Dorothy says goodbye to Oz and taps her heels three times, chanting, "There's no place like home." Dorothy awakens to a black-and-white world surrounded by the farm family, who resemble the characters in Oz. She tells of her quest, but Aunt Em says it was all a dream, and Dorothy reiterates that there's no place like home.

In *The Wiz* (also starring Nipsey Russell, Richard Pryor, Ted Ross, Lena Horne, Mabel King, Thelma Carpenter, Theresa Merritt, and Stanley Greene), Dorothy Gale, schoolteacher, lives in a Harlem apartment with her aunt and uncle and refuses to get out on her own. After a Thanksgiving dinner, Toto runs into a snowstorm and Dorothy catches him but is whirled into Oz, smashing a sign that falls onto the Evermean, the Wicked Witch of the West, and freeing the park inhabitants, who are Munchkins transformed to graffiti by the witch. Miss One, the Good Witch of the North and a numbers runner, gives Evermean's silver slippers to Dorothy, telling her if she wants to go home she must follow the Yellow Brick Road, which is not immediately seen, to the Wizard in the Emerald City. Dorothy is in despair. She discovers a Scarecrow made of garbage, who wants a brain, and together they manage to find the Yellow Brick Road. They collect other companions: a Tin Man (who wants a heart) from a long-ago amusement park and a Cowardly Lion (who wants courage) banished from the jungle and hiding as one of the New York Public Library's stone lions.

Their journey takes them past puppets controlled by a homeless peddler and prostitutes called Poppy Girls who want to put the companions to sleep with dusting powder (and not the talcum kind). Escaping all traps, they arrive at the Emerald City at the World Trade Center and meet the fire-breathing giant head which purports to be the Wizard and who sends them to kill the witch who runs sweatshops: Evillene, the Wicked Witch of the West, who also has control of the Flying Monkeys — a motorcycle gang. The gang captures the companions; Evillene "destroys" the Scarecrow (unstuffs him) and the Tin Man (flattens him), tortures the Lion, and threatens Toto with death by fire. Dorothy activates a sprinkler system, accidentally melting the "I'm allergic to water" witch, freeing the captive sweatshop workers (Winkies) and the motorcycle gang, which gives the companions a ride to the Wizard, whom they discover to be a phony politician from New Jersey who failed to be elected dogcatcher and whose promotional balloon flew him to Oz. The three companions who wanted their hearts' desires despair but Dorothy convinces them they had what they wanted/needed all along. Glinda, the Good Witch of the South, tells Dorothy she can get home if she finds her inner strength and uses the silver slippers. Dorothy, strong now, clicks her heels three times and finds herself back in Harlem. She, now strong and confident, and Toto, still a dog, enter the apartment.

The short story "A Murder in Oz" begins with the discovery of Ozma, dead. Glinda finds in the Great Book of Records that Ozma returned to her previous existence. The Wizard knows what has happened and has the guards capture a small boy, Tip. Ozma became Tip by enchantment (in Baum's series) and Tip also wanted to live and be with his old friends, the Sawhorse and Jack Pumpkinhead among them. The Wizard concludes that, when Ozma was restored as a girl, the boy spirit still existed and finally took back its life from Ozma. The Wizard tells Tip he can continue to live and the Wizard will restore life to Ozma who will be Tip's twin. All ends happily as it should in the Land of Oz.

A Barnstormer in Oz is based on the premise that Dorothy visited Oz once and only once, as in *The Wonderful Wizard of Oz*, the other books being the works of a fertile imagination and not true recountings of Dorothy's adventures. The pilot is Hank Stover, who is the son of Dorothy Gale and who knows the original story is true. He lands in Oz and meets Glinda and her female army, to one of whom he is attracted. He gets involved in the battle against the latest foe of Oz, Erakna the witch. Stover, as a scientist pilot, tries to discover what made Oz into Oz. He also discovers that his inadvertent landing in Oz might become the first of a deliberate number of U.S. government incursions made in the hopes that Oz would provide weapons and procedures that would help the U.S. in any future conflict. Stover, who is now invested in Oz, refuses to accede to government demands and succeeds, for the nonce, in fending off what amounts to invasion.

The Korean comic *Dorothy of Oz* begins in a town in which Mara, Toto, and three companions stop. The inhabitants are threatened by monsters and the town garrison seems unable to help. The three companions, Abee, called Scarecrow; Namu, AKA Tin Woodman; and Tail, also called Cowardly Lion; and Dorothy battle the monsters, which turn out to be the members of the garrison, developed as monsters and controlled by the head of the garrison. It is in the next volumes that the reader finds out the story begins when Mara Shin loses her dog Toto in a Korean town and searches for him on a yellow brick road only she can see. The road takes her to Oz, where people keep calling her Dorothy and she keeps insisting she is Mara Shin.

The yellow road, on which she is safe and unseen, may be the way she can go home. She meets Selluriah, a witch who gives her witch's boots that, if Mara stamps, turn Mara into a witch. Sellurian is killed by an assassin, but Mara is found with the body and suspected of murder. Mara also has a glove, Thyros, that turns into a destruction-causing staff. Toto is frequently forgotten and searched for. Abee is one of the Wicked Witch of the West's clones whom Mara rescues from a pole. He has memory and speech problems. Namu is half-person, half-machine — a cyborg who cannot remember his full mission, which originally was to locate Mara (which might prove to be an ominous occurrence). At the end of Volume Four, the reader meets Tail for a few short frames. Tail, created by the Witch of the North, is a lion chimera with ears, tail, and claws of a lion and looks most feminine (even as a boy), is hungry (like the Hungry Tiger of another Baum book), and short-tempered.

The Tin Man mini-series (also starring Alan Cumming, Raoul Trujillo, Kathleen Robertson, and Richard Dreyfuss) continues and redefines the story of Oz. D.G., living in a small town in Kansas, unhappy with her life and with visions of a woman telling her a storm is coming, wants something different. Through a storm, the ruler of the O.Z. (the Outer Zone), Azkadellia, sends soldiers to kill D.G., who escapes into the O.Z. through that same storm. She finds companions: Glitch, who had half his brain excised by Azkadellia; Wyatt Cain, a "sheriff," or Tin Man, who opposed Azkadellia and who lost his family and was locked in a metal suit for years; and Raw, who is an animal/human combination whose people are enslaved and used as "seers."

D.G. learns a number of things in her journey around the O.Z. and in her session with the Mystic Man, a half-crazy prophet: her Kansas parents are androids; her real mother sent her warnings in her dreams; she is the sister of Azkadellia. We discover that Azkadellia killed D.G. as a child, but her mother revived her and gave her a secret to hold. We also discover someone in Cain's family is still alive. Azkadellia captures D.G. and Raw and the troop captain, Zero, shoots Cain, who falls into icy water, from which he is rescued by Glitch. Glitch and Cain go to the city to rescue D.G. In the city, the Mystic Man advises D.G. and is killed by Azkadellia. D.G. is freed by a dog/shapeshifter named Tutor, AKA Toto, who is secretly working for Azkadellia even as the four travel to find the Emerald of the Eclipse, the secret entrusted to D.G., who relearns her magic, discovers that Azkadellia's evil came upon her when D.G. left her alone after releasing an evil witch from her imprisonment, and finds that Tutor is a traitor to the group but keeps him with the group in his dog form. Glitch, Raw, and Cain are captured but freed by Cain's son — who is alive and leading the resistance. Azkadellia's plot is to use the Emerald with a device which is already in her possession and controlled by the missing part of Glitch's brain in order to imprison the O.Z.'s two suns behind the moon during an eclipse and keep the O.Z. dark forever.

D.G. finds her real father and travels with him by balloon to the O.Z.'s area of royal interment where Dorothy Gale, D.G.'s ancestor, is entombed and where Dorothy Gale gives the Emerald to D.G. as they meet in a black-and-white "Kansas." Azkadellia captures D.G.'s father and the Emerald and leaves D.G. to die. However, D.G. escapes to join her companions and they reach Azkadellia just as she completes her heinous plan. D.G. reaches for Azkadellia and releases her from the witch's thrall as the suns are also released and destroy the witch forever. D.G. and Azkadellia, now a good girl, reunite with their real parents.

In *The Emerald Burrito of Oz*, the Emerald Burrito of Oz serves only "goomer" meat, goomers being the only non-intelligent and non-speaking animal in Oz. Oz is reached through a "gate" in a barn in Salina, Kansas, which might transport a person to Oz, leave that person on the Kansas side of the gate, or kill the person. Originally, the "gate" was a matter of national security, but its existence was leaked by a member of the CIA. Gene Spielman, entering Oz for a vacation, and Aurora Quixote Jones, working at the Emerald Burrito, meet on the internet and then in person. Aurora wants Gene to smuggle her musings on events out of Oz. Gene wants to make Aurora happy, with ulterior romantic notions.

Contrary to expectations, Gene is able to carry a laptop — that continues to work, albeit with some lively, living quirks — into Oz. The laptop plays an important part in the subsequent events, being sentient and aware of the events in the "black cloud," which menaces the Emerald City and the Land of Oz. The two partners fall into a situation: Ozma and Glinda, rulers of Oz, are under attack by the Hollow Man, who is supported by elements of the U.S.

government and a fast food/entertainment corporation and wants to rule—or destroy all existence in—Oz. The Hollow Man's scheme is not actually in the best interest of the corporation because the corporation wants to take over Oz and make it a theme park. Gene has to learn to adapt to a place where guitars grow on trees, bushes talk and provide leaves that allow visitors to understand all languages, and cars travel in packs.

The book is told by two alternating narrators, Aurora and Gene, who write out their adventures as if in blogs. Gene meets Nick Chopper, who is the head of those resisting the Hollow Man, and Ralph, originally a representative of the U.S. and an ally of the Hollow Man who converts to fight for Oz. Mikio is a genius at Oz "science" and aided by Dr. Pipt (of Life Powder—from an Oz canon book—fame). Mikio fights the war for Oz from a rooftop and science perspective; Ralph, Aurora, Gene, Nick Chopper, and the "good" inhabitants of Oz fight a battle. The battle ranges far, and part of it takes place in a compound set up like an Earth video game. Ultimately, the good guys—Ozma, Glinda, Nick Chopper, and, of course, Gene and Aurora—triumph with the aid of the entities which originally created Oz. Gene takes the two narratives back to Earth and will post them so Internet browsers will know the difficulties in Oz were caused by elements in the U.S., which may cause him some difficulty. However, his laptop may give him a way back to Oz.

In the comic series, *The Oz Squad*, the first problem with which we see the Squad dealing is Tik-Tok's loss of morality. Dorothy is grown up. When Tik-Tok, now in the USA, becomes violent (even to the point of killing babies), the Squad leaps into action and takes Tik-Tok back to Oz to be reintegrated into Oz society. The second problem is Rebecca Eastwitch offering Tik-Tok blueprints to bidders. The Hungry Tiger joins the hunt, and the Squad recovers the plans. However, Tik-Tok kills Jack Pumpkinhead and heads back to Earth. The fourth issue ends with Tik-Tok at large and the appearance of a new character: the Pincushion Man. The series continues, probably with more black-and-white mayhem, and can easily be avoided.

In the Fumetti *Dorothy*, Dorothy arrives in Oz, having jumped from a car twirling in a tornado, her arrival prophesied in the "evil queen's" dream. Her first companion, after her confrontation with a flying monkey, is TO-2, a mechanical kind of doggy thing. With water, she revives a witch who tells her there is evil afoot and gives her a necklace with a glowing green stone and tells her to look for a blue cobble road and a man named Boq. The "evil queen" tells her gray minion she wants her lost necklace which her dreams have prophesied will find its way to Dorothy. With the necklace the queen can finally defeat the Wizard.

Dorothy, wishing for a cheeseburger and a compass, travels with TO-2 and meets a talking, but incoherent—and needing a brain, ET-faced scarecrow whom she promises a hat. Hungry and tired, she enters a cave behind a waterfall, the lair of a dragon she defeats with pepper spray as he bites her, leaving her with a nasty wound. She follows TO-2 back to the scarecrow to ask for friendship. The scarecrow walks with Dorothy and tells a story about a boy who refused to take education pills (an allusion to events in Oz far past the Wonderful Wizard) and who opposed the evil queen but was captured and transformed into — a scarecrow — maybe. The transformation is shown to a woman who is shocked and then "goes away." The scarecrow, carrying an unconscious Dorothy, begs her not to go away and the novel ends.

In Search of Dorothy/Witch's Revenge/Dorothy and the Wizard's Wish begins the series when Joshua, Tamara, Tommy, and Laura end up in a strange land through freak weather. Joshua knows where they are — Oz. Their only hope of getting home is some little girl and her magic shoes, but entering the action will change the book/current events/whatever it is that's happening, which, of course, is a mystery to the characters who find that their copy of the *Wonderful Wizard of Oz* is now blank. Tracking Dorothy down and then trying for possession of the shoes, the four friends meet adventure after adventure, including meeting and not eating talking bugs who give them meal-berries; meeting and eating talking fish; meeting the Kalidahs, merpeople, fairies, Jack Pumpkinhead, and others; battling the Witch of the West and her flying monkeys, controlled by a cap; and trying to discover the whole of a prophecy about their presence in Oz, which is causing a problem with Oz history and with the future. Finally managing to get back home, they find they've been gone two years rather than a week and end up in an institution, where they meet Alice (yes, of *Alice in Wonderland* fame).

The second book begins with the friends breaking out of the asylum, with the exception of Joshua who has to experience shock therapy. The other three find Dorothy and begin their quest to find Glinda's Great Book of Records to erase the story of their presence. However, the Dark Wizard also wants the Book so he can prevent retribution as he plots to overthrow Oz. The books refer to many of the characters in the Oz canon, including Professor H.M. Wogglebug, T.E. (H.M.: Highly Magnified, T.E.: Thoroughly Educated), Sir Hokus of Pokus, Kabumpo, and others, as well as Alice and the Jabberwock from *Alice in Wonderland* (the early Disney film version at any rate). Book Two ends with Joshua's sudden rearrival in Oz, looking for that pesky prophesy, and with Tamara's finding she has power.

In *Wicked: The Life and Times of the Wicked Witch of the West*, Elphaba's parents are not entirely happily married, her mother (Melena) having married "beneath her" and her father (Frex) being gone often because he preaches to various populations. Melena takes a "green elixir" and a lover and subsequently gives birth inside the Clock of the Time Dragon, which travels around the land and occasionally gives prophesies. Her baby, Elphaba, is green, has wickedly sharp teeth, and is afraid of water (even as a newborn). The mother asks for help; and Nanny, an old family retainer, arrives. Frex continues to travel, and Turtle Heart, an itinerant glass blower arrives to keep Melena company, which might have resulted in Nessarose, a daughter with no arms, who becomes a convert to Frex's religion and is his favorite child.

Elphaba goes to university at Shiz, meeting a professor, Dr. Dillamond, a talking Goat. She ends up with Galinda as a roommate since Galinda has no chaperone with her, Ama Clutch being ill. Galinda and Elphaba, unlikely as it is, become friends. During classes they discover the increasing discrimination against talking Animals, a sentiment with which the headmistress Madame Morrible agrees. Galinda and Elphaba enroll in the sorcery section of the university and also become friends with Boq, a Munchkin boy, and Fiyero, a Vinkus prince. They rescue a captured Lion cub. Dr. Dillamond, who calls Galinda only "Glinda," is murdered by Grommetik (a "Tik-Tok"), witnessed by newly-arrived Ama Clutch, who is magicked into a coma. Nessarose arrives at Shiz with a pair of glass bead-covered shoes, which Galinda enchants so Nessarose can walk. As Ama Clutch is about to die, Glinda (who adopts Dr. Dillamond's name for her) revives her long enough to learn about Grommetik's murder of Dr. Dillamond. Madame Morrible almost persuades the three friends, Nessarose, Glinda, and Elphaba, to join the Wizard in his plans to unite the four regions of Oz.

Glinda, tempted, still joins Elphaba on a quest to Emerald City to convince the Wizard, who refuses, to remove the discrimination against Animals. Glinda returns to Shiz; Elphaba remains in the City and becomes part of the resistance against the Wizard and his policy to suppress Animals. Years go by, Elphaba meets Fiyero again and they become lovers and coconspirators but are betrayed and Fiyero is killed by the Gale Force, the Wizard's secret police. Elphaba escapes, becomes mute, and takes refuge in a "mauntery," where she meets Yackle, a very creaky old maunt.

After a number of years, Elphaba, now speaking and with a child named Liir, whom she does not recognize as hers since he was born to her during her unconsciousness, goes to Vinkus and lives with Fiyero's family: widow (Sarima), three children (Manek, Irji, and Nor), and widow's sisters. Elphaba wants to tell Sarima about her life with Fiyero. Sarima refuses to listen. Nanny shows up. Elphaba discovers a book of magic, the Grimmerie, and uses it to create/manufacture a flying monkey (Chistery). She causes Manek to die of an icicle after Manek leaves Liir in a well, where a fish tells Liir he is Fiyero's son. As Elphaba travels to see her father and Nessarose, who is now the Wicked Witch of the East and who promises to give Elphaba the beaded shoes when she dies, Fiyero's family is taken by soldiers. Nanny remains at the castle. A house containing Dorothy and Toto lands on Nessa, killing her and making her unable to fulfill her promise about the shoes since Glinda hands them over to Dorothy.

After Nessa's funeral, Elphaba goes to Shiz and bashes the already-dead Madame Morrible on the head. She claims the murder. She also discovers the Wizard to be her father. Ick. Elphaba returns to the castle, fearing Dorothy and her friends are conspiring to kill her at the Wizard's behest. She thinks the Scarecrow is Fiyero and sends dogs, crows, and bees to lead him to her, but all her representatives are killed by the companions, as is she, by accident, when Dorothy, who was tasked to kill her but only wants to apologize for inadvertently killing her sister, attempts to put out a fire. Dorothy returns to the Wizard with the green elixir and without the Grimmerie. Dorothy may or may not have returned to Kansas. The Wizard plans to leave Oz and kill himself.

The story continues in *Son of a Witch* with the tale of Liir, who, wounded, is taken to the mauntery where he was born, where he becomes close to a young maunt named Candle. Candle heals him and they pick up life at Apple Press Farm. We find out that Liir, on a quest to find Nor in Emerald City, meets Princess Nastoya, a talking Elephant enchanted to be human but ill and desiring to become fully Elephant before she dies. Liir asks the current ruler of Emerald City, Glinda, for help. Glinda introduces Liir to Shell, Elphaba's and Nessa's younger brother, who is not entirely ethical. Shell gives Liir access to the prison Southstairs, where Liir searches for Nor, who has already escaped.

Liir enlists in the Home Guard. The Guard goes to suppress the Quadlings. Because Liir's group is not aggressive enough, they are ordered to act. The events lead to the burning of a village and the death of many. Liir is disgusted and returns to Nanny. He is asked to attend a conference of Birds, who are now threatened by the Wizard's laws on Animals, but on the way is attacked by dragons and wounded. This leads him to the Mauntery where Yackle locks him away with Candle, who saves his life by physicality and ends up pregnant despite Liir's assertion that he never had sex with her (more unconsciousness). He is tasked to recover Elphaba's broom from the dragons who menace the birds.

Liir goes to the Emerald City, where Shell is the current ruler, where "Elphaba lives" is written on surfaces — in Nor's handwriting, and where he meets an old soldier friend, Trism, who is a conflicted dragon trainer. The two poison the dragons, steal the broom, and flee to the mauntery where they are discovered but escape. Liir sees Candle and persuades her to use her music to turn Nastoya back to an elephant and allow her to die. Liir goes to Nastoya's funeral but on returning to the farm finds Candle gone and a green newborn abandoned.

In *A Lion Among Men* we see more parallel stories. We have the story of the Lion cub (Brrr) rescued by Elphaba and her friends. However, the Lion no longer has a family or pride connections and feels disenfranchised. We revisit Yackle, who is old and asks to be buried in the crypt, where she does not die, and who seeks only her origin and the way of her death. We discover Nor, damaged but alive, and with the dwarf Mr. Boss and the Clock of the Time Dragon, who are looking for the Lion. Brrr and his pet, the Glass Cat (Grimalkin/Shadowpuppet) meet Yackle, who arises from her wrappings. Brrr tells Yackle he met Jemmsy, a soldier trying to trap Animals but caught in his own trap, who asks Brrr to go for help. Instead, Brrr stays with Jemmsy until he dies and takes his books and medal to give to Jemmsy's family in Tenniken.

On his way to Tenniken he has adventures with a Bear tribe, tries and fails to save trolls, decides he is a coward, flees to Shiz, flees to live with Lions, flees to a tribe of Tigers, and then flees and meets Dorothy, the Scarecrow, and the Tin Woodman (Nick Chopper). Together they go to the Wizard, go to Elphaba's, witness her death, and return to the Wizard, where Brrr gets a medal and promises Dorothy to take care of Liir, who disappears. Brrr becomes a broker and is arrested for aid to Animals but granted lenience if he agrees to hunt down the Grimmerie, which he seeks to find with Yackle's help.

In the musical *Wicked*, Glinda begins by telling the story of Elphaba, who was unhappily conceived, born green and thus discriminated against, and with the additional burden of a sister who cannot walk and for whom she must care. Galinda; Nessarose, with the gift of jeweled slippers from her father; and Elphaba go to Shiz where Madame Morrible singles out Elphaba as special and as a candidate for serving at the side of the Wizard. Dr. Dillamond, a talking Goat with a speech impediment who cannot say "Galinda," but only "Glinda," convinces Elphaba that Animals are losing their speech.

Elphaba thinks the Wizard can fix the problem and vows to see him. She and Galinda meet Fiyero and Boq. All of them attend a party where Fiyero celebrates hedonism, Boq chases Nessarose in an attempt to score with Galinda, Madame Morrible tells Galinda that Elphaba wants her to be part of the sorcery class, and Elphaba looks good in a hat. Galinda and Elphaba, after initial mutual abhorrence, become friends. Dr. Dillamond is removed from his position, and Fiyero and Elphaba, feeling attracted to each other but guilty about it because of Galinda, rescue a Lion cub. Elphaba, ambitious and hopeful, is granted a visit with the Wizard; Galinda sees Fiyero's attraction to Elphaba and decides to become "Glinda"; Nessarose discovers Boq wants Glinda; and Elphaba asks Glinda to go with her to see the Wizard.

The two see the Wizard who has Elphaba use the Grimmerie to make flying monkeys and who asks her to serve him. Elphaba refuses and is denounced. Elphaba asks Glinda to join her; Glinda refuses, and Elphaba escapes on her broomstick, earning the soubrette of the Wicked Witch of the West. Fiyero and Glinda break up. Elphaba enchants Nessarose's shoes, turning them ruby-colored. Nessarose, piqued at Boq's lack of feeling for her, makes his heart shrink so he will die. Elphaba makes him a Tin Man to save him, which onlookers think is an evil action. Elphaba is blamed. She tries to free the flying monkeys and is almost captured by Fiyero, the captain of the guards, who lets her go and runs away with her. Glinda tries to trap Elphaba with rumored danger to Nessarose, a danger the Wizard and Madame Morrible make real so that the weather they create causes a house to fall on Nessa and kill her. Glinda gives Nessa's shoes to Dorothy, the passenger in the house. Elphaba is almost captured and Fiyero actually is. Fiyero is tortured; Elphaba tries to save him but thinks she has failed and decides to actually become the wicked witch she is purported to be, capturing Dorothy in order to get the shoes. The Tin Man and the Cowardly Lion blame all their ills on Elphaba, forming a killing mob to chase her.

Glinda discovers Madame Morrible's role in Nessa's death. She tries to convince Elphaba to release Dorothy, telling Elphaba she will clear her name. Elphaba refuses. When Elphaba receives a letter, things change. She tells Glinda not to mend her reputation, to rule Oz, to take the Grimmerie, and to hide it. As the mob arrives, Dorothy throws a bucket of water on Elphaba, melting her. Glinda confronts the Wizard who admits he sired Elphaba and agrees to leave Oz. Glinda says she is not "Glinda the Good" and will rule wisely. Glinda mourns Elphaba even as the Scarecrow, the result of Elphaba's spell to save Fiyero, opens a trapdoor and helps Elphaba emerge. They have faked her death and now leave Oz together.

Alice Summaries

The original Alice in *Alice's Adventures in Wonderland* falls through the rabbit hole to a vestibule with a small door. She finds a "Drink Me" vial and an "Eat Me" cake, making her various sizes. When she is gigantic, she cries and makes a pool of tears. With a fan, she becomes small and swims in the pool with a mouse, who is offended by her talk of her cat. Other animals are also in the pool and the mouse tries to dry them with a talk about William the Conqueror, but the Dodo says a Caucus-Race, around and around with no winner, will dry them. Alice's talk about her cat runs the animals off.

Again Alice sees the White Rabbit, who wants her to find the Duchess's gloves and fan. However, Alice outgrows the White Rabbit's house. The animals throw cakes at her. She eats them and becomes small again. Alice meets a caterpillar on a mushroom, one side of which will make her grow and one of which will make her shrink. Finally she reaches the "correct size" and, seeing the Duchess receive an invitation from a Fish-Footman, goes into the

Duchess's house. The Duchess's cook is putting too much pepper in the soup: all sneeze. The Duchess gives the baby, who turns out to be a pig, to Alice.

Alice meets the Cheshire Cat who guides her to the March Hare's house where there is a tea party with the Hatter, and the Dormouse (mostly asleep) as guests. Senseless riddles irritate Alice, who leaves and goes to the palace garden where live playing cards are painting the white roses red. The Queen invites Alice to a croquet game with flamingos as mallets and hedgehogs as balls. The Queen wants the Cheshire Cat beheaded and, because he is only head, has to release the Duchess, who owns the cat, to help. The Duchess cannot help. She introduces Alice to the Gryphon who introduces her to the Mock Turtle who tells her story, which is interrupted so the Mock Turtle and Gryphon can dance, which is interrupted so Alice can attend the trial of the Knave of Hearts, accused of stealing the Queen's tarts. The very strange jury is composed of animals. The judge is the King of Hearts. The witnesses include the Duchess's cook and the Hatter. Alice is called as witness but because she has grown is ordered to leave the court, then sentenced to execution, but big Alice calls them all a "pack of cards" and is awakened by her sister to take tea.

In *Alice Through the Looking Glass*, Alice falls through the mirror to find her house is reversed; she can only read, including "Jabberwocky," by holding the book up to the mirror. She sees small, live chess pieces also. She leaves her reverse house and finds a garden with talking flowers that think she is a flower. She meets the bread-and-butterfly and a life-sized Red Queen who can run at fantastic speed and who informs Alice that the place she's entered is a giant chessboard. Alice, who is now a pawn, can become a queen if she makes it to the other side of the board. She rides a train over spaces and meets Tweedledum and Tweedledee who recite "The Walrus and the Carpenter," tell her she is the dream figment of the Red King, and begin to prepare for battle but are frightened by a crow.

Alice meets the White Queen with whom she advances over a brook. The Queen becomes a Sheep in a rowboat. Crossing yet another brook, Alice meets Humpty Dumpty who tells her about words and translates "Jabberwocky," then falls. The White King, the Lion, the Unicorn, and horses and men come to put Humpty together, and Haigha and Hatta come as messengers, but, as the Lion and the Unicorn fight, Alice leaves, crossing another brook into the realm of the Red Knight who wants to capture her. She is rescued by the White Knight who, reciting a poem and constantly falling off his horse, escorts her to the last brook which she crosses and becomes a queen. The White Queen and the Red Queen meet her and tell her they're going to the party she has invited them to, of which Alice has no knowledge. The party is a jumble and finally Alice shakes the Red Queen and wakes herself up, wondering if she is, in fact, a figment in the Red King's dream.

In the 1951 Disney film *Alice in Wonderland*, Alice is bored by her sister's reading and follows a White Rabbit down a rabbit hole, finds the "Drink Me" vial and an "Eat Me" cake with the help of Doorknob, gets small and then big, makes a tear lake, gets small and falls into the "Drink Me" bottle and floats through the doorway through which the White Rabbit disappeared. She gets to shore where the Dodo runs in the Caucus-Race. She meets Tweeldedum and Tweedledee who recite "The Walrus and the Carpenter," and goes to the White Rabbit's house where she grows large and gets stuck but escapes by eating a carrot. She enters a garden with talking flowers that think she is a flower and meets the bread-and-butterfly. She then meets the Caterpillar who introduces her to the growing big/small mushroom sides.

The Cheshire Cat directs her to the March Hare, celebrating his "unbirthday" with the Mad Hatter and Dormouse, then directs her to the garden of the Queen of Hearts where playing cards are painting the white roses red. The Queen invites Alice to play croquet with flamingo mallets and hedgehog balls. Alice is put on trial for the trick the Cheshire Cat plays and the Queen orders her executed, but Alice eats a piece of mushroom and grows gigantic, scolding the Queen, but she shrinks and all Wonderland chases her back to the Doorknob who tells her she is already out of Wonderland. Alice sees herself on the riverbank and she wakes, thinking that all nonsense might not be a good thing.

The 1999 Hallmark *Alice in Wonderland* film, starring Robbi Coltrane, Whoopi Goldberg, Ben Kingsley, Christopher Lloyd, Miranda Richardson, Martin Short, Peter Ustinov, George Wendt, Gene Wilder, and Tina Majorino, opens with Alice in her bedroom practicing a song she is to sing at a party. Partygoers and toys have semblances of characters which will appear in Wonderland. Alice runs away in fright and falls down that pesky rabbit hole where she has size issues but finally makes it through the tiny door, swimming in a pool of tears, meets Mr. Mouse and other weirdness, and runs in the Caucus-Race. At the White Rabbit's house, she drinks a growing potion and is trapped in the house until she shrinks.

She travels and meets Major Caterpillar, who becomes a butterfly, as she eats a piece of mushroom and becomes normal-sized. She meets the Duchess, baby (who becomes a pig), Cook (who throws pepper), and the Cheshire Cat, who sends her to the Mad Hatter, March Hare, and Dormouse at a party. She leaves to enter the Queen of Hearts's garden. The Queen invites her to play croquet and orders the Cheshire Cat executed. Alice convinces her to spare the Cat and meets the Gryphon and Mock Turtle who sing the "Lobster Quadrille." Alice meets the White Knight and some talking flowers, then Tweedledee and Tweedledum, who fight. She goes to the trial of the Knave of Hearts. Alice is called to the stand but eats some mushroom and becomes gigantic so she can see the intact jam tarts which makes the Knave innocent. The White Rabbit tells the court that he enticed Alice into

Wonderland deliberately so she could overcome her fear of singing in public. He sends her home where she sings the "Lobster Quadrille" and all ends happily.

In this 2009 televised *Alice*, starring Matt Frewer, Harry Dean Stanton, Tim Curry, Kathy Bates, and Caterina Scorsone, Alice gets a family heirloom ring from Jack Chase but he is kidnapped and, with the help of a stranger called the White Rabbit, goes through a mirror into Wonderland, which is not what the name implies. The Queen queries her son, Jack, as to why he gave the ring, the Stone of Wonderland AKA the key to the mirror-gates, to someone. Now everyone is after Alice. Through the mirrors, the White Rabbits kidnap people from the Oyster World, Earth, so the people's emotions from gambling can be made into a drug that pacifies the inhabitants of Wonderland.

Alice meets a resistance leader (Dodo) and fighter (Hatter, played by Andrew-Lee Potts, a total cutie) and a White Knight (Charlie) and is hunted by assassin Mad March, a man with the head of a rabbit. Alice, captured, tries to get Jack released, only to find he is the son of the Queen of Hearts and engaged to the Duchess, whose task is to find out why Jack gave the ring to Alice. Alice is rescued from Drs. Dee and Dum by Hatter and Charlie and they escape on pink flamingo flying motors until they are shot down. Alice meets Jack, who tells her that her father, who does not recognize Alice, can help send the captured Oysters back to Earth.

Mad March captures Alice and Jack. Hatter is captured as Charlie flees in fright. Alice and Hatter again escape as Charlie returns with a fake army that the Queen attempts to overcome with all her guards. Alice enters the casino and begs the Oysters to awake. Her father recognizes her and takes the bullet meant for her, dying. The Oysters awake, the casino collapses, the King of Hearts remains in the collapsing building, and the guards turn on the Queen. All is won. Jack stays with the Duchess. Alice uses the Stone of Wonderland to return, waking in a hospital, rescued by a construction worker who turns out to be Hatter. All is well.

In Walt Disney's 2010 *Alice in Wonderland* live-action version of *Alice in Wonderland*, Alice is expected to marry the son of Lord Ascot, but runs from the situation to chase a rabbit down a rabbit hole. She lands in Underland, meeting the White Rabbit, Dormouse, Dodo, Tweeledum, and Tweedledee, who discuss whether she is "the" Alice of the prophecy who will slay the Jabberwocky, overcome the Red Queen, and restore the White Queen's reign. The Caterpillar maintains she is not "the" Alice. Alice runs away as the Bandersnatch, the Knave of Hearts, and soldiers capture the group. The Red Queen is informed of Alice's presence in the land and Alice meets the Cheshire Cat, the March Hare, and the Mad Hatter, who is captured in place of Alice, taken to the Red Queen's palace, and becomes her personal hat maker. Alice has learned about the Red Queen and, enlisting Bayard the Bloodhound's help, infiltrates the Red Queen's castle to help the Mad Hatter.

Alice obtains the Vorpal Sword with which the Jabberwocky can be killed from the Bandersnatch, and escapes with the Hatter to the White Queen. All prepare for war, Alice with reluctance even though she is told she has been in the land before and that she has the ability to overcome the Jabberwocky on the Frabjous Day. On that day the two forces fight on a checkerboard battlefield and Alice faces the Jabberwocky, killing him. The White Queen, triumphant, gives Alice Jabberwocky blood so she can return home. Alice promises the Mad Hatter she will return. Returning home, she rejects her suitor and joins Lord Ascot's ship in an attempt to build trade routes.

Combination Works Summaries

In two acts of *Into the Woods*, also starring Joanna Gleason, Chip Zien, Tom Aldredge, and Robert Westenberg, we follow the stories of Cinderella, Little Red Ridinghood, Jack (of Jack and the Beanstalk), and Rapunzel. The first act opens with "Once upon a time" and we find a narrator who is "in charge" of the action. Cinderella wants to go to the festival; Jack wants to keep his cow Milky White and his mother wants her sold; Little Red Ridinghood wants to take goodies to her grandmother, those goodies from the Baker and the Baker's Wife, who want a child. Next door to the Baker lives the gnarled and warty Witch, whose "daughter" Rapunzel is locked in a tower. She tells the couple that the Baker's father stole vegetables from her garden, including some beans, and, in response, she cursed his family to infertility and took the child Rapunzel as her own. The Baker can lift the curse if he finds "the cow as white as milk [Can you see what's coming?], the cape as red as blood, the hair as yellow as corn, the slipper as pure as gold" before the third midnight.

All the characters enter the wood to achieve their hearts' desires. Cinderella goes to the festival in a dress furnished by her mother's tree-spirit. Little Red Ridinghood strays from the path at the behest of a Wolf; he swallows down both her grandmother and Red. The Baker buys Jack's Milky White, who later runs away, with beans he tells Jack are magic — and which turn out to be so, taking Jack up to the sky to bring back gold pieces to regain Milky White, who is gone. The Baker slays the wolf and is rewarded with the red cape. The Baker's wife meets Cinderella more than once, seeing the golden slippers and then trying to grab them from Cinderella, who has had a nice time at the festival and met the prince, who is "nice." A mysterious man appears and disappears, making what seem to be nonsensical statements, and stealing the gold pieces from the Baker but then giving him back Milky White. Cinderella's Prince and Rapunzel's Prince meet and talk about their quests.

The Baker's Wife finds Rapunzel and pulls out some of her hair. The Baker and Wife agree to work together now that they have three of the four necessities.

Jack, now with a golden-egg-laying hen, still wants Milky White, who is suddenly dead, The Witch discovers Rapunzel's illicit romance and begs her not to leave, but Rapunzel joins her Witch-blinded Prince. Since Red doesn't believe Jack visited the giant's house, Jack returns to steal a harp. Cinderella's Prince uses pitch to get her shoe (he wants her, but gets her shoe), and Cinderella trades her one shoe to the Baker's Wife for the Wife's two shoes. The Giant, pursuing Jack, falls from the sky. Milky White is revived by the witch, but the curse still reigns because the Witch has touched Rapunzel's hair, but the mystery man, whom the Baker discovers to be his father, tells the Baker to use corn silk (and then dies), and the curse is broken. The Witch is restored to youth and beauty; Cinderella's Prince finds her (the stepsisters lose a heel and a toe to try to catch the Prince); Cinderella is wed and the stepsisters and stepmother have their eyes pecked out by birds. A new beanstalk grows.

In Act II we see what happens after "happily ever after." No one is satisfied: the Baker and Wife have a baby boy but want more room; Cinderella has nothing to do; Jack thinks about how nice the female Giant was. Something threatens them all: noise, giant footprints. Red's mother is killed, and the Baker and Wife decide to escort Red to Grandmother's house. The inhabitants finally conclude there's a giant in the land. It's back into the woods for them all.

The princes have found new quests: Sleeping Beauty and Snow White. Rapunzel, with twins, is not quite sane. Homes are destroyed, and the Giant turns out to be the dead Giant's wife, come for revenge. The people of the palace say it's not their job to take care of Giants and the family runs away. The palace steward strikes down Jack's mother to silence her, killing her. The group sacrifices the narrator who tries to escape by saying he is telling the story. The Witch tells him, "Some of us don't like the way you're telling it," and he dies. The Witch says they have to find Jack and sacrifice him. Cinderella's Prince sees the Baker's Wife and they have some kind of "interlude" in the woods. The Wife, happily on her way back to her family, is killed by the Giant and buried by Jack, who is found by the Witch, powerless now that she has regained her beauty. All blame all for the predicament.

Finally the Witch leaves them to it and vanishes. The Baker starts to run, without his baby, but returns to face the trial. Cinderella, who leaves the not-too-faithful Prince; the Baker, with whom Cinderella and the baby make a family; Red, who discovers her grandmother is dead; and Jack, who first vows revenge on the palace steward and then realizes the futility of revenge, make a plan, which they carry out, to kill the Giant, with regret. They succeed.

The Tenth Kingdom (starring Kimberly Williams-Paisley, Scott Cohen, John Larrouquette, Dianne Wiest, and Daniel Lapain), begins with Prince Wendell, on a royal procession, who stops at the prison to deny the Evil Queen's parole. The Troll King, Relish, frees his children (Blabberwort, Burly, and Bluebell) and the Queen, who turns Wendell into a dog and a dog into Wendell. The dog Prince escapes through a mirror into the Tenth Kingdom, New York City, and the troll children are sent to recapture him. The Queen also frees a Wolf/man to send after him. A waitress, Virginia Lewis, finds the dog and she and her father, Tony, follow him through the mirror-gate to the prison in Nine Kingdoms, where Tony and Prince are captured and Virginia is kidnapped by the troll teens but rescued by Wolf who helps her rescue Tony and Prince.

They travel the Kingdoms as the Queen trains the DogWendell to be the Prince and uses magic mirrors belonging to Snow White's Evil Stepmother to track events. Since Tony and Virginia want to go home, they and Wolf and Prince go to find the magic-gate mirror which is lost from the prison. Facing curses, a Huntsman, wishing wells, dwarves, sheepherding trials against Bo Peep, conspiracy at the hands of the Peep family, and accusations of murder, they hunt for the mirror. They find it at an auction, cannot afford to buy it, and accidentally destroy it. Since they know who made the mirror, they continue the quest and discover the Evil Queen has the only other magic-gate mirror. Virginia meets a Snow White ghost who tells her she will defeat the Queen. Uhuh. Prince is captured. Tony discovers the Evil Queen is his wife and Virginia's mother. Virginia kills the Evil Queen (so Freudian), Tony stays in the Nine Kingdoms to make bouncy castles, and Virginia and Wolf go to New York City to have their "cub." All is well, at least temporarily.

Conclusion Again

Each of the versions of the classic tales has its own emphases, elements, and themes. Discovering those elements and themes and speculating about their values, relationships, and rationale can be the key to stimulating analysis, criticism, and critical thinking at many intellectual and educational levels.

Works Cited

Ahlquist, Steve, Andrew Murphy, and Mike Sagara. *The Complete Annotated Oz Squad: Volume One*. Providence, RI: Patchwork, 2006. Print.
Alice. Two 1½ hour episodes. 2009. DVD. Lionsgate, 2010.
Alice in Wonderland. 1951. DVD. Walt Disney, 2010.
Alice in Wonderland. DVD. Walt Disney, 2010.
Alice in Wonderland. DVD. Hallmark, 1999.
Alien Quadrilogy: Alien [1979], *Aliens* [1986], *Alien 3* [1992], *Alien Resurrection* [1997].DVD. 20th Century–Fox, 2003.

Anthony, David. *In Search of Dorothy*. Hollywood, FL: Frederick Fell, 2006. Print.
_____. *The Witch's Revenge*. Hollywood, FL: Frederick Fell, 2006. Print.
Asimov, Isaac. *I, Robot*. 1950. New York: Spectra, 2008.
Austen, Jane. *Pride and Prejudice*. 1813. New York: Oxford, 2004.
Austen, Jane, and Seth Grahame-Smith. *Pride and Prejudice and Zombies*. Philadelphia: Quirk, 2009.
Baum, L. Frank. *Tik-Tok of Oz*. 1914. Los Angeles: IndoEuropean, 2010. Print.
_____. *The Wonderful Wizard of Oz*. 1900. 100th Anniversary Edition. New York: Harper, 2000. Print.
Bester, Alfred. "Fondly Fahrenheit." 1954. *The Science Fiction Hall of Fame, Volume 1: 1929–1964*. Ed. Robert Silverberg. New York: Orb, 1998. *Google Books*. Web. 23 June 2010.
Bloom, Benjamin S., ed. *Taxonomy of Educational Objectives, Handbook I: Cognitive Domain*. 2nd ed. White Plains, NY: Longman, 1956. Print.
Brown, Rita Mae. "Writing as a Moral Act." *The Prose Reader: Essays for Thinking, Reading, and Writing*. 9th ed. Boston: PrenticeHall, 2011. 540–45. Print.
Buffy the Vampire Slayer. Seasons 1–7. 1997–2003. DVD. 20th Century–Fox, 2006.
Čapek, Karel. "R.U.R. (Rossum's Universal Robots)." 1921. *Toward the Radical Center: A Karel Capek Reader*. Ed. Peter Kussi. Highland Park, NJ: Catbird, 1990. 37–130. Print.
Carlson, Karyl, and Eric Gjovaag. *Queen Ann in Oz*. 1993. New York: Books of Wonder, 1997. Print.
Carroll, Lewis. *Alice's Adventures in Wonderland* [1865] and *Through the Looking Glass* [1871]. New York: Puffin, 1997.
Clarke, Arthur C. *2001: A Space Odyssey*. 1968. New York: Roc, 2000. Print.
Crichton, Michael. *Eaters of the Dead*. New York: Harper, 2009. Print.
Dark Knight. DVD. Warner, 2008.
Doctor Who. BBC. Broadcast. 1963–89. 2005–present.
Dudley, Joshua Patrick. *Lost in Oz*. Raleigh, NC: Lulu, 2007. Print.
_____. *Lost in Oz: Rise of the Dark Wizard*. Raleigh, NC: Lulu, 2008. Print.
Durand, Kevin. "Introduction." Buffy *Meets the Academy: Essays on the Episodes and Scripts as Texts*. Ed. Kevin K. Durand. Jefferson, NC: McFarland, 2009. 1–5. Print.
Farmer, Philip José. *A Barnstormer in Oz*. New York: Berkley, 1983. Print.
Fein, Esther B. "Book Notes." *New York Times* 20 Nov. 1991. Web. 2 June 2010.
Gjovaag, Eric. *The Wonderful Wizard of Oz Website*. 2010. Web. 6 June 2010.
Hee-Joon, Son. *Dorothy of Oz: 1*. Trans. Haksan Publishing. Ontario: Udon, 2007. Print.
_____. *Dorothy of Oz: 2*. Trans. Haksan Publishing. Ontario: Udon, 2008. Print.
_____. *Dorothy of Oz: 3*. Trans. Haksan Publishing. Ontario: Udon, 2008. Print.
_____. *Dorothy of Oz: 4*. Trans. Haksan Publishing. Ontario: Udon, 2008. Print.
I, Robot. 2004. DVD. 20th Century–Fox, 2004.
Into the Woods. DVD. Image, 1997.
Jekyll. 2007. DVD. BBC Warner, 2007.
Lackey, Mercedes. *The Five Hundred Kingdoms: The Fairy Godmother, One Good Knight, Fortune's Fool, The Snow Queen, The Sleeping Beauty*. Toronto: Luna, 2004–2010.
The League of Extraordinary Gentlemen. DVD. 20th Century–Fox, 2003.
Mary Reilly. 1996. DVD. Sony, 2000.
Maquire, Gregory. *A Lion Among Men: Volume Three of the Wicked Years*. New York: Harper, 2008. Print.
_____. *Son of a Witch: Volume Two of the Wicked Years*. New York: Harper, 2008. Print.
_____. *Wicked: The Life and Times of the Wicked Witch of the West*. New York: Harper, 2007. Print.
Mannino, Greg, and Mark Masterson. *Dorothy, Volume I*. Mountain View, CA: Illusive Arts, 2005. Print.
Mead, Rebecca. "Onward and Upward with the Arts: Adaptation." *The New Yorker* 27 Sept. 2010: 44–49. Print.
Moore, Alan. *The League of Extraordinary Gentlemen, Volume 1*. La Jolla, CA: America's Best Comics, 2002. Print.

Moore, Alan, and David Lloyd. *V for Vendetta*. 1989. New York: Vertigo, 2008. Print.
Singer, P.W. "War of the Machines." *Scientific American* 303.1 (July 2011): 56–63. Print.
Skipp, John, and Marc Levinthal. *The Emerald Burrito of Oz*. Northridge, CA: Babbage, 2000. Print.
Snow, Jack. "A Murder in Oz." 1958. *Spectral Snow: The Dark Fantasies of Jack Snow*. San Diego: Hungry Tiger, 1996. 83–93. Print.
Sutton, John William. "Beowulfiana: Modern Adaptations of *Beowulf*." *Camelot Project*. University of Rochester. Web. 1 Oct. 2010.
The Tenth Kingdom. 2000. Five two-hour episodes. DVD. Lionsgate, 2002.
The 13th Warrior. DVD. Touchstone, 1999.
Tin Man. Three episodes/six hours. 2007. DVD. Rhi Entertainment, 2008.
Transformers. DVD. Dreamworks, 2007.
Transformers 2: Revenge of the Fallen. DVD. Paramount, 2009.
2001: A Space Odyssey. 1968. DVD. Warner, 2007.
V for Vendetta. DVD. Warner, 2006.
Wicked: A New Musical. Stephen Schwartz, composer. 2003 Original Broadway Cast. CD. Decca, 2003.
The Wiz. 1978. DVD. Universal, 2009.
The Wizard of Oz. 1939. 70th Anniversary Edition. DVD. Warner, 2009.

Conclusion

Jim Ford

Integrating pop culture in the curriculum does not have to detract from the classic texts. Used properly, works of fantasy enhance and enrich students' encounter with canonical works. There are still works that every educated person should know, but the list is fluid rather than fixed. The essays in this volume suggest a number of New Classics, fantasy and pop culture works that are particularly well-suited for the classroom. They include literary works like *The Lord of the Rings* and the Harry Potter series, films like *The Matrix*, *Memento*, and *The Dark Knight*, television shows like *Buffy the Vampire Slayer* and *The Simpsons*, and graphic novels like *Watchmen* and *Blankets*. Sure, these recur in part because many of the contributors really like them (for a variety of reasons), but also because they are all conducive to cultivating the kinds of skills and talents expected of high school and university students today. These are worthy vehicles for critical and creative thinking, for close analysis and repeated viewing.

Adding fantasy to the classroom helps students reflect on their own education. The confrontation with a new and unusual work often prompts students to wonder what makes a work worthy of study. By making that question explicit, teachers engage students more deeply in their own education. Even for students who are suspicious of or resistant to fantasy materials, this can be a wonderful opportunity. As students begin to take more seriously the question of what they should learn, and why, they take greater responsibility for their individual education. We have found time and again that this inspires student enthusiasm, and often leads students to suggest new pop culture works for use in the classroom. Some of those suggestions produce new discoveries, and a fair number of the ideas in this book began as suggestions from eager students. Even when those suggestions are not worth developing, the conversations they generate are great teaching moments. Developing and refining those student suggestions is an ideal way to build on the assignments, topics, and works in *Teaching with Fantasy*.

Students are bombarded with the images, ideas, and noise of popular culture. By teaching them to think critically and creatively about leading contemporary works, faculty can help students to develop their own identity. This enriches their lives as it enhances their education. Creating lifelong learners is a common goal of universities, and students who see fantasy as part of their classroom are much better positioned for a life of learning. They become more aware of the complexities of their favorite films and shows, as they develop deeper appreciation for more traditional texts and authors.

Whether in high school or college, teaching freshman composition or a senior interdisciplinary seminar, using works of pop culture is a powerful way to enhance teaching and learning. Fantasy films, graphic novels, and television shows expand the curriculum and provide numerous opportunities for engaging student interest, refining critical thinking skills, and deepening their appreciation for literature. Our three sections suggest the range of possibilities. Fantasy material can be used to illuminate a standard issue or text. Traditional classes are enhanced by adding fantasy material as significant in its own right. Or professors can develop new classes that focus strictly on fantasy materials. Either by implementing the specific ideas and techniques described in this book, or by using them as a model for developing your own, we hope that your own teaching will be inspired by fantasy.

About the Contributors

Jacqueline **Bach** is an assistant professor of English education and curriculum theory at Louisiana State University. Her work has appeared in *Changing English*, *The English Journal* and the *Journal of Curriculum Theory*, and she is a co-editor of *The ALAN Review*, a journal dedicated to the study and teaching of young adult literature. In addition to her work on *Buffy the Vampire Slayer*, she studies the representations of classrooms in school films and television shows.

Jessica **Broussard** is a PhD candidate in gifted education at Louisiana State University. She teaches courses in creative and critical thinking at Axia College. Her current research deals with how game playing shapes students. She has presented at several conferences including the Louisiana Association of Computer Using Educators and Popular Culture Association/American Culture Association.

J. Renee **Cox** holds an MA in English from Northern Arizona University. She teaches at Rogers State University, where in addition to teaching she is a costumer and seamstress for RSU's major theatre productions and serves as the faculty advisor for a student organization known as the Gay-Straight Alliance. Her essay "Got Myself a Soul? The Puzzling Treatment of the Soul in Buffy" appeared in *The Truth of* Buffy*: Essays on Fiction Illuminating Reality* (McFarland, 2008).

Emily **Dial-Driver** is a professor of English at Rogers State University. She has published textbooks, articles, and poetry; had plays and media produced; and has acted as editor for books, articles, and periodicals. She serves as fiction editor of RSU's *Cooweescoowee: A Journal of Arts and Letters.* She is editor (with Carolyn Anne Taylor, Carole Burrage, and Sally Emmons) of *Voices from the Heartland* (University of Oklahoma Press, 2007; nominated for the Oklahoma Book Award in Non-Fiction in 2009), and (with Sally Emmons, Jim Ford, and Carolyn Anne Taylor) of *The Truth of* Buffy*: Essays on Fiction Illuminating Reality* (McFarland, 2008).

Sally **Emmons**, an associate professor of English at Rogers State University, received a doctoral degree in English from the University of Oklahoma. Her academic specialties include Native American literature, contemporary American literature, technical and business writing, and creative writing. Her book (with Carolyn Anne Taylor, Emily Dial-Driver, and Carole Burrage) *Voices from the Heartland* was a finalist for an Oklahoma Book Award in Non-Fiction in 2009. She was co-editor (with Emily

Dial-Driver, Jim Ford, and Carolyn Anne Taylor) of *The Truth of* Buffy*: Essays on Fiction Illuminating Reality* (McFarland, 2008). She serves as managing editor of *The Cooweescoowee*, RSU's literary and artistic journal.

Jim **Ford** is a professor of humanities and philosophy and director of the honors program at Rogers State University. Host of *The Meaning of Life* on KRSC 91.3 FM, he was editor (with Emily Dial-Driver, Sally Emmons, and Carolyn Anne Taylor) of *The Truth of* Buffy*: Essays on Fiction Illuminating Reality* (McFarland, 2008).

Laura **Gray** is an associate professor of English and the Writing Program liaison at Rogers State University. She has taught at RSU since 2002. She teaches courses in women's studies and the humanities as well as English and rhetoric. She is the co-author (with Jim Ford) of "Team Teaching on a Shoestring Budget," published in the 2011 edition of *Honors in Practice.*

Kenneth S. **Hicks** is an associate professor of political science at Rogers State University and heads the Department of History and Political Science. He has been at RSU since 1999, teaching many of the upper division political science courses and pursuing research interests that transcend the narrow confines of conventional political science.

Melanie K. **Hundley** is an assistant professor of the practice of education at Vanderbilt University's Peabody College of Education and Human Development. Her work has appeared in *Language Arts* and in a number of books. She is a co-editor of *The ALAN Review*, dedicated to the study and teaching of young adult literature. She studies the composing practices of pre-service teachers as they transition from writing for print to writing for digital environments, as well as the relationship between pre-service teacher candidates' performance assessments and early instructional practices and student learning outcomes.

Mary M. **Mackie,** who holds a PhD in American and Native American literature, is an associate professor of creative writing and literature at RSU and the advisor for the Rogers State University student newspaper, *The Hillpost*, as well as poetry editor of the *Cooweescowee*. Her one-act plays, *Unrequited to the Nth Degree* and *Closing Time*, have been produced by the RSU Theatre Program. Her academic writing has been published in journals such as *Journal of American Studies of Turkey*.

Shaka **McGlotten** is an assistant professor of media, society, and the arts at Purchase College, where he teaches courses on media, ethnography, and digital culture. His research focuses on the intersections of media technologies with categories of gender, sexuality, and race in particular. He also works in "affect studies," or the study of the ways feelings are central to individually-lived and shared social experiences.

Frances E. **Morris** is an instructor at Rogers State University. She has been a medical technologist, English bulldog breeder, and cattle rancher. Several years ago she decided to return to school to study literature, a move that led her to an MA from Northeastern State University and subsequently to teaching composition at Rogers State University.

Jesse **Stallings** is a teacher of English at the Tulsa School of Arts and Sciences. He earned his bachelor's degree in liberal arts at Rogers State University, and is co-author of "Texting *Buffy*: Allusions of Many Kinds" in the nonfiction collection titled *The Truth of* Buffy*: Essays on Fiction Illuminating Reality* (McFarland, 2008).

Carolyn Anne **Taylor** is a professor of political science at Rogers State University. Her areas of academic specialty include American federal, state and local government. She served in the Oklahoma House of Representatives from 1984 to 1992. She was the managing editor (joined by Emily Dial-Driver, Carole Burrage, and Sally Emmons-Featherston) of *Voices from the Heartland*, a finalist for the Oklahoma Book Award in 2009, and co-editor (with Emily Dial-Driver, Sally Emmons, and Jim Ford) of *The Truth of* Buffy*: Essays on Fiction Illuminating Reality* (McFarland, 2008).

Index